STILL WATER BENDING

By

Wendy Mitman Clarke

For Johnny

Still water bending moment: "Primary stresses arise from considerations like the *still water bending moment,* a mechanical engineer's snapshot of the gross effect on a structure of all of the forces at work on a ship at rest on the water arising from its basic hull design. There's a bending of the entire hull that you have to think about first just because of the shape of the hull in the water and the distribution of the weights within it... large pieces of equipment, or even lots of smaller pieces in one place, can, by their cumulative weight, affect buoyancy (and thus the bending moment) by changing how much of the hull area is exposed to the water, and where."
—Michael Sanders, *The Yard*

Still Water Bending

Part One

"How I have loved this house in the morning before we are all awake and tangled together like badly cast fishing lines. Too many people have been born here, have wept too much here, and have laughed too much, and have been too angry and outrageous with each other here. Too many have died in this bed already, there are far too many ancestral bones propped up on the mantelpieces, there have been too damned many antimacassars in this house, she said loudly, and oh, what accumulation of storied dust never allowed to settle in peace for one moment."
— Katherine Anne Porter, *Pale Horse, Pale Rider*

Chapter 1

The screen door on the back porch slammed and Jines Arley Evans walked down the oyster shell path toward the dock, his shoulders hunched deeply into his jacket. It was just past dawn. Steam purled up from his coffee mug like the mist swirling off the glassy river. He was running late. Hadn't slept worth a damn, and when he finally did nod off on the davenport in the front room it must've been only a couple hours before he had jerked awake and saw the clock said nearly six. Slack water was at seven. Hadn't taken but a couple minutes to take a leak, tug on some long johns, corduroys and a sweatshirt, and shove a cup of day-old coffee into the microwave. Then out to the back porch where he pulled on a pair of rubber bib overalls, a yellow oilskin jacket, and the tall, white rubber deck boots parked right by the door. Didn't matter much that he was still half-asleep. It was the same gear every day, left in the same spot. Same path to walk down to the *Jenny Rae*.

The workboat's diesel was already rumbling as Jines stepped aboard. "Not too cold after all this morning," said Kenneth. "S'posed to push sixty, and no wind to speak of." He took a huge bite out of a fried-egg-and-scrapple sandwich and waved what was left at Jines. "I got two. G'ahead."

Jines shook his head. "Not hungry." He took another careful sip of the stale coffee. "Boys asleep?" he asked, jerking his head toward the little cabin house that sat forward of the wide open cockpit. Kenneth nodded. "Who all we got?"

"Robbie," Kenneth mumbled around his sandwich. "Ronald. Calvin wouldn't come, said it was too damned early in the year for fishin.' That boy Joe, though what you hire that thing for I'll never know. Boy's not right."

Jines pitched what was left of his coffee overboard with an irritated flick of his wrist and tossed the stern line to the dock. "He's all right."

"He's a goddamn idiot."

Jines throttled up *Jenny Rae*'s engine, effectively silencing any further conversation. He'd already talked more than he liked, but Kenneth was like that, always wanting to chitchat early in the morning. The boat's high, sharp bow carved into the sunrise, and Jines felt the relief of leaving land behind, as if the hands that had been squeezing his chest finally let go. He knew it was too early in the season, really, to be out here and expect much. Most of the other men were still getting their boats and gear ready and wouldn't put anything overboard for another three weeks at least. Jines didn't care. He was always the first out of Little River to set a pound. He could count on Kenneth, and there were always a couple of boys looking for work after the long, tight winter. Even if he barely broke even on the day, he was out here. That was enough.

He turned back once to look at the tall white house he'd left behind on the point. Force of habit, even though there was nobody there in the big kitchen window that faced east toward the river. The house looked grey as an old lady in the early light. Sometimes at night he swore he could hear it breathe, its sighs and moans the only sound to accompany his footsteps.

The noise of the boat's engine beneath him was a blessed relief. After a bit they cleared the jetties at the river's mouth and headed southeast, straight into the pale morning sky. Below them, the water revealed a bottom of sandy white flats scalloped by the dependable ebb and flow of tide, darkly brushed here and there with meadows of seagrass. Before them, the Chesapeake Bay spread outward like a great open palm. The long fetch from the Atlantic Ocean invited all sorts of things, dolphins, sea turtles, sharks. When they caught a sea turtle, Jines would take extra care with it. Then he'd give a call over to the Virginia Institute of Marine Science and tell them to come on over and get it. He was a practical man who understood there was no place for sympathy in his world of water and sky. Yet something would stir in him when he saw a sea turtle or the rare seabird like a shearwater, blown off course. Their journeys mystified him, made him restless for some infinite distance. It was as close as he ever got anymore to longing.

It always surprised him a little, that pang for something other than what he'd been born knowing. He'd chased his daddy down the back porch steps, the screen door slamming behind him just the way it had this morning. Same sound from sixty years back, a hundred. What did they call it when sound got stretched out like that? He couldn't remember just now. He didn't think it was supposed to stretch that far, but aye God, it did. He remembered running down the path in his oversized boots, tripping over the rolled-up rubber pants that tangled his ankles, frantic not to miss his daddy's boat. Some days he had to miss it—he had school, or the weather was too wicked, or the men were heading out in the middle of the night when he was deep in what his mama always called old-dog sleep. On the days he could go along, he would sit on the cabin top and watch and listen. When they'd come in off the water and gather under the tin-roofed shed on the dock, his daddy would turn over a milk crate for him to stand on. He could just see over the edge of the culling board where the crew would stand for three or four hours, sorting, icing, and boxing the catch, their stories and cuss words and laughter rippling over and through him like a breeze in a wheat field.

This morning, the Bay was blown glass. No breeze at all yet. Most days he worked hard not to let his mind travel back, but the sound of the screen door and the grey face of the house never left him. Jines didn't consider it memory. More like ghosts, waiting for him in the kitchen window, the way his boots waited by the door.

He always came back. One morning, when he was twelve years old, it was blowing dogs off chains and his daddy was already gone with the other watermen. They were looking for his Uncle Henry, who'd gone north up to St. Mary's River the night before and wasn't answering his radio. Jines had looked out the window and saw the river prowling up the front yard like a feral dog, creeping forward and back, side to side, but never, ever, quite stopping. Before long, it was up the steps and through the door, brown as Ovaltine. They never named that storm, and why should they? Nightmares don't have names. It drove the water as high as the counter at the Ophelia General Store and blew birds up the Bay no one had ever seen before. That tide beached eight-ton workboats half a mile inland, and it swept his daddy away. Jines had sat in the big house as the neighbors came and shook his hand, murmured assurances about whatever he might need, whatever they could do. They brought crab casseroles and oyster pies and cornbread and cole slaw. He looked out the window at the sparkling river, and they held his mama while she cried.

The *Jenny Rae* was coming up on the pound net, and as soon as Jines throttled back, the crew stumbled out of the little cabin up forward, yawning and stretching. Kenneth walked aft and started hand-over-handing a thick line attached there, drawing close the thirty-foot open bateau they had towed along behind. As Jines pulled *Jenny Rae* alongside the pound head and the crew made her fast to the tall poles, Kenneth pulled the bateau's bow up tight to the bigger boat. The crew clambered onto the bateau and pulled it from pole to pole until they were on the other side of the pound head. Jines, alone on the *Jenny Rae*, killed the engine, and the limpid stillness of the morning rang in the silence. Not even a wave to kiss the hull. In the quiet, some of the boys lit cigarettes, some leaned on the bateau's gunwale and closed their eyes. They waited.

"Water clear some," Jines finally said. "You see any, boys?

Huh?"

"Water's clear as I've seen it, I b'lieve, in my life," Kenneth answered. He peered into the bottle-green water that was as still and secretive as a mountain pool. "Pound's lookin' pretty good, Jines."

Jines grunted. This was the only pound he'd set so far; he'd wait another few weeks for spring to settle in and the fish to start running in earnest before setting another further offshore. It consisted of a long row of pine poles pounded into the bottom and strung with a continuous net that dropped to the sand. With the top of the net sticking a couple feet above the surface, it looked like a fence line stretched across the water. The fence ended in a wide, heart-shaped net whose narrow end led into the pound head, a corral about forty feet square made of more poles and seine net that hung to the bottom where it attached to a net floor. On the surface, it looked pretty simple. Underwater, it was a complex network of ropes, pulleys, chains, and thimbles that could loosen or snug the net tight, raise it and lower it back down. A fish, or anything else swimming along, would run into the long fence. It would turn and follow the net, trying to get around the end. But the end eventually funneled into the pound head. For Jines, it was just a matter of closing off the funnel, tightening the head, and scooping out the catch.

"Slack water." Kenneth said. He looked closely at Jines. "You all right? You look like shee-it."

Jines grunted. His head was suddenly throbbing, and his right arm felt strangely heavy and numb. "Probably shoulda taken you up on the sandwich." He had a biscuit and some chicken and gravy back at the house left over in the icebox. That'd surely help. For now, though, he wasn't sure he could eat anything without puking it back up, the way his head was pounding. "Let's go, boys. We're burnin' daylight." The crew in the bateau set to work. The four of them started hauling the net slowly into the bateau, ropes wrapped around the backs of their thighs so they could lean into the pulling, making levers of themselves. Below, the still water of the pound head began to stir, sheens of silver shivering the water's surface like cattails ruffled in a breeze. Then the flickering jets of silver flashed brighter and faster as the bateau pulled deeper into the head and the net came up tighter. A panicked, fluttering mass of fish crowded the net's southern end. The men were mostly silent. Now and then, one of them would groan at the weight as they hauled the net, hand over hand, into the bateau. As the net edges began to lift, the frantic fish pooled to its center. Watching from the *Jenny Rae*, Jines finally cranked up the engine again, this time to raise a huge dip net hanging from the gaff pole attached to *Jenny Rae*'s stubby mast. As if they were scooping ice cream, the men pushed the net into the squirming mass until fish spilled out the top. Jines kicked the gear to raise the pole and swung the net over the center of *Jenny Rae*'s long cockpit. Then Kenneth yanked a line, the bottom of the dip net flew open, and a flood of fish poured into the cockpit hold, where they slapped the deck and each other, frantic at first, then slower and slower. The men repeated the scooping until the pound head was empty and the hold was a writhing, frothing sea of expiring fish. A single eel snaked through them, and a cormorant that had been diving into the pound to steal fish and couldn't escape the net was now scrabbling across the pile. Desperately it tried to fly, but its body and wings were coated in thick foam and slime. Finally, it found a corner and cowered there, quivering.

Jines grabbed a metal snow shovel and pushed it along the gunwale, flicking errant fish into the hold. Then he killed the engine again. The only sound was the men's heavy breathing and the wet slapping of the dying fish. Without a word, the men reset the net, brought the bateau alongside, and clambered aboard the *Jenny Rae*. They eyed the catch. The boat could hold about twenty thousand pounds of fish. Today, it looked like they might bring home less than a quarter of that.

"Not much to write home about," Kenneth said. "Mostly bait."

Jines grunted agreement. "Pretty poor. Couple rockfish, anyway."

"That's a purple eel there, he ain't no account for nothin', " the boy called Joe said. Jines peered over to look.

"I don't think that's a purple eel, Joe," he said.

"That's a purple eel right there, Jines, damn if it ain't!"

"All right." Jines walked back toward the helm and sat down hard on the engine box. He felt like the sky was lowering itself on him. His shoulders hunched and he rubbed his forehead with one hand as he fired up the *Jenny Rae*'s engine once again, stood up, and leaned hard on the tiller. The boat slid through the water, its sound and motion marking the steadiest rhythm in Jines's life. Some days he was lucky enough to see a calm, peaceful morning like this one. Others it was a hell-fired blast furnace out here. Sometimes it was still dark when they headed out, so clear the stars rained down over their heads and the southeasterly blowing up from the Atlantic was like a warm, wet kiss. The restless water made it hard to work the nets, but he loved to watch the birds on windy nights. Seagulls and pelicans, fish hawks and terns, they would hang up there in the big breeze, wingtips balanced on the darkness, waiting for their world of wind to settle down. That's what you had to do sometimes when the wind gets up, Jines thought, just wait it out.

He felt sometimes that he'd been born knowing what the birds knew, how to just plain endure, to survive. That he had known already, before that storm had taken his daddy and uncle and half his town, that you can't hold a tide, you can never hold a tide. He was wary in a way that other people misunderstood. He knew people called him ornery, or even arrogant; it didn't bother him. Only Jenny Rae had seen beyond it. She always had, even when they were youngsters growing up just down the river from one another. She knew him, without ever having to say a word about it. When they married, he basked in the lightness of her and let that wariness go for a bit. They watched their son and daughter learn to crawl, walk, and run in the big house. His son Danny had chased him down the back porch steps in too-big boots and flapping pants. His daughter Lily Rae met him at the dock with hands full of wildflowers and turtle bones. His wife's voice was like music.

It was going on ten o'clock, and he was suddenly grateful that he hadn't set that first pound too far offshore, and he was almost back home. He was feeling no better. The sunbeams bouncing off the water skewered his head, and the boat seemed to be shrinking. For a moment he squinted hard offshore, thinking he saw fog rolling in. Couldn't be right, though, fog on a morning like this. They were nearing the dock and Jines had throttled back when Joe started climbing down into the fish hold. He shoved through the dead fish, hanging onto the coaming, and headed for the corner where the cormorant shuddered.

"Joe," Jines said. "What are you doin'? "

"Whaddya mean, Jines?" Joe reached down for the bird and grabbed at it. It slithered free for a second, but Joe caught it by one wing, held it down with his boot, and then wrapped his fist around its neck. It hung there in his grasp, exhausted, flapping feebly. Joe grinned. "Don't you bite me now. There he is."

"Don't y'all hurt him," Jines said.

Everyone turned to look at Jines. "The hell's bit you this morning?" Kenneth said. "Better for target practice than anything else, those thievin' birds."

"Let 'im go, Joe."

Joe looked disgusted and flung the bird over the side. The cormorant dove quickly, then popped back to the surface splashing and preening, trying to cleanse itself of the blood, oil, and slime.

"He was a lucky one," Joe muttered. "I swear you gone right round it this time, Jines Arley."

"Could be."

He eased the *Jenny Rae* alongside the pier next to the tin-roofed shed and icehouse where he had once stood on a milk crate listening to the watermen while they culled fish. The boys tied the boat fast to the pilings, drew in the bateau and tied it off as well. Then they began offloading the fish with the dip net and shovels. It would take a few hours to cull, ice, and box the catch, and suddenly, Jines knew he couldn't do it. His head hurt so bad he was finding it hard to keep his eyes open. His whole right side felt weirdly heavy and slow. The wide-open sky, where on any other day he would find something like solace, seemed to be draping itself around him, threatening to buckle his knees.

"Damn," he muttered. "Kenneth, think you could help the boys finish up? I think I need to get somethin' to eat. Feelin' right strange."

"Yeah, no shit," Kenneth said, shaking his head. "I'll stop in when we're done."

Jines turned, waving a hand of thanks in Kenneth's direction, and started to walk up the oyster-shell path toward the back porch. His white rubber boots felt like they were full of water. He didn't know how it was possible, but damn if that wasn't fog, right there. Dirty looking, though, black, not grey and soft. Live long enough, you never know what you might see. Workboats perched in trees. Prehistoric fish in your nets. A house full of ghosts.

Danny had passed, just nine years old. Leukemia. And when the cancer got hold of Jenny Rae and crept through her body, Jines thought about that storm tide, and he knew just exactly where he stood. He had nursed her in that cold metal hospital bed they put in the parlor. It always stank of disinfectant no matter how many quilts he threw over it. And then, after a while, she was gone. He had no memory without her. The way she stood in front of her family's house while he'd pass by on his way out the river when he was still a young man, her dress swaying with all of summer in it. The way she came in from the garden, laughing, dirt all over her knees and face and her hands holding something she'd just dug up, maybe an arrowhead or a piece of old pottery.

His ears were ringing now, and he realized he couldn't hear the gulls squawking over by the pier. Instead, he heard Jenny Rae's high sweet laugh, opened his eyes wide to try and see his wife, dead now these twenty-four long years, and fell to his knees. He barely felt the oyster shells as they sliced through his rubber work pants, corduroys, and the skin beneath, and when they tore his face he didn't feel that at all. Behind him Kenneth was running, yelling his name, but Jines could only hear Jenny Rae's laughter.

It was dark, and he could not see. That could be all right. Some places near Ophelia never even got the electricity until he was halfway through junior high. Even now, few streetlights to speak of. That kind of darkness was familiar, though. You grow up with a thing, you learn how to live alongside it. Night has a way of making its own light, Jines knew, if you keep your eyes open. Starlight glinting off the river. Foxfire in the grass. Glow-balls in the water like silent firecrackers in the boat's wake. The county had come and put a streetlight at the end of the driveway where it met the county road. Hung it up on a telephone pole, and it put out a light like a pool of piss. His daddy shot it out once, twice, three times. They kept replacing it. After a bit it just stayed there, and pretty soon Daddy set up one more or less like it down at the boat shed so the men could see what the hell they were doing if they went fishing at night. That thing was a bug magnet. Moths as big as your hand, beating themselves to pieces on it, making little wet thumps with their bodies and wings. Too much light could be hurtful, that was sure.

But this darkness. He didn't recognize it. There was no light at all here. Now and then he could feel his eyes move, he'd think they were open, but still no light. Drowned. I must be drowned, Jines thought. Took goddamned long enough. Oh, he'd thought about it, thought it over long and hard. It'd have been so easy, just go out there one day and leave her in gear, step right off the transom and watch her slip away. It wouldn't have been so bad. He felt his eyes growing wet, at least he thought that's what he was feeling. Tears in his eyes where he remembered his eyes to be. He tried to wipe them away but his arms were like sacks of potatoes. His whole body, really. Felt that way he'd feel in dreams sometimes, when something bad was about to happen. It loomed there in his subconscious like a growing storm, and he knew he had to run away, but his legs felt just like a tractor bogged in the mud, and his chest was waterlogged and heavy as if he were breathing seawater instead of air.

So the tears just pooled up in his eyes, and he seemed to be spiraling down into the dark pool of the past, one bitter cold winter night when Mary Virginia let herself into the kitchen with a big noisy "Halloooh!" and some kind of a casserole. It'd been too cold to oyster and anyway the river was froze up, no way to go out now. They'd asked the state to bring in an icebreaker, but the icebreakers were having a hard time just keeping the channels out to the islands open. Matter of life and death out there, they were told, those channels don't stay open the ferries can't run and those folks won't have food nor doctors. Like it wasn't a matter of life or death for Jines, getting out through the ice. But here was Mary Virginia with her casserole, and she was spooning it into a big bowl and shoving it under his nose. She sat at the other end of the kitchen table, fluffing her clothes around her like a broody hen settling in. She had bright blue eyes and cropped, curly white hair that had been, when they were young, blonde as a summer wheat field. It occurred to him that this woman had looked like a grandmother her whole life.

"My land, it's cold! That fire feels nice, Jines." He nodded. She fiddled with a button on her jacket. "I'm wondering," Mary Virginia had said, "if you think Lily Rae shouldn't come stay with me awhile. Just till this cold spell breaks."

"Ain't you havin' any?"

"I made some for myself and ate earlier, thank you. With your truck broke down and all, it's a long way to the bus stop for her from here. And it's so cold early in the mornings, as you know."

"I had to walk twice as far."

Mary Virginia settled herself a little deeper into the chair and regarded Jines the way a schoolteacher might look at a particularly stubborn pupil. "Why yes, Jines Arley, we all know what a rough growing up you did have. But we're not talking about you, are we?" She spun the lazy Susan at the center of the table until the salt and pepper were in front of Jines, stopping it there. He grabbed the saltshaker and showered his casserole with it. "My Lord, Jines, Dr. Rayburn would have a *fit*. Are you trying to kill yourself?"

"She ask you?" He stabbed a carrot with his fork and wedged it into his mouth.

"Ask me what?"

"To come stay with you. She ask?"

"Not in so many words."

Jines snorted. "Yeah, I know, she don't have too many words lately."

"And I wonder where she learned that from." Mary Virginia sat up more primly in her chair the way she always did, he knew, when she was getting ready to make some kind of speech. Back in grade school, he'd started calling her Mary Poppins when she sat this way. Lord, she hated that. He leaned back, clinked his fork loudly into his bowl, and sighed. He waited. She leaned across the table toward him. "She's lonely, Jines, loneliest thing I've ever seen, like a bird fallen out of her nest. Fourteen years old and so beautiful, beautiful as her mother ever was, and so wordless it scares me. She looks at me sometimes with those big brown eyes so wide open and dark, it's like she's haunted."

Jines reached for the lazy Susan and spun it slowly with one thick finger. Around it went with a little clicking noise, salt, pepper, Old Bay, the butter dish with the smiling Guernsey cow, the wooden napkin holder, the honey jar, the sugar bowl, circling like a bizarre carousel.

"You'd have to be blind not to see it," she said, sitting back up straight. Inside the woodstove at the far end of the kitchen, a knot made a soft whumping sound as the fire's heat split it apart.

"I ain't blind."

"Well then why don't you do something! Look at you, Jines. Living in the downstairs, sleeping in that parlor all these years! Fishing sunup to sundown whether you have to or not. When's the last time you had breakfast with her? Kissed her goodnight? Talked to her about school, about anything? She's just a child, Jines, but she's going to be a woman soon, and you two are all you have left."

"She has a house to come home to, doesn't want for nothin.' "

"A house is a house, Jines. It's a home she needs. It's you she needs."

"She needs her mother and her mother's gone."

"And how long are you going to use that to punish her? It wasn't her fault Jenny Rae died."

Jines slammed his fist into the table so hard his bowl jumped, knocking the fork out and splattering Mary Virginia's casserole. The lazy Susan jerked to a stop. The Guernsey cow smiled at him.

"I was twelve years old when my daddy died and two years later I was makin' my own way, taking care of my family!"

"What does that have to do with anything?"

"On my own. And I made it all right."

"You weren't on your own." Mary Virginia shook a finger at him. "That's you changing history again just to suit yourself. You had your mama. You took care of each other."

"Makes no difference." He smacked the table again and she turned on him, full of scorn.

"You don't scare me, Jines Arley Evans, never have, never will. Break the damned table for all I care. But don't you think it's time you stop feeling sorry for yourself? Do you think you're the only person on this river who's ever lost someone?" She was angry, no doubt, her short curls shook with it, but her eyes were bright with tears. For James, of course. They'd all grown up together. She and James had married the same year as he and Jenny. Good man, James Cockrell, good fisherman. Fell overboard they all figured, though you could never be sure it wasn't a heart attack or something without an autopsy, and by the time some weekend warrior had found him drifting in Fleets Bay there wasn't much left to take apart. Mary Virginia wiped her eyes brusquely and straightened a napkin on the table. "Let her go, Jines," she said. "Just put one foot in front of the other and keep going."

And hadn't that been what he'd been doing all these years? All these long years, aye God, putting one goddamned foot in front of the other, walking through this empty house, walking down to the boat, walking back, walking to the Grove where the pines shaded the graves in the hot summer?

"It won't work," he told her flatly that cold night, staring at her down the long table. "James had it easy, and so did she."

"You can go to hell, Jines Arley Evans," Mary Virginia spat. "They didn't want to die. You want to live your life like you're dead already, go ahead. But don't take your daughter with you."

She had slammed the back door so hard the plastic clock that chimed the hours in different bird songs bounced off the wall and onto the floor. The hell had happened to that clock, he wondered now. Had he thrown it in the river? Was it still up on the kitchen wall? Had he put it back there, or did Lily? He couldn't remember, time was sliding together like beads on a string, the necessary spaces between them vanishing. Lily. Every year, every day, the distance where he held himself from her and she from him, growing. He willed it to grow. He couldn't stand seeing her eyes, watching her move; she was her mother all over again. It was like living in a house of mirrors where you could approach a reflection, run to it, and smash yourself senseless. He reeled in the rip of the tide. What good was it to know where to find the fish, or how to build a boat, or make it home in a storm? He despised this knowing he had. What good had it done any of them? Where he had once found compassion and light he found only a void, a darkness like this one he was in now. A place of things gone missing, so deep and silent that eventually the darkness itself became the only thing he felt comfortable knowing. He watched as Lily became like one of those moths beating themselves to death on the light down by the dock. After awhile, the carnage grew more unbearable than the distance. He could not see her. He could only see the water and the sky, those things he didn't have to touch for them to go on living.

Here in this strange new place came another image of her, so young, when his family was still whole. He'd gotten a bad flu, laid him out for a week. Jenny had slept on the couch and hadn't let either of the children into the room where he lay in bed sweating through the sheets night after night. But one morning, just as the sun was breaking over the windowsill, he saw the door open a crack, saw her gamine face, all eyes, peering at him. "Lil," he had croaked, and she put her fingers to her lips swearing him to secrecy and pointed toward the night table beside the bed. He looked. Beside the glass of water from the night before was a piece of bright yellow construction paper folded in half. She had drawn two figures, a small one and a big one, riding on the back of something that looked like a dolphin. The water was green, the dolphin purple, the father and daughter bright blue. Next to the card was a slender vase holding a sprig of blue asters. The morning sun shot through the tiny blossoms. They flickered like captive stars. Here in his new darkness, he could see them perfectly. Where in the hell had she found them, he wondered now. When was it he'd been so sick, had to be winter or near to it. Where had she found the blue asters to bring to him? And then, with the burning, bursting lungs of a diver who has miscalculated the time he has spent at depth and claws wildly for the surface, he needed to know, where had they gone?

Chapter 2

Lily reached up for the rail of her sailboat as a gust of wind sliced across the harbor. She felt the smooth teak beneath her hands and took a deep breath, focusing on that reassuring steadiness under her fingers. Sheltered in the sailboat's lee, the yard skiff was less skittish than it had been coming across the harbor; still, she saw Willy's big hand grab the sailboat's rail as well, his tree-trunk arm holding the two boats apart in the cuffing wind

"Ah don't know, Miss Evans, you know ah don't think you should be going out today." Willy's accent seemed even flatter against the thin, cold air. "Weathuh suhvice has a small-craft advisory out for the hahbah. You'd be better off waiting for this front to pass. Why, ah saw that Satuhday's going to be lovely spring weathuh. Fifty degrees they're calling for, if you can imagine. Hahdly any wind to worry about, maybe fifteen knots."

Lily smiled. Her boat moved around its mooring ball in the breeze, restless as a racehorse. The white hull gleamed in the brittle sunlight. "She looks great, Willy. You didn't have to wax her."

She heard him behind her making the snorting sound he did when one of his customers was foolish enough to ignore his hardearned know-how. Without looking, she could see him shaking his head under the blue wool watch cap, his wrinkled neck skinny and white beneath the turned-up collar of his pea coat, his long nose wagging like an admonishing finger. Willy Perkins had owned his scrap of boatyard in South Portland for fifty years, after he'd decided he didn't want to spend a lifetime lobstering. He had a soft spot for her, she knew. He enjoyed a boat with classic lines. "Your little boat, Miss Evans," he would say, "that's a fine boat. Carl Alberg design, you can see it a mile away in that sheerline, those overhangs. That's how God meant for a boat to look." She knew he would never launch her boat for the season—even this early—without first polishing the winter off her, making her look pretty for spring. Even if it wasn't really spring. This was Maine, after all, and spring was more a frame of mind than an actual season.

Lily pushed herself up enough to get one knee onto the rail, then swung all the way and nimbly climbed over the lifeline onto her boat. She smiled back at Willy. He frowned at her. "Ah guess ah'm not talking you out of it?" he yelled over the breeze. He shook his head one more time. "I'll be waiting on thirteen when you're ready to come in." He twisted the throttle, and the outboard sputtered and whined as he turned the skiff downwind. She watched him go for a moment, the skiff's boxy stern rising up to meet the waves, Willy's sturdy back rounded against the wind.

She slid open the hatch and poked her head below; it was even colder there than outside, the fiberglass hull seeming to absorb the water's chill and hold it. She tossed her backpack to the small settee, then got to work. She raised the mainsail, dashed forward to let the mooring line slip into the frigid water, then unfurled the jib with a snap. The sails slapped and banged around momentarily, then suddenly they filled and the boat heeled over sharply as if swatted by a huge paw. She winched the sails in, double-checking their trim, and maneuvered her boat through the small field of mooring balls that dotted this end of the harbor like mushrooms. They were all empty still, awaiting the boats whose owners had better sense than she, or perhaps just less stubborn desire. A wave slapped the hull and the wind needled the spray into her face. "Come on," she taunted under her breath. "Show me what you got. I could use an honest fight." She felt better already. It was a fact that a boat was an inanimate object, an organized aggregate of fiberglass and wood and fasteners, but Lily never questioned the fundamental truth of how alone she felt when she was apart from this one. It was a Cape Dory Typhoon, small, capable, and simple enough for her to take out for a quick afternoon sail, but with an efficient, tiny cabin that afforded basic comfort and necessities for a weekend away from the city. Within the boat's nineteen feet, Lily found life distilled to its minimum, a clarity that eluded her on land. The little boat's elegant lines were deceptively sweet. For all its grace, it was tenacious as a bulldog. She had named the boat *Pelagic* for the wandering, solitary creatures whose home was the sea.

As she passed a shelf of rocks, a pair of seals watched her. Great manes of seaweed lay draped over the granite waiting for a rising tide to lift them and transform them into swaying green forests. She breathed the rich, musky smell of the ocean's edge, a million things living and dying at once within its tentative web of water, rock, and air.

Beyond it came the clean, clear scent of the sea. She'd probably have to stay in the harbor today; Willy was right about it being rough out in the bay. She loved that about Maine; there was no mediocrity to it, no middle ground. All was contrast, a constant battle of extremes. One moment she could stretch her vision across the water until the horizon's edge simply quivered and disappeared—no wonder there was a time people believed you could fall right off it—the next the fog could narrow that wide world to a fleecy cocoon that bent sound, smothered the sun, and defeated all sense of direction. One mistake here and you and your boat were smashed to bits or left high and dry on a ledge with the seals and gulls, waiting through a humiliating low tide. She appreciated this lack of forgiveness, this decisive world. It helped to know where things stood.

Willy, for instance. They had always understood each other, from the first time she had driven into his hardscrabble yard looking for a place for the boat she'd just bought. She found his concern for her safety today kind. Even though he knew he couldn't deter her, they both knew he had to try. It was a ritual they had; she was forever going sailing alone at all hours, disappearing for a weekend or even three or four days when she could string them together, and he would sit next to his muttering outboard as he ran her out to her boat, grumbling about how a young woman such as herself should be more careful, that just because she was on the water didn't mean she was safe, that no amount of sea sense could help her if she took the boom in the head one day, for instance, and got knocked overboard, alone out there as she was. And then he'd turn the skiff around and say, as he had today, "I'll be waiting on thirteen when you're ready to come in," and she knew he would be, the portable VHF tucked into his jacket pocket. Willy may have been right that she wasn't safe alone out here, but she knew he understood why she had to go. And if he had seen something different in her face today, some narrow pinching in the carriage of her shoulders that wasn't there before, he would never say so. Like the rocks and the seaweed, he would wait for the tide to change.

Michael, on the other hand, had no such discretion. "You are completely fucking nuts going out." She was sitting in his office. The door was closed, but the walls were glass so that he could keep an eye on the worker bees in his bureau, and they, in turn, could spy on his personal and professional life via the same transparency, using his body language as an indicator. For this reason, when she and Michael had begun their affair nearly a year ago, they had never been able to go at it on his desk or even so much as slide an arm around one another while at work lest the entire staff at The Associated Press's Portland bureau know that one of the staff writers—the senior female on the staff, in fact—was fucking the boss, who in turn had the bad judgment to dip his pen in the venerable company ink. That he was married only exacerbated the need for caution. Lily didn't feel especially guilty about it; she'd encountered the wife at the usual office social functions like the annual Christmas party, and she'd come away with the clear impression that Mrs. Michael Johansen was a glowing example of the women she dubbed the Vapid Divas—maintained as meticulously as their husbands' stock portfolios and Porsche 911s, enhanced and diminished in all the necessary places. Sweating, breath heaving after another round of raucous sex in Lily's apartment, Michael would run his hands up and down her damp body, pull them along her wet hair, and talk about how much he loved her passion, her lack of inhibition. Invariably, he would also bring up how much he disliked his wife, really, how inane she was, how Lily made him feel alive, how much he wanted out of his marriage. Thank God, Lily thought, he'd never have the nerve to really pull the ripcord. There had been men like him before, craving what was free and unreachable in her, but always shying from it in the end, running home to mama instead. She preferred to make her commitments to boats. They were so much easier to be with, in the long run.

"Lily," he had said this morning in his office, "I am so sorry about this, I know you're upset, but just go home. Go home and pack and make your plans. I'll come over later when I can get out of here."

"I have three hours left of my shift, I'd rather stay here and finish. Then I'm going sailing."

"You need some time for this to sink in. I can't believe that crazy old man put your boat in the water already. He should know better even if you don't."

"He's not crazy," she snapped. She stood up quickly and walked to the door before her raised voice would invite even more eyes into the inner sanctum. On the other hand, she realized she wasn't sure she really cared who knew anymore. "I'll call you when I get in."

She glanced up and checked the telltales, little strips of

parachute material attached to the jib's leading edge that let her know if she needed to ease the sails or trim them in, or if the wind had shifted slightly. Paying attention to them was like taking a pulse of the boat, the wind, this little crucible of the world. In the bigger gusts, she had to let the boat's nose come up and spill the sails a little. The whole boat would shudder at the tension of the forces being thrust upon it, then charge off again when Lily eased it back down off the wind. A sharp gust caught her by surprise and buried *Pelagic*'s rail in roiling water before she could regain control. "Blowing the dogs off the chains," she said, surprised the words had come out that way. That was her daddy talking.

She settled the boat back down, thought about heading in, and kept going. A tanker was making its way down the channel toward the waiting gantry cranes of the port. Rust sheeted down its sides like rain. She tacked the boat to let the ship cross well ahead of her. "They say he's like as not going to die, Lily Rae," Mary Virginia had said to her on the phone this morning. "You need to come on home now." As if she were an errant child who had run away on a whim and peanut butter sandwiches. Come on home now, as if she'd been gone a night and a day, rather than fourteen years. As if it could be called home. The phone call had come right at the busiest point of her morning shift. She wasn't sure she had heard the voice on the other end of the line quite right; no one around here called her Lily Rae or even knew her that way, given name and middle, always said together as one. Never just Lily, not down in Ophelia. Where the dogs blew off the chains. Where people had that peculiar way of putting extra words around what should have been a simple enough concept—"he's like as not going to make it." Why not just say he might not survive? Or, things look grim? Or, he's dying? Ophelia, where nobody ever ran away, and where fathers were always called daddies, no matter what kind of stone cold sons-of-bitches they might be.

Beneath her, *Pelagic* slid through the choppy water with the easy grace inherent in something completely at home with itself. She sailed just outside the harbor, up to Big Diamond Island, glancing toward the houses there. She had thought about renting a place on one of the Casco Bay islands, liking the concept of being separated from the city and closer to the sea. But she scuttled the idea when it became obvious that the ferry schedule would be too undependable for her work at the bureau with its changing shifts and unpredictable emergencies. She watched a school bus crawl along the shoreline road, stopping now and then and popping open, the kids bursting from it like seeds from a jewelweed flower. She knew they must be shouting with their freedom, but the wind tore their voices away. A line of cars followed the bus like ducklings. The trees along the road swayed in the breeze. Some of the houses on this side of the island were new, big and brassy with enormous windows that flashed in the sun. Most, though, were older cottages built low and tight against the elements. Smoke curled up from their chimneys until the wind caught it and whisked it instantly away. She imagined its scent against the firs, mingling through the delicate fingers of green. She imagined the snug rooms below, the fire glowing somewhere—in the living room, maybe, or in a woodstove in the kitchen—and the warm cooking smells of cinnamon and vanilla. From out here on her boat, a chilly fleck of white in the gunmetal water, the whole island seemed to her like some kind of diorama or one of those elaborate tiny landscapes you could see at Christmastime in the shop windows down in the Old Port. Here, perhaps, she could reach out and change things, move the white-steepled church over to make room for a lighthouse high on the hill, add some trees sloping down to the west, give the town a little beach instead of just rocks. Make sure all the little bulbs in the houses didn't burn out so the windows kept that warm, perfect, happy glow.

There was a time when she had thought often about Jines dying. Maybe he would wrap his Ford pickup around an oak tree down on the road to the post office, or simply step off the washboard of the *Jenny Rae* one day, a little flick of a wave when he was alone out there and poof, gone. Alone in her bed at night as the wind howled around the corner of the big white house, she would let her young imagination weave the whole grand tapestry of her father's untimely, yet poetically just, demise. They would search for him. They always did, no matter the weather. They would find the *Jenny Rae* still afloat, tow her in, empty and forlorn. But they wouldn't find Jines. The tide would take him, pull him along under the surface moonfaced and wrinkled, so his glassy eyes could stare up at the arching sky until one day, weeks or months later, some beachcomber or maybe another waterman would see something floating, something odd. Because he had drowned, there would be no laying out for Jines in the parlor. What was left of him, what the crabs hadn't gotten, would have to go straight to the casket and then into the family cemetery, the Grove. Everyone would say how it was a blessing that the Bay had given him up, that he could come home and lay to rest in the good earth with his wife and his parents and the rest of his kin, not be doomed to the fate of some who float on forever.

But Jines had not stepped off the *Jenny Rae*. He and his Ford hadn't eaten a tree on the way to the post office. The stubborn bastard had just kept on living, such as it was. And so had she, avoiding his silent, brooding bitterness, and when he fell asleep in front of the television after dark she would creep in and stare at his indecipherable face that looked creased and worn as an old glove. How had her mother loved this man? And how had she known how to make him love her, no matter what? What was the secret? Lily would watch his face in the blue TV light and then creep back to bed and dream of another father, another life, far from the big white house on the point where Evanses had lived for as long as anyone could remember. And so, it seemed, would she.

The sharp blast of a ferry's horn startled her; it was the four o'clock boat from the city, and she was straying into its path. She tacked *Pelagic* quickly away. Willy would have given her no end of grief for that, she thought, getting run down by a ferry. It probably surprised the hell out of the ferry pilot to see a small boat out here on a day like this, at this time of year. The greasy scent of diesel lay thick on the water as she crossed the ferry's wake and pointed her boat toward Willy's boatyard. What little there was of warmth in the feeble spring sun was fading entirely with the late afternoon. Her hands were stiff, and she shivered as she made up the sails and tidied her boat, but neither the sound of Willy's laughter when she told him about the ferry nor the stream of hot air from her truck's heater did much to warm her.

Michael came over with take-out from her favorite sushi place down in the Old Port. Lily set pillows on the floor and between them placed a small cloth to serve as a table, a vase with a single daffodil imported from some place far from here, and a candle. Her hands ached when she squeezed the chopsticks. The warmed sake slid down her throat like fire. They ate quietly, without saying much, and Michael poured more sake. Lily slid her feet out of her clogs, stretched her legs toward him and then eventually, just for the hell of it, started sliding them slowly toward his crotch. She tucked her toes as far up as she could, playfully feeling the outline of him through his khaki office pants.

"I can't believe you," he said. She tweezed the last piece of tuna to her mouth, letting the cool smoothness of it slide over her tongue, her eyes never leaving his face.

"Can't believe me why?"

"I can't believe that you'd be thinking of sex when your father's in the hospital." She felt him hardening.

"Seems like some of you believes me all right."

"Yeah, well, you know how it is when I get near you." He set his chopsticks down and tipped the small sake cup back to his mouth. "Still, it goes against my better judgment tonight."

"Why's that?" She hadn't eased up with her toes, and she could see the outline of him pressing against the khaki.

"I think we should be talking about what's happened, how you're handling it. What you're going to do. Seriously." He pushed her feet down his thigh and held them there.

"That's very noble of you, wanting to help." She imagined the feel of him inside her and felt that slippery looseness deep within. He had a point; she wasn't sure why she suddenly wanted him so badly when the sound of Mary Virginia's words were still banging around in her head. Even the sailing and the noise of the wind hadn't stilled them. She wiggled her feet free and pushed her toes firmly against him.

"I'm not trying to be noble." He closed his eyes. "But it's a little disconcerting. Jesus."

She came around the pillows and sank her tongue into his mouth, her hand moving to his waist to undo his belt, unzip the pants, and then sliding down the flatness of his stomach, the raspy patch of hair and the silky hardness of him within it. "You don't seem disconcerted," she murmured into his mouth. Maybe this was what she was after, just this, his fingers unbuttoning her shirt and pushing it open wide, his mouth on her nipples, his hands pulling her jeans off and lifting her up on top of him so that she cried out loud when he pushed into her all the way, one long fluid thrust that took her breath away, his hands on her hips, pulling her, pulling her. Her legs wrapped around him so that they rocked together in a fierce embrace, his teeth bit the skin of her lower lip, his mounting cries finally drowning out, for a moment at least, that voice telling her, "You need to come on home now," drowning out the sound of her name the way her daddy always said it until he pretty much stopped saying it, "Lily Rae, Lily Rae, Lily Rae." Don't stop, she wanted to say, don't stop, but not because she loved him or even the idea of them together, but because she needed the feel of his hands on her skin, she needed to know she was human, she needed to make contact.

He lifted her slightly and rolled out from beneath her, away, and stood up to pull up his pants and fasten them. "Jesus," he said again. He was still breathing hard. He looked at her as if he didn't quite know her, walked over to the refrigerator and pulled out a pitcher of water, poured a glass.

"What, no afterglow?" she said. She reached for her jeans. "That's not very noble of you."

He took a long drink of water. "I didn't come over here to make love, Lily, I came to see if you were okay. If you needed to talk."

She poured herself another cup of sake and considered telling him that he needn't have worried, that what had just transpired more accurately fitted her definition of sport fucking than actual lovemaking, but then, hadn't this been really the case since they had started? Or at least for the last couple of months? She had felt, early on, that perhaps Michael was different. She had been truly drawn to his intelligence, his wit, and yes, she would admit, his handsome, almost aristocratic New England good looks. She wouldn't have potentially jeopardized her career for nothing more than a lively roll in the hay; something about him had compelled her on a level far deeper than the physical. For a few months she had let herself be swept into his words when he told her how she made him feel. It was enough to know she could please him, make him laugh, rescue him, if only briefly, from the Vapid Diva. It was enough to let herself feel safe within the confines of the world they made together when they managed to get somewhere alone. And that in and of itself, that piece of him that allowed her safety, was enough to make her love him. Or at least think she loved him.

"Do you love me?" he would ask, and she would say yes, while what she really wanted was to ask him to define that, exactly, love. Do you love me.

Then one night eight weeks ago, they had driven up to a hole-in-the-wall Mexican place in Brunswick for dinner together. The bitter winter landscape outside the restaurant's bay window seemed like the surface of the moon. "It's the one thing I hate about Maine, don't you?" she said over margaritas in giant glasses frosted with salt. "This time of year, I mean. When was the last time you felt like the sun was really putting out? It rises, yes, and it crosses the sky, and if there are no clouds, its rays evidently reach us, our skin, our faces—" she took a long sip from the glass—"but do you really feel anything like actual warmth? Doesn't it seem like some kind of cut-out sun? It's not even trying up there. Do you want guacamole?" She pushed a dish that was shaped like a chili pepper toward him and he stared at it.

"I can't keep going like this," he had said. He had looked at the pulverized avocado in the chili pepper dish the whole time, she remembered. Not at her. At the stupid, kitschy dish that she probably could have found at the local Goodwill with the green glop that they had put way too much garlic and not enough lemon juice in. "It's too complicated. I can't lie to her anymore. She's been going through this whole in vitro fertilization thing, and it's wearing us down. I…she…."

Lily pushed the guacamole away and reached for another dish, this one shaped like a tomato. "Try the salsa," she said "It's better than the guac." They drove back to Portland in silence, only about forty minutes in the car since the roads had been well cleared of the latest snow, forty minutes that lasted approximately forty days and forty nights as she recalled, when she would have given anything to be alone since at least then she could have screamed out loud. She could have felt far less lonely by herself than sitting next to him during that endless, dark drive. It was so familiar, the isolation that slid between them, that she almost had to smile. How easy it was to remember that solitude was a far more acceptable state than being with someone who had reacquainted her with the basic truth that she was alone, that she carried solitude on her like a scent. How careless she was to have allowed it to slip her mind, like leaving the woodstove door open and burning down the house.

If pressed, she wouldn't have been able to explain exactly why, when he'd shown up at her apartment a month later, she had let him back in. She might have given these reasons: The winter nights were dark, they were cold, she had waged an hourly war with herself trying to get over it while being forced to see him at the bureau every day (even after taking a week of sick days, during which she drowned herself in red wine and dark chocolate) and she was worn out with it. Fuck it, she told herself; she missed the physical presence of him. Still, though she wouldn't have said it out loud while looking at herself in the mirror, she knew she would never really let him back in. No more safe places. This was just a longer version of breaking up, the inevitable sinking of a boat already doomed by too much rot in its hull. In those rare moments she let her guard down long enough to face this fact, she despised his weakness almost as much as her own.

She tipped back the last of the sake and started clearing up the dishes.

"So, when are you leaving?" Michael asked.

She handed him the two plates with the small bowls for soy sauce balanced on them. "Careful. These bowls are really tippy. I love the shape of them but they're far more artful than functional."

"I've got them." They clattered into the sink. "Are you flying?

You'd have to go into where, Richmond? And then get a ride or something?"

'What makes you assume I'm going?"

"He's your father, Lily."

"Wrong, m' love. He's muh *daddy*." She exaggerated the deep drawling accent she had grown up hearing, the one she had worked purposefully over time to erase from her voice. "We don't have fathers down to Ophelia, we have daddies."

"Fine, he's your daddy. You don't have to be shitty about it," Michael shook his head. "No more sake for you."

"Says who? And yes, I do need to be shitty about it."

"Christ, Lily, be serious. Your father's had a stroke. He's in trouble. Don't you think maybe he needs you?"

"Please." She poked around in the Styrofoam containers the sushi had come in. "Did we eat all the cucumber rolls?"

"Why won't you talk about this?"

Lily sighed and closed the lids, shoving the awkward containers into the trashcan. They squeaked and snapped and she closed the lid quickly. "I *hate* that sound." She rinsed out the sake bottle and tipped it over in the sink to drain. "What do you want me to say? Yes, he's my father. We share the same DNA. That's it. I would have been better off being raised by a dog pack."

"People can change."

"Really. Been up to Five Islands lately, seen the lobstermen come in, the guys who look like they're a hundred years old? Seen their boats, about the same vintage? Their pickups that look like World War II surplus? That's kind of how Ophelia is. Things there don't change. And Jines, I can tell you for sure, doesn't either."

"How do you know? When's the last time you were there? When's the last time you talked with him?"

"A while."

"How long is a while?"

"What difference does it make?" She turned away from him and sat on the futon that served as a couch and, sometimes, as her bed. There was a skylight directly above it, and she liked to stare up through it at the night sky as she fell asleep.

"I just don't think it's right to keep judging a person so harshly for things that happened a long time ago. It wouldn't kill you to have a little compassion for the man."

"You're right, Michael, it wouldn't kill me."

He was still standing by the sink. She wished he would leave. "There you go again, Lily, falling back on the old standby."

"What's that?"

"Sarcasm. You use it like Dirty Harry uses his forty-five."

"Dirty Harry used a forty-four, honey. Forty-four Magnum."

"Right." He bit off the word. He leaned against the counter and regarded her with an expression she couldn't read. A long, uneasy minute went by. "How long have you been in the Portland bureau now? Six years? Seven?"

"Something like that."

"Why do you stay?"

"What do you mean?"

"Why do you stay here? You're thirty-two years old. You have a sailboat in a marina run by a crazy old coot, and a kayak, a bed and a kitchen table and some chairs in your apartment. Oh yes, and a futon, and one potted palm. You work every holiday shift, every weekend, every night trick. If it's a Friday afternoon and a story breaks, you're the one who goes, even if it means you don't get home till midnight."

"What's your point? Most bureau chiefs would be happy to have me, dedicated, unattached, no hubby and kids to interfere with being a good Marine." Not to mention, she thought, getting laid.

"You're not answering my question."

"I don't really need the interrogation, at the moment. Besides, as you were so kind to point out, perhaps I have had too much sake."

"It's not that hard a question to answer. At least it shouldn't be."

"Maybe. But I'm not even sure what gives you the right to ask it."

Michael leaned his head back and looked at the ceiling. "Ah, now we're getting to the real issue here." He looked back at her, and his eyes were dark. "You don't think that what just happened a little while ago, over there on the floor"—he pointed to where the makeshift tablecloth still rested with its candle still lit—"what's happened between us in the last year, doesn't give me at least a little bit of a right to ask?"

No, she wanted to say, no I sure as shit don't think it does. And by the way, how's that in-vitro project going? "Okay, then, turnabout is fair play. Why do *you* stay here?"

"I have a job here, a career."

"And so do I."

"And I have a family."

"Ah," she said softly, almost to herself, "now we are getting to the real issue, aren't we?"

"Jesus, Lily, what do you want me to do?" He couldn't stay still anymore and strode across the room, then back again. She watched him, and part of her wanted to just let it be, give him his answers, let herself soften to him. "All I'm saying is that it counts for something, family. It's important. It's worth some sacrifices, some risks. He's your father."

She couldn't trust herself to comment. She was motionless, watching the candle on the floor in front of her.

He stood quietly a moment more, then walked over, leaned forward and cupped her cheek in his hand, kissed her there very slowly, letting his cheek brush hers. He took one of her hands and turned it over. The palm was still raw from the afternoon's sailing.

"You do love that, don't you," he said. "You love *Pelagic*, and your kayak." He stood up. "That's easy enough."

She waited until the door had closed behind him and the apartment was finally silent, a giant silence that loomed in a way she hadn't expected. She was cold again. She'd left the windows open and the breeze off the water had scrubbed the room's air clean but had left a raw, damp texture on everything. She walked around slowly, closing the windows, all but the skylights. It had been the attic of a house in the Old Port part of town, converted into a loft apartment. Except for a small bedroom drywalled off, it was entirely open, all angles and corners with skylights opening in the roof and dormers to the streets. One whole wall was original brick; mortar would sift into her hand like salt from a shaker when she would run a finger along the grooves. The exposed rafters were the color of burned caramel, and even after all the years they'd held up the roof she could still smell the pine in them. It was an imperfect space, cold and drafty in winter, and all the weird angles made it hard to find things to fit. She loved it. She could have given that as an answer to Michael's question, a list of things I love, she thought, my boats, my apartment. Define love. Willy. She might love Willy.

She finished closing the windows and stood in the middle of the apartment, not knowing which way to move. She wanted to be angry at Michael. She thought she should be afraid or sad for Jines. But she felt nothing. She felt like she was floating, a shimmery piece of seaweed floating on the cool breathing of the tide, waiting to rise, waiting to fall. Or maybe, she thought, I'm sinking, but there wasn't even a sense of panic, that tingling on the backs of her hands when the adrenaline rushed through her to remind her of being narrowly alive. She looked around. There was her kayak leaning against the brick wall, the futon, her bed. The potted palm needed water. In his brief inventory of her intimate world, Michael had neglected to mention the bookshelves, as well as the apple crates stacked nearby, and the books spilling from them. It didn't seem fair he had left those out. Suddenly she was about to cry.

She walked over to an old, dark, bookshelf. She hadn't brought much from the house on the point, but her grandfather had built this piece long before she was born after a hurricane took out a willow oak that had stood in the front yard. Her eyes fell to the photographs without even knowing they were headed that way. They were side by side in a folding frame. She picked it up and carried it to the middle of the room, sat on the floor cross-legged, and held it in her lap. Both were black and white. In one, she was six years old and sitting at her mother's vanity, the smooth, polished wood of its surface as big as a ship's deck, it seemed to her then. In the image she could see the little crystal perfume bottles, the tiny porcelain ring dishes, the bright, star-shaped doily flared out in the middle, the silver brush and mirror, engraved with her great-grandmother's initials and passed to Jenny Rae when she and Jines married. The brush's bristles were soft and forgiving, easing out the tangles, and her mother would run them gently through Lily's long hair. Lily would tilt her head to the ceiling, close her eyes and smell the perfumes, the powders, the scents of a waterman's wife who somehow never forgot how to be soft and warm even in a world of hard edges. In the photograph, Jenny Rae was braiding Lily's hair. Her head was tilted slightly to better watch her work, and she had a little smile on her face as her daughter gazed into the mirror admiring her new dress, loving her mother's hands. The second image was a ghostly mirror of the first. In it, Jenny Rae was sitting at the same vanity, her mother behind her in her best dress with a fresh magnolia pinned just over her breast, her thick fingers fixing her daughter's hair, her eyes smiling at the lovely girl in the wedding dress. "Someday," Jenny Rae had told Lily, showing her the old wedding album from which the photo had been copied, "that will

42

be you sitting there, and me fixing your hair, just like I do now. And your daddy will walk you down the aisle, just like my daddy did for me."

Lily folded the frame and held it in her lap, rocking back and forth. Why do we make these promises, she thought. Why do we tell children these stories when we know there is every chance they won't come true? She tried to remember her mother's scent, but all she could smell was the pungent salty air still hanging in the apartment and the thickness of the old pine rafters. She wondered where that wedding album was, and the brush and the mirror, and the perfume bottles. She wondered what her mother would look like now. She couldn't remember her voice, and she wished she could hear it to tell her what to do. Somehow that was the most unjust thing of all, the shabbiest cheat of memory and time. After a bit, she looked down again at the photograph. She couldn't remember her voice, but she could almost feel the gentleness of her mother's hands working through her hair.

"Okay then," she said to the smiling woman in the photograph. "Okay. I'll go see to him. For you."

It took her about half an hour to pack. Lily tucked the folding frame deep in the middle of her suitcase wrapped in a soft black sweater. She left a message on the machine at the boatyard, asking Willy to please keep an eye on *Pelagic*. The potted palm looked pretty far gone, but she carried it down the steps and placed it next to her neighbor's door with a Post-It note stuck on the pot asking her to keep it watered. The hardest part was the kayak; it was awkward, and she was sore and tired, but she wrestled it onto the roof of her pickup and strapped it down. When she closed the apartment door for the last time, the sound echoed in the empty space she left behind.

The old house waited at the end of a long, straight lane, as it had done all these years. Lily stood in the drive, facing it square-shouldered. On bright days, its tin roof would throw the sunlight back up to the sky. On days like this, the roof and even the clapboards would fade into the pewter clouds and water beyond, as if the house could become even more a part of this place of low land and wide sky than it already was. It seemed the kind of house to want a picket fence, but it never had one. Nothing much around here could be fenced in. Not the water. Not the men like her father who worked it. Not the long fields of corn and soybeans that stretched alongside it, the salt marshes or dark stands of loblolly pines that framed it.

Oyster shells crunched beneath her boots. The sound made her look down, as if to verify the ground she was on. She bent down and picked up a few of the crushed shells. She squeezed, and their sharp edges dug into her skin. She stood quietly, nothing but her own breath in her ears. It was going to snow. She could feel that much. If she could reach down and pick up the oyster shells, feel their sharp edges, then why not the silence? The air here was made of it, all the weight of what was left unspoken compressed into something tangible yet unreachable. There might have been birds—gulls and crows, perhaps a late wintering loon on the river—but they waited for the weather, hidden. She let the oyster shells slip through her fingers.

The swing was still there at the porch's far end, a wicker loveseat that her father had pared the legs from and fashioned to fit onto a tongue-in-groove pine platform, just so her mother could swing in her favorite wicker loveseat on a summer evening. The way he adored her. The seat was secured by a raised edge of cedar whose corners were precisely dovetailed. Lily lowered herself into it carefully. It creaked, and when she swung gently what was left of the seat's most recent coat of white paint whispered downward like the flakes that were beginning to fall out of the sky. Snow in March in Ophelia. She remembered the fitful nature of spring here, a petulant season of hope and doubt. The farmers, fearing too much cold and rain, would hesitate to plant yet fret that they'd waited too long as their tractors sagged in the mud. The watermen would tar their nets in the cold wind and rain of a late nor'easter churning the Bay, then lean over their coffee down at the Seaside where Jeanette would cut them thick slices of warmed apple pie, brew another pot.

The front door was unlocked. Despite the damp air it wasn't swollen shut; Lily had to push just a little to open it. She was already one step through before she suddenly considered the implications. The front door was really only for letting in strangers who didn't know any better. In summer it would often stand open to let the breeze off the water pass through the house, but family and friends used the back door facing the dock, the boat and ice sheds, and the water. Most friends came by boat anyway. Plenty of people around here still felt that cars and roads were something of a hazardous nuisance. Water was safer, and so was the back door. She was surprised that she had forgotten this. She didn't think she'd forgotten anything.

Inside, the only sound was the hush of her boots across the wide-plank pine floors, and even then the house seemed to absorb the noise, as if it were filled with cotton. For a moment Lily felt as disoriented as she had in the driveway, wondering if she really was there. The air was musty and thick and smelled of sleep, wood smoke, and dirty dishes.

To the left, the front room and kitchen behind it. Straight ahead, the hall through to the back porch and the dark steps that climbed two more flights. To the right, the parlor where her father had sat for three days with Lily's dead mother. She'd been taken special care of, Mr. Taylor, the funeral home director from over in Heathsville, had assured Jines while Lily listened on the landing above. She had stood there fingering the ragged braids she refused to take out because her mother had plaited them with fingers so weak they could barely move. Her daddy had thanked Mr. Taylor, closed the front door after him, and turned to the parlor. Lily watched his hunched back and thought of the pictures she'd seen in her schoolbooks of the Appalachian Mountains, ground down, the books explained, by enormous glaciers. She stood frozen on the landing when her daddy had closed the parlor door behind him, but when she raced down, too late, and sat outside the door sobbing and calling, he did not come.

It was Miss Mary Virginia, who lived just down the road, who finally found Lily some days later, asleep on the landing. She washed Lily's face with a cool, white cloth, helped her down the back steps, and drove her to her house. She fed her vegetable soup thick with okra and tomatoes, ran a hot bath, and slid her between sheets as crisp as a fall morning. Held there, imagining herself in a cocoon from which she might emerge to find things as they had been, not something frightening and new, Lily listened to Miss Mary Virginia's voice suddenly sharp into the phone: "You tell Walter Taylor to get that poor woman out of there and into the Grove where she belongs! Jines Arley is out of his mind." Lily heard her shush her son Jamie when he came home from school. They were in the same class, born just a month apart. They were best friends, but now he wasn't allowed to disturb her. When she woke up later, her hair lay loose on the pillow, brushed out smooth and soft. Miss Mary Virginia fed her soup and cornbread and ice cream and spoke to her softly. It would be all right, she crooned, everything would be all right. When Lily went home a few days later, she left on the pillow of the cocoon bed a fine, blonde rope of hair which her awkward, eight-year-old hands had found easier to cut with the sewing scissors than to weave and caress into a braid.

Jines said nothing about any of it, not even her hair. It was like she wasn't there. Over the course of a day he shoved the parlor furniture to the walls, moved the big couch to the front room, and carried an old bed frame from the attic down three flights, banging it against the newel post at the bottom hard enough to take a chunk out of the walnut as he swung it into the room. He carried down his clothes and threw them on the coffee table and on the chairs that matched the outcast couch. He never went upstairs again, at least not that Lily ever knew.

To the left, the front room and kitchen. Straight ahead, the hall to the back porch and the stairs up. To the right, the parlor. She fingered the dent in the newel post and looked at the parlor door, pushed wide open. She knew if she looked in there she would probably see his bed still unmade, clothes on the chair.

She sat down on one of the steps. It curved beneath her, the wood worn into a smooth saucer by the footfalls of her family's generations. She traced her fingers along the wood, carving little tracks in the dust. They had called her because there was no one else, not because she belonged here. Outside, the snow was falling in fat, wet flakes that fell straight down, and the kayak she had strapped to the roof of her pickup looked absurdly bright and blue.

Chapter 3

The hospital where her daddy was like as not going to make it looked brand new. The Tri-County Medical Center and Wilcox Memorial Rehabilitation gleamed in the fresh light like a space ship in the middle of a cornfield. Lily checked in at the front desk and learned that Jines was in a room on the fourth floor. There were six floors in all. Where in God's name did they get all the people to fill this place, she wondered. Even wrapped up as one and throwing in some long-distance strays from Norfolk, the "tri-counties" had more soybeans than residents. The elevator glided to a stop and a soothing ding announced her arrival on the fourth floor. At the nurse's station a slender man wearing dark blue scrubs reassured her that this was, indeed, the right place; her father had been released from intensive care early that morning.

"You are surprised? It is good, very good. Less than two days in ICU," he said to Lily as he led her down the wide hall.

He looked over his shoulder and smiled as he walked. He wore those rubber clogs that nurses always wore, and they squeaked on the polished floor.

"Your father is a strong man. You must be proud."

He whisked her into the room and was headed for the bed before she could slow him down.

"Here we are, Mr. Evans, are you awake? Yes? Excellent. Can I get you some more juice? Look who I have brought with me!" And then he was back out the door—"I will let Mr. Evans's doctor and caseworker know you are here at last, yes?"—and suddenly the only thing between Lily and her father was the thick plastic arm of the bed with its indicators and switches for changing one's orientation—head up, feet down, how convenient, she thought, to have something else besides yourself to maintain equilibrium in the world—a snowy mound of blankets and a dazzling sense of unreality. That was Jines, under the snow mound. Snow in March. In Ophelia. The lacework of tubes and thin wires made her think of an old tree felled in the woods being overtaken by greenbrier and poison ivy vines. His face was hollow, its wrinkles like crevasses in a glacial field. A crosshatching of cuts etched his forehead and one cheek, and her hand tightened as she remembered the oyster shells she'd picked up in the driveway. Yesterday, it was. When she had come back to the old house. His hair had gone pure white. One arm lay on top of the blanket; she expected to see its ruddy tan but it too was white, almost glowing like mother of pearl, except where the iodine cleanser had turned it a sallow yellow near the port for the various IV lines. He looked small, and this was the most unreal thing of all. It was like walking into your first-grade classroom after graduating college. The blackboard never really took up the entire wall, the way you'd remembered. The chairs and desks could never have held you.

But his black eyes, these had not changed. They watched her approach the side of the bed, where she wrapped her arms tightly around her waist and tried to summon up something like nerve. Something to show for all the fourteen years she had avoided these eyes.

"Hey," she said.

Nothing about him moved. The monitor off to the side of the bed made a steady beeping sound. One corner of his mouth was drawn down a little, as if he'd been to the dentist and gotten a shot of novocaine that hadn't yet worn off. Maybe he couldn't talk. So what else is new, she thought. Even when he could have talked, he never did. She let out a long gusty breath and wondered again why she had even come here. Family is worth some risks, Michael had told her. He had no idea. Nobody leaves family. Not down here. Nobody left Ophelia, for that matter. They were all stuck in a 1950s

B-movie tractor beam. She had done what she'd needed to do to survive; she'd gotten the hell out. It didn't surprise her one bit that Jines had never called, never tried to get in touch with her. She'd sent the obligatory Christmas card every year, and she didn't even know why she did that, except that she always sent one to Mary Virginia and so it was easy enough to send one to him. She made no mystery of her return address. How hard could it be to call information and ask for a phone number? But had she ever really expected some response? How ironic that a stroke had finally taken away from him what he had so purposefully taken away from her: his voice.

"Heh," Jines croaked.

A trickle of saliva had pooled in the slack corner of his mouth. My God, she thought. It wasn't just that. Tears had filled his black eyes and were spilling down the valleys of his face. Impossible. She couldn't ever remember seeing Jines cry. Not even after Danny, or her mother. He hadn't taken his eyes off of her. She didn't know what he was seeing. Was he dreaming? She wondered if he was still knocked out but dreaming with his eyes open. She'd heard of people doing that, and who knew what kind of drugs they'd pumped into him? He could be staring at the Virgin Mary for all Lily knew. Somehow this was easier to believe than the idea that he was crying at the sight of her. There was a box of Kleenex on the rolling table near the bed and Lily snatched a few to give to him, but his arm just lay there, his eyes boring into her. She would have to wipe his face herself. Jesus. She leaned forward and dabbed brusquely at the tears.

"Okay?" she said, thinking about how ridiculous that sounded.

What could possibly be okay about any of this? There was a trashcan near the window, and Lily drew back from the bed to get rid of the Kleenex. She looked around the room. It wasn't half bad, a fairly open space that managed to avoid feeling institutional, despite such obvious clues as the outlets for oxygen on the walls behind the hospital beds. If you had to be stuck someplace inside for weeks on end, trying to teach your brain how to relearn the motor skills of a toddler, how to get a spoonful of applesauce successfully down the hatch, this was a nice place to do it. She pulled open the blinds. The view was expansive. Immediately below was a garden dotted with decorative ponds that, from this height, reflected the sun like mirrors. Paved paths wound gracefully past benches strategically placed beneath big shade trees, some maples, sweet gums, willow oaks. The driveway leading to the outside world passed by here with a post-and-rail fence running parallel, and behind it, a line of young white pines. Beyond that, winter wheat fields of stunning green. The parking lot was off to the left. She could see her kayak strapped to the top of the truck. It pulled her with an intense longing to be anywhere but here.

Behind her Jines made a noise. He was squinting hard against the bright sunlight.

"Oh," she said. "Sorry."

She closed the blind and felt the room drape over her like a cloak. She sat down and looked at him, not knowing what else, at the moment, to do. There was a tap at the door, and then a tall man, at least six foot three, strode into the room. He had an easy, open face and was wearing blue jeans and dark brown clogs, not the rubber kind but leather, which seemed weirdly disconcerting attached to his long legs. He held out his hand; the other arm clasped a laptop computer. "I'm Cliff Wyatt, the neurologist here. You must be Mr. Evans's daughter." She shook his hand and wondered how he knew this. "Your father's neighbor, Mrs. Cockrell, told us she'd contacted you. Up in Maine? Great country. I went to a summer camp up there as a kid, up on Sebago Lake."

"That's pretty there, yes. My name is Lily Evans."

"Good to see you. And your dad, too." He leaned over the bed and put his hand on Jines's arm. "How are you feeling, Mr. Evans? Those ICU nurses are tough, aren't they?" He turned back to her. "Mr. Evans's response over the last twenty-four hours has been excellent. Your dad's a fighter."

"Okay."

"And he's got a lot to be thankful for. His friend—is it Mr. Raley?—was right there when he collapsed and they got him in here quickly. This is so critical in stroke recovery, quick response. We were able to treat it with t-PA within about two hours."

"That's the drug that dissolves the clot that blocked the artery in the brain."

"Very good." Dr. Wyatt's eyebrows arched up appreciatively. "You know something about stroke, obviously?"

"Occupational hazard. I'm a journalist. I learn a little about a lot of things."

"Wonderful." He pulled open the laptop and tapped the keyboard a few times. "Of course, you realize that the stroke's onset probably occurred before he lost consciousness. So there's some time we can't account for. Evidently he was out fishing, and had complained of not feeling well. He's lost some function on his left side. But as I said, he's responded well so far. "

"You think he will survive it."

He looked at her with his head tilted a bit to one side, as if he'd heard an odd noise.

"Why, of course. You can quote me."

He grinned. She hated it when people felt compelled to say things like that once they'd learned she was a reporter. She turned her head to the window and then remembered the curtains were drawn.

"The light seems to bother him," she said.

"That's not unusual at all." Dr. Wyatt peered at the laptop again. "There will be changes, and some of them may seem quite strange. We have a lot of great information here about stroke and its effects, as well as how to recover from them. Great team over in the rehab wing. I think we can get you over there by tomorrow. But I don't see you spending much time there, really," he said smiling at Jines.

"How long, do you think?" Lily asked.

"Hard to say. It all depends on how your dad responds to the therapies. They'll work him hard over there. Maybe two weeks. Maybe less."

Lily pulled back the curtain enough to look out across the brilliant green of the winter wheat. You never saw this kind of green in Maine, always darker. Never this surreal color so intense it almost hurt to look at it.

"But he'll need some kind of care at home, right?"

"More than likely, yes. The therapists and you and Mr. Evans will discuss your goals for his therapy; how much he can do on his own, cooking, shopping, what have you. But in most cases, yes, it's better if people have someone at home to help them readjust."

"—ing?" The sound came from Jines. Dr. Wyatt turned back to him, put one hand on his arm.

"Didn't catch that, Mr. Evans."

Jines squirmed himself up out of the blankets a bit and licked his lips. His brow furrowed in concentration or frustration, Lily couldn't tell which. "Fishing?" Though from his warped mouth it sounded something like "whush-ing."

Dr. Wyatt looked at his watch, then over to Lily.

"It's too soon to say, Mr. Evans, and really, you need to be thinking about getting better and nothing more."

"Fishing is what my father *does*, Dr. Wyatt," Lily said. "Can you be a little more specific?"

Dr. Wyatt snapped the laptop closed.

"For a moment there, I forgot you are a reporter, Miss Evans.

Direct questions, seeking direct answers. But sometimes, the question is premature. And in this case, the answer is as much that of 'if' as it is of 'when.' Best to take one step at a time."

He turned to Jines.

"I will check in on you tomorrow."

Then he was out the door.

Lily looked at Jines, and for the second time this day his stricken look rattled her. Was it just memory playing with her? Jines was a cold-hearted shit, yes, but he certainly had been through the grinder years ago; she was sure there must have been times when his face had taken on this same expression, as though suddenly nothing lay between his windbeaten skin and the bone beneath it. She didn't know what he was feeling, exactly—she'd given up trying to figure that out a long time ago, after she understood that it got her nowhere but hurt—but she knew what she was seeing. She was looking at a crippled, scared animal that had strayed out of its bounds and couldn't find a hidey hole fast enough.

When she was small, sometimes in the early mornings she could hear the crows carrying on in the pines, and she and her mother would follow their racket and find them clustered high up in the branches, harassing an owl who'd stayed out too late. Now the owl was caught trying to get home while being dive-bombed by a bunch of furious black harpies, all of its usual defenses of stealth, silence, and darkness rendered useless. If as much as when, the doctor had said. A not-so-subtle way of weasling out of saying that there was every chance that Jines was finished with fishing, the one thing he had always seemed to care about. Lily had always felt a little sorry for the owl trapped in the tree, even though its own arrogance had blown its cover. Looking at her father's pale, lost face, she was surprised to find herself feeling something like sympathy, and disgust with herself for pushing the question that had treed him.

Ophelia wasn't a town in the sense of a place with a main street of shops and businesses where people could exchange greetings. The local hello was often expressed from the driver's seat of an oncoming vehicle on a two-lane road—frequently a dirt road—and it could be a hand, a couple of fingers, a whole arm out the window. As a truck passed her and its driver lifted two fingers of the wheel, Lily waved at the last moment, too late for him to see. She was out of practice, and she felt suddenly foolish and regretful, a tourist in her own neighborhood who had thoughtlessly insulted a local.

She slowed at the crossroads of the Sunnybank Road and Route 14, the only geographical center Ophelia ever had. There was the dusty, boarded-up shell of what had been a general store, with the stump of a gas pump out front. She was surprised to see the vintage Esso sign hadn't been pirated by some antiques dealer from the next county over. Cattycorner was the sagging pile of what had been the post office. Sometime in the 1960s they'd centralized all the post offices from loose settlements like Ophelia in downtown Mathews Courthouse, a town with a well-laid street grid centered around a tidy common with a gazebo and a memorial to the Civil War dead. It was twenty miles from Ophelia and might as well have been Mars for the way the locals felt about the move. Beyond the crossroads, what constituted Ophelia were fragments and pieces, a scattering of families and homes spread over thirty square miles or so. If the town had anything like a heart, it was the river. As she drove she caught glimpses of it, unsullied and calm, across a field or through some trees.

The road wound around a long curve and suddenly ended at a black-and-white striped gate like a railroad crossing. The river lay beyond sparkling in the midday light. This was the Ophelia side of the one-car cable ferry that had, in various forms through nearly a hundred years, carried people, vehicles, and the occasional cow across the river to Sunnybank and back. She was in luck; it was running and the ferry was on her side. It would cut at least a half an hour off her trip home from the hospital. The ferryman raised the gate and waved her on, and as he throttled up the engine she peered out of her window watching the cable rise up, pass dripping over the metal roller, and then back down to lay on the river bottom until the return trip drew it up again.

It only took a few minutes to cross, and on the other side just up from the landing squatted the Seaside, a faded red-and-white awning over its only door. Somebody had painted a nostalgic mural along one wall depicting workboats at their nets, children playing on a silvery beach, oyster shucking houses and tomato canning plants, a visiting steamboat. The blue-green background mingled water and sky into a kind of magical, charmed ether. In the parking lot sat half a dozen pickups, all Fords and Chevys, she knew without even needing to take an inventory. The community may have lost its post office, but the Seaside had continued to serve as its nerve center, the place where all pertinent news and gossip was exchanged and debated, stories told, deals made, business partnerships born and dissolved—all over gallons of coffee as strong as jet fuel, the flat accents layering the air and giving shape to the place the way flour thickens a roux.

Inside it smelled of coffee, damp wool, grease, and bacon, and as soon as Lily walked in, the low hum of voices stopped as if she'd thrown a switch. For a long moment, the whole room was perfectly silent. Then she heard a soft sound—*wick, wick, wick*—and she knew without even looking at the long table full of men that Jimmy Pierce was still carving decoys on the side. There he was at the far end, his chair pushed out a little to make room for the small block of pale wood that sat on his ample belly. The *wick* sound accompanied each flick of his wrist, and fine shavings drifted around the foot of his chair. A handful of round white faces peered

56

up like moons from the table at her. They called it the liars' table, because that's where the men all sat and told their stories. She recognized most of them immediately; there was Billy Meekins, Jennings Haynie, James Pritchett, Edward Jett. And Kenneth Raley, her father's lifelong buddy and fishing partner. All the old school, no one of her generation. No sign of Jamie, but who knows what he was doing now or where he might be. With a conflicting sense of relief and disappointment, she turned quickly and took a seat at the counter that paralleled the table, and after a bit the rumble of voices resumed.

A young woman, welfare thin and pale with freckled sticks for arms, pushed a menu at her. "Coffee?" Lily nodded and she slid a mug across and filled it. Lily wrapped her hands around the mug. "Take your order?" The waitress snapped a piece of gum between her teeth, slung one narrow hip to the side.

"Yes, please, a bowl of crab soup. Is Jeanette still here?"

"Jeanette's off today." Snap, spin, and she was gone back into the kitchen.

The wall behind the counter was covered with photographs, some framed and some just tacked to the paneling. *Miss Emily, Miss Mischief, Full Moon, Pet, Bustd n Disgustd.* The local fleet of workboats over the years, each with her man at the helm or hauling crabpots or showing off an especially choice catch. There was the *Jenny Rae* and Jines in the cockpit. He was wearing a pair of green farmer-john oilskins, a sweatshirt and a sweat-stained baseball cap over a face whose expression was lost in the shadow thrown by the cap's brim and the photographer's distance. The *Jenny Rae* looked perfect, her white hull gleaming against the blue-green water. Jines had always kept her immaculate, a job that took him hours each week. For these attentions his peers had labeled the photograph "Pretty Boy."

Here and there along the wall were small shelves that held

various knick-knacks: Fossils and prehistoric bones the men had found in the hauls, a taxidermied crab the size of a serving platter, arrowheads and pottery shards, beautiful old medicine bottles thick and narrow, their glass etched by sand and shell. There were framed, yellowed newspaper clippings: "Ophelia Waterman Finds Mastadon Tooth;" "Hazel Wipes Out Packing Plants;" "New Ferry Makes First Run."

To the right of the counter was what the locals called the boneyard: rows of coffee mugs on a series of shelves, each with a name and some with a photo curled inside or propped behind. There was Mary Virginia's husband, James, whose body didn't turn up for weeks though they'd found his boat, bright and empty, the same day he'd gone out. There was Lily's grandfather Walter Dandridge Evans, drowned in a hurricane while searching for her Great Uncle Henry, who had gone fishing the night before like a stubborn fool, she'd heard it said over and over, like a *fool*. And her mother's father too, Andrew Hudgins, who dropped stone dead of a heart attack right there in his cockpit one bright autumn morning just after sunup. Everyone agreed, at family picnics year after year, that if they could choose it, that's how they'd go. The little porcelain tombstones. She looked down at the mug in her hands.

She was halfway through her soup when she heard a chair screech behind her. She felt Kenneth Raley coming before she saw him; he seemed to push the air in front of him the way a road grader shoves dirt off to the side. Then his breath, close enough that she could smell the coffee and Red Man. She silently kicked herself. All she'd wanted was to get away from the hospital and try to sort out her thoughts. She should have known Kenneth would be here. She should have known he never would just let her walk in without some smart-ass comment about it. He'd always taken Jines's side on everything.

"Well now, will you look what the cat dragged back. Ain't you even gonna say hello, Lily Rae?"

She took another spoonful of soup and nodded her head briefly. "Hello, Kenneth," she said.

"My God girl don't they feed you where you're at? You look skinny enough to wrap up in one hand. Better eat two bowls of that while you're at it. " He grinned. "Where *are* you at these days, anyway? Inquiring minds want to know."

"Up north." Her voice sounded so small she hated it. She cleared her throat. "Portland, Maine."

"Portland, Maine, that's a long way. Mighty thoughtful of you to come so far just to see your daddy. After all these years." In his mouth "daddy" sounded like "deddy." He had leaned up against the counter next to her, resting heavily on one meaty arm and leaving the other one at his side. Her whole body tightened. "We think mighty highly of your daddy, don't we, boys. Helluva fisherman." There was a low rumbling of assent from around the table.

Lily was trusting only small spoonfuls in her mouth.

"So what do you do up there in Portland, Maine? Got yourself a fancy job? I don't see no ring, so I guess you stay busy some other way."

"I'm a reporter."

"A reporter!" Kenneth turned a little toward the table behind them, drumming up his audience. "You hear that, boys, we have a reporter in town, a gen-u-wine journalist. Now alls we need's one of them Washington lobbyists and a couple lawyers and we'll have all the chum we ever needed, with some shit left over for the farmers!" He guffawed loudly at his own humor and then turned back to Lily and draped his free arm around her shoulders. He squeezed. Chaw oozed from under his lower lip like a wad of tar washed up from some oil spill. "You know I'm just kiddin', don't you, Lily Rae. Just a little joke with us old friends."

59

Trapped beneath his arm, Lily felt like she'd had just about enough of men who thought they could pin her like this: Michael with his hypocritical guilty games, Jines with his silence, even Dr. Wyatt with his polished delivery that revealed so little but the fact that he was in charge. She shrugged from under Kenneth's arm and reached into her backpack for her wallet. Her hand felt a tube of lipstick. She must've left it in there from her last date with Michael. She pulled it out and uncapped it, turned the end and applied it lightly to her lips. She was buying time, but also figured anything overtly feminine might back him off. Everybody knew his record with women was a disaster. "So Kenneth," she said. "How about you? Still fishing with Jines?"

"Every day except Sundays in the season."

"Of course. Some things just don't change, do they?"

Kenneth quit leaning on the counter and stood up, a full foot taller than Lily and, she figured, about a hundred and fifty pounds heavier.

"Why fix what ain't broke?"

"Exactly right." She leaned back, trying to look casual while her heart hammered away in her chest. She knew how to do this, overcome intimidation, anger, isolation. It didn't matter that this was Ophelia, she told herself. Kenneth Raley wasn't any different than some blowhard governor or state's attorney she'd locked horns with in her job. It didn't matter that it was her father's photograph on the wall, that a person's history piled up here like tide wrack on a beach. Who she was, who she had been, didn't matter at all. She was suddenly furious with everything that had landed her back here in this situation. "Lord knows it's hard to have the discipline and, you know, just the know-how to run your own operation. I mean, you said it yourself: Jines is better than anybody around here when it comes to fishing. Why not just stick with him? Why run the risk of being your own man? After all these years."

The room had gone stone silent, even the *wick, wick, wick* of Jimmy's drawknife down at the end of the table. Lily held tightly to her coffee cup to keep her hand from shaking.

"I'm not sure I catch your drift." Kenneth said.

"I'm not surprised."

Kenneth took a step toward her, his face flushing an alarming shade of red. "You got some nerve, little girl. You leavin' your daddy alone, with all he's been through, then walkin' in here with that mouth. Hadn't been for me he like as not would've died right there in his own back yard. And where the hell were you? *Nobody* leaves family. Why'd you even bother coming back here anyway?"

"Good question. Sure wasn't for the local color."

"Jesus!" Kenneth spluttered.

"Well, Kenneth," came a drawling voice from the end of the table. "She *is* Jines Arley's daughter, after all. Maybe you should have figured there's bound to be more'n one hornet's nest in that tree." A relieved laugh rippled around the table. Jimmy resumed his carving.

Lily took a five-dollar bill from her wallet and tucked it under her half-finished bowl of soup. She took one more swallow of coffee and nodded to the men at the table. "Gentlemen," she said. "So nice to see you all."

The keys shook as she turned them in the truck's ignition, and she gripped the wheel with both hands for a moment and took a long, deep breath. Then she tilted the rearview. She wore lipstick fewer times in a year than she went to church, and she never put it on without a mirror. She took a look. Perfect. Well that was something, anyway. When she pulled out of the parking lot, she let the gravel go spraying behind her.

Outside, some old wind chimes jangled in the breeze that was whipping down the river. The rain had started as Lily drove back from Seaside, and now it slatted against the window at the end of the hall. Across the top of the upper pane a layer of stained glass squares glowed in yellow, blue, green, and red. She stood before the white door of her mother's bedroom and felt the familiar cool curve of the porcelain knob. She didn't know quite how to go in. It didn't seem as simple as a matter of one step after the other and then—whoosh—over the threshold and there you are. Something held her back.

She used to sneak in here after her mother died. Jines had moved down to the parlor, and when he was out on the water or working in the shed she would creep in, one ear listening for him on the walk or at the porch, always afraid he would catch her. Sometimes she would sit at the vanity and brush her hair with the heavy silver heirloom brush. She would unfocus her eyes so that everything would go soft, even the hard little knuckle in her throat, and she would feel nothing but the long, slow strokes. Sometimes she would curl herself up in the middle of the big bed and breathe deeply, trying to find her mother's scent. Now she didn't care whether Jines knew she was in the room or not. But it still felt like sneaking.

She pushed the door open gently, her hand held straight out before her as if she were releasing a bird into the worn-out air. The room occupied the southeast corner of the house, and the long double-paned windows that reached nearly to the floor admitted the feeble light through prisms of rain. Dust lay across every surface like a fine grey fur making her sneeze, and despite the rain, she slid open the windows a few inches, cracking their swollen seals with a flat smack from the back of her hand. Locking up her mother's room tight as any coffin had never felt right, not for the woman who loved to fling open the doors and windows at the first hint of warm weather. "Come on, my Lily, why don't you give me a hand and we'll let the old house take a deep breath," she would say, and the two of them would dash from window to window, throwing them as wide open as they could reach. Her mother always did it with a theatrical kind of flourish, stretching her arms wide at each pane of winter vanquished and inhaling dramatic lungfuls of air. "And now the old house can hear the birds again and smell the tide and feel the wind. It's a miracle every time, don't you think, Lily? Spring? Every time, I can never quite believe it." And few things seemed to make her as happy as the simple act of tossing open the windows.

It was the small things, Lily thought now standing in front of the windows and listening to the rain, always the smallest things that pleased her mother the most. A bunch of flowers freshly cut and placed on the table. The sound of a whip-poor-will or a pair of owls hooting back and forth through the nighttime pines. A good soaking rain when the garden desperately needed it. A fat red tomato sliced thick. Coming home from an afternoon in the skiff with a dozen fresh soft crabs, their backs smooth as silk.

The thought of the skiff swept her into a memory of a summer morning about a year after Danny died. She had heard the screen door slam and her father's steps on the path below her window. This time, though, the door creaked open and closed again. Curious, Lily had gotten out of bed and gone to the window, standing just next to it so no one would know she was watching. "Jines." Mama was still in her robe and slippers and she was following Daddy down the path. Daddy seemed angry. He always seemed angry after Danny died. Every stride of his rubber work boots was a stab at the ground. He looked like a turtle when he hunched up like that, a turtle pulling into its shell. The bottom of Mama's robe fluttered open like a pair of blue wings as she hurried down the path. "Jines, please just talk to me. *Please.*" Lily wondered what she wanted so badly that she would sound like that, like she had to have it even though she knew she wouldn't get it. Daddy didn't stop. He stomped across the dock and stepped onto the boat. Mama's voice was louder and Lily was shocked to hear her swear. Usually that was Daddy's job. "Dammit, Jines!" Lily heard the diesel turn over. Mama was on the dock and she was still saying something, but the engine noise drowned her out. Daddy threw off the lines and throttled up the diesel so hard a thick plume of black smoke rose up off the water and hung there in the still morning air. The boat's wake was frothy and white. After a bit, the sound faded and Lily could hear birds again, the noisy little Carolina wrens who lived in the woodpile and the musical swallows who nested under the porch eaves. Mama sat on the dock a long time facing the river where the boat had gone, one hand slowly coiling one of the lines into a wide spiral, then pulling it back out, coiling it again. She was crying. Lily knew what that looked like, even from the back.

A little while later, Lily came down to breakfast and Mama scooped her up and held her tightly. Then she said she had a surprise, and led her out to the little beach beyond the dock where the crabbing skiff was pulled up on the sand. The two of them pushed, climbed in, and then Mama rowed them along the shoreline past the woods where the deadfalls hung over the water and then the soft marshy edges beyond. She came up next to the sandy spit off the point and shipped the oars. The skiff floated quietly off the beach and her mother took a long, deep breath. It was hot already. "Mama?" Mama held her finger to her lips and shook her head. Then her eyebrows jumped and she pointed toward the water. There, not three feet away, a delicate grey fin sliced the surface. Then another, and another, like dozens of miniature sharks, but the fins were soft looking, not menacing and sharp. Sometimes they even flapped like they were waving. "Skates," Mama whispered, "they're scooping up the manoes. See those big plumes of mud in the water there?" Lily could see the dark cloudy places billowing up in the clear water. "There's a clam bed in there and the skates are having breakfast."

It was mesmerizing, like being in the center of a strange, silent ballet. Every now and then the bottom of the river would seem to be lifting up to meet them, but it was only the back of a skate gliding on its wide wings right underneath the skiff. Mama reached her hand over the side to try and touch one as it flew by, and Lily did too. They were smooth and supple, but the touch only lasted a second before they darted away from her hand. They floated there a long while. Lily lost track of the time. Eventually the skates moved off and the fins stopped waving.

"Wouldn't it be wonderful to be able to glide like that?" Mama said as she rowed them back to the house. "To just soar without making a sound, without hardly moving."

Lily tried to imagine that. The skiff's oak seat was hard under her behind. She shifted a little and leaned over to drag her fingers in the water. "Do you think Danny is like that now?"

The oars stopped their steady dipping and Lily looked up to see that her mother was starting to cry again. She felt awful. What a stupid question to ask. But Mama smiled a little and rested the end of an oar in her lap to put her hand on Lily's hair. "Yes," she said. "I think Danny was there the whole time flying right along with them. I'm glad you could feel that too."

Lily squinted across the water back the way they had come. Even in the summer the deadfalls were bare and spooky. Their branches looked like claws against the hazy sky. The day was already harshly bright, the glare hard and unforgiving as she looked down the river toward where it met the Bay. "Daddy can't feel that. Can he."

The oars resumed their rhythmic slipping into and out of the water. "No," Mama said, and her voice sounded tired, as tired as leaves at the end of a long, hot summer. "I don't believe he knows how anymore."

The rain was starting to slant sideways outside and the sills and floor were getting wet. Lily pushed the windows closed a little, leaving them open just enough to still smell the air and hear the thrumming on the porch's tin roof. She sat at the vanity, and when she slid her damp fingers across the glass top, they left little channels where the golden burl of the birdseye maple peeked through. The dust stuck to her wet fingers like lint. She felt suddenly half-made, as if critical parts of her just weren't there. Had they ever been? She had come into the world with ten fingers and ten toes, but then things had happened. A silence came to live in the old house, and despite what she could understand was her mother's best effort to protect her, it bled into them all. Maybe that was why, Lily thought now, that at the center of everything she had known there was a void, like what was left behind after the crabs had shed themselves soft. You could find them on the beach or floating in the shallows and they looked just like the whole animal, all the parts and pieces intact, but when you picked them up you felt the unnatural lightness, and you realized they were entirely empty inside.

Her mother had shown her the grace in the smallest, most unassuming details. But like the rest, it was only half done. She had never explained the alliance she must have made with the sadness that came with that sense of wonder. How else, Lily thought, could she have endured the loss of her son, the growing distance of her husband? Watching her mother crying on the dock that morning, Lily didn't know the coldness in Jines's turned back. Only later did she begin to understand, when his loneliness bound her as well. Yet somehow her mother had found a way to live with the silence and still find something like hope in watching skates glide under a skiff, in opening a window on an early spring day. If she stayed here now, Lily wondered, would she be able to do the same.

Chapter 4

She is kneeling on the dock. Splintery planks under her knees and shins. The river frozen in great sheets, jagged seams between them etched like the lines in a skull. The ice groans as the current moves beneath, pulling little strips of dead grass and tattered leaves toward the Bay. She leans over the ice watching the ebbing tide, cold air raw in her throat. The foghorn at the lighthouse offshore moans. Suddenly Jines is floating there, his face like a bright moon pressed up against the ice. His eyes are open, his hospital gown blooming around him like a pale exotic flower. His mouth opens as if he is speaking but all she can hear is the slow call of the foghorn, filling her with melancholy. Just as he is about to slide from view a seam in the ice opens with a snap. She wants to reach to him, but her arms are paralyzed; the harder she tries the heavier they seem. Suddenly his hand clamps on her leaden arm and she is down under the ice with him, floating in the frigid silence, her lungs filling. His hand is like a vise but she is too cold-stunned to struggle. Above her, above the ice, the sky is the purest blue she's ever seen. He turns to her, his eyes silver and flashing like a rushing school of mackerel, and she thinks: This is how the world looks through eyes of ice. When she looks up through the frozen surface, she sees her mother, walking away into the sky, her body silhouetted against the blue.

Lily awoke gasping, her body sweat-soaked and freezing. For a moment she was too terrified to move, completely disoriented. She turned her head to the window and saw the edge of light creeping into the sky. Around her the house, bound in silence. She was in her mother's room, on her bed, still in her clothes from yesterday. She remembered coming in here, the rain on the windows, the silver hairbrush. She must've fallen asleep and slept through the whole night. Then the image of Jines's pale face under the ice, the vise of his grip on her arm, shuddered through her again.

The sound of a diesel pulled her to the window in time to see a solitary workboat disappear into a low mist. Time and distance seemed to slip along with it leaving their own corrugated wake of memory. The slap of the screen door. The thump of Jines's boots on the steps, the crunch of the oyster shells as he walked down the path. The brief roar as he fired up his boat's engine and the low rumble that followed. And then the steady fade, just like this one, into silence.

In the first smudge of light she could see the *Jenny Rae* tied up at the dock next to the jumbled complex of sheds and outbuildings that were the base of her father's fishing operation. The boat shifted restlessly on the low swell that had moved across the water following the passage of the early waterman. Beside one of the sheds a small mountain of arrow-straight pine poles lay against one another, all of them hacked into points on one end like enormous pencils. Shrugging beside them was a heap of net, probably already patched, painted, and ready to go. Jines liked to get his pounds set early, she knew. He prided himself on it. She saw the rusty red of the old Farmall tractor and beyond it the woodpile and the wood crib, nearly empty. There was the shed, framed by loblolly pines, where her father had turned out skiffs and small boats when times were tight and fishing wasn't quite enough. He was known for his Little River crabbing skiffs, for the sweetness of their lines and the precision of their construction. She drew in the moist scent of the river at dawn. All was quiet but for the fading drone of the workboat's diesel. Time seemed to have flown back on itself, and she had never left, and suddenly she needed out. The front door banged on its hinges and her feet left a path of shadows where they disturbed the wet grass. She wrestled the kayak off the roof of her truck and carried it to the beach.

Lily slid her kayak into the silent skin of the river and let it take her. Daybreak. A deep breath, the cool air making a cloud of it as she exhaled, the damp chill of night still clinging to the earth. The water was like mercury, silver and thick, as it slipped off the bright yellow paddles. Against the limpid river the world doubled itself. She paddled across a mirror so perfect and endless that looking down into the water gave her the sense of vertigo, as if she might fall away entirely if she looked too deeply. Sliding into the boat's narrow cockpit had always seemed to be a kind of transformation, and she wished this morning she could stay forever in this more supple, graceful skin. With each stroke she could feel her body easing, the fearful dream receding. She took another deep breath and heard the sharp chirp of a cardinal as she rounded a curve by the marsh. Without even looking she knew where the bird would be, and when she turned her head she saw the brilliant dart of color against the dark grasses, the strand of cattail bending under its fine weight. A flash of recognition passed through her, and a strange, unexpected gratitude at knowing the bird would be exactly there. There was the rank smell of the river edge awakening to spring, the quick pat-pat-pat of a flock of diving ducks as they scrambled for flight on their stubby wings.

She paddled steadily. Where once she could have waded for miles along the shoreline netting soft crabs or poking about at low tide, rows of docks jutted into the water like a set of bad teeth, each one seemingly attached to a new or rebuilt house overlooking the water. Her family's house and all the other old places were set well back from the water's edge on the highest ground. She knew the practical reasons for this. In the old days, air conditioning Ophelia-style meant lots of fans and open windows and doors. The higher the homes were the better they could catch the summer southerly, the sea breeze that funneled up from the Atlantic nearly every day. Like the other old homes, her family's house was situated so that with the front door and back door open that steady breeze passed through, and even on the hottest days the rooms would feel cool. Length from the water and proximity to the breeze meant fewer mosquitoes and no-see-ums. More than that, no one on the river with any kind of history would ever underestimate it. Giving it a respectful distance was just good judgment based on hard-earned experience. But these new homes, Lily saw, seemed to have no compunction at flouting tradition or common sense. Oversized and ostentatious, they crowded the low shoreline like impatient children, shouldering each other and everything near them out of their way.

Not far downriver she passed Jenkins Boatyard. The two thin rusty arms of the railway still stretched out of the enormous barn down the ramp and into the water. Addison Jenkins, of her grandparents' generation, had installed a Model T Ford engine to hoist the boat cradle up the railway, and it had hissed and spat and squealed as if it needed an exorcism rather than motor oil and fuel. She wondered if it still ran. She pictured Addison's son Angus, who over the years had stacked the dusty barn to the rafters with everything from adzes to outboard engines as living proof that he was not one to part with a tool or piece of machinery simply because it had a few miles on it. The railway probably ran as ornery as ever. At least two dozen boats were tied up under the covered sheds on the water. She noticed as she glided by that of those, only a handful had the high bows, long, low cockpits, and rounded transoms of the local working fleet. The rest were runabouts and a few cruisers but mostly fishing boats, the recreational kind, small and plastic and forgettable with names like *Reel Estate* and *Nice Asset*.

As she left the railway behind she was paddling out across the broadest part of the river, passing the Sunnybank Ferry. Up on the hill she could see the Seaside, half a dozen pickups in the parking lot. Coffee would be good, but she had no desire to run into Kenneth again, and so she paddled on. She was headed for Piney Island. It sat near the river's mouth, a pancake of earth fringed with white sand. In the middle on the only high ground was a small forest of loblolly pines whose skinny trunks and tufted tops always reminded her of the kind of trees Dr. Seuss would draw. It wasn't much bigger than an acre, probably, but when she was a kid it seemed huge and mysterious. As she grew older it became her favorite place to poke around with Jamie. They had found arrowheads and Indian tools; they had watched terrapins dig their nests in the sand. As she approached she could see that the island was nearly gone. Of the forest nothing was left but a few thin trunks sagging over the eroded edge. A single pine still stood upright, and a pair of osprey nesting among its high branches took off with angry shrieks when she approached. A few low scrubby bushes, mixed with cattails and the invasive phragmites, clung to the swatch of marsh and sand that the water and time hadn't yet taken.

The kayak's bow hissed to a stop on the beach and she climbed out, hauling it up so just its stern hung in the water. She jumped when a pair of mallards bolted from the grasses, almost crashing into her as they took off. A wisp of breeze rustled the grass then moved along, its handprint darkening the water briefly. Lily walked a few paces along the beach, remembering how it had been.

She thought about the new houses and docks, the new people coming to live here. No doubt it was great for the economy, having a bunch of rich retirees finding their little patch of river heaven here, maybe buying a nice new boat from Jett's Marine, dining on the crabcakes once or twice a week at the Seaside, contributing all that fresh tax revenue from their newly assessed properties. Come-heres. That's what the locals called them, people who moved to the river from Richmond or Norfolk or Washington, D.C., or anyplace else. You could live in Ophelia eighty years, but you'd still be a come-here if you weren't born with your toes in the river. Change was inevitable as the tide, but Lily had seen what had happened in many of Maine's small fishing villages when the outsiders discovered them. She wondered if the same was happening here. On the face of it, the new properties would drive up the taxes, making it impossible for older people on fixed incomes to live in the houses they'd been born in and even owned outright. But it went deeper, too. Many of the new people would begin to want Ophelia to be something different than it was, all the while proclaiming how much they loved it for what it is. They'd say that they came here because the workboats on the river were so charming, although they'd rather the watermen did not crab off their waterfront. In fact, they'd insist they didn't, complaining about the engine noise and the watermen's FM radios turned up full blast belting out Reba McIntyre and Waylon Jennings at six in the morning. And sure, they liked how quaint the old machinery was at Jenkins', but could he just ask those crabbers to keep their boats somewhere else, because that bait on a hot summer day, my God the stink! And even though local kids had forever soft-crabbed and made campfires on the beach that happened to be on the land they'd just bought, they'd post the land up and down with No Trespassing signs because, they would regretfully say, their homeowner's insurance wouldn't cover it if some youngster got hurt out there.

Of course, they would want to preserve the local history and traditions, even while their own histories took over the river like kudzu overrunning the edge of a summer field, obscuring everything beneath. Maybe it was inevitable, as natural as the turning of the seasons, but Lily had seen the donated black-and-white photographs and old Bibles and chamber pots and fishing gear in little local museums in Maine, and they'd always made her feel simultaneously curious about the past and uneasy about its rendering in the present. Here in Ophelia, how would they honor that past without tydying it up too much, without mentioning how back in the day Jenkins Boatyard and everybody else routinely dumped oil and trash and anything else they didn't want overboard? That everyone once went to school in one room, which seemed charming until you realized that for a long, long time, there was hardly a future past tenth grade that didn't have something to do with working the water? They would try to find the appropriate distance and perspective through which to view the stories that made Ophelia what it was. And maybe they would sanitize it, clean it up, to make it something else.

It was better than nothing, Lily supposed. Better than just eroding into nothing. She pushed her toes into the wet sand. Still, there was something melancholy about it. The river seemed to her like an old woman who has outlived everyone, all her friends and family, until it's just her left looking out the same familiar window, surrounded by strangers who nod and smile at her stories but think she's a little touched, and tuck them safely away to be retold in a more coherent, acceptable fashion.

The osprey pair had returned to the single tall tree and eyed her warily. She was about to head back to the kayak when she heard an engine. In the distance, a boat was emerging from the creek to the southeast. It seemed to be headed straight for her. She couldn't quite see it yet—the sun was fully risen now, the flat planes of light firing the water—and she'd rushed from the house without her sunglasses. Even with her eyes squinted and her hand hooded across her forehead all she could make out was an outline against the glimmer. As it approached she could see the hard chines and plumb bow of what had to be a local skiff. She saw what looked like the round head and stout legs of a dog perched at the prow leaning into the boat's wind. A tall, broad-shouldered figure was standing to one side where the vertical tiller would be. There was something familiar about that stance. The man looked almost casual leaning against the gunwale, she could swear one leg was crossed in front of the other, as if he were leaning on a signpost waiting for a bus. But there was a steadiness also, a firmness in the shoulders. One hand, the one not steering, was stuffed into a pocket. Casual, but not. Relaxed, but poised. As if he were simply an extension of the boat, an integral one of its parts, ready to do what was needed.

The boat was rushing toward her now—Jesus, was the guy asleep or what?—and at the last minute it slowed, its bow pushing sharply up onto the beach as the driver throttled into a quick spurt of reserve, then neutral. The dog, a yellow lab, leaped to the beach and jogged immediately to Lily, snuffling her legs and hands. The two osprey took off again screeching. The wave that followed the skiff shushed up onto the beach and rocked the stern of Lily's kayak. As the driver shut off the engine she realized what had seemed so familiar. Jamie Cockrell swung one leg over the gunwale and sat, straddling the skiff's side like a horse, and nodded toward her. "Thought that had to be you out here, this hour of the day," he said. "Still mudlarking? Find any treasure?"

"Not much left to find, it seems," Lily said. She had wondered whether she would see him. Now that he was here, she felt as flustered as the osprey. She steadied herself patting the dog's broad head. "That was quite an entrance. I thought maybe you were asleep on your feet."

"Well it's nice and deep coming up from that side. The poor old island, she's been washing away a little bit every year, especially in the winter when the nor'easters hit her. But this side is still deep. You remember. Current sweeps right by here, scours it out. Good swimming hole, even now." He was looking at her so straight and steady. She ducked her head down. "Damn, Lily, you look just like you did in high school. How long ago was that now? I can't remember."

"Fourteen years." She hadn't even brushed her teeth. She twisted her uncombed hair into a ponytail with one hand, tucking the stray pieces that were teasing her face behind her ears with the other. Did he really not remember how long it was?

"Man." Jamie shook his head.

He wore a baseball cap over his short dark hair. Even in the brim's shadow she could see the roughness etched into his face; he was aging like everyone did here, windblown and sun-blasted. He hadn't fixed that one tooth that he'd chipped falling out of the magnolia tree in her front yard. Now the imperfection complemented his face, all those pieces had come together. His eyes were as she remembered, a striking, nearly turquoise blue. He was wearing jeans and white rubber work boots, and he rooted around with one hand in the pocket of his flannel shirt until he fished out a pack of Marlboros. He pointed it at her, offering, but she shook her head.

"I only smoke when I've had too much wine to drink," she said.

"Yeah." He mouthed the word around the cigarette as he lit it. "I only smoke when my daughter and my mama's not looking. Probably a good thing for me that's not too often." He gestured toward the boat. "Have a seat. Go on, Mags," he said to the dog, who jogged off into the grass.

Lily climbed over the side, suddenly conscious that she was still in the clothes she'd slept in. She stepped gingerly across the plywood floor of the cockpit and climbed onto the small triangle of deck at the bow. Her bare feet were freezing and damp from the inside of the kayak, and she tucked them tightly beneath her.

"You have a daughter?"

"Look here," and Jamie dug his wallet out of a back pocket and pulled out a small snapshot. His big hands and fingers held it delicately out to her. He wasn't wearing a wedding ring, not even a tan line where one might have been recently. "That's my girl. Isabelle. Belle for short."

Even from the small image Lily could see the girl was pretty. She had Jamie's black hair but her eyes were a darker blue, almost grey. Despite the gap where two front teeth had fallen out her expression had something in it that made her seem older, more knowing.

"She's beautiful, Jamie. Wow. An old soul in those eyes."

"That's just exactly what Mama says too! What is it with you women?"

"It's not meant to be a criticism."

"I know, I know that. I'm just sayin'. You and Mama I swear, so much alike sometimes. Always were."

She handed back the photo. "How old is she?"

"She'll be nine next month. April baby. And you're right. There is somethin' about her that's different from other kids. Although I am biased, of course." He smiled and carefully tucked the picture away. "How about you?"

"Kids?" She shook her head. "No."

"Why not?" He deflected the sensitive nature of the question by not meeting her eyes, instead reaching down into a duffle bag and pulling out a thermos, as if they were just talking about the weather and crab prices. He handed it to her. "If you didn't stop for shoes you probably didn't stop for coffee." She poured a cup into the cap.

"Oh, that's good." The coffee heated her inside, and she began to feel the sun's growing warmth on her legs and face. Why in God's name would she want to have kids, she wanted to say. Bringing them into a world full of promises bound to be broken. "My job isn't too conducive to what you'd consider a stable family life."

"Married?"

"Nope, not that either." She sipped the coffee, held the question out there with her voice nice and steady. "You?"

"Not anymore, thank God." His expression tightened, a slight gesture so quick it seemed almost involuntary. She wished she hadn't asked. "Mama tells me you're living in Portland, Maine, working for the wire service."

She nodded quickly, happy to be off the marriage and kids topic. "You'd love it up there, Jamie. The ocean is so open, wild. When I'm out sailing sometimes I see whales, seals. And the seasmoke and fog. It's so, so—" she waved one hand around as if she were trying to catch the word she was looking for—"so *alive*."

"I don't know, Lils,"—her stomach jumped a little when he said the nickname he'd always used with her—"I'm a Bay boy, you know, through and through. You can go a lot of places and not see anything prettier than the sunrise from this spot right here."

A workboat pushed along out in the channel trailing a bateau behind it. Jamie waved; in the boat's cockpit, a burly figure raised one arm in steady salute back. "That's Gerald Haynie from over on Bloxom Creek. He's got a couple of pounds down south a bit. Besides him and Jines there aren't too many boats runnin' pounds out of here anymore." He turned back to Lily. "So how's he doing?"

She pushed a long breath between her teeth. "The doctors tell me that he has a good chance of nearly a full recovery. He'll be in that new rehabilitation center for a couple of weeks, learning how to deal with weakness on his one side, how to get around at first, use a walker, stuff like that."

"Jesus. Jines with a walker."

"Yeah, I know. Doesn't seem possible, does it."

Like you being married, she thought. Like you having a daughter. Like me, sitting here in my bare feet and slept-in clothes looking at you. She poured some more coffee and handed the cup to him.

"When will he be able to work again?"

"They won't say, but even in not saying, what it sounds like is they don't want him to go back out at all. They say his sense of balance is affected and it would be too easy to go overboard. His blood pressure is out of whack too, and he's on all kinds of meds. They could affect his depth perception. He could have another stroke out there."

"What's he going to do?"

"I don't know."

"Man," Jamie said. "He's not gonna want to hear that he can't go fishing."

"I know."

Jamie held out the thermos to her, and she gratefully took another cup of the black coffee. She must have slept ten hours straight last night. Amazing how tired she still felt. "So what are you going to do?" he asked her.

"I guess I'm hanging around here for a while. I took a leave of absence from work, I have about a month."

"That's great! You'll get to meet Belle."

"I'd like that." She wondered about the ex-wife. "So what are you up to? What brings you this way so early on a fine day?"

"Work, what else. I'm over at the yacht yard there in Merrymeeting Creek. Quicker in the skiff. Besides, the owner—you remember Tommy Wilson?—he can't be using my truck to do errands all day long if I don't bring it."

"Tommy Wilson? Owns a yacht yard?"

"His daddy bought the old Rowe place when Miss Emily finally passed. Nobody'd been doing anything with it for years, you know, she'd just been knockin' around in the old house all alone after Old Man Rowe died. They didn't have any kids, nobody to pass it on to. The wharf was falling apart. Tommy's pop bought the place at auction and put in a whole bunch of new docks, got a new lift, poured a ton of money into it, and just when it was really getting off the ground he keels over with a heart attack. Stone dead. You believe that? Tommy inherits the whole shebang."

"Must be nice. I guess."

"Must be."

"How long have you been there?"

"I worked there over the winter, couldn't get out with anybody oysterin'. Most of the old beds are pretty well shot, although I hear they're making a comeback up on the Rappahannock, so maybe we're next. Even so, the state puts a cap on what you can take now, and believe me, there isn't much left to take. All those scientists and they still haven't figured out how to stop the MSX and Dermo from killing the things. And so many people buying oysters from all over the place—Louisiana, even Oregon—there just isn't enough market for the locals. Anyway, Tommy had a decent amount of winter work and wanted someone to ramrod it cause he's too damned lazy, and I needed the money, so there you go. It's a job. And Maggie gets to come with me." He pointed to the yellow tail waving like a flag in the marsh grasses.

Lily looked around at what was left of the island and then back at Jamie. "I was thinking, before you showed up, that it seemed like everything around here has changed so much in some ways and not at all in others."

"Well, you know, Lily Rae, some things on the river won't ever change."

He was looking at her in that way he had, straight and steady. She held his gaze. He smiled and swung his leg back into the boat.

"I better get going." He whistled for the dog.

"Me too." She stood. "Thanks for the coffee." She hesitated a moment, then leaned into him awkwardly, quickly. She felt his big hands on her back then she pulled away and hopped from the bow into the sand with a wet thud.

"Listen," he said, "why don't you come on over to the house for dinner tomorrow night? You got any plans?"

"Oh yeah, my dance card is burning up."

He grinned. "I know Mama wants to see you, and Belle and I

usually have dinner with her couple nights a week. Tomorrow's one of them."

"You don't think she's still mad at me for leaving?"

"Ah shit, Lils, once you walk in her door all will be forgiven."

And what about you, she wondered.

"That sounds great."

"All right then. Around six at Mama's. You know the way."

The boat's engine started up with a low, wet rumble. Maggie raced across the beach and jumped in. Jamie hit a little reverse to nudge the bow off the beach, then leaned in toward her once more.

"Mama said she'd called you," he said, "but I sure didn't expect to see you here again, Lily Rae."

He pulled away from the island and throttled up, turning the boat's bow toward Merrymeeting Creek across the river. She saw the name painted in gold letters across the transom: *Belle.* Jamie's skiff ran sweetly through the water, and she kicked herself for not asking him about it. She watched the outline of him going away against the morning light, then pushed her kayak off the beach and slid in, paddling quickly away from the island. The early spring sun was warm against her back now and it wasn't long before she was sweating. Water sparkled and flashed off the paddles.

God, he had grown into a handsome man. When she'd left he'd still been on his way, still fighting all the battles of high school— acne, pre-calculus, trying not to get caught smoking pot and necking at the drive-in movie theater off the road toward Mathews (it was, she had noted now, a U-Store-It). They had run together for so long, everybody in Ophelia just assumed that they'd go on and get married, and perhaps it was just that expectation that she began to resist.

Jamie had always been her best friend, but by the time they hit junior high she began spending less and less time under Mary Virginia's roof. It was embarrassing, always feeling like some kind of an orphan. What was left of her family was so dysfunctional she was certain she carried it on her skin like a kind of scent, the way you could walk into a house and know if too many cats lived inside. Even if it weren't as obvious as she dreaded, this was Ophelia, after all. Everybody knew that Jines Arley was one of the best watermen and certainly the best boatbuilder on the Little River, but they also knew that he practically had to be separated from her mother's corpse with a crowbar. Everybody knew that ever since Jenny Rae had died, Jines slept in his front parlor instead of his bedroom like a normal person, and that he refused to set foot in church like a decent Christian, even on Christmas Eve or Palm Sunday. Because it was Ophelia, everybody knew that most of the time he wasn't even home, and if it weren't for Mary Virginia feeding and clothing Lily she would have ended up like some kind of ragamuffin, a street Arab in a place with no streets. Was it any wonder, she would ask herself as they grew older, that Jamie wouldn't want to have a thing to do with her? He knew more of her secrets than anyone, but as they moved out of childhood—where such secrets could be safely told and kept—she began to wish she hadn't entrusted him with so much. By the time they were in high school, Jamie spent most of junior and senior years dating Margaret Pritchett, the kind of girl who would have been a perfect candidate for the Junior League if Ophelia had ever dreamed of having anything even close to such a thing. She was the exact opposite of Lily in every way, and so it was easy to despise her and resent him when they passed her in the hallways on the way to class. It was easy to meet Jamie's eyes with a look of defiance instead of vulnerability, and it was easy to get a full academic scholarship to the University of Maine and get as far away as soon as she could from all of them—from the ghosts that ran rampant in the old house and in what was left of her father's heart, from Jamie and Mary Virginia, from a way of life on the river that she didn't want any part of.

And yet, here she was again, and there he had stood in his long legs and jeans and boots, married, divorced, a father of a beautiful girl. Still on the river, still trapped in Ophelia. Still knowing more about her than she wished he did. She skimmed in her kayak like a swallow across the flat water, bright and quick. This is how you'll survive, she told herself as she paddled, flying like the swallows. Only touching the surface for a second, never diving deep like the ospreys or terns. Only leaving a tiny footprint on the mirror of water, one that will vanish before anyone notices, so you can do the same.

Chapter 5

That afternoon she knelt in what had been her mother's garden. Strands of hair snaked around her sweaty neck and lay stuck across her forehead, and every time she pushed them back she was swiping dirt there as well. It wasn't even hot here yet and she was a mess. Something about her blood thinning or thickening from too many long New England winters, she could never remember which. Still, the hard work of tilling up even part of the garden felt good. There was no way she could do the whole thing. When it was under Jenny Rae's full-time care, the garden was big enough to feed a family of four with plenty left over for canning and pickling to tide them over the winter. She planted everything from herbs to eggplants, and there were large swatches set aside for rhubarb, strawberries, asparagus, and potatoes. When Lily had returned from paddling, she'd stopped at what was left of what had once been her mother's pride and joy and saw a field of weeds. It looked like the rhubarb and asparagus patches had simply been mown over and grass allowed to grow up in them. Jines had never spent time in the garden, even when Lily was young, but she was still angry with him for letting it go. It was disrespectful to her mother.

She dug the trowel into the giving soil and tucked in a Big Boy tomato seedling, gently patting the earth around it. She moved down the row a foot or so and scooped out another cup of dirt, then gently tipped another tomato plant from the flat beside her and settled it in. Afternoon sunlight skipped off the river and lit up the tin roof. It glinted off the slanted doors of the cold frame that hugged the house's southern side. It was set down near the foundation so you had to step down into it once you'd lifted the glass doors, which were really just big framed windows taken out of somebody's house. Half-dug into the ground like that the cold frame absorbed and held heat even on the most bitter winter days. Inside, rows of shelves flanked a center aisle where a gardener could move around and tend to things, watching the sky through the glass, waiting for warmer weather. Every now and then a storm would hurl a tree branch and maybe break a pane of glass that would have to be replaced, but everything else about the cold frame was exactly as her grandfather had built it. The pine shelves and mossy floor smelled as old and full of secrets as an attic.

It had been her mother's cold weather haven, and later her own. In late winter Lily would start her seedlings under artificial lights—zinnias and petunias, butterfly flowers, snapdragons, marigolds, sunflowers, summer squash and zucchini, eggplant and cucumbers, tomatoes and cantaloupe, watermelon, peppers and lettuce, parsley and mint and mounds of nasturtiums, not to eat but just to look at because they were pretty. All the things her mother had shown her how to grow. Sitting on the shelves in the cold frame, the plants' delicate necks would unfold from their beds of soil and Lily would sit with them, absorbing the dense earthy quiet and the wonder of the seeds. No one bothered her there; it seemed she was in another world entirely, a place that defied the cold and overcame it, where small things wanted nurturing and came to life under her attentions. As the sun would grow higher and hotter and the cold frame began looking and feeling like a jungle, she'd start moving her tender charges out, planting them alongside the carrots and beets and potatoes and onions that had waited patiently in the warming earth. Out there, although she could still look after them, the seedlings were on their own. Little warriors, battling aphids and Junebugs and the withering sun.

She moved methodically down the row, nestling more Big Boys in. They were sturdy little plants, their distinctly tomato smell strong already. They weren't hers. She had arrived too late to get

84

anything going in the cold frame; as it was, this was a little early for putting in tomatoes. The whole idea of planting anything in her mama's garden was silly, really, a nostalgic impulse that made no sense. Nevertheless, after tilling up a corner of it she drove to the House of Deals in Reedville and bought two flats of tomatoes and a mixed flat of squash, zucchini, eggplant, and peppers. The House of Deals was, ostensibly, the Trustworthy Hardware store, but everybody knew it as the House of Deals.

"Lily Rae!" Mamie Hardesty had crowed when she walked in. "Bless your heart, how's your daddy doing? House a Deals!" she barked into the portable phone, waving Lily to walk with her as she talked. "Yes ma'am, just got some in this morning." Pause.

Mamie pointed her bony finger toward a set of wind chimes hanging from a nail stuck into a shelf loaded with oil lamps, kitchenware, and scented candles. She looked back at Lily, her eyebrows raised as if to say, "What do you think?"

"Five-seventy-five a pound," Mamie said briskly into the phone. "How much you need?" Pause.

Lily gently pushed the wooden paddle under the chimes and smiled at their round tone.

"Fifteen dollars' worth? That's fine." Pause. "Yes I got petunias in and about half the annuals, all the vegetables." Pause. "No ma'am, no zinnias yet. Not till late May for those. Okay."

Mamie clicked off the phone looking harassed. Then her face brightened again seeing Lily. "What do you think of those chimes, aren't they the most beautiful sound you ever heard? Come from Vermont."

"I love them, Mamie, can I buy a set?" They would be perfect up in her loft apartment, under one of the skylights where they could catch the breeze.

"Why of course, darlin', I knew you'd like them. It's so good to see you, Mar' Virginia told me you were on your way home. Now do you want some of this rockfish I got in here this morning? Jimmy Pierce brought it in and it looks awful good. Better get it before it's gone. I got good red potatoes too, look at these," she was leading Lily over toward the front of the store where wooden crates sat plumped with ruddy potatoes and pale white onions. Lily could still smell the dirt on them.

"I thought I might plant a few things in the garden at the house."

"Well here you are, honey," Mamie said and walked out front to the flats of plants wedged in between the bicycles, Radio Flyer wagons, Adirondack chairs, and wooden whirligigs.

"Hardware" was on the sign out front but that was just the tip of the iceberg. The House of Deals was two stories tall and seemed to stretch back about half a block, and every inch of it was jam packed with everything from wood screws and engine oil to porch furniture and frying pans. Lily had always loved it when her daddy had to go to the House of Deals; she knew that while he went rummaging down the aisles getting distracted by power drills (in the hand tools section, next to paint and fasteners) and planers (in heavy equipment, back with lawn tractors and plywood) she would find, depending on the time of year, baby bunnies, fat pumpkins, bright kites and, near Christmas, plastic lawn Santas, ornaments, trains, and Flexible Flyers—not that anyone in Ophelia could actually ever use a Flexible Flyer since it hardly ever snowed, and the only thing that resembled a hill in the vicinity was a pimple of dirt the state highway administration had made when it excavated for a new off-ramp on Route 202. Now, since it was spring, half the parking lot was taken up with racks of vegetables, as well as annuals, perennials, and even tubs of roses for those hopeful and foolish enough to try to outwit the humidity and grow them. Lily had carried her flats of veggies inside to the check out and then darted back out again, this time returning with two flats of strawberry plants.

Looking at the delicate green tufts sitting beside her now, she didn't know what the hell, really, she'd been thinking. It would take at least a year for the strawberries to settle in enough to produce any berries, maybe more. Exactly who did she suppose would be caring for them by then? Jines sure as hell wouldn't be crawling around out here bedding them with the requisite straw. The garden had never been his thing. The new wind chimes, hanging from a branch on the silver maple tree, rang as the river breeze cooled her face. The real reason she'd started on this project, she decided, was to avoid going back to the hospital and sitting there with him.

Lily heard the crunching of a car in the drive out front and rocked back on her heels. She waited. There was someone at the front door; she could hear the knocking. A stranger. She stood and brushed her hands off on her jeans, then strode around the side of the house. In the driveway sat a nifty little blue BMW convertible, top down. On the porch its driver knocked on the door once again, peered through the window, and then jumped when Lily said, "Over here."

"Oh! Hey, hello," he said, turning and springing down the steps with the limber smoothness of someone who had spent a lot of time on some playing field somewhere.

He seemed familiar, or maybe that was just because he looked like a walking Nautica ad. His blue jeans appeared to be pressed, his oxford shirt crisp from the dry-cleaners, the cuffs rolled precisely halfway up his forearms. Down at the beltline she saw three monogrammed initials, BCW. At the beltline? What was up with that? His boat shoes were fashionably worn, just scuffed enough to not look new though she guessed they probably came that way. His ankles were bare. Even his hand, when he held it out to her, was perfectly clean. Probably manicured, she thought. She felt a certain wicked glee shaking it with her filthy sweaty one. He had a neutral hand, a cocktail party grip, easily extended, easily withdrawn, so that it didn't carry any meaning or emotion. He smiled, big and GQ and white, even while she could tell he was trying to figure out how to wipe off his hand.

"You must be Lily Evans?"

"And you must be?"

"Bradford Wilson," he said. "I'm a friend of Cliff Wyatt."

"Is everything okay?" She was alarmed and confused; why would Jines's doctor send someone out here?

"Okay?"

"At the hospital, is something wrong?"

"At the hospital?" His tanned brow, broad and smooth as a tennis court, furrowed, then suddenly cleared. She wondered briefly if he'd Botoxed it. "Oh, no, I'm not a doctor, I'm not affiliated with the hospital. Cliff and I went to school together at Virginia."

"Virginia."

"Yep. We pledged the same fraternity, same class. He had the brains, I had the lacrosse scholarship." His laugh was self-deprecating in a practiced way, a cocktail party laugh to go with the handshake. He was either a politician or a salesman. She felt the sweat of her gardening on her back; she craved something cold to drink but that would mean inviting him in too. "Cliff and Marita—that's his wife, have you met her?—they came up here a couple years ago and bought that house they're in. They invited me up here last fall—well, for me it's really over here, since I'm in Richmond now—and I mean to tell you, I've been pushing the hospitality envelope. I love it here. This place feels more like home every time I come. Working in the garden?"

"Tomatoes."

"Oh yeah," he said. "I stop by the produce stand out there on Route 202 every time I'm down here in the summer. Amazing tomatoes you folks grow around here. Do you know the stand I'm talking about?"

"Edward Hudgins," she said. Why did outsiders always assume calling people "folks" let them in? "His family has farmed here forever. People go to that farm stand like they go to church."

Bradford Wilson laughed. "The guy wears knee socks and a long-sleeved shirt no matter how hot it is, too funny."

She suddenly wanted to skewer him for even standing here in her family's yard.

"The shirt is because he's scared of skin cancer; there's a high incidence of it among watermen and farmers here. Because they're so exposed to the sun in their work. Johns Hopkins did a study about it years ago." She pulled her hair off her neck with one hand, keeping her eyes on him. "The socks make it easier to see the ticks when they come up out of the field. There's a lot of Lyme disease around here too. Or maybe they're just a Northern Neck fashion statement. What do you think?"

Bradford Wilson looked a little uncertain, as if maybe he'd just stepped off the smooth turf of his lacrosse field into one of his buddy Cliff's human anatomy classes.

"Oh, hey," he said, waving his hand, "I wouldn't know. I just love the man's tomatoes."

He looked up at the house, then across the side yard toward the river and back the other direction toward the meadow and forest beyond. She could almost see him regain his mental footing as he took it all in, found familiar ground again in his practiced appraisal.

"This is a beautiful place you have here," he said. "How many acres?"

"Fifteen, give or take."

"Wow! Terrific! You must have been here when the Indians were still around. Your family, I mean."

She pushed her hands into her back pockets. "Are you in real estate, Mr. Wilson?"

"Bradford, please. How'd you figure that one out?" He acted surprised, eyebrows high.

"Just a guess," she said.

"Cliff said you were sharp, that you're a reporter. Must do a lot of people watching, huh."

"You could say it's part of the job description."

"Then you've probably already guessed why I'm here."

"Why don't you tell me anyway."

He gestured toward the porch. "Mind if we sit down? It's pretty bright out here."

"I'm fine, thanks." She was feeling a slow burn and it wasn't from the sunlight. What right did Cliff Wyatt have to tell his fucking GQ frat buddy anything about her?

"Well, Cliff kind of keeps an ear to the ground for me about properties that he thinks I might be interested in."

"Interested in."

"Sure, you know. Local knowledge. I call him my Northern Neck mole." He laughed.

"And why would you be interested in this property?"

"Well look at it, it's beautiful! You must have a half-mile of riverfront right here. This point is amazing, water on three sides, what views! Any idea what that's worth on the market these days? I mean, it's hot. I'll bet you could subdivide into three or four lots easy, half of them on the water, you're talking good money. You and your pop could retire and head to sunny Flor-ee-dah, never have to work again. Or hey, keep the old house and stay, what the heck. Do the snowbird thing. Winters down there, summers up here."

The sweat from gardening had dried on her back; now she felt like she needed a shower just because of Mr. Lacrosse Scholarship's proximity, standing here as if everything he looked at was his already. "I must say, Mr. Wilson, you take my breath away. You and your good friend Dr. Wyatt, who keeps his ear to the ground for you."

"Please, call me Bradford. And hey, don't be mad at Cliffy, please."

"'Cliffy' is my father's neurologist. He has no business discussing anything about his patients or their families with you. Even if you did pledge the same frat at Virginia."

"He didn't discuss anything about your dad or his case with me, hey," Bradford Wilson said, waving his hands around as if batting away an annoying fly. The sun glinted off his gold Rolex. "He would never do that. The man's as straight-on professional as anyone I've ever met. I mean, come on. You can see that. He just knows that I'm always looking for possibilities down here, and over a beer he mentioned that he'd met you and that your family has been here a long time."

"And?"

"And what? That was it. Oh, and that you were a reporter."

"And from that you deduced that my father might be interested in selling his property? Seems like a bit of a leap, doesn't it?"

"Hey, look. Don't take offense, please. It never hurts to ask, right? It's all good."

"Isn't it nice to know the old-boy network is still alive and well."

He grinned like a twelve-year-old caught rifling through his father's *Penthouse* stash. "No harm in it," he said. "It's how things work."

"Maybe where you come from."

"Look, hey, I'm sorry if I offended you. But please don't take it out on Cliff."

"Right. He can't help it if you exploit a conversation between buddies, is that what you're saying?"

"Boy, I'll bet you're hell on wheels at a press conference."

Bradford Wilson took an exaggerated swipe across his brow and laughed. Lily looked over at the blue Beemer and nodded.

"Nice ride."

He completely missed the sardonic tone in her voice.

"Oh, hey, thanks. I love it. Wanna go for a spin?"

"I'll pass."

"You sure? Beautiful day. It's a hoot taking it over that little ferry with the top down. Better than owning a boat and a lot cheaper!"

She couldn't believe this guy. He was giving her a headache, or maybe it was just the sun shining off his teeth and his watch.

"I was just thinking how good it must look going up the highway. Back to Richmond. Where you come from."

Bradford Wilson looked overly hurt and a little baffled. Not chagrined, not the least bit ashamed of his trespass upon her family's property or even her brains, or the fact that he had driven out here like he already owned the place—you couldn't just stumble upon the house, after all, the driveway was about a mile long off a one-lane road, you had to set out to get here. He was clueless. It had never occurred to him to be otherwise. It had always worked before, she was sure of it. She watched him take one more long look around and, once again, shrug off his temporary uncertainty. He shook his head slowly as if someone was talking in his ear and had said, "Now, display an expression of deep regret." He reached into his back pocket and extracted a leather wallet, pulled a business card from it, and scribbled something on the back. He handed it to her.

"Just hang onto this, okay?" he said, rolling his shoulders a little under his shirt. "You never know, you might change your mind. Might want to run it past Dad Evans. These old folks, winter's hard on them, sometimes Florida starts to sound pretty good. That's my number in Richmond, and my cell and email."

"No wifi out here, Bradford. Not much cell, either."

He laughed again and shook his head, as if this was simply too delightfully Leave It to Beaver backwards.

"I love it down here, God I do," he said. "Too much."

After the blue Beemer had beamed out the driveway she walked up onto the porch, turning the business card over. Bradford C. Wilson had written three numbers, and it's a good thing her mama's favorite wicker loveseat was there to catch her when she nearly fell into it. Next to "house only" he'd written $700,000. Next to "five three-acre lots" was $250,000 each. And after "property whole," $2 million.

"I'd have kicked his yuppie Richmond ass right outta there."

"Jamie!"

Mary Virginia scowled at him and then threw an exaggerated nod toward Isabelle, who sat at the other end of the table stirring a butter lake into her mashed potatoes. She didn't bother to look up at her father's remark.

"Well I would have!" Jamie said, setting his beer down a little too hard on the table. It was a Budweiser longneck, the staple hops product of choice among the men of Ophelia. "These assholes come around here with their money and their slick shit and start buying up the land and building these butt-ugly big houses practically right in the water and next thing you know the river's getting polluted from all the runoff, property taxes are going up and people like you, Mama—" here he picked up his beer again and pointed the neck at Mary Virginia—"can't even afford to live in the place where you were born and raised. Then you end up where you have to sell something just to survive. It's bullshit."

"Jamie Cockrell!"

"Give me a break, Ma, I'm thirty-two years old, I can state my opinion." He took another pull of his beer.

"You can state it all you want but I don't care how old you are, you are under my roof and when you are under my roof you will mind your language! This isn't the boatyard!"

Jamie pushed up from the table abruptly and went to the refrigerator. Lily tried not to look at the pleasing stretch of his long legs as he bent over and clanked around in the Frigidaire's shelves. The man could wear a pair of Levis, good God. He had always been good looking, and as he'd gotten older his roughness and imperfections had only made him more attractive somehow. Years became him. Would that it could be the same for women, Lily thought.

"You got any more beers in here or are they in the fridge on the porch?"

"On the porch," Mary Virginia said, "although I am not at all sure you need another one."

He leaned over and kissed the top of his mother's head as he walked past and out the door, and she shooed him away, flustered as a bird. She moved some silverware around her plate and her mouth was set in a tight little line. "Isabelle, dear, I don't want you to think that that kind of language is acceptable, especially for a young lady. Sometimes your daddy just forgets where he is and who he's talking to."

"I don't, Grandma," Belle said quietly.

She'd been quiet the whole dinner, Lily thought, and hadn't eaten much either. Lily wanted to talk to her, but the girl's self-possessed distance had thrown her. The photograph Jamie had shown her hadn't begun to convey his daughter's fragile depth, as if she were walking a minefield and, although she knew how to place her feet with care and read the land, the knowledge did little to diminish the trepidation in her steps. What was she afraid of? Lily wondered. Nine years old. There were so many possibilities. Lily wanted to ask Belle; she wondered whether anyone ever had. If someone had asked her, all those years ago, what might have been different? But it was almost as if the moment Isabelle had said hello and looked up to meet Lily's eyes, she had recognized something familiar in the older woman, and it wasn't something she wanted to know anything more about. What she knew already was enough.

"There you go again, eating like a bird," Mary Virginia said. "Don't you like the nice rockfish Miss Lily Rae brought over?"

"It's very good, thank you, Miss Lily Rae," Belle said obediently, risking a glance up at Lily.

Lily smiled back quickly, trying to catch her. "Lily, okay? Just call me Lily. It's a lot easier than all those names put together, don't you think?"

A fleet little smile crossed Belle's lips. Then she went back to her butter lake, carving a gap in one side of the reservoir so the butter, now melted, could trickle through the breach and into the surrounding valleys and plains of mashed potato.

"How was school today, honey?" Mary Virginia asked. "How'd that spelling test go?"

"Good, I think."

"Well, you mean. It went well."

"Well."

"Did you get 'poison' right? That one was giving you a tussle, I know. And what was the other one that you had to practice on?"

"Courage," Belle said.

"You got them both?"

"I think so."

"Of course she got 'em, Mama, the girl's head and shoulders above everybody else in that class, I swear. They ought to move her up a grade." Jamie banged back into the kitchen, pulling the porch door shut behind him. He had two beers this time, one in each hand, and he put one in the fridge and sat back down with the other. Lily smelled cigarettes on him. It suddenly struck her as ridiculous; a grown man sneaking out for a smoke after his mother slapped him on the hand for swearing at the dinner table.

"Well, I was over to see Jines Arley this afternoon and I think he looks terrific, really," Mary Virginia said. "Do you want a little more wine, honey?"

"Yes, please." Lily said. She took a sip and let its coolness settle her down. She could feel Jamie's eyes on her. "They plan to move him to the rehabilitation center tomorrow, so that's good, they tell me."

"It's a wonderful facility. They finished it just two years ago, and they say it's so outstanding that it draws people from as far away as Washington."

"Cost a pretty penny, I'll bet," said Jamie. "Wonder how Jines'll manage."

"What do you mean?" Lily asked, looking up at him and feeling startled, again, at the blue of his eyes. Had they always been this amazing turquoise, or had they changed? Or had she changed in the way she was seeing them?

"Well, most of these guys don't have medical insurance, you know. Can't afford it. It's not like they have a union or anything."

Lily set her fork on her plate. The thought had never crossed her mind, but it made sense. Her father was old school, and she doubted old school included setting aside cash every month to pay an insurance premium on anything but boats, a truck, and gear. The men themselves? They were indomitable, unless they were unlucky enough to die on the water, in which case they wouldn't need much of anything but a funeral, and certainly no medical insurance. She looked at Mary Virginia.

"Did your husband, did Mr. Cockrell have medical?" she asked.

"No," Mary Virginia shook her head. "Never saw a need for it, even though I nagged him enough." She sighed. "Not that it would have done him any good."

"Grandpa died fishing, didn't he, Grandma?" Belle asked.

"Yes, honey, he left this earth doing what he loved." She put her hand on Belle's cheek, then turned to Lily. "It wouldn't surprise me at all if Jamie's not right about this in regards to your daddy. As far as stubborn goes, Jines Arley makes my James look like a pushover."

"My God," Lily said. She sat back in her chair. "Maybe it's a good thing this real estate guy came by today after all."

"Lily Rae, you're not suggesting Jines sell out!" Mary Virginia's eyebrows went right up into her curls. "Honey, you must know he won't do that. He can't. It'd be like selling his history. It'd be selling his soul."

"Jines has a soul?" She laughed, meaning to make a joke of it, but it caught in her throat like a knife burr.

"Lily Rae."

Mary Virginia set down her fork and put her hand on Lily's arm. Lily shrugged her shoulders and felt startling hot tears in her eyes. Shit, she didn't want to cry, not in front of Belle, not in front of Jamie. She had done it too many times before, always the pathetic waif all those years ago, begging for affection like a dog begs for scraps.

"I know he can be a hard man, honey, God knows I do. I've known your daddy all my life and more than once I have had to resist smacking him with a good solid frying pan. Everybody said your mama was either a saint or crazy to marry him, but she wasn't either. I think she loved him because it was like loving a thunderstorm. It wasn't easy, but it sure wasn't boring—your mama hated being bored." Mary Virginia smiled. "But she was a grown woman. She knew what she was getting into, and if she'd wanted she could've gotten out. She had choices." Mary Virginia sighed heavily and wiped the corners of her mouth with her napkin, then tidied it up and placed it neatly on the tabletop. "I know you have reason to be bitter. But that can only take you so far down the road. And if you want to see just how lonely that road is, you don't have to look any farther than right here." She gently tapped Lily's chest with a finger twice at the "right here." Lily couldn't speak.

"Mama," Jamie said, his voice low.

"Now wait, Jamie, we are like family and sometimes you just have to say these things. Lily, honey, I want you to consider something, and consider it long and hard." Mary Virginia fixed her with her bright eyes. "Jines needs you. He always has, no, don't shake your head, honey, because it's true even if you don't have the eyes to see it yet. Now I won't argue that he's a stubborn fool about the insurance, and that he's put himself in a bad spot. But that's the way it is, nobody can change it now. But Lily honey, Jines would sooner die than lose his house or his family land, you might as well just shoot him like a horse with a broken leg. You know it. He's only going to get better in that old house, because that's where his heart is. And he's only going to get better with you helping him."

"There is no way, Mary Virginia." Lily's voice was shaking. "I'm only here to figure out what needs to be done to get him settled down somehow. And if he's got no insurance and selling some land is the only way he can pay what are bound to be huge expenses, then that's what he should do. There's no other reason for me to stay. My life is in Maine."

"But your family isn't, Lily Rae. You're family is right here."

"I don't have a family anymore!" Even as she said it she wished she hadn't. Mary Virginia's lips trembled. Jamie was staring at his plate. "I don't mean that as an insult to you, Mary Virginia, you know I don't. If it hadn't been for you letting me stay here all those times—" She hated where this conversation was going, into a past she wanted to keep well behind her. "I'm sorry I had to go. But I couldn't stay here. And I can't stay here now. He doesn't want my help, he never has. I can't, Mary Virginia."

"Well, yes, you can. You can." Mary Virginia straightened herself a little in the chair, her chin firm again. "He's your family, and you're his, like it or not. You have a responsibility to each other. I know, you're going to tell me where was Jines when he was responsible for you." She was leaning over the table now, gripping Lily's hand hard. "But honey that just isn't good enough anymore. You're a grown woman now too, Lily Rae. You can choose, like your mama chose. You can choose to be like Jines, thinking you can run away from sad things. Thinking life is hard, but you're harder. You look in here"—she tapped Lily on the chest again—"and ask yourself who you really need to do this for."

Lily did not dare look up from the food on her plate. All the fierce aloneness she had depended on for so long, the willful contradictions of her life, seemed to wash out of her with these words at this table, and she was left standing with nothing to hold her up. As it had always been. Mary Virginia had always meant the best. But Lily had always come away weakened, embarrassed, and eroded, and always in front of Jamie. She was never strong enough to stand on her own, not until she got far enough away.

"Grandma, may I be excused?" Isabelle asked. She had stood up at her place at the table and was giving full attention to her plate, which was still mostly covered with food. It looked like all she had done was move things around, not actually eaten them.

"Well I wish you'd eat more, honey, are you feeling poorly?"

"No, Grandma."

"Leave her be, Mama, she's tired out. They work these kids hard in that school. And she's probably got more homework to do for tomorrow, don't you?"

Lily didn't know if Jamie was changing the subject for Belle, himself, or her, but either way, she was relieved. Belle nodded.

"Go on then, clear your dishes," Jamie said. Belle whisked her plate off the table and took it to the sink. She was almost out of the kitchen when she turned and said, "Thank you, Lily, for the fish."

Lily looked up at the girl, the only person here who knew her as someone other than what her past had dictated. "You are welcome," Lily said. She cleared her throat, thankful that Belle had given her a reprieve. "You'll have to come over and help me with my garden one of these days after school. Do you like gardening?"

Belle nodded.

"Okay, then, we'll set a date," Lily said, and with that the girl was gone, up the stairs two by two.

Mary Virginia listened, staring up at the ceiling as if to see through the plaster and framing and insulation to make sure the girl had settled in well away from the adults. Then she sighed and moved to clear the plates. When she turned toward the sink, Jamie reached over and briefly touched Lily's hand. Lily saw the strong curve of his neck disappearing into the collar of his flannel shirt. She wanted to bury herself there, just burrow in and disappear, the way she had once been able to do when they were very young and something had scared her.

The phone rang, and Mary Virginia picked it up.

"Hello?" Her face darkened. "Oh. Yes, he's here." She handed the phone to Jamie. "Regina."

"Christ," he muttered. "I'll go in your bedroom." He stalked off down the hall. Mary Virginia waited a moment, then hung up when Jamie picked up the other extension.

Regina. The ex-wife, Lily thought. Belle's mother. She felt a sudden angry pang that it took her a moment to place. Jamie was hers, Jamie had always been hers, from when they were babies. But she had left. And he had become someone else's. Coming back here was such a mistake, nothing but a daily trip through the haunted house of all she had lost.

Mary Virginia sat down at the table, her lips pursed with disapproval. "His ex-wife," she said, her voice low. She shook her head. "Trash, just trash. Ran around on him from the get-go."

Lily felt immensely tired. She took a long drink of the wine left in her glass. When Jamie sat back down he drained the longneck that was in front of him and opened another. Carefully, Lily kept her eyes away from him.

"Well, what is it?" Mary Virginia asked in a voice that had heard this before and expected to hear it again.

He let his breath hiss out between his teeth and stared up at the ceiling.

"She's coming over here. Wants to take Belle tonight instead of Friday," Jamie said, looking down at the placemat in front of him. To Lily he added, without looking at her, "Regina is my ex."

"Who is supposed to abide by the custody agreement the court helped you two negotiate, and here she goes again breaking it, putting it on her schedule, and here you go again letting her do it."

"Mama   ."

"Well I'm sorry, Jamie, but it's the plain truth." Mary Virginia's curls bobbed from side to side as she lectured him. "I never could see how that woman got such a hold on you in the first place, and I truly can't see why she still does after what she put you through."

"*Mama.*" Jamie looked sharply at Mary Virginia.

"Maybe one or two fewer Budweisers would help you put her in her place," she said primly.

"Give me a fucking break!"

Jamie slammed the longneck bottle onto the table and the beer in it sprayed out the top, splattering Lily's blouse. It was a gauzy cotton, robin's-egg blue, peasant style with long flowy sleeves. She'd worn it with Levis, her favorite calfskin cowboy boots, and silver-and-turquoise teardrop earrings, thinking, as she had checked herself in the mirror before dinner one last time, that the blue of the blouse almost matched the color of Jamie's eyes. Maggie, who had been sleeping under the table, slunk out from under it and headed for higher ground up the steps. Lily wished she could follow her.

"Aw hell, Lils, I'm sorry." Jamie started to come out of his chair to help wipe up the beer and she held up both hands as if to ward him off.

"I've got it," she said. "Come right out with a little club soda."

Jamie sank back, flattened. "Jesus H. Christ," he said.

"Let me get you some, Lily Rae," said Mary Virginia, starting to bustle out of her seat.

"No!" It came out too sharp, sharp enough to push Mary Virginia back into her chair. "No, thanks, Mary Virginia, I've got it." She shoved away from the table. "You know, it's late, I've gotta go. They're moving him to the rehab wing tomorrow, and I'm sure it's going to be another long day."

"Lily—" Jamie said.

"Please tell Belle I'd love to have her come help me in the garden some afternoon, okay?"

"Let me walk you out."

"It's okay."

God knows, I know the way, she thought, but he was with her anyway, out the back door, and she walked her favorite calfskin cowboy boots across the porch and down the steps under the star-struck night sky.

"I'm sorry about all this tonight, Lils. You know Mama, sometimes she just doesn't know when to shut up and mind her own business." He barked a short, humorless laugh. "What am I saying; everything is her business." He stood before her, both hands pushed into the pockets of his jeans. "Nothing turns out the way you think it will, does it?"

Lily looked upward. There was so little ambient light here, the Milky Way foamed across the sea of stars as broad and thick as a boat's white wake on a cobalt sea.

"No," she said, "not much."

"I didn't think you were comin' back. Seemed like, the way you left, there was no turning around in it."

"There wasn't."

She tried concentrating on the stars overhead. There was Orion, easy to spot. And Polaris, easy too despite its relative dimness, thanks to the Big Dipper pointing the way. Cygnus, now, the Swan, that one was always tough when there were this many stars scattered like spilled sugar, blurring the constellation's outline.

"I would have waited."

"There was nothing to wait for."

She saw him duck his head, and she thought, see, this is why coming back to anyplace you have said goodbye to is just a bad idea. You can leave, but you can never come back. Not without hurting people. Not without hurting yourself.

"That came out wrong. What I was trying to say is, getting on with your life was the right thing to do."

A bit of light caught her eye and she glanced at the house to see that someone had pulled back the curtain in one of the bedrooms and was outlined in the window.

"I think Belle is looking for you."

Jamie turned around to look up at the window. How many times had the two of them come out here on a night like this and lain back in the cool grass, counting shooting stars, picking out the constellations? Sometimes she would deliberately blur her vision so that all the stars melted into one great shimmering ocean of light, shifting reality just by changing the way one viewed it. Was there a way to do that with the past? Only, she thought, if you kept your distance from it. Here he was, so close to and so far from the boy she had known, and suddenly her loneliness had no limits. She touched his arm, then turned and walked quickly to her pickup. The whole way home along the dirt road she left her window wide open, hanging her head out of it like a dog until her eyes streamed in the rust of the cool night air.

Chapter 6

For the first time in his life since the passing of his wife, Jines had a roommate. Could have done worse, he supposed. At least he was a waterman, or used to be anyway, not some insurance salesman or fast-talking shyster lawyer. His name was Linwood Parker. He looked like a dried-up cornhusk. Made Jines wonder how he himself came across these days. He felt like an old husk of something, that was sure. Sometimes, he would wake up in a cold sweat, not even know where he was. Then he'd see the glint of that metal walker by his bed grinning like someone about to rob you, and he'd know how things were. Sailed right off the charts this time. And he would remember, in a world with sharp edges, how the old mapmakers would write in a trembling hand across those unknown waters, *Here Be Monsters.* They'd brought him over to this fancy new rehab center and when he got here, Linwood Parker was ready and waiting.

"Goddamn," he said, "finally some decent company."

And that was it; the gusher started. He'd been here three weeks, he told Jines, waving his hand like a claw for emphasis. Well, he tried to wave it. More or less it just made it a couple inches off the table there by his bed, a table and bed exactly like the one Jines was stuck with. The man was some kind of pack rat, Jines could see that right off the bat. His table was a mess of boxes of candy, water cups, cookie tins, fading flowers, a pair of socks, glasses, hand moisturizer, lip balm, a box of Kleenex, and a miniature model of a workboat, the kind a child might buy in a museum gift shop. Jines wasn't exactly a clean freak himself, but something about that table bugged him. It was like Linwood Parker was making himself too comfortable here. Jines's table had the Kleenex and lip balm (the rehab center included that with the price of admission, he figured), but that was about it. And that's how he intended for it to stay.

Linwood Parker had ten children, and they all visited at one time or another, a different one each day, it seemed. None ever came empty-handed. Every one of them talked like pecking chickens, not unlike Linwood himself. He was eighty years old, one of his daughters, named Dotty, had explained to Jines, while repeatedly offering him candies from a Whitman's Sampler, over and over like a nervous tic. Jines was pretty sure there was some reason why he shouldn't have a piece of candy, and he wasn't too partial to chocolate truth be told, but he finally took one just to make her stop waving that yellow box at him. Mr. Parker, Dotty had said, had been a menhaden captain from down in Gloucester for many years, and when the menhaden boom ended he went to work at Norshipco in Norfolk as a shipfitter. He had still crabbed a little on the side, down near New Point Comfort, but when he got prostate cancer three years ago he went to live inland, up near Tappahannock, with his oldest daughter, Candace. She was an executive with a pharmaceutical sales company and made good money, Dotty said, although she traveled a lot. It was Candace's husband, Jim, who'd found Mr. Parker this last time, crashed in the kitchen, his arms and hands bloody from the glass he'd been carrying when he fell. The dog had licked some of it off, Dotty said, the thought of which just made her stomach turn. Along with the prostate cancer, Mr. Parker had undergone, in just the last three years, two surgeries and subsequent rounds of chemo for melanoma, as well as a stroke last year. This latest stroke, Dotty had said, seemed flatly unfair—she'd started crying, Jines was horrified to see—and while the doctors and therapists kept telling them they thought he could regain enough function to return to live with Candace, it seemed to Dotty and her siblings as though he'd given up. It was the depression, she said, she was sure of it. Time and again he'd refused the therapies they were asking him to do, saying he couldn't, it was too hard, or sometimes, she said, not saying anything at all, just sitting there close-mouthed.

"He's so stubborn," she had said, sniffling. "Always has been. Once he gets his mind set, you can forget about changing it."

All of this was way more than Jines ever wanted to know. All he really wanted to know was when he could get the hell out of here and back home, back out on the water. Oh, he'd heard what that young doc had said. He'd made his point a few more times for good measure. Jines just nodded, all the while thinking there was no way some wet-behind-the-ears come-here doc who wore shoes you'd see on some queer from Germany or one of them foreign countries was going to tell him he wasn't supposed to go fishing again.

That doc was right about one thing though; they worked you hard here. Place ran on clocks. Every morning with his breakfast tray Jines got a schedule that set down where he needed to be when, and for what. No one came here to sit in bed. You came here to get better, to pull yourself back together, if that was possible. This meant, for Jines, a daily regimen that made his days on the water seem almost leisurely by comparison. Physical therapy in the morning for an hour. Speech therapy for an hour right after lunch. Occupational therapy mid-afternoon for an hour, and usually another half an hour of PT after that. In between, visits from doctors, psychiatrists, nurses. Meals. Aye God, the food. What he wouldn't do for some of Jeanette's strawberry rhubarb pie. Had to know the right time to take this pill or that one. Trips to the bathroom. They were the worst, just the mechanics of moving from the middle of the bed to the edge of the bed, from the edge to the walker, from the walker to the bathroom (a mere six feet away), onto the commode, off the commode, back to the walker, back to the bed. When he stopped to think that it sometimes took a half an hour just to take a shit, he almost got depressed enough to wish he were back in the ICU where he'd been more or less so out of it he couldn't think about anything.

That was another thing, the crying. Damnedest thing. Come on him like a freak wave on a flat calm day, no warning and no reason so far as he could see, an overwash of emotion that he could no sooner explain or put words to than he could fly like a seabird. Had happened the other night over his dinner tray, one minute he was doing a half-decent job of getting his beef stew to his mouth, the next he was blubbering in it. Linwood waved his claw and told him not to worry about it, happened all the time to him now too. "Involuntary emotional expression disorder," the resident head shrinker had told Jines. He had a bad comb-over and narrow eyes that bored into Jines like a drill press, and every time he came in the room Jines actually found himself thinking that young Doc Wyatt maybe wasn't so bad after all, even with his foreigner's shoes. "We used to call it reflex crying, or emotional incontinence." He patted down what he had of his hair a little and looked away, as if this wording embarrassed him. "The stroke can cause miscommunication between the part of the brain that controls how we label feelings, and the part that controls how we express them." Jines had no idea what the hell all that meant. All he knew is that most of the time he felt a weird looseness in himself like a boat slipping around on a greasy sea, a shiftiness that set him on edge. He couldn't trust his own self anymore to not just bust out bawling like a baby right in front of anybody.

He wondered how long that would last. He could feel himself getting a little stronger in other ways, although some days were better than others. This whole place was set up to make it so you could go home and get yourself around without much help. They had an entire kitchen. Cabinets stocked with boxes of Cream of Wheat and Jell-O mix, drawers with silverware, plates and glasses in the cupboard overhead, an oven for baking, a sink, and a dishwasher. Jines thought it was a bit of overkill. All he needed was a microwave and a fridge and he'd be fine. Downstairs, on the way to the gym, there was a door off the hallway that opened to an entire apartment. It had a living room with a couch, a few La-Z-Boys, an entertainment center with a television, sound system, the works. There was a bedroom with blinds that you could raise to look out across the parking lot. Double bed, alarm clock, night table, chair to throw your clothes on. And a bathroom too, with a walk-in shower and a tub. Commode, sink. All day long, patients practiced climbing in and out of bed, stepping in and out of the shower, getting up and down from the toilet. Everything was organized and laid out to mimic an ordinary living space in an ordinary life. Aye God, what he'd give for ordinary.

Lily Rae came now and then. She always looked like a highstrung young horse about to bolt. The physical therapists asked her to come along when they went down to the gym and put Jines through his paces. "You need to learn how to help your father with these exercises, so when you get him home you can both do it on your own." This is what they told her as they placed her hands on his bad arm and showed her how to guide him with the barbell curls, when they had her cover his hand with her own to help him grasp a pencil. Her touch was skittish as a bird landing on his hand. Those therapists, they were nice enough but they were living in a dream world if they thought he was anything but on his own.

One day she surprised him, though, when she showed up with dirt all over her knees and a piece of pie on a Seaside plate, covered over with plastic wrap.

"Jeanette sends her love," she said, setting the plate on his table. "Says the next one will be strawberry rhubarb but for now you'll have to content yourself with lemon meringue."

"Aye God," he whispered.

Lily looked at him and shook her head, a weird little smile on her mouth. "You know Jines, you're the only person I've ever heard use that particular expression."

He shoved a fork into the pie and aimed a huge piece at his mouth. It was almost there when the meringue trembled, his hand twitched, and the whole piece capsized onto his sweatshirt. Lily reached for a napkin and the fork. "I'll get it," she said.

He snatched the fork away and scraped the gooey mess off his shirt. A whole piece wasted, damn. Then he went after the pie again, focused his intent on his hand. Much as he wanted a big bite, he made this one smaller and navigated it safely into his mouth. Heaven. He wanted to kiss that Jeanette right then and there. He wouldn't even say hello first when he saw her again, he'd just plant one on her.

Lily looked angry, but the pie was so good he just thought about that. Then he remembered the dirt on her knees. He pointed to them.

"Whose garden you been tillin'?" he asked.

"Mine."

"Yours?"

"Mine."

"Didn't know you had one."

"The garden's still there, Jines. Mama's garden. Even though the strawberry plants are pretty much gone and the asparagus patch too. It's too bad you let it grow over." She brushed some of the dried dirt off her knees. "I figured I might as well put a little life back into it, as long as I'm here."

"And who's gonna tend to it when you're not?"

"I don't know. Maybe Belle, Jamie's girl. She and Mary Virginia could come over and look after it. She's been helping me get some plants in."

The glorious taste of the lemon meringue was leaving Jines's mouth like a sweet dream lost upon waking. What the hell was she about, planting Jenny Rae's garden?

"What makes you think I want Mary Virginia up my ass every day?"

"Delicately put as ever, Jines." Lily rubbed the sides of her head as if she had a headache brewing there. She left little streaks of dirt on her temples. "Look, it just seemed wasteful to have that beautiful patch there just full of weeds. I didn't think it could hurt to get something growing in there again."

"That soil's been setting there just fine without anybody digging it up."

Jines started to take another bite of pie and then put his fork down. Aye God, this girl made him tired.

"Well you can let it go to hell again, okay? I just didn't like looking at it so empty. It didn't seem right."

There was a long silence. From the hallway came the sound of the lunch tray cart being wheeled past the door. Linwood was down at speech therapy and Jines wished he were here instead. Lily seemed a little less feisty when he was around.

"So you're goin' back."

"To Maine? Of course. I have a great apartment. You can see the sunrise over Casco Bay from the bedroom window."

"When?"

"I don't know. After you get back in the house, I guess." She shifted impatiently in the chair and it squeaked beneath her. "Look Jines. We need to talk."

"Thought we were."

"About you, not me. About this new situation."

"What's to talk about? I get back fishing. You get back to Casco Bay out your window."

He had to struggle to say this much at once and a thin thread of saliva spooled out of the weakened corner of his mouth as he finished with the words. She snatched a Kleenex from the box and leaned toward him brandishing it. Startled, he pushed his head deeper into the pillow.

"Your mouth," she said, roughly wiping. "I don't know why you're even still thinking about fishing. You're going to need physical therapy, maybe for a couple of months. You'll have to take certain drugs all the time now, and Dr. Wyatt's right, they can fool with your whole system, balance, depth perception, all of it. And what if you have another stroke out there, or even just black out? It's pretty common after what's happened to you. There are facts you have to start being realistic about. Your life has changed. A lot."

She hurled the Kleenex at the trashcan and it twirled away in all its white lightness and landed on the floor.

"I've had hard fights before, little girl," he growled.

"Not like this one. Do you even have medical insurance, Jines? Mary Virginia told me she was pretty sure you don't. I told her I couldn't believe that, not after what happened to Danny and Mama."

Goddamn that Mary Virginia Cockrell! Always butting in where she didn't belong. He was feeling pinned like a bug by the look Lily was giving him, and he was sick of it.

"That's right."

"You are uninsured?" Lily slapped her hands on both her legs.

"Bunch of slick men in suits gettin' rich off scarin' people."

"Jesus!" Lily stood up and stalked to the window. "That's just brilliant, brilliant. I hope the fishing's been good, because if not, you are screwed. I'll bet you didn't even sign up for the new Medicare program under the deadline, either, did you. You might have to sell the house or some of the land."

"Bullshit."

"Then how do you plan to pay for all this?" She swept her hand around the room. "Do you have any idea how much one day costs in this place? And what comes after? You're probably going to need a physical therapist to come to the house a couple days a week, maybe more. Any way you slice it, you're looking at a ton of money."

"That point's named after your great-grandfather. Your mama and baby brother are buried in that dirt. It may not mean nothin' to you up there in Maine, looking over Casco Bay or whatever it's called, but as long as I'm breathing only Evanses are living there."

His breath was ragged and his chest felt pinched. He wiped the corner of his mouth again with a napkin. What did she care anyway, he wanted to say, but he was suddenly totally exhausted. He just wanted her to leave him alone. He'd managed before; he'd manage again.

Lily turned to him before she walked out the door. "I guess it's a good thing I planted that garden after all," she said. "You're probably going to need it."

When Jines came back from physical therapy later he was still pissed off. He was sick of these exercises. Puny weights he was supposed to lift with his arms, a long rubber strap for working his legs, a little rubber ball they gave him to squeeze with his left hand. Him, a goddamn waterman, third generation! Could they pound poles into the bottom all day long and still lift their arms at the end of it? Could they spend eight, ten hours hefting tongfuls of oysters on a frigid winter day and still walk with a straight back? And they give him a rubber ball. What was worse, his left hand sometimes could barely squeeze the damn thing.

The therapist—she was a cute little thing, there were a bunch of them here, which was one of the place's few attributes, in his opinion—looked at his schedule.

"Looks like you're off for the rest of the day, Mr. Evans. Dinner will be in about an hour. You want to sit in the chair by the window or take a nap?"

He was too keyed up to lie down, though his whole body felt like a wet sack. He pointed to the chair, and she settled him in there and pulled the rolling table close by.

"Thank you, honey," Jines said.

"Oh you're welcome, Mr. Evans," she giggled. "You're doing so well. You'll be out of here in no time, and then I'll miss you."

Outside, a beautiful spring day was settling in toward evening. Linwood's curtain was drawn around his bed. Jines was about to ask if he was okay when he heard the voice of Candace, Linwood's eldest daughter and what they called the primary caregiver. Jines had seen her before. She was a tall drink of water. She dressed like a woman who was trying hard not to look like one. He never did like seeing a woman in a business suit like that. Even if it was a skirt there was nothing feminine in it. He had always loved Jenny Rae's cotton dresses. They made her look like a part of the breeze when it blew. Candace's voice came from behind the curtain. She sounded less like a pecking chicken than the rest of them, but that didn't mean her voice was more appealing. Jines thought she sounded like she'd practiced how to talk in front of a mirror just to get rid of the sound of who she was, where she came from. Like she'd put a suit on her voice, too.

"You have a choice here, Pop," she was saying. "You either do what they tell you and get yourself better, or you go to a nursing home. You want to be in bed the rest of your life?"

What did she think, he was deaf? That he couldn't hear what she was saying to her daddy through this flimsy curtain? He was embarrassed for Linwood. He fixed his gaze out the window and saw a hawk making a lazy circle over the field.

"That's what's going to happen if you don't do what they tell you to do." Candace's voice lectured. Jines heard Linwod murmur something. "Well I don't want to just hear you say yes, Pa, I want you to do it. Actions speak louder than words. This is the third time I've had to leave work and come in here and talk to them about you refusing therapy!"

Must be a red-tail, Jines thought. Only a red-tail could be that big.

"I can't take care of you all the time, Pa. I have to work, you know, I have my own family to support. You have to be able to at least use the bathroom, get yourself out of bed. Basic stuff."

He didn't know as much about hawks as he did about the water birds, but he knew enough to know this was a big raptor out over this field. Probably looking for some poor old mouse. They said those birds had eyes that could spot their prey from half a mile up. It'd be like getting hit with a meteor.

"I mean, for God's sake, Pa, what do you want me to do? Jim still can't get work and it's all up to me! I need him to be working, I can't have him home all day, and if you can't take care of yourself, he'll use that as another excuse for why he shouldn't go get a job!"

A couple years back a pair of bald eagles had a nest down the road from Jines's driveway. They put it high up in a big stand of pines, looked to be as big as *Jenny Rae*'s cockpit. Sometimes he'd walk down there and just watch those big birds set their wings the way they do. That's how you could tell the difference between them and the turkey buzzards. The buzzards looked about the same way up there in the sky till you made out the way they held their wings, always in a V-shape. Not those eagles. Wings as flat and straight across as a two-by-four, like a plank flying in the sky. They nested there for many years in a row. Mated for life, eagles did, until one of them died. From here, he could see the way the hawk over the field banked its tail to make a turn.

"It's up to you, Pa. Your choice. You want to sit in a bed in a nursing home the rest of your life, that's your choice. But I'm done here. We're not having this conversation again."

Jines heard the hiss of pantyhose against fabric.

"I'll see you later, Pa," Candace said, and her heels clicked smartly out of the room and down the hall.

Jines kept his eyes out over the field and saw the wind moving through the winter wheat like a brushstroke, the color shifting with each little gust. By now the southerly breeze would be filling in up the Bay, its moist fingers touching his skin. The man was eighty years old. He'd raised ten kids. And worked hard all his life. And cancer, surgery, strokes. And now they come in here and tell him he has a choice? A choice to do what?

"Hey," he said. "Linwood."

"Yeah, Jines Arley."

"You ought to look over here. There's a big red-tail hawk over the field out here." He heard the sound of the curtain being pulled back. He kept his eyes out the window. "See it over there?" he pointed.

"I'll have to take your word for it, Jines Arley. I can't see much anymore, you know. Leastaways not that far." He sighed. "I used to be the eagle eye on my boat. They said I could see over the horizon."

Jines shook his head. "It's been a day for pissed-off daughters. I got an earful too."

Linwood tried to laugh, but it didn't come out as such. "I guess they've just got to be mad at somebody, you know. That one therapist called Jeannie, the one with the curly hair? She says kids get scared seeing their parents get old. Then they get mad at what scares 'em."

Jines grunted. That may be true, he thought, but it didn't give them the right to come in here and start trying to run things. Sell some of the land, she'd said. Like he could sell his own arms and legs. He couldn't believe the nerve of her.

"Anyway," Linwood said, "I'm just tired, Jines Arley, do you know? A man lives long enough, he just gets tired. And nobody can just let him go."

It was a couple days later, when Jines returned from yet another round of physical therapy, Linwood Parker was gone. Or rather, his bed was empty and his table was clear of all of his stuff. An empty bed wasn't out of the ordinary—he could be at therapy or in the bathroom—but the empty table, as impersonal and cool as a coroner's slab, stopped Jines cold.

"Where is he?" he asked the cute girl who was helping him along in the walker to his bed.

"Oh Mr. Evans, you know I can't discuss other patients."

Jines gripped her arm. "Is he all right?"

She sighed. "Well, I know you two were friends. His family discharged him this morning. Moved him to a place near Tappahannock."

"What kind of place."

"An elder care facility there."

"A nursing home, you mean."

"We don't call them that anymore." She helped him into his bed. "I'm sorry, Mr. Evans, that's really all I can say."

Jines looked out the window to the late afternoon light and thought about Linwood Parker, captain of a menhaden boat, who could see so far they swore he could see over the horizon. He tried to hold him this way in his mind, not in some place that smelled of piss and old skin, of metal bedpans and televisions that droned on night and day, where a man could never feel the warm breath of the water. Jines reached for a Kleenex, and his hand fell to an unfamiliar shape on his table. It was the little workboat model. Jines cupped it in his hand. His rough fingers ran over its lines. Linwood's choice had been made for him. He was damned if his would be. He'd flat-out rather go overboard and drown than end up trapped like that. He placed the model carefully on the table, and set his eyes over the field, looking for that hawk.

A week later he was home. There was the *Jenny Rae* at the dock safe and sound and his poles and nets behind the shed ready to go. The old house seemed just the same, even its creaks and groans and the way the wind hooted around the northwest corner. Worked out now, his sleeping in the parlor, on account of there was no way he could handle a flight of steps. Here it was mid-afternoon, and he'd been sleeping again. Seemed like all he did these days, unless he was sitting on the back porch or putting up with the physical therapy. He could see why they had him on that schedule at the rehab center. But it seemed like he'd lost some steam when he came home. He thought it would be the other way around. He eased himself up and swung his legs heavily over the side of the bed. He could hear Lily moving around out in the kitchen, probably cleaning the cupboards or some damned thing. She'd been cleaning everything in the place, every corner, every sill, bookshelves, cabinets, swearing when she scrubbed out the fridge and hurling crusted, burned up pots and pans into the trash. Couldn't hardly smell the saltmarsh and the loblollies for the Lysol she was slinging around, buckets of it. It was driving him crazy, her prying into places that had been dark and unused long enough to be safely forgotten. Truth was, having her in the house was like snagging onto a bluefish when you were expecting nothing but stripers. Sometimes it felt like you had a goddamn shark on the line they fought so hard, you'd be breaking into a sweat despite yourself because they were so pissed off and stubborn. And then you'd get it done, in the boat and there it was, something half the size it had felt like on the line, fierce and silver, all teeth and thrash. Doing its best to take your fingers off even while you were trying to cut it loose.

He reached for the walker and slowly scuffed his way out the door, down the short hall and into the john. It was a narrow little room under the stairway, the ceiling slanted overhead. He'd never used it much before since the head just off the mudroom in the kitchen—the summer bathroom, they used to call it—was bigger and had the shower. But that was a long way from the parlor now, might as well be miles. And there were the two steps down from the kitchen into the mudroom and then across. He'd have to ask her for help every time he wanted to take a leak. The toilet under the stairs was closer, easier, and he could use the edge of the vanity to steady himself.

He left the walker in the hall and eased into the little room hanging onto the doorframe, then pulled the door shut. Worked his pajama bottoms down and sat down hard on the commode. Couldn't even piss standing up anymore, he didn't have enough hands. Needed two to hold himself steady, one on the vanity and one against the wall, and where did that leave his pecker but flapping around like a garden hose on full-tilt with no nozzle. So he sat. Still beat a plastic funnel, or worse yet, a diaper. He felt the trickle stop, leaned down to grab his pajama bottoms, and suddenly everything was swirling and black. His guts somewhere up in his throat. He grabbed the edge of the vanity with his good arm and leaned the weak one against the wall but it just gave way, the room spinning and the blackness dotted with bright jabs of light. When his vision cleared—had he passed out, he wondered—he found himself slumped against the wall, one cheek of his butt about to slide off the seat. Good thing, he thought, the room was so skinny, otherwise he might have fallen right off the can. Still, there he was. Weak as a baby and no way to get up.

He sat a moment, still hearing her bashing around out in the kitchen. If he had passed out, it wasn't for long; not much had changed. He called to her. Once, twice. Voice as feeble as his legs. Finally whacked the bathroom door with one foot hard enough to make her go quiet, and a moment later he heard her outside the door.

"Jines? What is it?"

"Stuck."

"What?"

"I'm stuck in here, dammit!"

There was a long silence. His breath rasped in his ears. The door opened. She didn't look at him. Her mouth was thin and set.

"What happened?"

"How the hell do I know!" he snapped.

"You can't move?"

"I can't get up, for Chrissake! My legs…" he smacked them with both fists.

She moved toward him and bent over, wrapping her arms around him beneath his armpits. He was startled to feel her small, warm body so close to him, and the sweet scent of lavender in her hair made his throat tighten; suddenly he was close to tears and had no idea why, only that he couldn't bear the scent of her, the fierce tightness of her arms around him. He steadied himself with his good hand on the vanity, the useless one on the wall. He'd put up the wallpaper in here—aye God he hated wallpaper but Jenny Rae had asked, had chosen a country-home type pattern of blue spinning wheels on a creamy background. It felt puckery and damp beneath his fingers.

"We'll go on three," Lily said. And on three she lifted, her chest squeezed against his so he thought for a second he could feel her heartbeat through the thin veil of his pajama top. He did his best to push with his legs and then suddenly he was standing, hands splayed on the vanity and the wall, rickety as a newborn colt. He let out a breath in a long whoosh, glad to be upright again. That wasn't so bad. She had released her grip on him and was standing there, her eyes still somewhere over his shoulder. Then he felt something wet on his leg. He looked down. His pajama bottoms pooled at his feet. He'd forgotten about them completely. There was his pecker, limp as a flag with all the wind gone out of it. A thin short trickle of piss was wheedling down his leg. He willed it to stop but it just kept going, a pathetic little stream betraying him drop by drop. He couldn't take his eyes off it, couldn't begin to bring them to her face.

"What's wrong?"

But he just spluttered and then she looked down and saw him, the pajamas, the piss, all of it. She snatched off a wad of toilet paper and held it to him, but he was afraid to let go with either hand for fear he'd go down again. Why couldn't she figure that out? Why'd she have to make him say it out loud?

"Dammit, I can't—" he blurted, his fingers clawing the wallpaper.

She reached down and quickly wiped his thigh, then knelt and pulled up the pajamas, fumbling a little past the rubble of his knees, her hair inadvertently brushing his rubbery thighs as she slid up in front of him and let the waistband go with a little snap. She helped him turn and wrapped an arm around his waist, her firm shoulder propped under his armpit. He draped one arm across the brace of her shoulders and they crabbed sideways out of the bathroom, their small steps scuffling along the hardwood down the hall that had never seemed so long and deep before, past the stairway and into the parlor where she helped him sit on the edge of the bed. He felt as if everything that mattered had leached out of him. She lifted his legs, swung him into the bed.

She left and he heard the toilet flush, then her steps coming back into the room and the thunk of the walker as she placed it beside the bed. When he opened his eyes a little later the cold metal gleamed in the late-day light stammering across the floor. From outside he could hear the sharp smack of an axe splitting wood. He closed his eyes and felt the stretch and heft of the axe looping overhead, the smooth hickory of the handle, the tingle from his palms to his shoulders as it cleaved the wood. He smelled the sweet clean scent of freshly split oak, that secret perfume of forest and earth, rain and wind all blown wide open by the axe. He pictured Lily out there by the woodpile, her ponytail swinging past the dark clouds of her eyes, the fierce, compact strength of her all slicing down and narrowed into that single fine, curved arc of the axe blade as it met the wood. Just like he taught her.

He reckoned then that he knew just exactly how that bluefish felt, hooked deep, ripped from the water, twitching on a hard deck with all its power and grace gone in an instant, gasping for breath in a world of unforgiving, airless sky.

The next morning Jines managed to dress himself—a heavy cardigan and a pair of sweat pants Mary Virginia had brought from the thrift shop a few days ago, dropping them off in her usual yappy way: "You know those come-heres from Richmond who bought Eddie and Elsie Haynie's house out on Mundy Point? Anyway it was her, you should have seen the diamond on that woman's hand my *Lord*, and she had six pair of these pants, all brand new. Said she'd got them for her husband but he refused to wear them because they'd been made in China or Thailand or someplace"—Mary Virginia had rooted around briefly in the pants for a label and then gave up, refolding and setting them on the chair instead—"and I says, honey, I know just the home for them don't you worry." Jines didn't care where they were made. Fact was they were soft and warm against his prickly chilled skin and a far sight easier to put on than his work pants.

He eased himself out into the hallway and saw that Lily had already opened the door out to the back porch. A feather of breeze was moving through the hall, bringing with it the river's scent. Like a hound he followed it, making his way down the hall and out the door, settling into a wicker chair.

"Jines?" Lily's voice from the kitchen.

"Yep."

"You okay?"

"Yep."

"I'm off to the store. You need anything before I go?"

"Nope."

Out here on the porch the mid-morning sun warmed him all over, and he noticed the daffodils along the side of the house and out at the edge of the garden. Daffadowndillies. That's what Jenny and the kids had called them. Not too much longer for the shadbush and wild azaleas to start flowering, and that meant the shad run, good fishing. He watched a couple of fish hawks working the river, admiring their deadly aim as they dropped from the sky and shattered the water. More often than not they came up with a nice-looking fish. They shrieked and whistled, shaking water from their feathers and fighting for altitude as the fish squirmed in their talons. If it was a small catch they could sometimes do it with one foot, but the big ones gave them a tussle, no doubt of it. Could hardly blame them, Jines thought. Bright light, smooth water, lazy breeze, daffadowndillies in bloom. Bad day to be a fish when a couple of osprey, hungry from their long travels north, were hanging in the sky.

He heard Kenneth's shit-heap Ford that was missing both bumpers and half its rusted-out bed coming up the drive around front. Still hadn't fixed that fan belt. He'd known Kenneth all his life and had decided long ago that even though they were friends, Kenneth's troubles were his own. He knew Kenneth's daddy had been a cruel bastard with a fondness for Jack Daniels and the buckle end of his belt. And he was aware that Kenneth knew how a beer tasted by the time he'd barely cleared the seventh grade. Hell, who didn't? They all ran together, sneaking beers after school and at the football games on Friday nights over in Mathews and down to Gloucester. But with Kenneth, the sneaking didn't stop the next day. And by high school the beers were chasing Jack.

Still, Kenneth was loyal and always had been. After Jines's father had drowned, it was Kenneth who'd put in the months of nights and weekends helping Jines get Benny Pruitt's deckboat into shape enough to fish a pound. He still had his daddy's three sites just inside the Potomac—Big Betty, Seven Brothers, and Twenty-Footer were their names—but his daddy's fine deadrise and all the nets and poles had been lost along with so much else in the great storm. Jines was starting more or less from scratch, and after Benny Pruitt had agreed to sell him his old deckboat on a two-season note, it had been Kenneth who had helped him rebuild the rotten mast step, build and rig a new mast and replace a good half of the bottom, as well as get the rest of the gear ready. It had been Kenneth who'd somehow scrounged up enough net from somewhere and patched it over and over, and Kenneth who'd gone out with him that first lonely season, helping him with the backbreaking work of pounding the long pine poles into the bottom. Jines knew Kenneth was always there probably because he just wanted to get clear of his daddy, but he didn't care. He split things fifty-fifty with Kenneth in those early years, and they'd made some serious money together.

Then Kenneth got married and left the boat for a while. The first baby had come six months after the I-dos, and the wife had dreams of a split-level in Norfolk with regular trash pick-up and shopping malls around every corner. Kenneth took a job down at the refinery in York County trying to make union money with the benefits and vacations and whole nine yards. Didn't last, not the job nor the marriage. What lasted was what his daddy had taught him. When he came back Jenny Rae had been all against it; he wasn't trustworthy, she told Jines, he was dangerous and unpredictable.

Drunks always were. She'd seen his wife down at the Food Lion when the sunglasses and Revlon didn't quite cover the damage, and those children were skittery as rabbits, always hiding behind their mama's legs. But Jines could not put away the past. It wouldn't be fifty-fifty anymore, he told Kenneth, he'd get paid his share like the other crew, and if he showed up drunk he stayed on the beach. But Jines would always have a place for him.

Kenneth lumbered around the side of the house and hauled himself up the porch steps, slapped open the door and stopped abruptly, evidently surprised to see Jines there. "Well look at you old man," he crowed. "Takin' in some slack, ain't ya? Where's your TV so you can watch *Dr. Phil* and *American Idol*?"

"Ain't got her rigged up out here yet."

"I guess not." Kenneth lowered himself into the love seat, which groaned beneath him. He poked one sausage finger into the wicker. "Ought to get yourself a real couch out here. La-Z-Boy, now we're talkin'. "

"Didn't get to fixing that fan belt yet, I reckon."

"It's on the list." Kenneth eyed him. "You look pretty damned good, Jines Arley, I gotta tell you. That Lily Rae I saw headin' out the driveway?"

"Headed for the grocery." Jines shook his head. "Girl wears me out."

"Yay-uh." Kenneth barked a humorless laugh. "I can see that easy enough."

They sat quietly. Jines watched a barn swallow zooming in toward the eaves on the far end of the porch, a beakful of dried grass flying behind it like streamers. Over the river the fish hawks keened. From a distance came the whine of an outboard, and pretty soon a sleek, brightly painted fishing boat sped across the water in front of them, its cockpit bristling with rods. Kenneth snorted. "Come-heres," he said. "Goddamn lazy sons a bitches can't get outta bed early enough to find a self-respectin' striper."

"I b'lieve that's that Micky Carr, fella who built that big house up on Whitestone Creek. Owns a lumberyard somewhere near Richmond. Seems all right. What I hear does all right with the rockfish. Top in the tournament last fall."

Kenneth pulled an empty Coke can from his pocket and squirted a molasses-colored stream into it.

"They running yet?" Jines asked.

"Jemmy Owens come in two days ago loaded. Whole party hooked up huge out on the Middle Ground, nothin' under forty inches. He says it's been going that way for about a week now."

Jines shook his head. "Just my luck it'll be a killer season. You remember that year we hit into all them down-run herring? Aye God, how many pounds we took out of the Seven Brothers that one week, something like forty-, fifty-thousand in two days?"

"I b'lieve it was moren that, Jines Arley, moren that. We had to tie off the pocket funnel, remember? Didn't want no more fish to go *in*." Kenneth laughed.

"Thought it was the bluefish chased them all in there, scared them into one spot." Jines sighed. With one stiff arm he adjusted a pillow down near his hip. "You just never know how it'll go."

Kenneth spit into his can again. Then he slapped his knee suddenly. "You're not gonna believe this, I forgot to tell you on the phone the other night. You remember that deckboat *Eliza M. Bell*, big boat, sixty-some footer old Grover Parker built out of Locklies? She's been over to the Eastern Shore for years, drudging oysters for Tolly Parks. Anyways, some rich guy from Washington, D.C., buys her from Tolly, says he wants to turn her into a pleasure yacht." He stopped to spit again. "This damn fool evidently don't know the pointy end's called the bow and decides to cross the Bay with her clear from Tilghman two weeks ago. Gonna bring her into Deltaville to one of them yacht yards. Except he don't listen to his weather, takes her out on a Thursday morning when it's fixing to blow hard into a nor'easter."

Jines was fiddling with the pillow again, already shaking his head at the way this story was going.

"Well I guess he run down on that breeze all right, lucky enough he didn't spring no seams in that sea, which Jimmy Pierce told me he heard was running six feet anyway. But then what does this boy do? Instead of making Stingray Point, he's looking at Windmill Point and thinking he's seeing the barn. And evidently it's going on dark and raining hard, and he manages to run her right up on the spit in three foot of water on a falling tide. They can't get her off. Seas are pounding her, driving her right into the bottom. Have to get the Coast Guard to haul their sorry asses off. It didn't stop blowing for three days, and you know what that must've been like. Nothing but sticks left." Kenneth shook his head disgustedly. "Died in sight of the creek where she'd been put overboard some seventy years earlier. Can you believe that?"

Jines pictured the old boat battered by the wind and waves, taken apart bit by bit while the gulls and terns watched. And nothing anyone could do once she was grounded, the bottom slowly torn out of her. "Well," he said finally. "At least she was home."

Kenneth spit into his can. Out on the river another quick little fishing boat buzzed by, its wake folding back the water.

"So Jines," Kenneth said, "when you reckon you'll be ready to get back out? I can get some boys to set the Twenty-Footer next week, get her all good to go."

Jines leaned his head back and felt immensely tired suddenly, his whole body like lead. He was stiff all over, as if he'd been hauling nets for days on end, and his muscles felt like sodden sacks on his bones. The worst was morning. Had a hard time waking up, and some days it was ten, eleven o'clock before he opened his eyes, and even then it was another while before he could get himself moving. Aye God, he missed the sunrise, the way the light ribboned long and gold down the water to his dock, a straight shot into the new light of day. Even out here on the porch he felt closed in, pinched deep inside for the need of water, the settled breath and expectation of the open horizon.

"Fact is, Kenneth, I don't know," Jines said. He pointed to the walker. "I'm getting around better, but don't know as I'd be any good on the *Jenny Rae*." He didn't feel the need to go into details. Tired him out just thinking about it.

"Well shit, we can give you a hand. Me and the boys'll do all the grunt work, you just need to get us out there."

Jines kneaded his hands. How could they be cold on a warm morning like this? He remembered his mama when she got old, always asking him for more quilts and tea, the cup clattering in the saucer. "That young doc told me no way I should go out yet. Says it could make things worse, maybe bring on another stroke."

Kenneth stood up and walked over to the door, leaned out and with a flick of his forefinger scooped out his chaw into the boxwoods. He came back, wiping his finger on his pants. Sat back down. "Damn," he said. "Damn." He looked out through the screen, squinted a little. Then he said, "I can see how you'd be scared to go then."

Jines stopped working his hands, laid them flat and hard on his thighs. "I don't recall saying I was scared, Kenneth. I ain't scared of shit. I just said I need some time." There was a glass of water on the table next to him, and he drained it and set it back down a little harder than necessary.

Kenneth seemed to be considering the empty glass, then the pile of nets behind the shed across the yard. He reached into his shirt pocket and pulled out a sack of Red Man, tucked another wad into his cheek.

"Jesus, Kenneth, that shit'll rot your whole head, you know that, don't you? How long you been chewing now?"

Kenneth looked back at Jines. "What if I take her out for you. Set the second pound at Twenty-Footer, or Big Betty if you think that's gonna be better this year. I could get some boys. Everybody knows the boat." He looked back over at the pile of gear, waved one hand at it. "Seems like a waste having everything ready to go and just letting it all set there."

Jines followed Kenneth's gaze out toward the shed, the *Jenny Rae*, the river beyond. The spring light bounced off the water, a certain softness to it now. No more the hard mica glint of winter. It made sense, letting Kenneth take the boat. God knows he could use the money if the fish were running and everything went okay. If the boys Kenneth brought with him had half a brain among them and didn't do anything stupid like get drowned. If Kenneth didn't bully the boys the way he always had a mind to. If Kenneth didn't have a drink or five and pile his boat up.

If he could stand watching his boat, the one he'd built with his own hands and sweat, leave the dock without him.

Jines thought of the *Eliza M. Bell* hard aground, waves pounding the bottom right out of her. Hour after hour, day after day, till nothing was left but the story. He thought about Linwood Parker, trapped like an animal. Suddenly he kicked the walker hard with his right leg, the leg that still had some of the old strength left in it. It skidded across the wooden planked floor and banged into the screen, startling the swallows out from under the eaves. Kenneth's eyebrows went up his forehead. "The hell, Jines," he said, reaching for the walker.

"Leave it," Jines snapped. He knew he couldn't get out of the rocking chair without the hateful thing. Not yet. All the same, he pushed his butt to the chair's edge and leaned his forearms hard on his knees, nodding toward the pile of poles and net behind the shed. "Don't worry about setting the others yet. Let's see what's going on with the Seven Brothers first. If the fish are running hard we'll set the Betty." The bony knobs of his elbows dug into his thighs and he ground them in harder, registering the pain. He was resentful, suddenly, of the gentling spring light, the flowers, the softness of the sweat pants Mary Virginia had brought him. "Give me a week and tell the boys, the regulars," he said to Kenneth, "I'll be ready."

Chapter 7

Jines looked to the southeast, and what he saw there unsettled him. The edge of the sky was like a black eye, bruised and swollen and speaking of trouble. The breeze that had been building all morning was just plain strange, no other word for it. He'd listened to the weather radio ahead of time; he'd been listening every day with a hand-held VHF that fit just as neat as you please in his palm. At first he'd thought to hide it from Lily Rae but then that idea struck him as just ridiculous—he was a waterman, for God's sake, he lived and died by the weather. And she was his daughter, not some schoolmarm going to whack him on the hand with a ruler. The thing was he didn't want to tell her he was going out to the Seven Brothers, wanted to save his energy for the doing, not the arguing. And aye God, he knew there would be arguing on this particular point. So he'd listened to the hand-held out on the porch every morning just as ordinary as having a glass of juice or a cup of coffee (even though he was only allowed to drink that pissant decaf now), hiding in plain sight you might say, and the weather people hadn't said anything about this ugly sky or this crazy wind. It wasn't regular, not at all, and that made him uneasy.

The *Jenny Rae* had cleared the jetties at the mouth of the Little River two hours ago and was well up into the Potomac. They were coming up to the pound, another five minutes or so. The tiller rattling under his right hand, it was rough and all business. He knew that feel of it in his sleep. Something in the water ahead caught his eye and he pulled the tiller a bit to change course slightly. They rolled past a lunker of a log, three-quarters sunk and half as long as the boat, drifting silently in the half-dark river like some kind of prehistoric crocodile. Don't worry, Linwood, he thought, my eyes still work fine out here.

"Jesus Christ, that thing looks like one of them saltwater crocs you see on the TV!" Kenneth said.

"Grab you and take you down, too, if you hit it just right," muttered Jines.

It was always a hazard this time of year, all the junk that the spring tides and rains washed into the big rivers like this one, and then on into the Bay. He'd seen refrigerators, tires, the framing of what appeared to be somebody's front porch, screens still on it, anything you can imagine. Usually collected along the tide line, the whole mess swirling with muddy bubbles. Tide lines were easy though, predictable. You knew pretty much where they were going to be and when. It was these solitary floaters, dark and secret as the river itself, that you really had to watch out for. They could punch a hole in a boat or rip off a propeller quicker than you could say goodbye granny I'm going home. Jines gripped the tiller and leaned on it a little. He felt more tired than he'd like. He hoped the Seven Brothers wasn't torn up with debris. But as they approached it and idled along beside the leader he thought it looked pretty good. There were two sections that he could see something had gotten to, some kind of logs or who knows what. They'd have to patch them up. Whole thing would have to come out soon anyway for painting again. All in all though, not bad so far. Cormorants, narrow and dark-shouldered as goblins, shrugged on the poles. They took off as the boat came alongside.

"Rats with wings," Kenneth said. "You oughta take a couple pops at 'em, Jines Arley, it'll make you feel better."

"I feel fine," Jines said. "Get the boys up and let's get her done. I'm not liking the look of that sky much."

Jines slid the *Jenny Rae* alongside the pound head and made her fast. She rubbed against the poles in the swell that quickly became more noticeable as they came broadside to it. Running downwind he had known it was there some, every now and then her stern would give a little kick on a quartering wave, but in his haste to get up here he realized now that he'd been downplaying the wind in his mind, hoping it wasn't what his gut was telling him. He knew how it could roll up out of the south, send a big swell right up this river, and when the tide started falling, look out. Still, the swell could help the boys haul the net, once they got the rhythm of it. The wind was steadily building. When they'd cleared the jetties it was maybe ten knots or so. He'd guess the gusts at about twenty-five now, and it wasn't even barely ten o'clock. He stretched his eyes as far as they could see south, toward the river's mouth and the open Bay. He could see the flecks of white already down there. It was going to be a rough ride home.

"Come on, Kenneth!"

"Keep your fuckin' pants on," Kenneth growled, pushing the sleepy crew ahead of him out of the cabin house.

There were two of the boat's regulars—Robbie and Joe—and a third man Kenneth had brought named Tyler. Jines didn't know if that was the man's given name or last, but he knew he didn't much like the look of him. When he'd gotten on the boat he'd glanced up only for a second with glittery, narrow eyes set close together in a face that seemed to be caving in on itself. A sweatshirt and torn jeans hung off him. His whole body looked like it was skidding into some cracked seam somewhere deep inside itself. What Jines could see of his teeth reminded him of rotten dock pilings. Jines wondered what bar stool Kenneth had dragged him out from under. But the fact was he needed the bodies. He'd been out of commission long enough to lose most of his regular crew to other work. Nobody was sure he'd get back out here. He had no idea what was in the pound but he suspected it could be full and heavy. He was willing, for now at least, to make do with what hands he could get.

"All right boys, let's get on it," Jines said.

They climbed into the bateau and pulled it around to the other side of the pound. A wave slapped the hard chine of the smaller boat as it left the protection of the *Jenny Rae*'s side, and the one called Tyler fell hard to the floor, butt first.

"Fuck!" he yelled over the laughter of the others.

"What's the matter with your legs there, Tyler, you leave 'em and your balls with that skank at Stoney's last night?" yelled Joe in his too-high voice.

"Fuck you!"

Tyler lunged at Joe as he came back to his feet when Kenneth intercepted him, wrapping a ham-sized fist around his neck. Kenneth must have outweighed Tyler by about a hundred pounds. He looked like a wrung-neck chicken there in Kenneth's grip.

"Knock it off, asshole," Kenneth hissed. "You save it for the beach. Understand?"

Tyler tried to nod. Kenneth flicked him away. Tyler rubbed his neck sullenly. The wind was whistling now, setting up a steady whine through *Jenny Rae*'s VHF radio antenna and around the gaff pole. The rigging and blocks slapped against the pole and the short mast, and every now and then a box of a wave caught the boat's side square on, jolting Jines. He watched as the men struggled to maneuver the bateau into place and begin the labor of hauling the net. He heard the cry of the gulls as they swooped and dipped near the boat, their calls sounding like jeers, as if they saw the whole exercise as foolishness and him as the king fool. The hell was the matter with him today? He should be happy out here. For a while he had wondered whether he'd ever be out here again, hearing these damned birds and feeling the boat moving under his feet. He should be grateful. But the whole thing felt as strange and ominous as the sky, out of kilter. The way clouds sometimes moved in two directions at once, some current up there you couldn't see making things uncertain and hard to read. Didn't help knowing he was probably going home straight on into another storm, this one by the name of Lily Rae. He had told Kenneth to keep this first trip under the radar until the last minute. Kenneth had laughed at him.

"I didn't know better I'd think you were scared of that girl," he'd said. "What do you care what she thinks?"

Kenneth never did know when was a good time to poke at a man and when not.

"Just leave it," Jines had said.

At least Kenneth had the sense to keep his mouth shut this once. When Jines had woken up this morning and found her and that skinny blue kayak gone, he'd entertained the brief notion of a clean getaway. Almost did it too. He'd kept his eyes straight ahead and his hand firm on the tiller when the *Jenny Rae* had gone past her; she was on the way in while he was on the way out. Didn't even look at her. He didn't want her to think he was too weak to go out. He didn't want any of them to think it. But the truth was, he was hanging on to the tiller for more than steering. He'd been three hours or so on the water now. His left leg felt like a waterlogged branch hanging off his hip. His left arm hung at his side when he didn't keep his hand tucked into the bib on his rubber overalls. He could situate his left thigh against the side deck as he drove, put the weight on his good leg instead, and that helped. But this wind, damnation, did not. He reached into his pocket for a Hershey bar he'd stashed there, along with some peanuts. He had some egg salad sandwiches waiting in his cooler, a couple of Cokes and some brownies Lily had made yesterday. He'd eat after they'd hauled the net. Maybe give Kenneth the helm for a bit. He'd feel better then.

Across the pound the bateau started pulling closer as the men hauled away on the massive net. The gulls' cries grew more shrill as the surface of the water began to froth and quicken. Jines chewed the chocolate and watched the men. Maybe he shouldn't have just gone past her like that this morning, he thought. He had no doubt she'd be mad that he went fishing. She bought that young doctor's bullshit all the way; he could have another stroke if he so much as sneezed too hard, the way that pup told it. Even if he got his strength back the water was no place for him, that doc had said, too dangerous. And she believed that shit. Wanted him to spend the rest of his life puttering like an old man, working his hands with little rubber balls so he could do what with them? Fill out the crossword in the *Mathews County Intelligencer*? Whittle decoys to sell at the hospital auxiliary? As if that was a life. He shoved the Hershey wrapper into his pocket. Going by without even so much as a look, though, maybe that wasn't the best thing to do there. Just pissed her off even more probably, if that was even possible. But hell, why should she be mad at him for going fishing? Didn't she understand that being out here, it was all he was? And she herself was the one who was all fired up about his not having any insurance, and how he was going to need money to pay for all those medical bills. Well, he'd had enough to cover a chunk of it, hadn't he? He wasn't a complete fool. He'd worked hard over the years. It was true that he still owed, but all the more reason for getting out here while the fishing was hot and making some cash. If things went well, he could pay off the last of it in a couple years and be free and clear again. She couldn't have it both ways.

The boys almost had the net up, and Jines fired up the engine again to lower the dip net from the gaff pole. The empty dip net swung hard in the breeze, almost smacked Kenneth in the head before he got hold of it. The pound was thick with fish. Jines could see their flickering sides, and in all that shimmering energy he felt a sudden surge of strength run through his bones. Everything seemed suddenly sharper, clearer, the thick salty scent of the sea breeze, the smell of oil and diesel and a million fish embedded in the planks and floorboards of this sweet boat he had built, the hiss and whip of a swell as it moved under him. All the tiredness of these last endless weeks was gone. Hadn't he known it would be, out here? Hadn't he known it? Aye God, this is where he belonged, no matter what. He lowered the dip net toward the writhing fish. "What do we got, boys, what do we got?" he yelled, as they pushed the net down to fill it. He flicked the lever to raise it and with his good arm pulled it slowly over the *Jenny Rae*'s cockpit. Kenneth tugged the tether line holding the dip net's cinched bottom and with a rush like a waterfall the fish spilled downward in a silver torrent, thumping on the hard wooden floorboards. In a quick glance, Jines saw rockfish and perch, bunkers and even what looked to be some early mackerel. He busied himself with the dip net again, and over and over the men pushed it down to fill it, swung it over the cockpit and flooded pile after pile of fish into the hold. Jines crowed. It was a decent haul by God, maybe ten-, twelve-thousand pounds. They'd have to throw some of the rockfish back to satisfy the state, and a lot of the bunker would go to crabbers for bait. But still, Jines was jubilant. He'd checked the market yesterday and knew prices had been holding steady and pretty good for the rockfish. This was only the one pound; he still had two to set. Just to see the boat filling up again exhilarated him. He looked across to the men in the bateau and saw the weariness in their faces.

"Hang in there now boys, she's almost done," he called.

The one called Tyler looked totally played, his narrow chest heaving. Jines would get him off the boat as soon as they were home. Once word got out that the *Jenny Rae* was back up and running, he knew he wouldn't have any trouble finding good crew.

"How much more you got there, Kenneth?" he called over the wind.

"One more good one, I reckon," Kenneth yelled.

"Thank Christ," the one called Tyler said.

His face was pallid and shiny as a hard-boiled egg. Another

couple minutes he'll be going green, Jines thought, and then be puking. Key-hrist, where did Kenneth find that sorry son of a bitch? Kenneth was struggling with something in the net, his low cursing coming across the water in a wind-torn mutter. Jines waited, trying to be patient. The *Jenny Rae* was moving more violently under him now, making it hard to keep his footing. He took his eyes off the pound and looked around him. The whitecaps that he'd seen downriver an hour ago were all around now, tipping the short, sharp waves that were setting up on top of the bigger swells below. He could feel the unsettled boat beneath him wrestling with the breeze on the surface and the current beneath, now ebbing against the southeasterly wind. It was a strange feeling, the uneasy movement of something caught between two equally compelling forces. As if she were twisting a little beneath him, almost squirming, anxious, pinned here as she was against the Seven Brothers' poles.

"What's the problem, Kenneth?" he yelled.

"Something big and heavy in here and it's tangled in the net. I just about got it." Kenneth grunted and suddenly lurched backwards. "What the hell? Holy God that's foul! Shee-it!"

The one called Tyler ran for the leeward side of the bateau, puking loudly. Upwind, Jines couldn't smell anything at first, but when Kenneth pulled the net again he saw a head as large as a man's emerging from the water. For one horrible moment he thought they'd netted a corpse; then he saw a wide flipper and the broad, curved back of a sea turtle. It was huge, looked to be as big across as a rich man's desk. Limp and dead, the exposed neck half gnawed open by crabs, the eyes gouged out. There was a crab still right there, hanging onto a pale piece of gristle with a defiant claw. Jines heard Tyler puking again, and then a wave grabbed the *Jenny Rae*'s starboard stern and twisted her against the poles hard, knocking Jines to his knees. He struggled back to his feet, pulling himself up on the side of the cabin house. He looked into the net again. A loggerhead. What the hell was it doing up here this early? And that big? He'd known young loggerheads and other sea turtles visited the Bay come summertime; they came here after spending their earliest years down in the southern gyres of the Gulf Stream. Fattened up here all summer on clams and crabs and then headed out again into the big blue yonder. Travelers of the world. He had no idea what a full-grown loggerhead was doing in the Potomac River in water that was by all rights this time of year too cold and too fresh, but he knew for sure that his nets had caught it and killed it. He felt sick.

"The hell is it?" Tyler gasped from the far side of the bateau. His face had gone from greasy white to a pale yellow-green, not unlike the color of the turtle's barnacled carapace.

"It's a loggerhead turtle, is what it is," Jines said. "Probably thirty, forty years old, maybe a lot older."

Kenneth was still trying to free it from the net. "How'd you get to be such an expert?" he yelled, wrestling with one of the flippers. It was as long and thick as his forearm.

"How'd the hell it get stuck in there, Kenneth?" Jines said. "That mesh isn't big enough for something that size to get caught in there."

"Looks like there's a hole here. Something tore it open, who knows what. This big bastard got halfway in here and musta got snagged. All his thrashing, goddamn thing trashed this part of the net. We gotta haul her and patch her."

Kenneth yanked and pulled. Jines was reminded of a show he'd seen on TV once, one of those documentaries about an emergency room where the doctor had to set some woman's broken leg and looked like he damn near pulled it off to do it. He felt even more nauseated watching this.

"Aw fuck it," Kenneth said suddenly. "Give me that knife in

the pilothouse, Jines Arley, I don't have all day for this."

"You are not cutting that flipper off that turtle, Kenneth," Jines said.

Kenneth shot him an incredulous look. "Why the hell not? Stupid thing's dead anyway! And we gotta get this net out of here and patched up or you can forget about catching anything else."

Jines was suddenly furious. At Kenneth, at his nets for killing this animal, at the turtle itself for being where it shouldn't have been, at the bitter wind that just kept insisting on its way, never easing up, at his useless left arm and leg, which were both numb and heavy now, as limp as the turtle and just as wrecked.

"Goddammit, give him a knife and let's get the hell out of here!" yelled Tyler from the bateau.

"You shut up, you worthless son of a bitch," Jines said, and he heard a wet crack as Kenneth snapped the joint of the animal's flipper. Something in Jines broke at the sound of it. He sagged against the boat's cabin house.

"Robbie and Joe, give me a hand here," Kenneth yelled, and the three of them dragged the turtle out of the net and up on the side deck of the bateau where they paused for a second, gasping. "Fucking thing stinks," Kenneth said, and with a shove of his boot he pushed it overboard.

Jines watched it settle slowly into the roiled water, its pale, round head glimmering briefly before the dark river pulled it under.

The men said little on the way home. Joe and Robbie headed into the cabin house, getting out of the worst of the weather. Tyler slumped in one corner of the cockpit, rousing himself now and then to heave over the side. Jines considered going inside the cabin house to helm the boat where he could get out of the wind and water, but the spray pinging his face like needles kept him alert. Kenneth had wanted to stay and patch the net but Jines refused. It was going to be a bad enough ride home. He doubted with the seas getting up like they were that they'd be able to clear the bar safely with a hold half-full of fish. They'd have to go out and around the lighthouse, and while the deeper water would mean more regular seas, easier for the boat to handle, it would also mean a longer distance around and then more time exposed with the waves dead abeam once they'd cleared the lighthouse and headed for the jetties and the safety of the river. He wasn't afraid of it; fact was he kind of liked it sometimes when it got nasty out here, and this blow wasn't anything he and the *Jenny Rae* hadn't handled before. But he hadn't looked for it today. He was tired in his bones in a way he'd come to dread. He knew she could handle it. He wasn't as sure about himself.

"So how come you know so much about sea turtles to know that was a loggerhead and all that?" Kenneth asked again.

Jines wished Kenneth would just drop it. "I did some studying," he said. It was Lily, he could have said. But he didn't want to risk the memory by giving it to anyone, least of all Kenneth. He heard again the sick snapping sound of the turtle's limb and lowered his head.

He'd found turtles before in his nets. Most of the time they were unhurt, swimming around in the pound and just as panicky as everything else when it was time to come up. But there was a morning many years ago when he'd found one in serious trouble. It had a deep gouge across its shell, like it had been hit with a boat's propeller, and one rear flipper was nearly cut in half. He didn't know why he'd kept the turtle there in the hold with the rest of the catch, why he didn't just toss it over the side the way he'd done all the others. He and the boys just got busy with emptying and resetting the nets, and he just plain forgot about the thing. Then Lily saw it. She'd come down to greet him home, the way she always used to do when she was little, and as the boys were scooping out the catch and starting the culling she saw the turtle there in the corner. Jines figured it was dead by then. But when Lily climbed down into the cockpit and squatted next to its head, running her hands over its back, the animal's deep liquid eyes opened and gazed at her with a look Jines had never seen before in his life, some ancient look well beyond human understanding. It unsettled him and intrigued him, all at once. "She's alive, Daddy, she's alive!" Lily was yelling. She was begging him to let her keep the turtle, to nurse it back to health. Her bedroom was chock-a-block with stuffed animals, she kept every single feather she'd ever found, her dressers were covered in shells and rocks and the bones of animals she'd discovered in her little girl's curious wanderings. But this was real, he could see. This was urgent in her, and he found that he couldn't say no although it went against all of his instincts.

That first night they set the turtle in a tub of clean river water out in the culling shed. At dawn the next morning Jines went out expecting, again, to find the creature dead. He found instead his daughter sound asleep on the hard wood of the shed floor, a blanket wrapped around her legs, her hand on the edge of the tub. That morning he drove up to the House of Deals and came home with a flat of petunias for Jenny Rae, a couple hundred feet of small-mesh chicken wire, and a couple dozen wooden stakes. He and Lily spent the day building a pen in the shallow waters of the marsh just beyond the dock, her small, firm back rounded intently as she held the poles so he could pound them. Soft crabs skittered around their feet, and he remembered the ache of his back, the cool of the water on his arms, the twining of the eelgrass around his fingers as they worked. She had named it Granny. Because she was certain the turtle was a she, Lily told him, and her eyes reminded her of her grandma's, wise and wrinkly.

The next day Jines came in from fishing and found Lily and her mother at the marsh along with a fellow with a big duffle bag on the ground next to him. Jenny Rae had been talking to someone at the Food Lion about Granny, she said, and the check-out clerk overheard and suggested she give a call down there to the marine biology school in Gloucester, that those folks knew everything there was to know about what swam around in the Bay. The man's name was Jack Baker. He said that Granny was a loggerhead turtle, about ten years old, maybe less. Scientists were just starting to really study sea turtles in the Bay, he said, and he was excited Jines had found this one. He wanted to take her back to his lab in Gloucester where he could keep an eye on her, make sure she got better. Truth was, he told them, they couldn't keep her because she was an endangered species.

Well, Lily about fell apart. Granny had come to her, she pleaded, she would help her get well. Wasn't the pen the perfect place, with all the eelgrass and jellyfish and clams and soft crabs? Jack Baker had to admit it was turtle heaven. Couldn't she stay, and Lily would care for her, and Jack Baker could come back anytime and check up on her? And when Granny was better, they would release her back into the Bay, or even way down at the Virginia Capes if that was better, her daddy could take Granny down there in his boat. Jack Baker studied the intent young girl for a bit, a quiet smile at the corners of his mouth. He looked at Jines. Jines nodded. And then watched and helped as Jack Baker drew some blood from the turtle and put it in a little vial, examined the wounded shell, stitched up the flipper, injected Granny with some antibiotics, measured her front and back with a tape measure as Lily wrote down all the numbers in one of his notebooks. Last but not least he attached a tag to one of her front flippers. That way, he explained, if she turned up somewhere else people would know she'd been tagged, and they'd let him know where she was and how she was doing.

Well, damned if that turtle didn't take over the whole place that summer. Every day Lily would run to meet Jines at the dock, her long legs flying across the yard, and pull him by the hand down to the pen. Wouldn't even let him go get a Budweiser first, and him dead on his feet after hauling nets. Half the time he'd have to patch where the thing had torn up the chicken wire, like he needed one more thing to do at the end of the day. Even Jenny Rae got sick of all the attention the turtle was getting. "You'd think there wasn't a room to clean or a garden to tend," she'd say, marching off toward the house. But it had been a long time since Jines had just sat by the water, just watching, not trying to catch something in it. Fact was he couldn't remember when he ever did that. Maybe when he was a boy about Lily's age. The two of them hung their feet in the water, swatted mosquitoes, and Lily would tell him all about her day.

Jack Baker visited frequently and brought all kinds of books and information about sea turtles. Jines liked the man. He was a plain talker, no bullshit, although on his business card Jines saw that he had the letters PhD after his name, along with a bunch of other stuff. He agreed with Jines that state regulators usually did more harm than good when they tried to mess with Mother Nature. He told Jines and Jenny Rae that their daughter had the makings of a hell of a marine biologist. And he asked Jines about what else he'd seen in his nets, listened to his stories about how some years the Bay was full of certain fish—sea trout, for instance—and then the next year nary a one, but a slew of Spanish mackerel instead. Who could figure it? In his own way, Jack Baker seemed to like the mystery of what was out there just as much as Jines did.

Toward the end of summer they put Granny back in the tub—had a hell of a time catching her, now that she was healthy—and placed her in the *Jenny Rae*'s cockpit for the trip south. Jack Baker wanted to release her down at Cape Charles where she could make her way easily to the open ocean. Lily sat by the tub the whole way, running her hands over the turtle's back. She was trying hard not to cry, Jines could tell. He ached for her. It was going on sunset when they neared Cape Charles. The water was a bright green, almost tropical, and rafts of seagrass floated here and there, little fish darting in the shelter beneath them. The air was thick and warm off the Atlantic. Jines and Jack Baker carefully lifted Granny from the tub and lowered her over the side, her flippers going like mad as soon as she saw the water. She didn't hesitate. Jines watched her fly, her dark form soaring into the deep. "You did a good thing, darlin', a good thing," he told Lily. She leaned against him, her tears wet through his shirt, as they headed home under a raven sky.

Now, his face stinging with the salt spray, Jines closed his eyes a moment and wiped them slowly with the back of his weak hand. It had been years since he had opened himself all the way to that memory. So much had happened soon after that fine summer, so much of his world had flown apart. He had closed himself tight against anything that dared to draw him close to that time. Now it saddened him that it had taken this ugly day to bring those warm images back.

Up ahead off the *Jenny Rae's* starboard bow Jines could see the seas breaking on the bar just north of the entrance of the Little River. Home was so close, and so far. On an ordinary day he could head straight south across those shallows and cut four miles off the trip into the jetties and safe water. Today he couldn't risk it. He kept his course for the lighthouse to the southeast. The spray was constant now, the seas big and confused as they entered the Bay where the Potomac poured into it, wide and unforgiving. He might as well have been on the ocean; the only land in sight was the Virginia shore to the south. Other than that, all around him was hissing water and a sky of torn clouds. Behind him he heard the rasping of Tyler's dry heaves. Kenneth dredged a wad of Red Man from a bag and shoveled it into his cheek with a finger. He flicked his head aft toward Tyler.

"Well, that was a mistake," he said.

"I guess," Jines said.

Kenneth squinted south toward the breaking waves on the bar. He ducked as a wave shot up off the bow, the wind whipping the spray straight at them. "Jesus, what a fucking day," he said. "I gotta say, Jines Arley, you picked a fine one to get back out here."

Jines focused what energy he had left on driving the boat. She was taking the seas okay, but he didn't like it. His eyes burned from the salt and he was having trouble seeing. His whole body ached. He knew there would come a point he would be too tired to continue steering and he'd have to hand the helm over to Kenneth. He didn't want that point to come until they were inside the river. Kenneth drove a boat about the same way he drove his truck, and that kind of loose carelessness in these seas could turns things the wrong way in a hurry. All you needed on a boat was one thing to go wrong and it wasn't long before that led to something else and then something else, and then you were in the shit. When it came down to it, Jines knew it was just him and the *Jenny Rae* out here, counting on each other. That's the way it had always been, really, and truth was that's how he preferred it. He wondered if that was why Lily had moved away, all the way up to Maine. Maybe it was just that, after all was said and done, they both knew he did better on his own. Safer that way, all the way around.

"Too rough to go over the bar?" Kenneth asked.

Jines nodded.

"You sure? I'm thinking we can make it. Be a little nasty but what the hell."

"I'm sure," Jines said. That was just the thing, he thought. Kenneth would push everything; a truck was just a truck, a dead turtle was just a stupid dead turtle, a boat was just a boat. And if it broke, well, he'd cobble something together to make do, he'd dig under some rock to find a Tyler-type who owed him something from some deal way back when, he wouldn't worry about the mess. More than Kenneth's affection for the bottle, it was this aspect of his character that Jines found the most disturbing. Somehow Kenneth never had anything invested. And so he had nothing to lose.

It was in the middle of a gust that was strong enough to push Jines's breath right back down his throat when he heard a thump and felt the *Jenny Rae* shudder a little beneath him. Up in her bow. It was harder than a square wave; it felt like the boat had hit something. He thought of the lunker log he'd seen earlier.

"The fuck was that?" Kenneth said. So Jines hadn't imagined it.

"I don't know. Go forward and check her planking."

Kenneth hustled into the cabin house and Jines felt a gnawing in his gut. What if he'd hurt her? He was tired, aye God he was tired he knew, but he swore he hadn't taken his eyes off the water. Even with the darkened sky there was still plenty of light. He figured it was probably only about one o'clock, maybe a little earlier. It felt like he'd been out here since midnight. If anything he'd been trying harder to stay on top of things, knowing he wasn't quite up to speed. But the idea wouldn't leave his head. Maybe there was something wrong with him, something wrong with the way Lily brought out the mean in him and the way he almost wanted it. He'd always thought he left all of that poison behind when he threw the lines on the dock and turned his boat east. But what if he was no longer allowed that small grace? What if that blackness was out here with him, had followed him like the bateau tethered to the stern of *Jenny Rae*, a part of him that he couldn't put aside anymore? What if he had brought it to his blameless boat, the one true thing he had left? His mouth was dry as talc.

"Kenneth!" he yelled. Looking forward, expecting to hear Kenneth yell back, he heard a sound just behind him instead and half turned in time to see Tyler bringing the hickory boathook pole down across his shoulders.

"You old fuck!" Tyler yelled at him. Jines doubled over, hearing Tyler's voice somewhere above him. "Get us over the bar! Fuck this, get us the fuck outta here!" He was screaming and reaching for the tiller. Jines fell sideways against the engine box as Tyler pushed him away. Tyler grabbed the tiller and yanked it hard to pull *Jenny Rae*'s bow sharply to the right. It only took a second for a swell to catch her full on the beam, and she rolled violently over to starboard.

The roll yanked Jines off the engine box and threw him hard against the gunwale. He heard water hissing next to his ear, and things slowed down in a way that reminded him of something elastic and stretchy, like a rubber band being pulled to its limit before bouncing wildly away. In the cockpit, the mess of fish he'd been so pleased about a lifetime ago slid hard over next to him and he looked down into the dead glassy eye of a striped bass. Probably a thirty-four-incher, his head thought in the strange distance. Nice fish. The *Jenny Rae* was still laid over, all those fish helping hold her down, and in the quiet part of his mind Jines was begging her back up onto her feet, willing her back up, but in his fear for her he had forgotten about himself. And when Tyler shrieked in his ear and grabbed at his arm Jines didn't realize until too late that Tyler had lost his footing and lost his grip on the tiller, that glittery-eyed Tyler was in a full-on panic and he was going over the side, and he was taking Jines with him.

The water surprised him; it felt warmer than the air. He looked up in time to see the bateau, which had stayed straight on its course when the *Jenny Rae* had slewed to the right, come racing down the backside of the wave that had rolled her and slam into Tyler's head, silencing his gargled screams like a switch being thrown. The bateau's hard chine slid by Jines and he tried to reach up, grabbing for any kind of hold. His arm barely cleared the water, flailing as the boat rushed past. He felt the water close over his head, and in the sudden silence he remembered Lily's girl-voice on those soft summer nights by the marsh, he remembered Granny's dim shadow flying off into the deep, seeming so certain of her journey. And he thought now that he must be the dead one instead, the dead stinking turtle from his nets, his pale head sinking into the muddy darkness.

He was sinking like a brick, like a streamlined brick. And he let it take him. Just for a minute, he thought, I'm so tired, just for a minute. It was so quiet here, a kind of peace he never expected. He'd always thought there would be panic and fear and struggling, what he'd seen a million fish do as he pulled them from their element. Shouldn't it be the same with the roles reversed? There was a rightness to the idea that made perfect sense. What was part of nature couldn't stay out of balance for long. The certitude of this was what he counted on most in his life of water and sky, the one thing that remained steady in a random world. If something was out of whack—if it was seventy-five degrees in January, for instance—you knew nature would come along to set things to rights. After the uncanny sun there would come a cold front like a freight train, wild winds, hail, thundersnow, a violent setting of things to right. Drowning is probably what he would do best. Go swimming with the turtles, let the current simply take him, out into the blue. A proper alignment of the elements, what should have happened a long time ago.

Then, he breathed. And there was no peace in the ripping in his lungs, no silence in the roaring in his head. Only atonement.

Chapter 8

Jines woke to something familiar, and it was a smell. Not that of his boat, or fish, or the tarry stink of his nets, or even the low-tide reek of the marsh. It was plastic, it was disinfectant. It was the absence of honest-to-god scent of any living thing. "Damn," was what he wanted to say, "Goddamn son-of-bitch," because he knew without even opening his eyes where he'd smelled that before, where he'd felt these scratchy dry sheets against his skin. But the only thing that came out of his salt-seared lungs and throat was the same raspy grunt a croaker makes when you haul it off the bottom and dump it on the dock.

He pushed his eyes open. Lily was there. She was asleep in the chair, curled up like a cat, her head on a balled-up sweatshirt. Aye God, Jines thought, will you look at that. She looked different. Not like her mother so much, not like that shadow of someone who was and was not. She looked like herself. He noticed there were freckles on her forearms, and the skin on her hands looked tan and weathered. Even closed, her eyes had some wrinkles at their corners. He could see them in thin veins of white where she had squinted against the sun, a map of places she had been, things she had done. He wondered that he hadn't noticed these details before. Always thought of her as an office puss with her reporter's job, somebody who spends all their time with their face glowed up by the computer screen. But watching her now, Jines wondered. Did she look different to him because he hadn't really looked at her before? Or had something about her changed to make the details stand out? Or him? As if maybe the sear in his throat from breathing water had scoured some things out, burned them raw and fresh.

He looked around the room. He couldn't remember how he'd

gotten here. His neck and shoulders throbbed. He closed his eyes, cast his memory back, and winced. There was the *Jenny Rae* beneath him, stoutly pushing through the seas. Steady, she was so steady. He remembered the noise he and Kenneth had heard up in the bow, and he felt a rising panic so the skin on his arms tingled with it. It came back to him, all of his fear that somehow he'd brought something bad onto her, some of the blackness in him had caused that wind and that sound and everything that followed. He couldn't remember whether she was all right. He didn't believe much in what other people called God; it was always Jenny who'd dragged them off to church every Sunday, and while he liked the pastor well enough and the community of the people there, the overriding theology of it seemed a bit far-fetched to him. It's not that he didn't believe in a greater presence in the world, he just didn't necessarily feel the need to call it "God" and give it all the freight that name carried. But it was a funny thing about the Bay. What happened there sometimes sure as hell could bring a man to his knees. Jines remembered the strain of his boat pinned on her side, the strength of the sea keeping her there. Here in the hospital bed he lofted up a little prayer to the God he didn't quite know how to talk to.

Then he looked back again at his daughter, still asleep in the chair. Her mouth sagged open just a bit, and she was snoring. Strands of her hair, that tawny blonde and brown she'd gotten straight from her mother, fell across her face in fine wispy rivers. He wondered at how she could curl up so small like that, the tight bundle of her. She'd always done that when she slept, he remembered, from when she was a tiny thing. Wrap herself up in her quilts like a bug in a rug. It pleased him that this hadn't changed. Listening to her soft snores, he felt his eyes closing. He fell asleep knowing she was there.

When he woke again it seemed to be night. The lights in the room were low, and the window was a dark rectangle in the wall. A nurse was taking his temperature, her hand cool and dry on his wrist as she examined the watch on her own arm, counting his pulse. He recognized her from the last time. She was a good one. Liked jellybeans, as he recalled, grew up over in Lancaster. Lily's chair was empty, but the sweatshirt she'd rested her head on was still there. He didn't recognize it, not something she'd worn before, but who could say? He hadn't really been paying any attention to her, he realized. Hadn't really even seen her. The nurse let go of his hand, pulled the thermometer from his mouth, looked at it. She was tapping what she'd learned into a laptop computer when he said, "Hello." At least that's what he was trying to say. His throat felt jagged as oyster bottom scraped over one too many times.

The nurse looked up from her writing, her eyebrows arched.

"Well hello to you too, Mr. Evans. Nice to see you again, although I'm sure you're not glad to be back."

Jines raised his hand, even the small motion making him nauseous. His whole body was immensely sore and stiff. He remembered the water closing over his head, remembered feeling surprised that it wasn't as cold as he'd thought it would be. And that was all.

"Beats the alternative, though," she said, finishing his thought. "I'll let your daughter know you're awake. She just went down to the cafeteria for something to eat."

But when he woke again the rectangle of window had light pouring through it, and it was that pup of a doctor, Dr. Wyatt, standing next to the bed, and from the look on his face Jines knew he was in for an earful. Well shit.

"Only cats have nine lives, Mr. Evans," Dr. Wyatt said. "Is there something especially feline about your physiology?"

"You tell me, you're the doc."

Dr. Wyatt made an exaggerated examination of the notes on the laptop in front of him, fiddling with his glasses as if to bring the writing into focus. "Shock. Hypothermia. Contusions." He sighed heavily and closed the laptop in front of him with both hands, rocked up on his toes a bit and then back. He looked just like a school principal doing that, Jines thought. "You know, Mr. Evans, the wind blew so hard on Thursday that a tugboat lost its tow coming into Hampton Roads and the barge pinned itself against the Bay Bridge-Tunnel for six hours before they could free it. The bridge was closed for half the day. You can imagine the traffic nightmare."

"What day is this?"

"This is Saturday," Dr. Wyatt said. "And what else, let's see. An oak tree fell in Reedville, smashing the town gazebo to kindling. Fortunately no one was in there at the time. They think the tree was better than two hundred years old. It's a great local tragedy."

Jines was impressed. "You mean that big white oak that stood there at the corner of Market Street?"

"The very same."

"Damn."

"Indeed." Dr. Wyatt raised his head to the ceiling as if searching up there for more news items. Rocked up and back again, musing. "The Coast Guard, from what I read in the newspaper, had a particularly busy time of it. Two people drowned off Smith Point, although what they were doing out there in that weather is beyond comprehension. I've only owned a boat for a year and even I know that's some of the most treacherous water in the entire Chesapeake."

"It can be a right bitch," Jines agreed. He remembered the bateau sliding down the wave toward him, the sound of it hitting Tyler's head. He didn't want to ask the question that he needed to.

He stared hard at the window and the pale light coming through it. "Who drowned?"

"A fellow from Richmond who owned a furniture store and

had set aside that day to take his sailboat from winter storage on the Yeocomico River to a mooring off his summer house in Deltaville. He went alone because his buddy who was supposed to help him got the stomach flu the night before and couldn't make it. They found his boat at the mouth of the Rappahannock. They haven't found him yet. His wife told the newspaper he was a very experienced sailor, had raced to Bermuda a couple of times, knew that part of the Bay inside and out."

Jines waited.

"And the crewman from your boat. A Mr. Tyler Jenkins. Forty-two years old, late of Winona. Also lost at sea, presumed drowned."

"Son of a bitch nearly got us all killed," Jines said. He looked up at the doctor. "Do you know if everyone else is okay? Did my boat make it in okay?" The way Dr. Wyatt was looking at him Jines wondered whether he'd suddenly sprouted antlers. Aye God, he hated lying in this bed. Everybody always standing over him, staring at him like he was a bug or something. He wanted out. He tried to push himself up a little so he could swing his legs out. Christ, was there any part of him that didn't feel like it'd been run over with an ice truck? He sank back.

Dr. Wyatt was waiting for him. "If you won't listen to anyone else, maybe you'll have to listen to your own body."

"I'm a little stiff is all," Jines said. He wondered how they'd gotten him out of the water. He wondered why he didn't drown right along with that piece of shit Tyler. "How come you're here, anyway?"

"I'm your neurologist, remember? I want to do another CT scan, make sure your brain is all in one piece."

"Nothing wrong with me," Jines said. "If I was gonna be dead I'd be dead. I had my chance."

Dr. Wyatt leaned close to him, any hint of the reprimanding principal gone. "You're a tough man, Mr. Evans, I will give you every bit of that. You get yourself set on something and you're determined to carry it out. Sometimes that's the only thing that stands between life and death. I see people who lack that quality give up all the time." He lowered his voice a notch, making his point close to Jines's ear. "But there are a lot of ways to be dead. Pushing yourself this way into another stroke or two, being strapped into a wheelchair drooling on your bib watching reruns of *The Price is Right*—that's a method of dying I think a man like you would want to avoid. Forgive my frankness, but you of all people I think can appreciate it."

He stood back up straight. "I've scheduled the CT scan for this afternoon, three o'clock. In the meantime, you might want to reconsider your line of work, since I'm sure you're already thinking about how soon you can go fishing again."

He had him pegged on that account, Jines thought, watching the doctor's back heading out the door. But he felt uneasy. He couldn't remember anything after he'd gone overboard. What if he'd blacked out again, like he had in the john that time? Maybe he'd hit his head going over the side and knocked himself out; he couldn't remember that either. He didn't feel that same numbness he had before, after the stroke, so that had to be a good sign. One thing was certain, it was a mess. And here he was again.

"Heaven won't take you and hell's afraid you'll take over," Lily said. "Isn't that what the boys say when somebody has a near miss?" She was standing in the doorway, still in the clothes she'd been in when he'd woken up that first time. He was expecting her to be angry, but that wasn't it. Her eyes were shadowed with dark circles. "There's a guy from the Coast Guard here to see you," she said. "You ready?"

Jines sighed. He nodded. What else could he do?

The straight-backed young man wearing the dark blue uniform of the U.S. Coast Guard didn't look unfriendly exactly, but the way he was watching Jines made him feel the same on-the-spot squeamishness he'd felt with Dr. Wyatt. Like he was some nice fish they'd just caught, and they'd laid him out and were sizing him up.

"This is Lieutenant Brian Westfield," Lily said. "He's from the station at Point Lookout. He was on the cutter that responded to Kenneth's mayday."

"Mayday?" Jines said.

"Why don't you tell us what you remember about Thursday afternoon, Mr. Evans." He opened up a loose-leaf binder he was carrying. It was white with the red, white, and blue insignia of the Coast Guard on the cover. He clicked a pen open and stood poised, ready to take notes.

"Why don't you tell me whether my boat's all right. I already know about that piece of shit that drowned. Did everybody else make it in okay?"

Lieutenant Brian Westfield's back seemed to straighten up a bit more. Jines had nothing against these boys in the Coast Guard, even if half of them seemed to come from Iowa or some other potato-growing place about as far from the water as the moon. Fact was he thought highly of them for the work they did helping out people in trouble on the Bay. There was an old saying he'd heard some of the veterans talk about, that no matter how bad the weather, if someone was in trouble the Coasties had to go, but that didn't mean they had to come back. And Jines knew some of them didn't come back. He wondered whether this young man ever heard that old saying. He doubted it. He looked like a by-the-book type. Probably liked steering a desk more than a boat.

"The boat's fine, Jines, she's hauled out at the yard where Jamie works," Lily said. "Everybody else is fine."

"All right then," he said. "All right." He felt suddenly emptied out. He was grateful for the bed under him to prop him up and leaned back deep into the pillows. He could have been about a hundred years old just then. "I don't even know how I got here. And they tell me I been asleep two days." He looked at Lily, remembering seeing her curled up in the chair by the bed.

"You got here by ambulance, after the cutter brought you into Point Lookout," the lieutenant said.

"I was drowning," Jines said.

"Yes you were," the young lieutenant said. "By all rights you shouldn't even be here. You've got some kind of luck, is all I can say." He seemed oddly cheerful about telling Jines this, as if Jines were an especially interesting case. "Can you tell me the events that led up to you going overboard?"

So Jines did, starting with the unforeseen weather, the dead turtle, Tyler getting sick, his decision to avoid going over the bar given the sea conditions and the weight of fish in the *Jenny Rae*, the noise he and Kenneth had heard. "The boat was handling the seas," he said. "I won't say it wasn't rough but hell, I been in worse and so's she. But I'd seen a lot of junk in the water, logs and stuff. I was afraid maybe I'd hit one and holed her." Even to himself he sounded on the defensive. For the first time he wondered whether the worry on Lily's face had less to do with him being back in the hospital than with this young lieutenant coming here to grill him. He told them about Kenneth going to investigate, Tyler and the boathook, the terrible feeling of his boat like prey with the seas at her throat. Tyler clawing at him on the way over. The bateau. "Funny thing was," he said, "when I went in the water it felt warm. You know, I thought it'd be cold this time of year."

"Warm compared to the ambient air temp, maybe," Lieutenant Westfield said. "It's up to about sixty-five degrees on the surface now. You were hypothermic when we got to you. You were probably already dehydrated when you went into the water, which wouldn't help. When conditions get rough, people never keep themselves hydrated or fed enough. They're usually preoccupied

157

with their vessels, the conditions."

Jines thought about it, realized the young man was right about that anyway. He'd been too busy keeping the boat on her feet to eat or drink a thing other than that Hershey bar and a Coke he remembered pouring down his throat just after they left the Seven Brothers. It unnerved him how this young lieutenant could know this small detail about him on that day. That someone like him, with his years and experience, could be as predictable as anyone else. "Don't remember anything after thinking about the water." His throat ached from the talking. He reached for a cup on the table. Lily pushed the table closer to the bed. He pressed the cup against his mouth to stop it from shaking but it trembled as he set it back down. Watching it, he felt like he was outside of himself, as if his stroke-weakened arm was not his own but some other pathetic SOB's. He remembered tucking it into the bib on his foul-weather overalls, how useless it was on the boat, just along for the ride. Had to belong to someone else, this feeble thing. But here was the young lieutenant watching him, watching his arm, watching the cup.

"Your daughter tells me you had a stroke about a month ago," he said. "Must be tough recovering from that."

"You gonna finish the story for me?"

Lieutenant Westfield frowned. "According to the men on your boat, by the time they came on deck you were gone. They couldn't see you or Mr. Jenkins at all. Somebody called in the mayday, but it was one of your crew—" he flipped a page in his notebook and ran his finger down about halfway—"Robbie Davis, who actually saw you resurface and went in after you."

Jines's voice was a scratchy whisper. "Robbie?" He closed his eyes tight. He couldn't remember any of this. How had they gotten him back into the boat in those seas?

"Mr. Davis got a line around you and they hauled you in," the lieutenant said, evidently reading his addled mind. "We already had two boats out there en route back to the station after answering a call further east. That's another bit of luck; normally it would have taken us a half-hour to get scrambled and out to your position, and in those seas probably add another fifteen minutes. You wouldn't have lasted that long." He sounded somewhat smug about this. "We transferred you to the cutter and took you to Point Lookout."

The lieutenant flipped over another page. "It would appear that your boat did hit something—we had her hauled out when your crew got in and there's evidence of a collision on the starboard bow, just under the waterline. But it wasn't bad enough to hole the boat or pop a plank. Who built your boat?"

"Me." He hadn't gone for the cheap-ass materials most builders did. Those were all white-oak frames with oak planking too, right up past the deadrise. No pine until higher up near the decks. Made her heavier, true enough, but she was tough as an ice-breaker. He looked over at Lily and noticed the corners of her mouth tick up a little. She wasn't much more than four or five years old when he'd built the *Jenny Rae*. It was hell keeping her out of the wood shavings and dust.

"Well, she took good care of you. So did your crew." He paused. "Your man Tyler Jenkins wasn't so lucky."

"He wasn't my man. He wasn't any part of my regular crew."

"But he was part of your crew that day, Mr. Evans, right? He was on your vessel. You were in charge."

Jines wasn't sure he could hear anymore. The crazy nature of the story was like a whirlpool. He was a bug in a drain spinning down, staring up at the maelstrom.

Lily's voice came to him from a distance. "The man attacked my father," she was saying. "You're not going to tell me that my father was negligent because this guy lost it. You interviewed Kenneth Raley, the rest of the crew. Did they think my father or the boat was out of control before this Tyler Jenkins hit him across the back with a boathook and nearly capsized his boat by turning it across the seas?" She had been standing quietly next to Lieutenant Westfield since they'd entered the room, but now she'd turned to face him head-on. She was a full head shorter than him. He took a step back.

"It's all right, Lily Rae," Jines said. He felt dizzy. The scene was becoming more surreal to him by the second. This was his daughter defending him, the one he was certain would give him what for because he'd ignored her admonitions not to go out again.

She spun at him for a second and then back at the lieutenant. "No, it's not all right, Jines. You could be prosecuted for negligence if that's what they're thinking. Or worse. Manslaughter."

Lieutenant Westfield held up his hands. "Slow down, Miss Evans. Everything your father has told me is spot on with what Mr. Raley and the others described, okay? If anything, it was a situation of self-defense after Mr. Jenkins attacked your father. And apparently it wasn't a first for Mr. Jenkins. He had quite the resume. Aggravated assault was the most recent conviction; he'd just finished his sentence a week ago." He closed his notebook and turned to Jines. "But I would ask you to seriously consider your judgment. I'm not saying you aren't an experienced waterman with a sound vessel. But it's pretty obvious, all due respect Mr. Evans, you're not a hundred percent health-wise. It's my obligation to remind you to consider carefully the safety of your crew and the people put in harm's way—myself and my colleagues among them—because you decided you could handle the situation instead of heading home and waiting for better weather. We probably wouldn't look kindly on it again."

He held out his hand and Jines shook it, suddenly aware of how feeble his grip must feel to this tall young man. "I'm grateful, I am that, for your help," Jines said, struggling to keep his voice from breaking. "Please tell the rest of your crew."

Lily walked him out. Jines was relieved to be alone, to have no one watching him just now. He remembered once driving down to Norfolk to pick up a part for *Jenny Rae*'s engine in the pouring rain. He stopped at a traffic light and watched in horror as a tractor-trailer behind him didn't see the light until the last minute, slammed on its brakes and locked up, jack-knifed across the highway and stopped not five feet from his pickup. He had the same breathless feeling now, as if all the air had gone out of the room. He was afraid to move for fear of everything flying apart.

It was just bad luck that the wind had come up the way it had, just plain shitty luck. If the weather had stayed clear the way he'd expected—the way it was supposed to, he thought in a flash of anger—everything would've gone smooth as glass. But that wasn't the whole truth, and as soon as he admitted this to himself the anger washed out of him and left him limp. He saw now, the whole thing had been wrong from the get-go. He'd gone out there for all the wrong reasons, even while he had told himself there was nothing in the world more right. Kenneth pressuring him to take the boat out, Lily hovering around the house nagging him about the stupid physical therapy, him feeling weak and useless. He hadn't gone out there because he needed the money, even though he did. He had gone out to prove something, to them and to himself, that he was the same man, just as capable and tough as ever. But the Bay had something waiting for him he hadn't expected, and aye God he should have expected that. He wasn't some furniture salesman from Richmond sailing to a swanky marina full of weekend warriors with their cocktails and yachts. He knew the water better than he knew the dirt. And in his haste to prove it, he had forgotten the most basic rule of all those years of hard-fought learning—his own, his father's, his grandfather's—never take anything out there for granted. Always be ready for the unexpected.

He shifted in the bed again, moving carefully. He gasped, and the gasp turned into a sob. Like an old man, he thought, you sorry son of a bitch, you're like an old man. Before the stroke, before his body began acting in ways he couldn't control or predict, someone like that character Tyler had tried any shit like that he would have knocked him flat. But that wasn't even the point, was it. Someone as low-life as Tyler never would have been on his boat in the first place. He could blame Kenneth for digging him up from under whatever rock, but the fact was Jines had gone along. Jines had allowed the trash onto the boat.

His blameless boat. The tears streamed down his face, and in his despair he didn't care anymore if someone saw them. His arms lay limp at his sides. He felt something slipping away from him. He couldn't give it a name, but he knew well enough that like anything you try and hold too close, the faster it would go. All those things he had clung to and which had done their best to sustain him, the graceful strength of his boat, the natural order of his world, his family's past and his place in it, he had betrayed them all. He had failed them. He didn't belong out there anymore. He was a boat that was rotted all through. He was no good for it. He felt like he was falling off a tall faceless cliff, and every stab of realization was another jagged rock he hit on the way down, another piece of who he once was torn away.

Part Two

Fishing in the Keep of Silence

There is a hush now while the hills rise up
and God is going to sleep. He trusts the ship
of Heaven to take over and proceed beautifully
as he lies dreaming in the lap of the world.
He knows the owls will guard the sweetness
of the soul in their massive keep of silence,
looking out with eyes open or closed over
the length of Tomales Bay that the herons
conform to, widely broad in flight, white
and slim in standing. God, who thinks about
poetry all the time, breathes happily as He
repeats to Himself: There are fish in the net,
lots of fish this time in the net of the heart.

— Linda Gregg

                    What
we know: we are more
        than blood—we are more
                than our hunger and yet
we belong
    to the moon

— Mary Oliver, "Blossom"

Chapter 9

The way to the lighthouse beach was down a narrow, lumpy road that rested on the uneasy low ground, past willow oaks and loblolly pines tangled in greenbrier and honeysuckle, past tidy cottages and brick ranchers. Lily and Belle drove the blacktop until it gave it up for dirt and oyster shell, where the trees ceded to swaying marsh grasses and the warm, moist air smelled of salt and mud. Lily pulled the truck to the side of the little track where a long dock led out to the lighthouse overlook, which was really just the end of the dock itself.

"Can we go out to the overlook first?" Belle asked.

"Sure."

They walked along the curving dock that poked into the side of what was called Motorun Creek, so named for the noise from all the workboats that used to rumble from the creek in the mornings heading for their nets and crabpots. On this late morning there was none of that vibrant racket of money being made, of lives being lived. Gulls and cormorants perched on what was left of the pilings where watermen once tied off their boats, and except for their occasional squawking cries the creek was silent. Peaceful as it was, the quiet seemed unnatural to Lily. It said as much as anyone or anything could about what had happened to the way of life that had made this place.

The tide was slowly creeping into the marsh flanking the creek, and Lily could hear the little pock-pock sound of fiddler crabs popping out of the mud. "Belle. Look." She pointed down into the mud where the fiddlers moved among the periwinkles and grasses, skittering in their sideways fashion from hummock to hummock like tiny commandos on a covert mission, their single big claw held up like a boxing glove. Belle giggled, a sound full of lightness that made Lily grateful she had planned this day for the two of them. Mary Virginia had agreed to keep on eye on Jines at the house—that ought to keep Jines out of trouble, Lily thought with a secret smirk—and she and Belle had packed a picnic lunch of peanut-butter-and-jelly sandwiches, Goldfish, Oreos, and apples.

Belle's laughter purged the tone of Michael's voice on the phone last night, sounding like a personnel administrator with her file spread out in front of him. "You can take an extended leave. You've still got a week of comp time, and there's probably a way to get some more after your month of family leave."

It was eleven at night, and Lily knew he was pissed at her. For one thing, she had called him at home. And every time she had returned his calls before this one, it had worked out that he was in a staff meeting or someplace where she knew he couldn't answer. She wasn't proud of it. But she hadn't been ready to talk to him.

"What about staffing?" she asked. "Filling the shifts?"

"It's working out. I'm borrowing a relief staffer from the Boston bureau for the time being. She's a pretty quick study."

She should have talked to him and said she was sorry for the night before she left Portland. The apology she'd left on his voice mail was a cop-out and she knew it, probably sounded like she knew it too.

"Do I know her?"

"No. She's new, fresh out of J-school."

Lily wondered whether the rookie was pretty. She asked, "What do you need me to do for paperwork to take the extra time?"

"Go on the AP website. There are some forms you can print out."

"That's a fifty-mile round-trip."

"What?"

"No Internet here, Michael, no e-mail. The closest Internet

access is the public library in Mathews. Twenty-five miles over, twenty-five back."

"Christ. Do they have electricity?"

"Oh yeah, we've had that a long time, at least forty years or so."

"You're joking, right?"

"Mostly."

"Karen will get a package to you in the fedex. They have fedex, right? Fill it out. Send it to…I don't know who you have to send it to. Karen will know."

"Michael." She picked at a piece of stitching that was working open on the quilt lying across her bed. Her mother had sewn this quilt. Lily had never gotten the hang of sewing. Her thread always got knotted or broke halfway through a stitch. Mama said she was just too impatient, that quilts were like gardens and stars, you had to spend time quietly with them to understand how they came together. She was suddenly desperate to have Michael close again. "I miss you," she said, her voice soft. "I wish you were here right now. Although it would be a little tight, since it's only a twin." The phone line hummed. "Are you there?"

"I'm here," he said.

She made a soft noise into the phone. "I'm wearing your shirt, you know, the one you always like to slide your hands up?"

There was a long deep breath on the line. "I'm at home, Lily. In my home. And it's been a long day. I'm beat."

"Do you miss me?"

"Lily—"

"I'm sorry I was such a bitch that night." There was a silence, then a short, humorless laugh. She pulled her legs up close, hugging them. If she picked at the quilt's stitching much more a whole block would need fixing. Already some of the ticking was puffing out. She shoved it back under the fabric with one finger. "I know I should have apologized sooner," she said.

"Oh I don't know, what's it been, almost a month?"

"I was angry with myself, not with you."

"Next time you're angry with yourself, try not to take it out on everyone else."

Her fingers worked at the loose thread the way you touch a wound over and over, just to make sure it still hurts. She idly wondered if her mother's sewing machine would still work; maybe if she was just fixing the quilt she could get away with using it instead of sewing by hand. Although that bobbin thing never worked for her.

"Look, I'm going to bed," he said. "Take as much time as you need with your dad. He probably needs you more than you know."

"Maybe like I need you?" she said softly.

"Lily," Michael said evenly into the phone, "I don't think you know how to need anyone. I'll have Karen send the paperwork." And he hung up.

Now, listening to Belle's silvery laughter at the fiddler crabs, she squirmed at the thought that she had tried to seduce him. Here was this beautiful day and this beautiful girl to remind her that she'd behaved anything but beautifully. Something about him brought out a side of her she didn't much like, a manipulative, thoughtless side. Michael had hurt her, yes; but in this bright light of the morning she knew she didn't need him. She might want him, but she didn't need him. And she didn't love him. From now on, she resolved, it was strictly business. Although from the sound of things, she wondered whether she'd even have a job waiting for her when this was all settled.

Belle scampered up beside her. Just past the marsh, what was left of the woods of the lighthouse point was a thinning forest of tufted loblollies brushing the sky. Beyond, the pure white beach glinted like mica in the sun, and Lily could hear the constant shush and hiss of waves breaking on it. And beyond that stood the lighthouse itself, stoic and alone on its mound of earth and rock where the great storm of 1933—the one that had drowned her grandfather—had left it severed from the mainland.

Belle followed her gaze out to the lighthouse. "Do you think we'll be able to get out there today?"

"Nope, not without a blowout tide or a skiff, and we don't have either one of those."

"We could take Daddy's skiff out there sometime." Belle looked thoughtfully at the lighthouse. "Have you ever been out there?"

"Not for a long time. When I was about your age my daddy and mama and baby brother and I would go out there in the *Jenny Rae* and have picnics. And then when I was older, a teenager, I'd go out sometimes in our skiff."

"What's it like?"

"Smelly. Lots of seagull poop."

"But did you go up the inside? What's it like from up there?"

"It's beautiful," Lily said simply.

The lighthouse wasn't the fanciest on the Bay, not by a long shot. It was kind of stubby, really, shaped like an octagon that slowly tapered to the top and ended with a round light tower. The Coast Guard had automated it when Lily was still a girl, but all the local kids knew how to pry open the door. Once inside she would kick aside the beer cans and trash near the door and look up into the staircase that curved upward in ever-smaller spirals like a chambered nautilus. She would think about all the things the lighthouse had withstood—hurricanes and nor'easters fierce enough to hurl whole trees to its doorstep, British troops who wrecked it during the War of 1812, and Union soldiers who doused the light to confuse Confederate ships. Its history was legendary around the river. Her father had told her that when he was a boy there was a lightkeeper's house and a barn, a meadow, and a pond.

All that, and now only bird shit and waves. She wondered if a lighthouse could be lonely.

"I didn't know you had a baby brother." Belle was looking at her with the same direct gaze as her father. In someone only nine years old, it was startling. "What's his name?"

"His name was Danny."

"Where is he?"

Good question, Lily thought. Was he in the sky? Was he in the waves hissing on the beach? Was he in the lighthouse watching the storms, or up in the tops of the pines, or was he part of the sea breeze pushing through the sibilant marsh grasses? She had been so young when he'd died she could barely remember him. The things she could describe—that he had bright blond hair, that he ate dirt out of the garden whenever their mother had her attention on the vegetables, that he fell off the dock when he could barely walk and Jines had jumped right off into the clear water and yanked him out by the back of his shorts, that he loved pulling the figs off the fig tree near the shed and squishing them in his little boy fists—all these things had come to her from her parents, not herself. Too much had come after that had sifted over her memory of the boy who was her brother like a fine, persistent snow, impassive and silent.

"He died when he was young. He had leukemia, do you know what that is?"

Belle shook her head.

"It's sort of like cancer in your blood."

"Oh." Belle studied the mud flat below them. "Look, there's another fiddler crab."

"Funny little buggers aren't they." Lily started walking down the dock toward the pickup to get the backpack. Belle trotted after her.

"Is that why you seem sad a lot of the time?"

Lily stopped. "Do I seem sad to you? That's funny. Most

people tell me that I always seem mad."

Belle looked at her with those level eyes that seemed to belong to someone much older. "No," she said. "I don't see that. My mom, she's always mad." And with a head-spinning transition she was nine years old again, only nine, scampering down the dock and yelling to Lily, "Come on, I want to run on the beach!"

The day was clear and warm and the two of them ran along the beach until they were out of breath and then walked and then ran some more. It wasn't easy with the backpack, so Lily ditched it near a mountain of driftwood that had piled up from the winter storms, though calling it driftwood seemed too insignificant; the huge, bleached logs looked like the shipwrecked bones of whales. They gathered up shells and feathers, stuffing them into their pockets, and they walked along the edge of the pine forest where Lily suddenly made Belle crouch down and be silent; in one of the trees about fifty feet away two bald eagles perched near a nest that must have been eight feet across and just as tall. One of them took off and circled, its oddly fluting cry warning them to stay away.

"Have you ever found any arrowheads out here?" Belle asked a little later. "My daddy says the Indians lived here a thousand years ago and sometimes people still find traces of them."

"He's right. They call the arrowheads points. And no, I've never found one, but I've always wanted to." They were walking slowly, their necks bent to examine the sand in front of them. "I think sometimes that things as rare and special as that find you, not the other way around."

"What do you mean?"

"I just think that sometimes if you're looking too hard for something you might just look right by it. Hasn't that ever happened to you? You know, you're so focused on looking for, let's say a fossil or a shark's tooth, and you end up seeing every kind of little piece of shell that looks like it might be a shark's tooth but it isn't. And then somebody else just walks along and finds a tooth just like that, right where you just were."

"My school had a field trip up to Calvert Cliffs in Maryland and we looked all day for shark's teeth and fossils."

"Did you find any?"

"No teeth. A couple fossil shells. But I had fun looking."

"Then that's just as good, don't you think?"

"Yeah, but I still wanted a shark's tooth." Belle kicked the sand up a little with her bare foot. "So you think maybe I just wasn't ready to find a shark's tooth that day?"

"What do you mean, ready?" Lily asked.

"That's what you mean, isn't it, when you say something special has to find you? It doesn't matter if it's right there if you're not ready to see it. You would just not see it at all. You'd be looking for it all wrong."

Lily stopped and stared at the girl in front of her, her dark hair in braids on either side of her head, arms and legs seeming too long for her young body, bare feet digging into the wet sand as the water lipped up to them. It was so simple, but she'd never seen it that way. It had nothing to do with the thing you were seeking, everything to do with the readiness of the seeker. She thought about her conversation with Michael last night, her cheap manipulation. It wasn't anything she hadn't already done before to every other man she'd had. She'd draw them in and then, when they got too close, she'd push them away, and then get angry and blame them for her loneliness. But it came from her. No one could make her more lonely than herself. So why did she do it? Because it was easy, it was safe? Because she was always seeking the impossible, yearning for a cosmic do-over, for her brother not to leave and her mother not to die, for her father not to turn his back on her? But perhaps she had been looking all the wrong way, looking too hard, trying to find the one perfect shark's tooth in a million miles of sand. While even if it were right there she couldn't have seen it. She wasn't ready. She was too busy nursing her outrage. She wondered if she could ever be ready, or if there came a point where readiness just took a walk, when it got tired of waiting.

Belle had resumed her perusal of the sand and squatted down for a moment to examine some oyster shells the high tide had mounded up and left behind. Lily couldn't figure it out, how the girl could perceive something so intimate and deep one minute and then just drop it for total immersion in something like a pile of shells the next. Kids had always made her feel like an elephant at a tea party, bumbling and awkward and yearning for the safety of silence and wide-open spaces. Belle was different. It was as if she bridged two worlds, that of the child and the adult. Somehow she knew how to travel between the two and survive the trip, not lose her innocence or wonder along the way. Lily was envious. How much better off she would have been, she thought, to have been born with the same ability. Maybe she had, but it never had time to fully develop. She'd grown up too fast. She looked out past the lighthouse where a couple of small fishing boats were bobbing in the light afternoon waves. To the south a workboat was running a line of crabpots in its stop-and-start way, belching a fat puff of diesel smoke each time the waterman throttled up to get to the next pot.

"You're amazing, Belle," Lily said.

"That's what my mom says, too."

So we have things in common, Lily thought; we both think this girl is amazing and we both had a thing for Jamie Cockrell. And she has both, Lily thought, and I have neither. She felt suddenly like a stranger at the dinner table, a stray brought in from a storm and given a bowl of warm milk.

"It must be kind of hard, having to live in two different houses," Lily said.

"I don't know. It was at first but now I kind of like it. I get two whole different bedrooms. And Daddy comes over a lot, at least when Max isn't around."

"Who's Max?"

"My mom's new boyfriend." Belle flicked away some shells. "I don't like him much. He's really loud, and he always wants the TV on stations I don't like. Like, when I want to see *Animal Planet* he always says it's stupid and changes it to wrestling."

Nice, thought Lily. She wondered if Jamie knew about Max. How could he not? But he still went over there. A lot, Belle said. Was he still sleeping with her? Was she that great in the sack? Did he *like* being two-timed? Did he still love her? Suddenly Lily didn't want to know anymore. She hadn't been here for fourteen years; Jamie had his own life and she hers. Just because they'd been inseparable when they were eight years old didn't mean they knew each other now. Just because when she saw him she felt that instant jolt of connection didn't mean she knew him at all. She could be stopped at a traffic light or walking down a sidewalk and meet some stranger's eyes and feel that same shock, that instantaneous knowledge that somehow this person *knew* her in a way no else could, and she knew them. That they were soul mates from some past life, crossing paths again. And they could exchange that look between them, acknowledge it, and move on. Because you didn't just drive your life off a cliff for a complete stranger, even one who could look straight into your soul. Even one who didn't seem like a stranger, or shouldn't have.

"Are you all right, Miss Lily?"

"What?"

"You looked funny."

"I'm fine," Lily said. "I was just looking at those workboats."

"Were you thinking about your daddy? He's a waterman too, isn't he? Like my grandpa. Like my dad wishes he was."

174

Jamie wanted to be working on the water? Then why didn't he? What was he doing running the marina dog-and-pony show for useless Tommy Wilson?

"Yeah. I wonder how he and your grandmom are getting along today."

Belle giggled.

"What?" Lily asked.

"When she thinks I can't hear, she calls him, 'That g-d Jines Arley,' but she doesn't say g-d if you know what I mean."

Lily laughed. "That's funny, I call him the same thing."

"How come you call him by his given name, anyway, and not Daddy like I call my daddy?"

"How come you always ask such hard questions?" She said it playfully, pushing Belle lightly on the shoulder, but she was skittering from the question like the fiddler crabs they'd seen earlier, racing for cover behind the closest shelter.

"Sorry," Belle said, dipping her head, her laughter dashed. "My mom—" She looked away.

"What, Belle?"

"She gave me a sign to put in my room. It says, 'Be Sure Brain is in Gear Before Opening Mouth.' "

Jesus Christ, Lily thought, what a terrible thing to say to a girl like this. This woman must be some piece of work. "Well, no offense to your mom, but that's pretty superfluous. You're brain is always in gear, that's obvious."

"What does superfluous mean?"

"Unnecessary in kind of a silly way." Lily crouched down beside Belle and ruffled her hand through the oyster shells. She pulled one out that glowed like copper instead of the usual pearly grey and turned it over in her hand. "I didn't mean to say you shouldn't ask questions, Belle. How else are you supposed to find anything out? It's the grown-ups who don't ask enough questions. We walk around being afraid to ask for fear the answers won't be the ones we want to hear. And then we spend too much time imagining what other people are thinking about us because we're afraid to just plain ask. So ask away. Don't ever clam up."

"Okay. Can we eat lunch now?"

Lily looked at her and burst out laughing. "Last one to the backpack is a rotten egg!"

They climbed up on the shipwrecked driftwood and ate peanut butter and jelly, throwing the crusts to the seagulls who squabbled and swooped until the sheer numbers of them became unbearable, and Lily jumped down to the beach and ran among them screaming and waving her arms. She didn't care whether she looked ridiculous; she knew Belle would not mind. Perhaps the footing of that boundary that lay between the adult world and the child's, the border that Belle seemed to traverse so fluidly and where Lily had only ever staggered, had grown easier. She could run along the beach and shriek at the annoying birds without concern, yell and carry on the way she would have, had she ever remembered the brighter shades of being nine years old. She couldn't say whether Belle trusted her; she wasn't even sure she wanted such a burden. It seemed to Lily that offering or accepting anyone's faith was like handling damp dynamite. She wasn't well trained in the art. But dropping this girl's heart was not an option. She knew that one thing, if she wasn't sure about much else. She knew it later that very day, as the sun was casting long shadows on the beach and down from the northwest came the skiff called *Belle,* and when Jamie rounded the point and came along past the beach toward the jetties his daughter raced across the sand stopping only to leap up and down, waving her hands yelling, "Daddy! Daaa-deee!" Lily stood watching, and when Jamie yelled back, "Isabelle, hey Muffin!" her eyes burned with tears for something she could not define—not sad, not wounded, not lonely—reasons she could not begin to put words to, maybe didn't even know.

Lily's truck rolled on the sloped two-lane road, and with the windows down she could hear what sounded like a thousand peepers trilling as they passed a marsh. That wild hopeful sound. All around the outrageous spring was happening. In the forests, the buds of the maples about to burst flamed red against the pines. The tulip poplars and dogwoods were tipped with a pale green that enveloped the trees in a fuzzy glow. The birds and peepers sang their overwrought songs, and everything seemed to be swelling, all of it on the edge of a great bursting. Her mother was right about spring around here; it *was* a miracle every time, an exuberant chaos of life. It held nothing back. In Maine, everything was more cautious. You never knew when a late frost or a snowy nor'easter would slap you with winter once more. It would be another month of colorlessness there and then, only a wary openness to the possibilities of change.

"I love spring," said Belle, apparently reading Lily's mind. She had wanted to ride back with her father in the skiff, but Jamie yelled across the water to meet him at the marina. Lily followed two SUVs—a Cadillac Escalade and a Land Rover—down the long driveway that branched off the road. It wound about a mile past corn and soybean fields, through a patch of woods, and then finally between two worn brick gate pillars that had marked the entrance to what had been Rowe's seafood wharf. The SUVs told her all she needed to know about the clientele; these were rich folk from someplace not here, probably ecstatic that somebody had opened an honest-to-god yacht yard with a nifty ship's store, tidy bathrooms, laundry, and a boat lift instead of a barn, an outhouse, and a demonically possessed railway—and all of it right here where they'd bought their retirement or investment homes. Pissant Jimmy Wilson had inherited a gold mine.

The weirdly sweet smell of bottom paint, like molasses and oil, was thick on the air. She parked the truck near the ship's store; it looked exactly as she'd thought it would with a freshly raked pebble path, a pair of white-painted anchors flanking the door, and thick hawsers instead of railings along the walkways. Wooden planters painted with jolly blue sailing scenes held daffodils, tulips, and pansies. She had to hand it to Jimmy; as much as she disliked the cutesy nautical motif, the place was groomed like a show dog. No derelict workboats mulching into oblivion on the back edges of the parking lot, no rusty tractors, stray farm equipment, or greasy piles of pistons and blocks that once resembled engines. There were drums of oil and paint and epoxy somewhere—it was a boatyard after all, and even expensive pleasure boats needed the same nasty products as workboats—but they were carefully out of sight. To one side just before the main dock was a small swimming pool, landscaped and mulched all around, with a picnic area and a dog walk, complete with a "Super Scooper" station where you could grab a plastic baggie to collect Fido's unpleasantness and dispose of it discreetly. It was a long way from Addison Jenkins and his demon Model T.

Maggie saw them first and came jogging to meet them, cupping her wet nose in Lily's hand, her whole body grinning somehow. Belle dropped instantly to her knees and wrapped her arms around the big dog's neck. "Mags, you should have come with us today," she said. "You would have loved it."

Lily looked up from the girl and the dog to see Jamie striding toward them in his loose way, an end-of-the-workday beer in one hand. He was smiling at her, his eyes reaching for hers and catching them. Smiling at the sight of her. The thought nearly knocked her down, how happy she was to see him walking toward her. All the distance she had tried to put between them in her thoughts on the beach vanished in a wave of recognition. He took her breath away, and she didn't want to be without that face, those eyes, that presence.

"Hey," he said.

She could smell the cigarette smoke on him, and a scent of oil and sweat, and she loved the way it suited him.

"Daddy!" yelled Belle, wrapping herself around him like an octopus, all arms and legs. He laughed and lifted her up, hugging her, his eyes across his daughter's shoulder never leaving Lily's. "We had so much fun!"

"I can't wait to hear all about it."

She wrinkled her nose. "You have bugs."

"It's been a long day." He rubbed the stubble on his chin. "Bugs," he said for Lily's benefit, "are what Belle calls it when I need to shave."

"What were you doing up the river in *Belle*?"

"We had a job up there, and it was too nice a day to go by car. Seemed like a good day for a boat ride."

"Can we go back out now?" Belle was pulling on him. "Please, can we go to Piney Island?"

"Tell you what. Let's stop there on the way home, okay? Why don't you and Mags head on down to the beach and play awhile, and Miss Lily Rae and I will take a walk around the yard and make sure everything's put away that needs to be."

"Okay," she said, and she raced off with the dog in hot pursuit, down toward a small beach near the marina's picnic area.

"We did have a lot of fun," Lily said. "She's an incredible kid."

"The single best, most perfect thing I have ever done in my life," Jamie said, watching her run. "Probably ever will do." He was quiet a moment, then said, "Come on, I'll get you a beer up in the office and we'll walk the yard."

Except for a few people loading supplies to cart down to their boats for the weekend, the place was empty. They walked through the working part of the yard, Jamie stopping now and then to check on jobs that his crew had done during the day while he'd been gone, cursing quietly under his breath when he came upon tools that had been left out or found that some detail or other hadn't been attended to. "Some of these boys haven't got a brain in their heads," he said. "All they remember is that it's Friday and that means payday."

Lily wondered whether he would see Regina later. "How long were you married?" she asked. If the question surprised him he didn't show it. She wondered if he'd been waiting for it.

"Two years. Two years and out." He picked up a small sander and handed it to her. "Can you carry this one?"

"Sure."

They walked on a bit. She waited.

"It's hard to think of it as a mistake when Isabelle was the result," he said. "But I guess it was." They passed a small stand of pines draped in wisteria, and the thick perfume washed over her. "I love that smell," he said. He kept walking. "You ever get married?"

She shook her head. "I think I scare them away. Too much Jines in me or something." Even as she said it, she realized it was the most honest answer she'd ever given to the question.

"Well," Jamie said. He stopped to pick up a plastic paint bucket someone had left under a boat. There was a pile of rags there too, and he stuffed them into the bucket. "You don't scare me."

Do you still love her, she wanted to ask, but she was afraid of what that answer might be. "At this rate we're going to need a cart," she said, her arms nearly full of tools and cans of paint they had found.

"Hang here a minute, I'll go get one." But when he didn't come back after a few minutes, Lily started walking in the direction of the office, looking for him. She heard voices raised and came around the corner in time to see Jamie standing before a short balding man whose face was bright red. His suit and wingtips looked completely out of place next to the jaunty flower buckets with their bright pictures. "You people," he was saying, "never get it right. I told you I wanted the boat totally detailed and waxed by this weekend. I have a major client coming into town and I need the boat perfect, and there's yellow dust all over it!"

"The boat was washed, waxed, and polished this morning, Mr. Solomon," Jamie said. "We can't really help it if it was a breezy day and there's a lot of pollen in the air right now. All it needs is a quick squirt with a hose."

"Well then I expect you to go down and do just that."

Jamie's back stiffened, all the easy sway of him gone. "The yard is closed for the weekend, Mr. Solomon. The crew will be back Monday morning, seven o'clock."

"Well I'm not paying for it until it's right! I just wonder what else you people didn't finish." He reminded Lily of a furious little rooster that would peck on your ankles until they bled, and she wanted to kick him just to get him to shut up. From the expression on Jamie's face, she figured he felt about the same.

"Everything you signed off on has been completed, Mr. Solomon. You already approved all the work yesterday; I was standing there when you gave the thumbs up. You need to write the check or give me your card before you can take the boat. It says it right on the contract that you signed, and not in small print."

"I told you, I'm not paying it!"

"Then you're not getting your boat." Jamie's voice was soft and dark. Lily wondered how long it would be until he lost it.

"I'm calling the state's attorney about you people, consumer division," he snarled. "I don't know why you think you can get away with this."

"Mr. Solomon," Jamie's voice was still as dark as a thundercloud. "Does your mechanic let you drive your Mercedes out of his shop without paying after he's worked on it?"

"My mechanic does what I tell him to do! When I tell him I want the car perfect, it's perfect!"

Jamie's voice, if possible, grew even quieter. "Mr. Solomon, you need to come with me into the office and pay your bill. Then you can get on your boat and get ready for your big client, and I can take my daughter home to dinner."

"Fine!" the little man snapped. "But you can bet that Monday morning, your boss and I are having a come to Jesus meeting over this, and I'm going to tell him exactly what I think of this kind of treatment. Then I'm going to tell every single person I know who owns a boat not to bring it here. And you'd better believe I know a lot of people!"

"I'm sure you do." And with that Jamie and Mr. Solomon disappeared into the office. Lily waited by the picnic table, watching an osprey soaring past, its wings locked in two tight V-shapes, wingtips fluttering. It swooped low and fast across the water and then, with a flick of a wing and tail, banked a turn across the breeze, gained altitude, leveled off, and banked and soared again, using the breeze to power its acceleration and turns. The bird lived in the wind, she thought, coursed its currents like a river. Nothing held it.

Jamie's voice came from behind her. "That bird makes it look so easy." He sat down beside her, handed her a fresh beer and rubbed his head in his big hands. "Jesus, these people. We did fifteen thousand dollars worth of work on that guy's boat. All of it complicated systems stuff, plus a new paint job on the hull. All of it flawless, on time, on budget. And he's pissed because there's some pollen on the deck."

"Do you get many like that?" she asked.

"Not too many, but one's enough. I'm so sick of it."

"Why do you stay then?"

He took a long drink of his beer and looked down at the beach where Belle was sitting in the sand, building some kind of castle with branches and feathers and shells and sand. "That's why. She's why. I gotta have steady work or her mother goes to the judge and says I'm not employed, can't pay for my own daughter's upkeep, can't be depended on."

"She doesn't trust that you want to do right by your daughter?"

Jamie laughed bitterly. "Trust isn't in her vocabulary."

So he was trapped, she thought. Or he thought he was trapped. Or did he want to be trapped? "Can't you do something else?"

He shrugged.

"Belle told me you wanted to fish. Why aren't you doing that?"

"It's not steady enough anymore, especially when you're working for somebody else. Last winter was a prime example; I wanted to go oysterin', but the market was so bad nobody wanted to take on any crew. They were all out there on their own, hanging on to whatever money they could make." He shook his head. "No. I missed my chance with that long before I even knew it. Mama sold Daddy's boat and all the bottom licenses after he died, she was so broken up about it. She made me swear I wouldn't do it."

"That was a long time ago, Jamie. Even Mary Virginia has to understand you have to live your own life. If that's what you want to do."

"Live my own life. Right." He turned to her. "You know, you and Mama were so pissed at Jines Arley for going out again like he did, but what else was he supposed to do? He was his own man. Now he's stuck in that house and might as well be knitting sweaters." He pulled a cigarette out and lit it. She heard the slight popping sound of his lips letting it go to exhale. "I think I know exactly how he feels."

Above them, the osprey sailed by again. Lily could see the bird's head turning toward them as it glided. They were always looking as they flew, always searching. "What if you had a boat, your own boat?" she asked.

"Well that ain't gonna happen. It's not like the old days, when you could pay off a boat in a season or two. And even if I could afford somehow to get one, the state isn't issuing new licenses anymore, part of their idea of fisheries management. That is, make it so no new people can fish. You've got to be grandfathered in, or buy your licenses from somebody else."

"What if you didn't have to?"

He turned to look at her. "What are you getting at?"

"The *Jenny Rae*. The Seven Brothers, the Big Betty, all of it. The gear, the licenses. It's all just sitting there."

Jamie looked incredulous and then burst out laughing. "Are you kidding? Your daddy would no sooner let me run his operation than he would fly to Mars."

"How do you know?"

"I can't believe you'd even ask that. You know him better than anybody, and you're asking that?"

"Look, Jamie, people do this. Isn't that how Gerald Haynie got his start? He leased Eddie Ellyson's boats, gear, everything, and it was like a purchase over time deal. I remember people talking about it."

"That was twenty years ago."

"What difference does that make? It could work." She grabbed his shoulders and turned him to face her. "It could be your way in." She swept her hand toward Mr. Solomon padding back to his Mercedes, loading what looked like a case of Pellegrino into a cart. "You said yourself, one of those is enough. You're so much more than this place, Jamie."

"What about you, you doing what you really want?" he asked pointedly. He ground out the cigarette on the bottom of his boot, then stuffed it into his pocket. He turned back to the sky. The osprey was gone. "My mama's already lost enough to the water.

And if I'm around to tuck my daughter in every night I can, I don't see it as giving up. Some hearts, there's nothing worth breaking for."

"What about yours?"

He was quiet. Lily sat next to him, watching the hurrying clouds. Feeling, in the wind's restless pull, the fragility of dreams, the yearning for flight. She knew he felt these things too. She wondered if, in all of her own restless anger, she had forgotten that emptiness, like the wind, is only revealed through what struggles to move within and against it. She got up from the table. "I'd better get back before your mama and my daddy kill each other, if they haven't already." She called goodbye to Belle, who waved a sandy hand. Jamie walked beside her to her truck. When she closed the door he leaned down into the window.

"Thanks for today, Lils."

"Anytime at all. I loved spending time with her." She paused. "I'm sorry if I pushed too hard. It's a gift I have."

"You didn't." When he stood up, he clapped the side of her truck with his hand, telling her it was okay to go. She watched the dust pillow up behind the pickup as she rolled out and wondered if she'd alienated him completely. Little Miss Fix-It, she thought, if only you could learn to fix things with Elmer's instead of napalm. Why was it her business anyway, whether Jamie was fulfilled or not? If he kept letting Regina run his life, then he had bigger problems than just a job that made him feel small. And he was right, Jines probably would turn him down flat. Why set himself up for rejection? Jamie was a big boy; let him figure himself out.

She let her breath out in a long sigh, then inhaled just as deeply and took in the rich scent of spring along the roadside. But he had asked her that question: Was she happy doing what she did? She'd always thought she was. By any professional standard she was successful, she could probably get a job as a writer anywhere she liked. Michael kept telling her she should get in the AP's management pipeline, that she'd be a natural for bureau chief somewhere. Michael. Well, she didn't have him, or anyone else for that matter. Her time spent with Belle today was still warm inside of her like a rock heated by the sun. But she didn't have anyone like Belle, either. Neither one of them—Michael or Belle—was hers to have. She thought about the way Belle had raced across the sand calling her father when he passed by in the skiff, a shout of pure love and joy at the sight of him, and she realized that she hadn't earned the right to have anyone as beautiful as Isabelle. The love of someone like that wasn't something you could just borrow, or even expect. She'd never thought farther than herself, and so, all she had was herself. It had seemed like enough. And what else? She had a great apartment. She had *Pelagic*. She had a sofa, books in crates, and a potted plant. Taking this inventory, it came back, the sound of the emptiness ringing in the apartment after she'd closed the door the last time.

Was she happy, is what Jamie had really asked her. And when she turned up the long driveway and the old house came into view with this question poised in her mind like a pitcher about to spill, she felt something she hadn't expected. The tin roof gleamed in the late-day sunlight. Yellow and red blooms burst from the camellias her mother had planted to frame the front porch. Beneath them, daffodils and hyacinths swayed in the breeze. Next would come the iris and then her grandmother's climbing roses cascading down the side of the house in great waterfalls of blossoms, the only roses that never seemed to succumb to all the heat, humidity, and bug life that was part and parcel of tidewater living. A deep blue sky angled through the white gingerbread at the eaves. The clapboards needed painting and the bushes needed trimming. But the house was beautiful. There was no blame in it. She had slept in her old narrow bed, sipped tea at the kitchen window watching the sunrise.

Opened her mother's room, dusted the dressers, and washed the quilts. It was something she hadn't known she had, something that had lain dormant. The old house had waited. And this peace with it she hadn't expected, this reckoning she hadn't known she wanted filled her with gratitude.

Chapter 10

The loblolly pines that surrounded the shed were straight and true as arrows shot up at the sky, and in the light of the full spring moon they had the silhouette of palm trees, skinny at the bottom, bushy at the top. Not that he'd ever seen a palm tree up close and personal. Hell, he'd never been further south than Beaufort, North Carolina, and that was when he was a young man, fishing for menhaden for a bit to make ends meet. He'd never wanted to leave the Bay, didn't see a need, and when the job was done he didn't let the door hit him in the ass. He skedaddled on home to these tall, sighing pines. Jines enjoyed the smell of them. Their needles made the ground silent and springy beneath his feet. Tricky too, even with the cane. Its fat rubber tip sank down a little in the soft needle bed each time he stabbed it downward just ahead of his feet, making his forward progress even slower than usual. He knew this path like he knew his own name but even so, he was more cautious now. He'd seen that about himself lately. Old man, seeing shadows where there'd never been any. Hanging on the railing by the steps even on days he felt strong enough maybe not to. They put the fear of death into you, these doctors and hospitals, they did. "You need to be more careful," the nurses told him, "the last thing you want is a broken hip on top of everything else." Broken hip, shit. He'd broken plenty of bones. All the same, he could blame them all day, and sometimes he did, but he knew good and well the simple fact was that he hung onto that railing not because they scared him but because he scared himself. Sad goddamn state of things, he thought, when a man can't even trust his own body anymore.

As he moved slowly down the path he could see the white hull of the *Jenny Rae* glowing like a pearl in the moonlight. It had only been a week since he'd confronted himself about what had happened out there, and the loss was still sharp as a treble hook in the hand. He tried not to look at her because every time he did he felt that betrayal again, and it opened a hole in his gut and made his knees weak. Lily'd been bugging him about not eating enough, but the last thing he wanted was food. He felt like he'd carved a chunk of himself out and handed it over. If he ate something like as not it would just slide down his throat and fall right out the hole. And now there was his boat, another victim of his failure. She waited at the dock like an orphan, and he couldn't stand to see her. He walked on, his head down, following his unsteady steps to the shed.

The shed's dark shape loomed in the moonlight, the trees casting their spindly shadows against the siding that had come from a neighbor's barn torn down years ago. Not one to see things go to waste, Jines had piled load after load of the barn board into his pickup and trucked it home. The structure itself he had framed from the loblollies he'd cleared to make room for the shed, and the roof was tin, shining now in the moonlight. It was hot in the summer, drafty in winter, and it worked out just fine. But for the sighing of the trees above and all around, or maybe because of that, it was quiet and peaceful, a good place for a man to get some work done. He wondered what the hell exactly he was doing out here now.

They'd given him sleeping pills. He tried them once, and once was enough. Oh he slept all right, all night and halfway through the next day, at least that's what it had felt like, like he was moving in slow motion and trying to talk underwater. Hell with that. He'd rather have the sleep when it decided it would take the time to come to him. Tonight wasn't one of those times. Maybe it was the moon. It was pretty, the light out here clear as liquid. He heard a barred owl hooting deeper in the woods—"Who cooks for you?" the owl asked—and then he slid the shed door open and flicked on the lights.

Empty of any big ongoing projects and poorly lit, since most of the bulbs hanging from the beams overhead looked to be burned out, the shed seemed cavernous and dark, and not particularly welcoming. He heard a scurrying down in one corner as some varmint or other realized the party was over. At the far end in the shadows his table saw, planer, drill press, and band saw hunched like trolls. In the middle the woodstove was a darkened lump. Beyond that the dark hovered like hunger. Got to change out those bulbs, he thought. He'd like as not cut off an arm trying to work in this piss-poor light. He shuffled over to the workbench that ran the entire length of one side of the shed, the dust and dirt of the floor poofing up under his steps like talc. He turned on one of the clip-on lights fastened there, squinting in its sudden harsh brightness. Sawdust drifted around the bench's legs and dust sifted like fine flour from the light fixture. A battalion of wood clamps marched across in front of him, hung from a beam along the wall, smaller to larger. The biggest ones were near as long as his leg, the smallest could fit into his palm. There was a row of saws, most of them even older than he felt at the moment, and a couple of levels and T-squares. He reached up and pulled down one of the saws, the worn wooden grip satin-smooth in his palm. At the back edge of the workbench against the wall was a series of short shelves he'd built to hold a variety of miscellaneous stuff. These were littered with stray woodscrews and penny nails, empty tuna fish and soup cans he washed out and used for mixing paints or resins, boxes of dust masks and sandpaper, small wooden squares for sanding blocks. His hands turned the things over, disturbing the dust. Mouse shit freckled the bench's wood. He'd never been a clean freak, especially out here, but this place was a mess. Been too long since he'd spent serious time out here. He could do that, he thought, come out here and clean the place up. How hard could it be?

The plain prospect of it slumped him inside out. Near the end of the bench was an old davenport Jenny Rae had given up on long ago. He landed in it like a ship dropping anchor, sending up a plume of dust that made him sneeze outright. The cover had once been a pattern of ornate roses. He had never liked it, too showy, too hoity-toity, but out here he could put it in its place. Now the whole thing was pocked with mouse holes where tufts of the stuffing had escaped. It looked like a cotton field gone to seed. He picked absently at a tuft and felt a despair wash over him that pinched his throat tight and made his eyes burn. Even this place, this shed he'd put up with his own hands, where he'd built the *Jenny Rae*, it was full of mouse shit and dust and shadows. All these tools that had come to him, tools that his grandfather had used to hack out a home in an untamed place, tools he himself had used to build a boat that was the envy of every waterman on the river and had saved his skin more than once (even that young Coast Guard lieutenant had said she was stout, hadn't he?) why, they would waste away right along with him. A bonfire. Now that would be a useful thing. A bonfire right about now, with him and all this other useless shit right in the middle of it.

"Jines?" Lily Rae's voice came from by the door, delicate for once, gentle like a bird. Or maybe she was just scared of the shadows. "You in here?"

Yes or no, he thought. Either way she'd find him. She'd been a little easier to live with lately, now that she had her garden in. She had that girl Belle, Jamie Cockrell's girl, over a couple times a week and they would spend half an afternoon on their hands and knees in the dirt out there. He had to admit it wasn't all that intolerable to watch them. Even to hear their laughter now and then. That Belle was a pretty thing, pretty in a hard-to-figure way. What you might call mysterious. Watching his daughter with her, their backs bent over some precious weed or another out there, sometimes his breath would catch, and he would have to turn his head away. He was always a little surprised then.

"Jines," she said. "It's dark in here."

A fine statement of the obvious, he thought. "Yep."

He saw her jump at his voice.

"What the hell are you doing out here? What's the matter with you?" Her voice sounded shrill.

"What's the matter with you?" he asked.

"Nothing's the matter with me!"

"Then what are you doing out here?"

"I'm looking for you, for crying out loud! It's one in the morning!"

He tapped one wrist with his finger as if he were trying to make out the time on a watch, though he never wore one. "Aye God you're right," he said. "I'll be go to heck."

She walked toward the davenport, into the small circle of available light. "You're wearing pajamas."

"Lucky for both of us, I reckon."

"Aren't you chilly?"

"Worried about me, are you? Afraid I might catch a cold?"

"More likely you'd catch some kind of communicable disease." She looked around on the workbench, wrinkled her nose at the mouse droppings. "When was the last time you worked out here?"

"Been awhile."

There was a stool at the workbench and she brushed it off with a piece of rag, then perched herself on it. She alighted there only a moment, then she was up again and scouting around further down the bench.

"What're you looking for?" Jines asked.

"I was wondering whether you had any light bulbs somewhere. We could brighten this place up a little."

Jines made a humphing noise. He'd been thinking bonfires, not light bulbs. Put light on the subject and he'd have no choice but to see the sad state of things more clearly. Lily was still rooting around on the bench half in the dark. She knocked something over and then that knocked something else over, sounded like fasteners were going all over the place—"Oh, shit, sorry," she said, and she kind of giggled, he couldn't believe she was over there giggling while tearing up his workbench—and then something really big fell like a clamp or something and she yelled, "Hey!" and that was enough. "Goddammit, a shop ain't no place for a woman!" he stormed, and with a great effort he heaved himself up out of the couch—by God he wasn't asking for any help for that, although it made his head swim at first when he finally got upright—and stomped as best he could over to where she stood, holding something in the dark that glinted a little but he couldn't quite see it. "The hell you doing over here anyway, making a mess of things."

She looked at him out of the gloom. "Me," she said. "Making a mess of things." And she swept one arm as if to take in the entire wrecked, neglected landscape of his workbench and the shed beyond it and then laughed out loud. "That's right," she said, "me and the mice, making a mess of things."

She was really laughing. Goddamn hooting. And it did seem, he had to admit, fairly ridiculous that he could accuse her of trashing the place.

"Yeah, well," he grumbled. He saw the glinting thing in her hand again. "What's that you got there?"

She moved toward him and held it into the light. It was an old soup can, the red and white Campbell's label faded almost to nothing. There were four or five crayons poking out of it. A blue one, he could see, a green. A yellow. He remembered, when she was a girl, how she'd sit out here with him while he worked and draw pictures, then insist that he stop whatever he was doing to look at her latest creation. How in God's name had that can of crayons stayed on his workbench all this time? In the hardness of the workbench light he could see the circles under her eyes, the tiredness etched all around them. "What do you know," she said. And she grinned at him.

He found a box of light bulbs in one of the tall metal cupboards that still stank of resin, even though it had been years since he'd used the epoxies stored in there. He'd need a backhoe to go through this place, there was so much junk lying around. She looked doubtfully up at the sockets in the beams overhead, and he moved to get a stepladder that was over in one corner. He started to drag it under one of the beams but the fact was he couldn't maneuver the stepladder along with the cane—it was like having five extra legs, none of them working particularly well together— and not only that, his arms weren't feeling any too good. She grabbed the ladder from him and placed it under a socket, then climbed up and unscrewed the bulb. It squeaked in the socket rustily. "Uh, that noise makes my teeth hurt," she said, handing down the dead bulb. He took it and gave her a new one. "So, if I get shot across the room when I screw this in, you'll give me CPR, right?"

"You ain't gonna get shot across the room." She started screwing the new bulb in gently. "Besides, I'm an old man. Might break my good arm trying something like that."

"Please," she said. The light suddenly popped on brightly over her head, making him squint.

"Well I'm just following doctor's orders, you know. That's what they told me—I have to be more careful."

"I believe they were referring to the idea that perhaps you shouldn't be gallivanting about on the high seas hauling pound nets all day."

"It's called working."

She climbed down and moved the ladder over to the next

burned-out bulb. He walked slowly along beside her. They repeated the procedure.

"I *know* you're not thinking about it," she said, stretching upward.

"About what."

"You know exactly what."

"No," he said, with some finality in his voice. "I ain't thinking about it."

She stopped what she was doing and looked down at him, her eyebrows arched up in a question. "I can't quite believe I just heard that," she said.

He didn't meet her eyes, just rooted around in the box for a fresh light bulb. "It won't work anymore," he said, and that was all he was going to say about it. He heard that owl call out again and for a moment he looked outside himself at the two of them, both in their pajamas in the middle of the night in a filthy old shed, replacing light bulbs. Imagine if Mary Virginia or Kenneth were to walk in right now. They'd think they were both crazy. Maybe they were. What was the point of replacing light bulbs when the whole house had already burned down?

"What are you going to do?" she asked.

"I ain't got that far yet."

She was quiet for a minute. They moved the ladder under another burned-out light and she worked the bulb out of the socket. Wordlessly she handed him the dead bulb and he handed up a fresh one. Finally she said, "Maybe you should sell some of the land."

"No."

"Jines—"

"Ain't gonna happen."

"Hospitals and doctors don't wait forever to get paid, you know. They will call collection agencies, and those inhuman bastards will mess up your life, believe me. They don't have blood in their veins, they have embalming fluid. They do not care about you, or the house, or the boat, or any of it. They will just take it, piece by piece."

"They can try."

"What do you think, Jines, that the rules don't apply to you? That somehow you're exempt from the reality that afflicts all the rest of us?"

He looked at her in a way he thought might knock her off the ladder.

"I believe," he said, "it's been made pretty damned clear that there ain't no reality, like you put it, that I'm exempt from." He looked around the shed and saw it was just as he'd expected; all the fresh lights did was expose more of what he didn't want to see. "That bright enough for ya?"

And he shuffled over to the ruined davenport and more or less fell backward into it. The glaring light over the workbench had gone out. He closed his eyes. He heard her climb down from the ladder and carry it back over to the corner where he'd retrieved it. Then he heard the sound of a tarp being pulled back, and a soft intake of her breath. She had found the cedar. With the tarp off it, he imagined he could smell the wood's sweetness from here in the couch, the smell of the forest and things waiting to be born.

"What's this?" she asked. Her voice had gone soft again, like she was looking at something wondrous that might just fly away.

"It was supposed to be for a skiff." His cracked voice.

"What?"

He cleared his throat. "That's white cedar from over behind the point, cut it myself. Tree must've been a hundred years old. I had it made into boards down at Bobby Sarles's mill. It was supposed to be for a skiff."

"For who?"

196

"Don't matter now."

For you, he wanted to say, but he felt too used up to hear any sarcastic comment she might have to make about that. It was all a long time ago anyway, a long, long time ago.

"Why don't you build it?"

He didn't answer. His eyes were still closed, but he could tell she was standing there, watching him. Before she stepped out into the cool night pines, she switched off the lights, so all that was left was the moon.

"Jines Arley Evans, am I going to have to tell on you?" Jeanette swished her sweet behind as she moved out from the kitchen with a pot of coffee and made a beeline for him and his mug, sitting at the liars' table in the Seaside. He had been a faithful husband, he had loved his wife more than any man could love a woman, but he was a man, after all, he told himself. And Jeanette Pritchett, owner and operator of the Seaside, that woman had a way of moving around her domain that made a man stop and take notice. It couldn't have been an easy living, slinging pies and coffee for a bunch of smelly watermen who tended to show up before sunrise wanting bacon, eggs, and no surprises, but Jeanette always had a smile on her face and a wiggle in her giddyup and for that Jines was thankful. She leaned over him as she poured the coffee and put a hand on his shoulder.

"Tell on me for what?" He put a grateful hand around the mug.

"Well"—she slung one hip out and clamped her free hand on it in the classic posture of females everywhere giving their insubordinates a talking to—"I know for a fact that you aren't supposed to be driving your truck. And I also know for a fact that you'd be long gone dead before you'd walk however many miles it is over here, not that my pie isn't worth it. And since I don't see anybody else around at the moment, I'm just wondering what shenanigans you pulled to get here." She gave him a quick squeeze on the shoulder and headed back for the counter. "Although of course I am happy to see you after all this while. I must've known you were coming because I finished up two lemon meringues just this morning. You ready for a piece now or you want to wait?"

"I been waiting too long already."

"I thought so." She laughed and pulled the pie out of the cooler, sliced him a piece the size of a grain barge, and slid it in front of him. The fluffy white meringue quivered, as well it should. It didn't stand a chance.

"Sweet Jesus, Jeanette," he said, plowing his fork into it, "now that's a pie."

It had been near sunrise when he'd finally gotten to sleep. He'd sat out there in the dark listening to the mice running around and thinking about what Lily Rae had said. "Why don't you build it,"she'd said. Aye God but she could be so cocksure sometimes it made him want to grab her and give her a shake. As if everything were so simple, just a matter of doing it. What did she know about it? On the way down here this morning he'd passed by a marsh where the bones of old workboats lay gray and sagging in the grasses. Sometimes when a boat was finally done in and couldn't be patched up anymore, the man who owned her would take out her engine and anything else worth a damn and then haul her up so she could die. That's pretty much how he'd been feeling ever since that Coast Guard lieutenant had pointed out his frailties. Although in fact he knew the old abandoned boats possessed more dignity passing the seasons with the geese and ospreys, a kind of noble sad beauty that he was certain he entirely lacked in his present situation. Why don't you build it, she'd said. And he'd sat there in that mouse-eaten davenport longing for sleep, and even after she'd left he kept hearing her tossing the idea out there.

Been a long time since he'd built a boat. There were two types of skiffs his daddy had taught him how to build, a flat-bottom and a deadrise. The flat-bottom was a lot easier, went a lot quicker. You could use a skiff like that for netting soft crabs in the shallows or hauling it out to your pounds, put an outboard on her and use her for rockfishing in the rivers when the young stripers came in late summer and early fall. Perfectly serviceable, useful boat, the flat-bottom. Nothing wrong with it. But the fact was he liked the deadrise better, and that's the type he had tried to perfect. It could be a right pain in the neck once you got up to planking the floor near the bow. Every single piece had to be measured and hand cut and measured and cut and measured again, and then shaped and fitted. Sometimes it would take a whole day just to get three or four planks finished. And even before that, you had to make sure that chine was cut just so, the angle exactly where it should be, or none of those boards would sit right and tight. You didn't even have to think about that when you built a flat-bottom. But that kind of precision pleased him. More than that, the deadrise was just plain pretty. It would turn out like a miniature version of his *Jenny Rae*, with that cheeky, no-nonsense look up forward and a sheerline so fine it could make dead man's heart beat. A man could get some satisfaction out of building something like that.

Jines took another huge bite of pie and followed it with a swallow of coffee. He'd been ugly tired when he'd finally woken up this morning, like he was a million years old, but he was starting to feel better. He had the pattern for that deadrise skiff, a long thin piece of cedar his daddy had used years ago to cut out the sides. After that it was oak for the ribs, oak for the stem too, then stretching those sides back into the shape he loved. That cedar under the tarp had been dry all this time. Unless some varmint had gotten to it, the stuff should be better than prime. He'd had Bobby Sarles cut it in twenty-foot lengths. You couldn't even begin to find that kind of wood around anymore. Nowadays the longest boards you could find were twelve, fourteen, maybe sixteen feet if you were lucky. More often than not you'd have to make the sides out of two pieces, sister them together. Not that cedar he had. That stuff was worth its weight in gold. One long, smooth, perfect side right there in each board.

He probably had enough oak lying around too. He might have to hunt around the county for a good piece long enough for the keelson, but maybe not. The rafters up in the shed were full of wood he'd stashed up there. He hated to throw away wood, even scraps. You never knew when some little piece would come in handy, and the scraps made the best kindling for the woodstove. Jines finished off the pie and leaned back in his chair. No, he knew he had the materials and the tools, and he by God had the skills. The question was, he had to ask himself, did he have the muscle? He stretched and flexed his wrists and forearms, first one and then the other. He was stiff as a piece of oak himself. There were some parts he knew would be right tricky to manage. Just hefting a drill and hammer all day, let alone handling the wood.

The bell over the Seaside's door jingled. "Well Jamie Cockrell!" Jeanette said. "It's not lunchtime yet, what are you doing here this time of day?"

"Hey Jeanette. Jines Arley." He nodded toward Jines. "I saw the *Jenny Rae* tied up next door at Edward's dock and had a feeling you might be in here. Is that lemon meringue?"

"It was," Jines said.

"The *Jenny Rae!*" Jeanette left the counter to walk through the dining room and look out the window. Jines grinned into his coffee when she came back through and whacked him lightly on the shoulder. "I knew I was going to have to tell on you."

"Well come on, now, Jeanette. Nothing wrong with a short trip down the river to taste the world's best pie. Anyway I gotta run her a little. Boat starts sittin', boat starts dyin'."

"Mm hmm."

It always tickled Jines how Jeanette could do that, make him feel like a little kid caught with his hand in his mama's pie safe. You could tell she had this fondness for men whom she disapproved of just slightly. The ones she disapproved of too much—Kenneth was a good example there—she would barely give the time of day to, and certainly none of those saucy hands-on-the-hips lectures. No, with boys like that she might just come out of the Seaside's kitchen with the cast-iron skillet she used for cooking scrapple, two hands on the handle and swinging. But evidently she thought highly enough of Jamie Cockrell to slice him a piece of her lemon meringue and pour him a cup of coffee without him even having to make another comment. This gesture was not to be taken lightly. Few people in Ophelia were as good a judge of character as Jeanette.

The two men sat across from one another, the long expanse of the otherwise empty liars' table stretching out from them like the deck of a ship. The day was growing warmer and birdsong filtered in the windows. By the squealing and squawking of gulls behind the restaurant Jines knew Jeanette had opened the kitchen door and tossed something out the back. Hope it wasn't the bread crusts, he thought. He could go for some bread pudding tomorrow. He was working on his second piece of pie and feeling an uneasiness he couldn't quite put his finger on, other than the fact that it seemed like Jamie was working hard on not looking over at him. As if he was nervous or something. This was the thing about the Seaside; you knew if you sat there long enough you'd see everybody you needed to see, but odds were equally good you'd see someone you didn't particularly want to see or just didn't feel exactly comfortable sharing a meal with. Most of the time eating at the liars' table felt just like you were sitting in somebody's kitchen, so you damned well better hope you more or less liked the people you were sitting with. Although God knew that wasn't always the case in your own house. Jines had nothing against Jamie Cockrell. He was a good-looking kid and a hard worker. Took good care of his mama. Lily certainly seemed to be getting on with his daughter. Jines stabbed away at his pie. Jeanette had a good point, though; exactly what *was* Jamie doing here at this time of day? The boy had a boatyard to run, hadn't he? If it was anything like running a workboat, you didn't just up and leave on a bright sunny spring morning to eat pie, even Jeanette's lemon meringue. Jines poured a little more cream in his decaf—that was another thing lately, he thought, his taste buds were all out of whack because instead of just blond and sweet seemed like he wanted his coffee peroxide and sweet. Must be those damned pills. He took a healthy swallow of coffee. Being the senior member at the table in this situation, he didn't feel a need to break any ice there might need to be broken.

Jamie cleared his throat. "I think Lily Rae's upset with me," he said.

Jines snorted. As icebreakers went this one wasn't all that imaginative or new.

"That don't make you special."

By the slight grin on Jamie's face Jines could tell that his daughter's cantankerousness appealed to him, the poor dumb son of a bitch.

"What'd you do to earn such approval?"

Jamie squirmed a little in his chair.

"Ah, I think she thinks I can do better than running Jimmy Wilson's yard."

"She's more like your mama every day, wanting to tell people what they ought to be doing instead of minding her own business."

"Jines Arley, you ought to be smacked, honest to God." This from Jeanette, who had swept back in from the kitchen behind the counter and was yanking the basket out of the industrial coffee maker to brew another pot. "What kind of way is that to speak about that beautiful girl of yours?" She whacked the metal basket against the trash can to dump out the old grounds and, Jines understood, to make her point.

"Don't start with me, Jeanette."

"You men around here, I swear." She slammed the reloaded basket into the coffee maker and put a new pot on the heat plate beneath it with less vigor, only because she didn't want to break it, Jines was sure. If it'd been a metal pot, forget it. "Try walking upright sometime. It's a whole new world." Then she stomped back out.

Jines looked thoughtfully at her receding shoulders, squared back with righteous female indignation.

"A fiery woman with a good vocabulary can be a wonderful thing," he said, "long as you know how to duck and cover." He looked over at Jamie. "I hope you're not expecting me to say something to Lily Rae on your behalf. You're on your own with that one."

"No, sir, I wouldn't expect that."

"Good." Jines examined his coffee cup and thought about his Jenny. He wouldn't have characterized his wife as fiery. Feisty, yes. You bet, and not above dropping a less-than-Christian word or two when the moment suited her. She was smart that way; she could completely disarm the crew with a well-placed, salty comment geared to ensure that they would realize she was both womanly, and therefore possessed of that particular female power that could be so intimidating and enticing, but also down to earth. This was a potent combination, Jines could attest. He suspected his daughter possessed it too, although she had an edge, a hardness, her mother never revealed. And if there was any one thing he could say he missed most of all about Jenny Rae it was her lack of harshness, her inherent gentleness. His life now seemed like all hard corners.

There was no give to it. He took a listless sip, not liking the extra cream suddenly. Made his coffee look like those frappuccino things they sold down at the Get N Zip. Pantywaist coffee.

"Jines Arley, I have a proposal for you." Jamie was leaning forward over the table. "I've been thinking on it for awhile and, well, when I saw the *Jenny Rae* here I thought I should come in and just lay it out to you."

Jines pushed his chair back some from the table and stretched his legs. "All right," he said.

"I felt bad about that day you went out, that day when that boy pulled you overboard and he drowned, and you almost did." Jamie's hands were clasped tight together on the table. Whatever it was he wanted to say, it was making him jumpy. "But I could understand why you had to go back out. It was like you just said to Jeanette, about how a boat not moving is starting to die. I think people are like that too. But now I have to ask you a personal question, and I hope you don't take offense at my asking." Here he paused, waiting.

Jines nodded.

"My question is, what are your plans for the *Jenny Rae?* I know you've got pounds still out there. I know they're sitting, all that gear just sitting there, and so's your boat. If it's true that you're not going to fish her anymore, or for awhile, I would ask if I could fish her for you. We could come to an agreement that could be good for both of us. I would lease her, and give you fifty percent of the catch. That would mean income for you, and your boat and gear wouldn't be wasted. Depending on how things go, you could decide further on down the road whether you'd be amenable to me doing a sort of rent-to-own thing. The lease payments could go into a down payment on the boat and gear. That's only if, of course, you're not going to come back to it."

"That what the boys are saying, that I'm out of it?" He hated the thought of the talk, most of it probably right here, all the men gossiping like a bunch of old ladies in a church sewing circle, speculating on his situation. His future, or lack of it. "They don't call it the liars' table for nothing, you know."

"That's why I'm talking to you direct, Jines Arley. I don't get down here too much anyway, I got no time to sit around telling stories. I don't know what they're saying. But it's no secret what happened, and it's no secret the *Jenny Rae* hasn't moved since. Till today." He pulled a cigarette out of a pack in his chest pocket and lit it.

"Those things'll kill you, you know."

Jamie grinned suddenly, a wicked grin lopsided by the cigarette tucked into the corner of his mouth, and Jines saw a handsome man there, straight and strong and a little dangerous in the way a young man should be. He looked away and fixed his gaze on the sparkling river outside the windows. For the first time in a long time he let himself think about his own son and where he might be now. Like as not this conversation would never be happening. God willing, Danny would have loved the water as he did and taken it up himself, be running the *Jenny Rae* or his own boat right now, this fine spring morning. Although who knows, a lot of this younger generation didn't want to work so hard for what was lately relatively little. They'd up and get out right after high school, go work at the shipyard down in Norfolk or at that paper mill over on the York River. Jamie was different that way, loyal to his past. Jines had hardly known Danny, and the hard truth was he was grateful for that. It was a bitter gratitude, and he felt cowardly in his acceptance of it. He could justify it all he wanted—he was working so hard back then, trying to make hay while the haymaking was good, it was the way he was brought up to be. None of that made things any different. That was the thing about how you lived your life, Jines thought; time was irrelevant. A man had no hold on it. For all the work, all the time spent away from his son and later his daughter (although that, he would admit, was deliberate, a desperate need to avoid all he had loved), here he was. Alone, half-crippled, in debt to a bunch of doctors, eating lemon meringue pie. This day. This fine spring day. He brought his gaze back from the river to Jamie.

"I'm not sure why you'd want to do it," Jines said.

"What?"

"You've got a good job, seems like. Plus you've got a fine daughter there, I get to see her sometimes when she and Lily are out in the garden. Fishing's a hard way to make it as it is, and with that kind of a deal you'd be making even less. Probably wouldn't even break even. You probably got stuff like medical benefits with the boatyard, vacation time, that kind of thing. None of that when you run your own boat."

Jamie stubbed his cigarette out. "I'm surprised you would put it to me that way."

"There isn't that much in it anymore, you know as well as I do, Jamie. The market hasn't held up, costs keep going up. It worked for me because I don't have the overhead—I own my boat, I own my land, I own my gear."

"But you don't own your own life anymore, do you?"

This stopped Jines cold, the stone truth of it. For a second he was furious, red-hot mad at this boy insolent enough to put it out there in spoken words. You put something like that out there, you say it out loud, it could become real in a way you never wanted. Didn't this boy know that? His expression wasn't lost on Jamie.

"Jines Arley, I don't mean any disrespect. You know I don't. But you know who I am. You know where I come from. All I ever wanted was the chance, and I never got it. I'm doing what I do now out of pure dead necessity, and I think it's killing me in a way that's ten times worse than cancer." He reached for another cigarette as he said this but he didn't light it, he just flipped it between his fingers, back and forth. "I haven't ever owned my own life. If I leased the *Jenny Rae*, if I fished her for you—" Here he stopped and pressed his lips together hard, looked out the window as if he were searching for the words somewhere out there in the water. The cigarette tumbled back and forth through his fingers.

Jeanette swirled in from the kitchen—"You boys okay?"—and then turned right back around and disappeared. She had a good sixth sense that way, Jines thought, knew when to stay and when to go. He let out a long slow breath and watched the river along with Jamie. He didn't want to be angry with him. The boy had stones to come ask him this, and he'd had the good sense to make it a real proposition. Not like Kenneth, who'd want it all for nothing, and whom he knew he couldn't trust to take care with his boat. More than that, it was obvious that Jamie understood the idea had to do with more than money. Fact was, when you got right down to it, money had nothing to do with it. Money wasn't the reason Jamie wanted to fish his boat. And money wouldn't be the reason Jines would let him.

"Who'd you get for crew?" Jines asked.

Jamie turned back to him and put the cigarette on the table. "I don't have a whole crew yet. I don't want to ask anybody until I know we're going to work something out. But there are a couple guys who work for me now who are good strong guys with good boat sense. I'd probably take as few as I could, you know. Less guys to pay." He had allowed some hope back into his face, and his voice took on a quick eagerness. "I was thinking that along with the pounds, depending on the market for crabs I might run some pots too. I can do that alone if I have to. Oystering in winter, I might need one other guy for that."

"Well, I don't know," Jines mused, "you're good and strong and if you're tonging that's all you really need, a back and shoulders like a brick shithouse. That and a healthy tolerance for being cold as a witch's tit most of the day."

Jamie laughed.

"I gave up tonging a couple years ago," Jines said. "It just seemed like one winter I couldn't take it anymore. You're lucky you're a young man, don't feel that cold the same way us oldheads do."

"You ain't old, Jines Arley."

Jines snorted. He looked up at his photograph framed on the wall behind the liars' table, the one of the *Jenny Rae* on a brilliant summer day, flag snapping sharp in the breeze, and suddenly he remembered that day clearly. He'd been doing just what Jamie was talking about doing—crabbing a little in the off days—and he'd caught a mess of crabs. They looked so fat he'd kept two dozen for himself, and that evening Jenny Rae steamed them up along with some sweet corn from the garden and fresh tomatoes sliced thick as his thumb with just a little pepper and salt sprinkled on them. Danny smeared a tomato around on his plate like it was a sponge, his fat little hand squashed down on it so the seeds squirted through his fingers, and Lily couldn't quite eat the corn on the cob because she'd lost most of her front teeth, so Jines had sliced it off for her. It had been hot, he remembered, but the breeze came off the river and they sat on the screened porch, and later that night he and Jenny Rae had wandered down to the dock. She was wearing one of those white cotton dresses she always wore—how the woman could wear white and not have it filthy dirty by the end of the day was a walking miracle; he always looked like he'd been rolling in a pig pen—and it shifted around her so she seemed like a part of the night itself, as if she wasn't quite real or a part of this world but already belonging to someplace else. She dropped the dress and jumped in and turned back laughing at him. "Come on, sweetie, come on," she said, and as she swam all the water was lit up like fireworks around her as her pale body moved through the water and bumped into the comb jellies. She was irresistible, she was magic, and when Jines jumped in beside her he pulled her to him. She wrapped all of herself around him, her arms, her legs, and they made love there in the water, him hanging onto a mooring line with one hand to steady them, her moving like flame all over and through him, the water lit up around their single body as if the stars had fallen out of the sky into the river. The memory was so clear, every detail so sharp, as if he were in a dream and didn't even need to breathe.

"Jines Arley, you all right?" It was Jamie, across the liars' table from him. He had put one hand across the table onto Jines's arm.

Jines wiped his eyes with a napkin, cleared his throat with a loud harrumph. He was too full of memory today, all of these days. They came at him like a herd of horses, thundering and wild and out of control. He wondered fleetingly if some of these pills that doctor had him taking were responsible for the crazy intensity of them. Sometimes it was like he was hallucinating. It would be better, he thought, to have an explanation like that, rather than what he'd been scared to think, that his mind was going back in a way he had resisted all these years, like a dam had broken inside of him and there was no stopping what was behind it anymore.

"All right," he said.

He reached for his coffee and it was cold. There was Jamie, waiting for an answer from him. He already knew the answer he was going to give, and he knew it was going to complicate his life in a way he couldn't possibly need right now. He knew Kenneth would be furious, and Mary Virginia too, probably. He was sure Jamie hadn't out sussed that part of it. There would be repercussions, no doubt. But it was the right thing to do. That wacky Mary Virginia was always going on about karma, how if you did something right for someone it would come back to you in a good way sometime. She was always telling Jines he needed to start thinking about his long-term spiritual health—that's how she would say it, his long-term spiritual health, as if it were a life insurance policy or something—that between the fact that he never went to church anymore and couldn't care less that his karma bank account was dead-ass empty, he was headed for the spiritual shitter. Or words to that effect. Maybe so, he thought, probably so. Anyway, he had his reasons for what he was about to do.

"I'll let you take the *Jenny Rae*," he said. "You pay the insurance on her—that's about five hundred dollars—and you pay for all your own expenses, fuel and what-not. You'll be responsible for her gear and all her maintenance and I guarantee you"—here he leaned toward Jamie, poking his thick finger into the big pine table—"I will be on you like fleas on a dog in this regard. No part of my boat goes short-changed. I worked too hard to build her and she's worked too hard to take care of me. She stays at my dock."

"I understand, Jines, I—"

"I ain't done yet. I'm gonna come in for a world of shit for this, you better believe that. I don't know if you've thought that part through. Your mama's gonna want my head, and she won't be the only one."

Jamie looked down at the table and nodded.

"You'll pay me half the catch, whatever it is. I can probably get Jimmy Laird to do any trucking for you on the cheap; we had a deal worked out and it still stands, far as I know. For now, I won't ask you for anything for the boat outright."

"Jines Arley, I appreciate that but it doesn't seem hardly fair. I'm prepared to pay you—"

"You ain't prepared for shit. This is going to be harder than you think. I'll help you how I can, but it's up to you, Jamie. It's gonna be up to you."

The two men stood up, and Jamie reached his hand across the table. Jines found some assurance in the rough, fierce grasp that met his own.

"I don't know how to thank you," Jamie said.

Jines looked out at the river again, sparkling and riffling in the growing midday breeze. It would be a fine ride home. Too short, of course. Maybe he'd poke up a creek or two on the way, take a couple plugs, see if any fish were biting. Not like he had somewhere else he had to be.

"You'll figure it out," he said.

Chapter 11

Jines pulled the tarp back with a snap. Amid the cloud of dust the smell of the cedar came at him like a freight train, pulling with it a carload of memory. The tree had stood down near the marshy point long before he was a boy. Most boys wouldn't have noticed it particularly unless they were thinking about climbing it or building a tree fort, and since cedar trees weren't much good for either occupation with their soft, snappy wood and bushy branches, it could have been just another tree. Your magnolia, now, that was a tree for climbing with its low, strong branches that laddered straight up to the top and the waxy leaves that provided a secret hideout and shelter from the weather even in winter. But Jines was the son of a man who loved to build boats as much as take them out on the water to work, and so his daddy never let him walk past a tree without pointing out its particular features, its uses, the merits of its wood as well as the flaws, the shape of its nuts and cones and even its inherent beauty. By the time he was nine he could identify the fine distinction between the Atlantic white cedar and the Eastern red, the shortleaf pine with its stubbier needles that poked out in pairs versus the loblolly whose longer needles came in bundles of three, the dappled bark of the sycamore that was a dead giveaway even in winter, the white oak with its round-lobed leaves, the red with its sharp-pointed ones, the willow oak with the long, slender leaves that gave it its name. "You want to keep an eye peeled for the good ones," his daddy told him, "and look after them. Help 'em along if they need it. Make sure none of that damned honeysuckle or wild grapevine gets up on the trunk and the branches, keep the damned maples and poplars from growing like the weeds they are all around it and shading it out. A good tree ain't no different than a good boat. You got to be responsible to it."

Jines's daddy had spied the white cedar out near the marsh and made a special note of pointing it out to his son. "Best boatbuilding wood there is, come from that tree," he said. "Easy to work. Strong as a bull but nice and light." Jines had watched that tree grow all his life, even as fewer and fewer of them seemed to be showing up near the river, and when the time came to build a boat that he wanted to be extra special, he made his peace with the tree and took it down. The wood was just as beautiful as his daddy had told him it would be, strong and straight, light and supple.

And here it had sat. Still protected, still his responsibility. Looking at it he felt the rush of years come upon him like a wave at the shore, almost knocking him down. He was an old man now, he truly was. Felt nearly as old as this tree had been when he'd dropped her. Never thought he'd get this far. Sometimes wished he hadn't. He tugged the tarp further back and uncovered the whole stack. Aye God, it was good stuff. He could sell it right off and make a nice bundle. You just couldn't find wood like this around here anymore; boatbuilders had to go as far south as the Carolinas, pay a pretty penny for it and then pay some more to ship it home. Selling it as is would be the practical thing to do. There was a builder down in Mathews he knew would be drooling for it. What was the point of trying to build a skiff now, even if he could do it? True, he could probably sell one for seven, eight-thousand dollars to one of these come-heres who thought it was just the bees knees to have a boat built by what they called a local craftsman. Jines snorted. Put me in the Smithsonian, he thought, I guess I'm old enough to be an artist and a relic.

He slid the top board out a little, testing its weight. And he had to admit it felt good in his hands. The roughness of the surface scraped his skin and he liked that prickly feeling, like this wood still had plenty of that tough old tree in it. And he knew his decision, it came to him loud as a bell. He wasn't so far gone as to forget all that had gone into making this wood what it was, all the days and nights, storms and calms, floods and freezes, bugs and birds. Maybe he should have been, but he wasn't so desperate for money that he would take a piece of his own history and sell it to the highest bidder. Wouldn't be any different than selling the house or the land or the *Jenny Rae*. What did he have but all that was past?

Jines set to work.

The first thing to do was dress the wood, get it ready for working. That meant pushing it through the planer, a despotic piece of machinery that dated from Jines's grandfather. He called it the Beast. Made of nothing but black iron, the Beast was unlike any other heavy equipment that Jines had inherited. The band saw, now it's true that thing wasn't much to write home about in the looks department. He'd seen the new ones at the House of Deals, seen them come and go. Shiny and sleek as sports cars, redesigned every other year and made of all kinds of new metals that weighed half as much as the old iron stuff, machines you could change the blades in slick as snot. He had no faith in anything that easy. Jines's band saw stood better than eight feet tall and was almost entirely encased in plywood to protect the moving parts, with the exception of the blade and small table itself. For lighting in the work area, it had a single bare bulb that you had to screw in to turn on. As tall and boxy as it was it looked like some kind of piece of dining-room furniture gone haywire, but when you turned her on she hummed and hummed, and he could slide a piece of wood through there and move it, bend it, shape it in ways that just weren't natural for your average band saw, not without snapping blade after blade. He didn't know what it was—maybe had to do with the way the blade itself was set in the saw, maybe with black magic—but he loved that saw.

The planer, well he loved that too, but in the way you love a mean dog that's too ornery to die. You had to respect it, even if you didn't necessarily trust it. It stood waist-high with about two-thirds that width and it had taken him and four huge men to get it into the shed, and afterward they all bitched at him for a week about what it had done to them. One of them took to calling it Christine after a demonically possessed car in some book by a horror writer whom Jines had never had the inclination to read, but Jines just called it the Beast. There wasn't a damned thing female about it, least of all its name. The Beast had been built in 1909 at the Josiah Ross Iron Works in Buffalo, New York. That information was stamped into one of the side plates just in case anyone had a notion to track down the hell-fired furnace of its birthplace. It had a density that seemed to define gravity. It didn't just occupy space, it consumed it. Jines had read about black holes in the *National Geographic*, and that's how he thought of the Beast: a black hole, a cosmic force. If you weren't careful, if you didn't approach it with the appropriate respectful attitude, it could pull your whole arm into its maw and devour it before you had time to keel over.

Acknowledging his weakened physical state, he did not attempt to face the Beast without a little help. He pulled a sawhorse over to where it sat about four feet in front of the planer. Then he placed another one about the same distance out the back and one more about another five feet out to catch the wood and support it as it came through. He'd figured on a skiff about sixteen feet. The boards were twenty feet long. He'd keep the extra length for now— could always trim it later—but he needed to plane the boards from their present thickness of an inch to about seven-eighths. That might mean as many as three passes for each board, and he was probably going to need two boards per side. And that was just the sides. He would still have to dress the wood for the keel, the chine, the keelson, the ribs. . . He shook his head, knowing if he sat there thinking about the task ahead like as not he wouldn't get through even one board. Back when he was young and strong he could dress nearly all the big wood for a skiff like this in maybe an afternoon of steady work. He didn't have any illusions about how long it might take him now.

Turning a small shiny wheel, Jines adjusted the planer's cutting surface to the height he thought would be about right to take off the first layer of wood but not have it snag up in the blades and kick back. He pulled the top board off the pile and positioned one end of it on the first sawhorse, moved it close to the short table that served as the tongue for the Beast's dark slit of a mouth, and pushed the switch. The lights dimmed for a second and the Beast came to life with a low roar, deceptively smooth at this point. He took a deep breath, steeled his shoulders and arms and slid the end of the wood into the planer.

When the blades grabbed the board's end and started chewing, the sound alone was enough to make you think a child of Satan was in there. The low roar instantly changed to a snarling r-a-a-a-w that made you want to clap your hands over your ears lest you listen too long and go mad. It always amazed Jines how something that sounded so god-awful destructive could produce at its other end a piece of wood that was fair and clean, something almost sweet. It didn't seem possible, but on the other hand that's the way life was sometimes; the hotter the fire the harder the steel and all that. He leaned hard into the wood and felt it kick against him at first; then the Beast took over and the wood simply trembled as he pushed it slowly through. As it emerged from the other end it slid over the first sawhorse. He hoped it would make it to the second one; either way, he was going to have to get over to the other side before the wood went all the way through. It was only a question of how fast he was going to have to move and, of course, how fast he could. He'd have to go without the cane, it would only get in the way. If he had someone on the other end he wouldn't have to play this game of leapfrog around the thing. A helper—the way he used to help his daddy—could just grab the end and pull her steady while he fed the last of it in. He didn't like to be thinking about these things when he was feeding the Beast. He didn't like to be distracted at all. The damned machine could sense weakness and fear like a high-strung horse, he was sure of it. Wouldn't that be just the thing, he thought, to show up at the hospital again but this time instead of a couple of bruises to have an arm halfway cut off. Wonder what that puppy Doc Wyatt would have to say about that. Jesus, just watch the wood you old fool. Get your timing right.

The far end of the slab of wood was approaching the second sawhorse.

"Come on," Jines muttered, "just get right on over that there now." He cackled a little as the wood nudged over the edge of the sawhorse like it knew where it was going. "That's it," he was talking to it, urging it along, "that's it."

With about a foot of wood left to go across the planer's table and into the blades he moved away and around the Beast's side, its snarling like a dozen chainsaws in his ears, his eyes on the prize at the other end and not on where his feet were going. It was harder than he'd thought without the cane. The wood was crawling through of its own accord as the Beast's blades chewed across its surface and nudged it along, and he was counting on that little bit of help, counting on that momentum, he just wasn't counting on the way his one foot caught the leg of the second sawhorse as he came around it, and so he staggered, his hand coming down hard on the end of the board since that was the only thing right there to grab on to. He heard the Beast's voice ratchet up a notch in irritation when the other end of the board flexed up into the planer blades, he felt the whole board vibrate and moan against the deeper bite as his hapless weight pushed the cleared end down. Then with a final snarl the Beast spat out the last of the board. It shot up a foot or so with the force of Jines leaning on the other end, and with this little buck of freedom the board dumped Jines unceremoniously and without hesitation on his ass, then skipped off the sawhorses and landed not an inch from his legs. As it was, the end cuffed his elbow hard enough for him to yell out loud, "You son of a whore!" although whether he was yelling at the board, the Beast, or the world at large was up for debate right about then.

Shed of its irritation, the Beast resumed its low, even growl. He thought it sounded rather pleased with itself, the rat bastard, no doubt waiting for the next victim. Jines gingerly rolled over to his hands and knees, crawled through the dusting of fresh cedar to the planer and punched the off switch. The Beast gave it up with a sudden deceleration, a downwinding of pitch and energy like a jet engine coming to rest. Its roar lowered to a whine and then a sigh and finally a quiet that seemed unnaturally loud. Jines sat there a minute, then hauled himself up bit by bit using the planer for support. When he regained his feet he leaned both hands on the Beast's table, then eased one behind to rub his lower back and butt, both of which already were paying dearly for his clumsiness and evident lack of judgment. He moved to reach for his cane, which was leaning on the first sawhorse, leaving damp handprints on the planer's iron. Ears ringing, legs shaking, hands sweating, Jines realized he didn't have the energy left to fight the plain unvarnished truth of the matter: He was going to need help.

The next morning he woke up to the sound of Jamie's boys walking by his window. He heard their sleepy, comradely voices and for a confused moment he thought they were his crew, that he was late for the tide. He sat up thinking he was who he used to be, and right about then is when his lower back stabbed at him as a rude reminder of just who he was now—old man on the beach, ass-kicked by a ninety-year-old, piece-of-shit planer. He wondered if Jamie or one of his boys would have the time to help and ruled it out almost as soon as he thought of it. They had enough to do. They'd set the second pound down to the Big Betty and between that and the Seven Brothers they were hauling in some good quantities of fish and working hard to do it. The market wasn't great—it hadn't been great in about twenty years, so far as Jines was concerned—but it was something. Anyway, once those boys finished the off-loading and culling and boxing after four or five hours on the water, they were thinking about one thing or maybe two: A cold beer and a soft La-Z-Boy. Last thing they were going to want to do is help him plane wood for some skiff. And anyway, he didn't even know how he could ask for something as falling-off-a-log basic as that. It was like asking for help unzipping your damned fly.

He pulled himself from bed and groaned as he bent over to tug on some pants. He felt his elbow; there was a knot on it where the board had clipped him. Mulling over a few choice words, he crawled into a sweatshirt and forgot to be grateful for the mere act of being able to get dressed. The sunrise was streaming in the eastern window, the one that looked out through the screened porch toward the dock, and he could see Jamie moving around the *Jenny Rae*'s cockpit. And huh, there was Lily down at the dock. She was leaning against a piling and the sun was glinting off her hair. "Aye God," he whispered. Did a child learn so very much at so young an age just by watching, by taking in every detail? Did they miss anything at all? If someone years ago had been in this room on a morning like this and taken a photograph of Jenny Rae seeing him off for the day's work, it could not have captured with any greater accuracy the exact tilt of her head, the shine of her hair, her hand around a coffee mug, the way she had her legs crossed at the ankles as she leaned there, as easy on the rough uneven boards of that dock as a duck on water. The only difference would be the clothing; there was no soft cotton flutter of a housedress in the image before him this morning. His breath hitched in his chest and he felt that unsettling weird sweep of emotion all out of proportion coming at him. He shook his head and stood before the mirror, used a soft brush to tamp down the mess that constituted what was left of his hair, and wiped his eyes. He heard the diesel throttle up.

Jines shuffled into the hall, took a brief detour to the john under the stairs, and then made his way toward the smell of coffee in the kitchen. Lily was coming in the back door just as he was sitting down at the table. She was fairly bouncing. She popped a couple of pieces of bread in the toaster and poured herself some more coffee.

"Did you see that sunrise?" she asked.

Jines looked out the window with eyes so tired it felt like they were sliding down his face. The dock was empty, like he knew it would be. He shook his head.

"Geez, Jines, you look like you got run over by a bus. What happened?"

"Had a little run-in with the planer yesterday afternoon."

"Oh great. Wait till Dr. Wyatt finds out you're playing with heavy equipment now."

"Well I ain't gonna take up crochet."

The toast popped up and Lily brought it to the table, setting it on the lazy Susan and sitting down. She spun the lazy Susan and he stopped it when the little Guernsey cow with the Half n Half came into view. Its jolly face was as plump and insipid as a cherub's. The spoon in his cup made a noisy clink as he stirred it. She pushed the lazy Susan again, sending the plate of toast his way.

"Want some toast?"

Jines grunted and shook his head.

"You need to eat something with the pills." The pill bottles, the whole damned battalion of them, were clustered on the lazy Susan too. Jines gave them his customary glare. "Mamie Hardesty gave me a jar of peach preserves last week. Some of her private stash. You ought to try it on the toast."

"Bribery."

She grinned. "Whatever works."

"You're right perky this morning."

She looked over at him, eyes narrowing. "And what's the matter with that?"

"Nothing the matter with that."

"Then how do you manage to sound annoyed that I'm 'right perky?' " She held up her hands and made quote marks in the air. "It's barely sunup for crying out loud. A little early for the usual petty grievances, don't you think?"

He gave her a long look. Spun the lazy Susan and watched the pills go by, let the toast stop in front of him, put a little butter and some of the jelly on a slice. "Pretty snazzy blouse you got on there. Snappy shorts. Didn't know the tomatoes expected you to wear earrings while you water them."

"Sunrise, Jines." She nodded her head at the window. "Beautiful day." She spread a fat dollop of jelly on her toast. Between crunches she said, "I'm flattered you care so much about my ensemble. Now that I know you're paying attention I'll have to plan ahead. Make sure I don't wear the same T-shirt two days in a row." She pointed to the pills again and he ignored her. "Do I have to take them out of the bottles for you?"

"I'll take them when I'm damned good and ready."

She rolled her eyes. "Do you ever get tired of being the classic crotchety old bastard? I mean, doesn't it take a lot of energy to always be pissed off about something?"

"You tell me."

For a moment she looked like she was going to let him have it, or at least stomp out of the house and take to that skinny blue boat of hers or throw some dirt around the garden, but then her mouth softened up from the thin line it was setting into and she shook her head. Her hair swung this way, that way. She brushed the toast crumbs from the table into her palm and stood up.

"Nope," she said. "Not going to do it today."

"Do what?"

"You're not going to wreck my day just because you want to wreck something. You want to be ornery, knock yourself out." Her voice was crisp and businesslike, although the dishes were taking a beating as she rinsed them out and smacked them into the drain rack. "Physical therapy appointment at two o'clock in Mathews. That therapist—the one who looks like Nurse Ratched in *One Flew Over the Cuckoo's Nest*—wants to give your arms a workout today. Maybe you can take it out on her, she looks like she might think abusive patients are fun. Truck will be running by one-thirty."

And with that she marched out the back door, snatched her muddy work gloves off the porch table and headed for the garden. The screen door slammed behind her and as she walked in front of the window he saw her slapping her right thigh repeatedly with the gloves as if she were quirting a horse. The girl could march and say plenty while she was doing it, that was for sure.

If fatigue and a body that ached like a gimpy knee before a heavy snow were good for anything perhaps they were good for keeping his sore butt in the chair and not pursuing his original hell-hath-no-fury daughter just to say something to make her even madder. Funny how things worked, he thought. Jenny Rae used to get so angry with him when he wouldn't talk to her, when he wouldn't engage her in some kind of argument she felt they needed to have. "Do you know how hard it is to live with a man who won't fight back?" she said to him once. She never quite understood that it wasn't that Jines wouldn't fight back; he just couldn't fathom the female compulsion to get it all out on the table—whatever it was— at the exact moment when they felt the urge or the need to do so. It was as if they thought about it for months, let all this time go by when they could have brought it up—perfectly appropriate times when everyone was in a good mood and the kids were in bed or whatever—and instead they waited until the exact wrong moment, at least from his point of view, to launch into the issue at hand. You don't tell a man, for instance, that you're mad he spent two-thousand dollars more than he said he was going to on a new engine for his boat, right when he comes in from a long day's work on that very same boat dragging his boots he's so bone tired and fish-reeked. Never mind that the engine re-power was six months ago, and she's had all this time to let it work under her skin like some kind of splinter. He didn't get that. And he didn't like being blindsided. And so he would do what he felt was the reasonable thing: Leave. He'd get in his truck or the boat and hightail it out of there for a couple of hours, give himself time to think about it before making any kind of comment one way or the other. It made more sense, didn't it, he would say to her later, for him to take his initial frustration away from her until he was calm enough to talk about the problem rationally? Even if it maybe took a week or two for him to get around to it? Well, it had always made sense to him.

He picked at his toast. Made perfect sense to him why Lily had left like that just now. Better to leave and go plug for perch or yank weeds than say something hurtful you would come to regret later. That's how he'd always reasoned it to himself when he'd done the same. He sipped his coffee, grimaced because it was tepid already. The kitchen was intensely silent, empty of everything. It was as if Lily had taken more than herself out the door and whatever was left in the room was gasping for air. He realized that emotion, whatever color it was, took up space. It was just like the Beast out there in the shed, just like a black hole sucking up all the energy near it. And what was left after the force of that emotion up and walked out the door, even for seemingly justifiable reasons? Nothing real good,

Jines thought, sitting there with his cold coffee and pill bottles. Nothing but a silence that just felt bleak and bad.

"Huh," he said out loud, but it still didn't fill the space, not near enough. He munched at the corner of his toast. Even with the jelly—which was terrific, he had to admit—the food just stuck in his mouth like old Saltines. He spun the lazy Susan until the pill bottles were in front of him and went through the demeaning labor of opening each one, his daily reminder of the recent past and the doubtful future. Even the caps seemed to imply infirmity; they had an oversized easy-grip top in case his fingers were too feeble to handle the standard pop-off kind. He tapped out the pills one by one onto the table and, knowing he was risking gastrointestinal havoc, swallowed them with the coffee. Then he headed out to the garden.

Lily was working on putting metal cages around the young tomato plants, which were already thigh high. She was having a time of it; should've put those things in as soon as she planted the seedlings, he thought, that's the way Jenny Rae'd always done it. If you waited too long it was like trying to wrestle a wet puppy, getting all those branches in between the cage's wire without breaking them. But he hadn't come out here to tell her how to mind the garden. Wasn't like he had any real clue anyway. He stood watching for a bit, long enough that finally she had to straighten up and walk toward him to get another couple of cages.

"You were right about Mamie's preserves," he said, "right good."

Nothing. She returned to the row where she'd been working and started wriggling a cage into the soft earth, rocking it back and forth and stopping to reach down now and then to move a branch of the plant out of the way. He leaned on the cane and looked over to the shed.

"Shit," she said under her breath as one of the branches

snapped.

"Bad luck," he said.

She kept working. "What do you want, Jines?"

"I'm just wondering how long you think you might be working here this morning."

"Why would you be wondering that?" She was still bent over the cage and the plant and he was kind of glad for the delicate nature of the task that allowed her to keep her attention focused on it, not him.

"I could use some help in the shed." He thought he saw her hesitate for a second but it was a fleeting thing; she was carefully tugging at the tomato plant's branches. He plowed onward. "I'm having some trouble with that goddamned planer, like I said, and I could use a hand. Wouldn't take long."

"What are you planing?"

"Cedar," he said.

She looked up at him finally.

"Well," she said.

She nodded curtly, the way you do when it's hard to make your mouth say the word yes. Then she bent back over her plants and her bit of earth, and Jines took his leave, figuring if he opened up the shed doors this early the warming breeze might just take the chill out of there by noon, anyway.

Chapter 12

In the morning at the old house, it seemed to Lily, the sun and the river forgave each other any differences of opinion and merged into one element, one long stream of liquid light from due east that flowed past the dock, across the lawn, through the big magnolia tree, into the picture window that took up nearly one whole wall of the kitchen, and across the table where she stood holding a cup of coffee. More than once she'd put on sunglasses to eat breakfast. She knew the eminently practical reasons her forebears had chosen this spot for the house, but she couldn't help wondering if the sunrise didn't have something to do with it, too. Beauty and wonder didn't make the land more fertile or the oyster beds more rich, didn't put food on the table or cool the house with the steady river breeze. But it counted for something. If witnessing this spectacle didn't make you want to get up and out of bed every morning, she thought, you might as well be dead.

She raised the mug to her mouth and grimaced. Even her fingers ached. They had planed wood, she and Jines, all afternoon the day before. Or rather, *she* had planed wood while Jines had bossed her around, enjoying it all the while, she suspected. When she had sat up in bed this morning a curl of cedar fell out of her hair, fluttered to the quilt. She brought it to her nose and drew in the clarifying scent. For all the infernal racket of that machine they had done battle with, for all the hefting and holding and wheedling of board after board, for all of Jines's cursory commands, there was this—this amazing smell that seemed to carry everything within it, the damp, low earth, the slow bend and shush of the loblollies in the breeze, the glow of this morning light.

Jines was parked in front of the lazy Susan, looking none the worse for wear. Out at the dock, the *Jenny Rae* was already gone.

Lily hadn't even heard Jamie or the diesel. This she regretted. It was always pleasurable to watch him walking across the lawn toward the dock in the morning, Maggie clipping along at his heels. She wondered whether he knew or suspected she watched him. He never looked at the house, only toward the river. Did he think about her as he walked by, or was he just thinking about fishing? She had gone down to see him off once or twice, on the excuse of being on her way to the garden or the kayak or something, but he was all business with her then, with his crew standing there half leering. So she just watched, apart. She wasn't sure what she would do if he looked up and saw her there in the window; dive for the floor probably. Stupid. Why couldn't a woman watch a good-looking man walk by? But even she knew that explanation only told half the story. Maybe she didn't want Jamie to see her in that window because he would know the rest of the story, all of it, just in the way she was standing there.

"What we got to do today," Jines butted into her thoughts, "we got to cut out the sides and see if we can't get 'em planed out, then start workin' on the stem. I think I still got a nice hunk of oak set by for the stem. It's a good shape and shouldn't need too much work."

"Good morning to you, too," she said.

He sipped his coffee and eyed her with some amusement. "Little stiff this morning, are you?"

"Right as rain," she said. "You?"

"That Beast'll wear you down, no doubt about it."

"What do you mean, cut out the sides?" She headed for the cupboard. "You want some cereal? Did you take your pills?"

He waved her off with one hand. "That's where you have to start with a boat like this, the sides. I got patterns out there for it."

"Patents?"

"Patterns." He accented the first syllable with some

exaggeration and shook his head. "You been gone from home so long you don't know the sound of your native tongue."

"Not *my* native tongue," she said. "You and all those boys talk like you have oyster shells in your mouths. Up in Maine, it's lobster claws or clamshells or something. Either way, it's all the same; that's waterman native tongue."

He rolled his eyes. "You done?"

"I suppose."

"Good. Patterns, like I said. It's just like sewing a dress, you lay the wood on those patterns and you make your lines and then you cut 'em out with a jigsaw. Then you got to hand plane 'em, make sure they are exactly the same—everything depends on that. You start making little mistakes early on, off a quarter-inch here, a half there, pretty soon you end up with a boat lopsided as a bull with one ball." He cleared his throat. "Excuse the expression."

She emptied out a box of Raisin Bran in a bowl. "I should probably make a run to the Food Lion today. And I need to get out to the garden for awhile."

Jines pushed back his chair, grabbed his cane and headed for the door with a spontaneity and swiftness that surprised her. "Let's get her goin', then."

"Can I eat, or what?"

"Burnin' daylight," he said over his shoulder.

In the shed, all Lily could do at first was wait. She wasn't accustomed to it. She rarely had to wait for anybody, let alone wait for anybody to tell her what to do, and when she did it made her wildly impatient. Here, though, with the smells of cedar and diesel oil and creosote from the wood stove's chimney all mingling in the air around her, she stood hesitantly near the workbench. One hand doodled with a carpenter's pencil on a scrap of paper. It had taken her all day yesterday to get used to what Jines aptly called the Beast. She hated having her hands even close to the mouth of that thing,

228

and either Jines realized that or he just wanted to be in charge because she would drag the wood over and lift it, but he would be the one to feed it in. Then it was her job to get on the output end of the monster and help the wood through, bring it back around if he deemed it unworthy still, or set it on the stack if it was finished. Dressing the wood, that's what he'd called it.

"Why are we doing all this now?" she'd asked after they'd fed what felt like a hundred miles of cedar and oak (cedar for the planking, he'd told her, like she was a pig-tailed student, oak for the frames) into the roaring maw of the Beast, and her arms were shaking from the effort. This, after he had pointed out to her the eighteen-foot length of oak that would be the boat's keelson—its backbone—and they had run that through the planer too. Three times, each side.

"I dress all the wood I can right off the git-go," he'd yelled back at her. "Then it's done and you know you got everything you need."

After a few hours of work she started getting used to the machine and the rattling in her arms, but now again, this morning, she was awkward as a new kid in school, not knowing even where to put her feet. She didn't want to make any mistakes in here. God knows how pissed he'd be at her if she broke one of his tools or messed up with the precious wood.

This shed had always been Jines's territory, and you only came if invited. He'd brought her out here with him when she was a little girl. She remembered the whine of saws, the pitched shriek of the planer, the way she always had to plug her ears whenever Jines worked around those ancient, heavy machines. He never had to. The noise didn't seem to bother him. Nothing out here ever seemed to bother him, she realized. She had sat on a stool watching him build things. Usually it was winter, when he decided against oystering for one reason or another and instead took on a project for someone, a skiff maybe, or some repairs to a friend's workboat. How young had she been? Maybe four, five years old? There was the faint smell of burning as the wood went through the planer. The glorious heat of the potbellied woodstove that despite its age and ample size still couldn't dispel the coldness in the shed's corners. The hum and sway of the pines outside, and the assured movement of her father as he created something strong and beautiful. She'd usually have a can of crayons out here to draw on the bench or on some scrap wood he gave her. Or he would bring her handfuls of wood shavings and sawdust and pile them on an unused portion of the workbench. She would carve entire civilizations in the soft, fragrant flakes, steep little alpine towns of shaved cedar and oak that curled like a baby's hair. "Plug your ears now, honey," he'd say before turning on a big machine, and she would. Every now and then someone like Kenneth would stop by and see how he was progressing, and she remembered the sharp scent of chewing tobacco and the dark squirts of it in the sawdust, brown as cockroaches.

She wished she'd brought another cup of coffee out with her; the night still wasn't out of the building and she knew it wouldn't be for a couple hours yet until the sun had time to work on the tin roof. Even then, it would harbor cold corners. It was like an old person, this shed, never quite able to shake off the chill. Until high summer; then, she suspected, it was probably the exact opposite, an oven. So maybe it was like Jines, contrary no matter the season. Well, he'd built it, she knew that. And she knew enough about building things to know that anything created by hand had some of the soul of that person in it. She'd always envied him that ability, to be able to take a pile of wood or a stick and turn it into something remarkable. She wondered if that was one of the reasons she'd agreed to help him with this. She wondered what Jamie was doing at that very moment.

"Well you just gonna stand there woolgatherin' or you gonna do something?" Jines was over by the stack of lumber aiming his dark-as-a-cave-pool gaze at her and waving her over. "Reach over there, just behind that bench, and see if you can't pull out that big piece of plywood there."

"This one?"

"That's the one."

It was long, at sixteen feet the exact length of the skiff to be. The piece was perhaps two-and-a-half feet wide, and while one edge was straight, the other held a long, graceful curve from one end to the other. It was thin, though, not heavy, and she carried it over easily.

"Careful now, don't want it to split anywheres."

"I am being careful." She laid it out by the stack of wood.

"There's your pattern, see, a template they call it," Jines said. "I've been building boats off this pattern since your granddaddy made it and showed me how to do it." He ran his hand over the thin wood like you would a favorite dog.

"I don't see a boat in there," she said.

"Well," he said, "you will." He ambled to the workbench, waving at her to follow.

"You know, Jines, if these boats are such hot items, I wonder how much you could sell one for these days," Lily said.

"Reach up there and get those clamps for me now. No, no, not those ones, those over there." He pointed with his gnarled finger toward a set of four clamps amid the dozens along the piece of two-by-four that ran along the wall almost the whole length of the workbench.

"How old are these?" she asked, climbing up on a stool to reach them. She handled each one like it was porcelain, carefully lifting them off and down to the workbench. Jines had never let her touch them before. They were covered in dust.

"Well these belonged to your great-granddaddy, so you figure it out."

"They're probably worth a fortune."

"Not a cent," Jines said, "cause I'll never sell 'em."

"So what do you think you could sell one of your skiffs for, like this one you're building?"

"Same thing. I ain't building this skiff to sell it."

"Even so," she said.

"I don't know, depends. I reckon I could get six thousand, maybe more for one nowadays. Not so many people know how to build these anymore."

Lily spun on the stool so quickly she almost fell off. "Jesus, Jines! Six thousand bucks is nothing to sneeze at! Why not sell it and build another one too?"

"Money ain't the point."

"It is when you don't have it and you need it." She thought about the fact that she had another month's rent due on the apartment, as well as the winter storage fees for *Pelagic* and the mooring fee, too. The weeks of half pay had been taking a toll on her bank account; when she'd checked it a few days ago she'd been shocked how quickly it was draining. She could see she wouldn't have enough for rent next month. And what was she going to do about *Pelagic*? Should she call Willy and ask him to haul her and block her for a while? It might save her a couple hundred bucks, but that wasn't going to be enough. She'd been buying all the groceries; it probably never occurred to Jines that maybe he ought to pitch in. Not that he ate very much anymore. She wondered how much he still owed the hospital and the rehab center; he refused to even talk to her about it. She resolved to just open his mail the next time one of the bills came. She had no idea if he was keeping up with it. For all she knew, he hadn't paid a dime, and the collectors were already salivating. Six-thousand bucks was a drop in his bucket, she had no illusions, but it was better than nothing.

He pointed to a suitcase-sized metal box on the shelf under the workbench. "That one, there, we need that."

"I'm serious, Jines." She tugged the box out, set it on the bench. "You have major money issues, and you're not facing it. I wish you would tell me how much you still owe. Have you even paid any of the bills yet?"

Jines opened the box to reveal a saw whose business end looked remarkably like an enormous version of a sewing machine's foot. Instead of a needle projecting through the foot there was a long, thin blade. The motor was encased in a thick, green, plastic cylinder darkened, Lily imagined, by some thousands of dirty hands that had gripped it over the years. Jines reached for an extension cord she guessed had probably been bright yellow at one time and plugged one end into an outlet over the bench and the other into the saw's cord, tying the ends of the two cords together before attaching the plugs.

"Why do you do that?" she asked, pointing to the knot.

"So when you're moving along the wood and your saw's runnin' and the cord gets stuck on the corner or some other damn thing the way cords always do, it don't come undone and you lose power right in the middle of your cut. You ready to quit asking questions and go to work?"

"How the hell am I supposed to learn if I don't ask questions, Jines?"

He stopped then and looked at her with something like surprise on his face, and she wondered if it was reflected in her own. She hadn't suggested this project because she wanted to learn to build a boat; she'd thought it would be good for him to have a way to occupy his mind and keep his body moving, something to get him out of bed and off the porch every day. God knows she practically needed a come-along and a tractor to get him moving for a physical therapy session. Maybe if he had something he wanted to do, he'd get at least some of that therapy without bitching about it or worse still, just blowing it off completely. The healthier Jines became, the better it was for her, the way she saw it. She'd had no intention of ending up out here in this shed with her father taking orders from him—as if she needed that bullshit anymore—and she wasn't quite sure how it had happened that way. But now that she was out here, she might as well be useful. She'd never dueled with anything like the Beast before yesterday, she'd never run a saw like this one Jines was holding, but she suspected she would before the day was out. He put up a good front, but he was far from the powerful man she had known who could work all day, every day. He was going to need her help to build this boat, and it occurred to her that out here in this dusty shed—deep in Jines's personal turf—might be the only place where he could be at ease at all in the asking, and she could be at all comfortable with the giving.

He held up the saw and handed it to her so she could feel the weight of it.

"This," he said, "is a jigsaw. It's what we're gonna cut the sides out with. That's one thing. Second thing is this: When you're out here, your head's in the work, not in some number cruncher's office, not watching Jamie Cockrell's blue jeans walking across the yard, not out gallivantin' in that little skinny boat of yours."

"It's called a kayak. And who says I'm thinking about Jamie Cockrell or his jeans?" She felt her face flush despite herself. She hadn't realized she'd been so obvious. She hadn't known, either, that Jines was watching her.

"Point is, your mind can't be wandering. That's how you lose a finger or worse. This ain't the A-ssociated Press out here." He said this last with a touch of smugness in his voice. Oh, was he ever loving this, having her on the rookie end of the stick.

"Fine." She gritted her teeth around the word.

234

For the next several hours Jines showed Lily how the boat's sides were formed. They spoke little as he traced the pattern out on each of the boards designated to be the sides; he was particularly pleased with these, because they were wide enough to comprise an entire side and would not need to be joined to another board to cover the width. "Any seam on the side's just a weak point, I don't care how strong you make it," he told her. "You try and find wood like this at any local lumberyard, I dare you. They don't make 'em. They can't." He was full of himself on this point, positively ebullient for Jines.

Once the patterns were traced on the boards he had her lay one piece aside and left the other up on the sawhorses, then fired up the jigsaw and carefully pushed it along the lines, cutting out the pattern. As the saw advanced, the extraneous wood started to sag and tug, and he had her nudge along next to him holding it up—so it wouldn't pinch the saw blade, he shouted to her over the saw's noisy whine. He made it through one whole side, had her take that piece off the sawhorses and replace it with the uncut second side, and he then he passed her the saw. He could barely lift it, and his hands were shaking. When she took the saw from him he massaged his forearm, and she wondered whether that was to make his hands and arm feel better or to hide his pain and tiredness from her. Maybe this whole skiff thing wasn't such a great idea, she thought. Wouldn't that be ironic, her pushing him into something that would stroke him out just as quickly as fishing could have. The saw was warm in her hands.

"Here's the switch," he said. "You push it up one more notch here to make it lock, so the saw will stay on. Elsewise it'll stop if you don't keep pressure on that switch, and your fingers'll get tired." He held up a hand, signaling her to wait, and shuffled to the workbench, returning with a pair of clear plastic safely glasses. He handed them to her.

"You didn't use them," she said.

"Put 'em on."

She wasn't going to argue. She was nervous about the cutting—what if the saw caught and snapped back, or what if she got off the line of the pattern and messed up the whole thing, this beautiful, perfect plane of wood about which Jines was so proud and happy? Did he have another lying around somewhere or was this one it? If she messed it up irrevocably, would he be able to join two pieces together in a way that would not be weak, that would be strong enough?

"What are you waiting for?" he asked.

She looked at him, and he took hold of her hands on the saw, switched it on, and moved it toward the edge of the board.

"Don't be shy with it," he yelled. "Keep her movin' or she'll bog down."

So startled was she to feel the raspy warmth of Jines's big hands across her own, guiding the saw into the side of the board and toward the pattern's line, that she forgot about screwing up long enough to feel the saw's movement through the wood. It wasn't hard; the blade gnawed quickly at the cedar, the dust of its passing jittering across the wood like tiny dancing bugs. The saw reached the line and they started pushing the blade along it, Jines's body bumping against hers still guiding her hands. After a minute he moved away, his hands holding the outer edge of the board as it started to sag. Only once, when she had to make a tricky corner, did he come in to correct her as she started off course, and she realized he was right; you couldn't be timid with this particular saw, you had to tell it where to go without hesitation. Around the pattern's long lines they went in tandem, Lily pushing the saw and Jines next to her making sure the extraneous wood didn't snag the blade, until she finished the final long stretch and the saw blade sang a little as she eased it out through the edge of the wood. She switched it off, and there was that sudden startling silence again, as when Jines had turned off the Beast the day before, a silence that was somehow loud. It took a minute before she could hear the birds outside and the early afternoon sea breeze starting up in the trees. Her hands were tingling from the saw, and she flexed them in and out.

"Okay," said Jines, shuffling to the workbench and picking up the cane that leaned there, then heading for the door. "We'll true 'em up after lunch and then see about that stem."

But after lunch Jines told her he could proceed that afternoon in the shed himself. "You said you had some chores in the garden, and the Food Lion too," he said.

"Are you sure?" she asked. "What do you mean, true up the sides?"

"You clamp them together and make sure they're exactly the same. Mostly using a hand plane anyway, one-person job. You go on with your errands."

And he pushed himself slowly up from the table and moved out the porch door and across the lawn like an aged bull ambling for the shade of an apple tree on a hot summer day. Lily found herself standing there in one spot holding a sandwich plate, watching him go. If it were only hand planes he was using that meant no power tools that could hack off a limb or a digit, presumably. She rinsed off the plates and put them in the drying rack, wondering what she'd expected—an attagirl, maybe, for her victory over the jigsaw? A thanks a lot, honey? Not likely. She might as well quit while she was ahead if she hoped for that from Jines. She stood on the porch, turning her attention to the river and the garden. It was a beautiful day, and she wanted to see if Mamie had gotten any zinnias yet; she had set aside two rows and could get them in this afternoon and work on her tan at the same time. Although she probably shouldn't stop at the House of Deals; every time she did she dropped another thirty bucks on plants for the garden. She frowned. Okay, maybe no plants. She'd see how much the grocery bill was. But she could talk with Jamie when he came back in, see how the fishing was going. Lily squared up her shoulders, grabbed the small leather backpack that served as her purse and headed for the truck, doing her best to push aside the strange, fresh tendril of loneliness that followed her from the open door of the shed.

She stopped at the mailbox on her way of out the driveway and found two pieces of mail mixed in with the weekly *Mathews County Intelligencer*, one from the Associated Press' bureau in Portland, the other from the Tri-County Medical Center and Wilcox Memorial Rehabilitation's billing department. Despite her earlier resolve about the bills, she didn't want to open either. What a week this had been already for shitty mail. Three days ago it had been the new property tax bill, which had doubled since the county had reassessed everything. Jines had been furious, ranting about "those rich rat bastards from that shithouse of a city, Washington, D.C.," moving to the river, buying up all the houses and land at insane prices, driving out all the locals who couldn't afford to pay the higher taxes. On this point she had to agree with him. She let these two new pieces of what could only be bad news sit there on the seat burning holes in it while she drove to the Food Lion where she forgot half of what she had intended to buy and had to go back in twice. She loaded the groceries and got back in the truck, looked at the mail and said, "Hell." She tore them open one at a time.

The first letter, from the AP, was from Michael telling her what she already knew—that her allowable leave was finished in two more weeks—and he wanted to know her intentions as to whether she planned to return to work or not. If her decision was the latter, he explained in exquisitely crafted office-speak, he could possibly facilitate a transfer to another bureau, perhaps Richmond or Norfolk, although he could only make a recommendation, as he

238

had no influence on their staffing situations. He was certain they would be pleased to consider a staff writer of her caliber, experience, and dedication. He had copied the letter to the personnel department at headquarters in New York. She shoved it back into the envelope. The new J-grad intern who had filled in during her absence must be working out just hunky dory for dear old Michael; perhaps she gave great blow jobs. Two weeks. No zinnias today.

The second letter was not a letter but a bill, which she had also expected. This, though, was worse than she had feared. Jines had evidently paid some of the initial medical expenses; there was a credit of ten thousand dollars. But he was thirty days overdue on the remainder, sixty thousand dollars, and from what she could tell, this bill didn't include the last full week of his time at the rehab, nor his more recent visit to the hospital after the Seven Brothers accident. Add to that the new property tax bill, another twenty-thousand, due in a month. Plus whatever might happen in the future. Lily felt a gnawing in her stomach that had nothing to do with hunger. She wondered if there was any way for Jines to get insurance now. Even if the answer were yes she was certain it would cost an arm and a leg. Rich men in suits, Jines had said, making money off scaring people. Well, she couldn't disagree too much with him on that point, even if he had been an idiot not to just swallow his pride and get the insurance. Now he was looking at a financial hole like he'd never been in. Or rather, he wasn't looking, and that's the part that alarmed her most. It seemed like he simply couldn't deal with it. She'd seen him pick the bills up off the table where she'd left them and shovel them into his pocket, never even open them. She'd find them later in the trashcan or crumpled up on his floor, still unopened. She knew that feeling of being completely overwhelmed by circumstances and events and how it could paralyze a person. But somehow she had to get Jines to wake up. He couldn't just pretend it would all go away.

She threw the bills onto the seat next to her. She picked up the *Intelligencer*. The little weekly had all the juicy local stuff, marriages, divorces, property transfers, and the ever-popular DWI page, which included photographs of those unfortunate enough to find their fifteen minutes of fame this way, as well as weekly specials at the Seaside (if there happened to be any), local tides, the fishing report, who was catching what, that sort of thing. She flicked irritably through the pages, not really registering anything; there was a grip-and-grin of some county councilman accepting the Boy Scouts' Silver Beaver award for his years of supporting the organization; the obligatory weekly wreck photo (this one of a tractor-trailer that had lost it on Route 202 and dumped an entire load of melons); and a big black-and-white photo of a fifteen-year-old from Reedville who'd caught a trophy rockfish last weekend off the lighthouse, forty-six inches long. He was holding the huge fish like he was holding a pile of lumber, barely supporting its dead weight in his arms. Next to the photo was an advertisement for River Realty. "Buy a Piece of Paradise," it said, right over a photo of Bradford C. Wilson himself. Even in the newsprint she could see the gleam in his overly whitened teeth. She reached into her wallet and took out the business card she had tucked there, looked again at those numbers he'd written on the back. There had to be somebody better to work with, someone less odious, but he'd already thrown the offer out there. She knew she didn't have the legal right to sell any of the property, but there was something called momentum. Nobody said she couldn't get the ball rolling. If she rolled it carefully enough, maybe Jines would have to pick it up. Out here in the Food Lion parking lot, her cell phone had plenty of signal. She started dialing.

"I've got one word for you. Power of attorney."

Bradford C. Wilson was leaning over the table at her in a close, conspiratorial fashion that Lily found completely disgusting. The arms of his perfectly pressed, dry-cleaned Oxford shirt looked wildly out of place on the red-and-white-checked plastic tablecloth. He had taken off his Ray-Bans and hooked them into a buttonhole on the front of his shirt, next to the pocket embroidered with *BCW* in cursive. Initials on the pocket this time, Lily thought. Must be summer wear. Down at the waist for fall and spring.

"That's three words."

He waved his hand. "Whatever. It's the concept. You need one."

"Not going to happen," Lily said.

Whatever else she may think of her father, he wasn't incompetent in a legal sense. The rehab center caseworker had talked with her about the possibility of a power of attorney, but Jines had recovered so quickly that they ruled out the necessity. And there was no way Jines would, at this point, ever agree to giving her that authority. She remembered the feel of his hands on hers as he had guided her with the jigsaw. Despite their roughness, he'd been quite gentle in the way he'd taught her what to do. She felt vaguely guilty even sitting here with Bradford C. Wilson and his gold Rolex and Ray-Bans and embroidered shirt, as if she were committing adultery and they were engaged in a secret tryst. Not that Pizza Heaven in Lively, Virginia, was what one would consider an ideal location for such an encounter. But she couldn't exactly meet him at the Seaside. Jines would learn about it before she even got back to the house. She shook off the sleazy feelings; she was doing this for him, so why should she feel guilty about it? If she could work with this guy and find a buyer for some of the land, get it all set up and then bring the proposal—and the promise of cash—to Jines, she didn't see how he could refuse. It made perfect sense. He'd be out of the hole, free as a bird to do whatever he wished with no worries about money anymore. He was just being stubborn, that was all, and he was scared of changing anything. If she could get a deal far enough down the road, maybe she could make him see that the change wouldn't be so bad, and in fact would have benefits that made it well worth it.

"I don't know whether I can get any buyers to bite if they know you don't have the legal authority to sell the land."

"Somehow I think you'll manage."

She waved to the waitress and asked for an iced tea, sweet. Bradford C. Wilson looked smugly back at her. She could swear he was preening.

"It's true I do have my methods," he grinned. "I can be quite convincing. I am passionate, after all, about what I do."

He took a delicate bite of his Greek salad. He'd piled all the olives to one side, like a little mound of cannonballs. She was willing to bet he pressed his Jockeys. A tiny bit of salad oil pinched in the corner of his mouth and began oozing. Lily didn't feel inclined to give him the heads up about it.

"Why won't your father just meet with me?"

"It's complicated," Lily said. "He's old school Ophelia, he doesn't trust anybody from the outside."

"Then I have to ask, if you don't own the place, why are you trying to sell it for him? Where's the fire?"

"I'm not trying to sell the place. And the fire's none of your business."

"Oh, hey," Bradford C. Wilson threw up his hands. "Don't take offense. The less I know about your private lives, the happier I'll be."

Not bloody likely, thought Lily. She sipped her tea and gnawed on a piece of garlic bread.

"How much are you thinking of selling?"

"One lot. At the price you quoted."

"Things change."

"Please," Lily said. "Don't patronize me. There's one lot, over on the north side. You could take the right-of-way off the main driveway. It would be far enough not to disturb the main house or the rest of the land." She tore off another piece of bread. "And, I would want covenants. Restrictions on the size of what could be built there, how many trees could be taken down, that sort of thing."

Bradford C. Wilson managed the hurt puppy look. "Lily—"

"It's Miss Evans."

"Sorry." He giggled like a mischievous schoolboy, then switched it to a little frown. "Miss Evans, now you're going to make it even harder for me to find a buyer. Who's going to want to enter a tenuous deal that dictates what they can and cannot do with their dream property?"

Lily put both of her hands on the edge of the table and felt the soreness in them. She leaned across the table at Bradford C. Wilson, her voice low and tight.

"That property, Mr. Wilson, was the dream of my great-grandfather. I won't see it turned into one of these obscene monuments to money and ego that are popping up all over this river like zits on a teenager. I won't see all the trees and habitat destroyed to make way for another ChemLawn wet dream, dumping its fertilizer into the river every time it rains. If that's the deal, the deal's off."

"Oh, hey." He leaned back, adopting his amiable look again. He waved his hands over his salad in what she thought must be his idea of a soothing motion. "I didn't mean to offend. I know the locals can be very sensitive about what is their birthright, after all. There's a certain defensiveness." He wiped his mouth, finally, and his eyes took on a more carnivorous look than she had seen in him to this point. "But you have to see it from the buyer's perspective too.

They are paying top dollar for the land. They are helping make some rather poor people quite wealthy. They're performing a certain service, after all. And regardless of what you say about the changing face of the river, people are lining up to sell."

Lily abruptly tossed her napkin on the table and pushed her chair back. She reached for her wallet.

"This was a mistake. Sorry I wasted your time." She wasn't even out of the chair before the predatory look was gone from his eyes, replaced again by the hurt puppy, and he was reaching one hand out to her.

"Oh, hey now, come on, Miss Evans. No need to feel that way. If you want covenants, we can require covenants. This is a sensitive situation, I understand."

You have the understanding of a gnat's ass, she thought. She ought to walk out of here right now and forget about this. But even while she considered it, she couldn't see another way out for Jines. And as hard as it had been for her to accept the idea, she realized her fate was linked to his, whether it involved money or not. If she simply headed back to Maine, to whatever it was she thought she still had there, she knew Jines wouldn't face this situation he was in. Things would get ugly. He could lose the house, the very heart of the place, if not everything. And the fact was, Lily had become too attached to the house and all it held for her to be able to stomach the idea that he might lose it simply because he was too willful or frightened to deal with the problem head on. She would have to do it for him, at least as far as she could. Whether he just didn't understand what he was up against, or he just refused to face it, the way was clear: Sell a piece of the land on the edge of the property, restrict as much as possible what could be done to it, use the proceeds to pay off Jines's bills, set some aside for him to live on, and invest the rest for whatever his future might hold. Then, and only then, could she see the framework of her own future. She stood from her chair, set some money down on the table.

"Come to the house tomorrow at three-thirty, sharp. My father has a doctor's appointment, and I can drop him off and come back to get him. I will show you the land. Then we'll see if we can proceed."

Bradford C. Wilson was saying something behind her, but she didn't care, she didn't want to hear anymore. She didn't like what she had to do. But she knew one thing: She could be as ruthless as her father if she needed to be. It was a gift.

Chapter 13

He put his hands on the wood, and for a time, that's where he felt they should be. Carefully he placed the boards together, the sides he and Lily had just cut, and clamped them as one with the big wooden clamps that had belonged to his granddaddy. This was not easy. The boards were bulky and long, heavy, and they fought him. He could have used her help, that much was true. She was doing all right. He could have done without all the chatterbox questions, and it did feel odd having her out here with him. It was as if she was two people at once, someone totally familiar, whose voice he didn't even need to hear to understand her every thought, and yet completely new. Damned confusing at times. All the same, she was doing all right.

He chose a hand plane from the bench and laid it against the edges of the wood. He pushed it briskly, trying to be firm, and was rewarded with several long peels of cedar and that satisfying tingle in his forearms and shoulders. Satisfying for now, probably be sore as a bastard by tomorrow. Still, it sure beat squeezing a rubber ball and doing curls with a weighted bar all day. The steady sliding of the plane made a whisking sound, and he finished one long edge of the sides and stopped to catch his breath. It had been a long morning, although when he thought about it against all the other mornings, what back in the day had been a long morning, it was nothing, it was a sneeze, and he felt ashamed and small and yes, he was angry. But it was only a moment of frustration that eddied up and then was gone like the swirl a fish would make on the water's surface when it was thinking about mayflies. It didn't go anywhere, it didn't last. He wondered briefly about this. He supposed it could be possible to just get too tired to be angry anymore. Worn out like an old engine that's been run too long and hard. But then what?

The headaches had been coming back. They scared him. He didn't remember much about the first stroke but he did remember the searing pain in his head, the fog across his eyes. Maybe they were just plain headaches. Man shouldn't be surprised to get a headache from time to time, should he? Anyway, damned if he was going to say anything to anybody about it. They'd have him back in that hospital quick as a cat, and he plain wasn't going. He'd had enough.

The wind made the tops of the loblollies outside the shed sing and sigh, he heard them in their long swaying breath. It was always windy here. Give a day enough time to really wake up, and there would be the sea breeze, always up from the south, unless there was something bigger to push it out of the way like a cold front or a nor'easter or heaven forbid a hurricane. He thought about Jamie and his boys out there on the *Jenny Rae*, moving in that wind. It had been hard, at first, to wake up in the morning and see the dock empty, or even to hear the diesel as Jamie fired her up and then moved off. But Jamie had been doing well, bringing in good loads of fish, and he made a point to come and talk with Jines about how the days were going, how the boat was doing. Every now and then he'd ask for advice on a particular aspect of the pounds or the boat. At first he'd been nervous about it, Jines could tell, probably didn't want to rub it in his face that it was him out there and not Jines. But Jines hadn't bitten his head off. Fact was, he liked the conversations. Made him feel he was still a part of things after all, when he could offer up a story or explain how to do something that Jamie hadn't quite figured out. It was a comfort to realize that all the old know-how wasn't just going to up and disappear along with him. And there was something good, too, about it knowing he'd arranged it so his boat was still working. At least the *Jenny Rae* could still be out there doing what she was born to do. It was like a piece of him was still out there, and aye God that was better than nothing.

Jines laid the plane along the other length of the sides, but his thoughts turned to the piece of oak for the stem. He'd need that before he could progress any further. Suddenly he felt so tired. His arms ached. Sixteen feet felt like sixteen miles. Should have carved a model instead. Maybe if he just took a little rest over there on the davenport. He shuffled over to it and got a nose full of dust when he got himself down onto the thing. He thought he heard rain on the roof overhead, but when he looked toward the door there was still sunlight streaming in. Maybe stuff falling out of the trees, pine needles and such. Who the hell knew? He'd seen rain and sun at the same time before, he'd seen snow and a thunderstorm all at once too. What was the weather doing today anyway? He hadn't listened to the radio to find out. He'd been thinking about the skiff, not the fishing. He tried hard not to think about the fishing.

And just like that she was there, Jenny Rae, standing in the door, and this didn't seem strange to him. Almost like he'd been expecting it. She was as beautiful as ever, but her hands were muddy. Not her dress though, her dress was still white as a cloud.

"Why are your hands all muddy, Jenny Rae?" he asked her.

"I've been in the garden of course."

Her voice was like music. In some far off place in his body he felt like he might be sick to his stomach. Some place in his body that was all wrong again, not buying the idea that his dead wife had just stepped in from the pea patch. He felt the searing in his head. She came toward him but he didn't see any movement that got her there. She was just there suddenly, next to him, like he'd blinked his eyes too long. He thought he should be so happy to see her, but it didn't feel to him as if she'd been gone.

"I don't understand."

"Don't understand what, Jines?"

"Your hands are all muddy, but your dress is clean."

She shrugged. "Why worry about it?" she said.

His head hurt. Throbbed and throbbed. "My head hurts," he said.

She reached out to touch him then as if to soothe him, but he didn't feel it. There was the slight pressure of her hand, but nothing more, as if he'd been shot up with novocaine. He felt suddenly robbed by this. Here was his Jenny Rae, reaching toward him, and he couldn't feel even the warmth of her fingers on his face. He started to cry.

"Why are you crying, Jines?"

"I'm weak, Jenny, I'm tired all the time." His head dropped to his chest and it heaved beneath him. Tears poured down his face and fell on his pants like fat raindrops. "I can't even feel you. I can't feel nothin'."

"Well I don't see why not. It's not as if you're dead, Jines Arley."

"Are you sure?" He could not stop weeping. The sound of his own blubbering filled his ears.

"Of course I'm sure. You're being silly. I'll be in the garden." And she turned and floated away.

No one had called him silly in a very long time. No one ever called him silly except for her. And suddenly the range of years stretched out before him, like a hundred doors had been thrown open at once and allowed light that was decades old to stream into him, and he felt the full weight of his loneliness again, of missing her. She wasn't really there, and even though he knew this he couldn't help himself from wanting to follow her.

Chapter 14

"Tell me about who the best boatbuilders were, Jines."

"Hold that now, just hold that for me."

They were getting ready to bend the chine, and Jines was fitting what he called a stretcher into the skiff's bow. It was a short piece of two-by-four and he'd angled the ends a little on the band saw. He was sizing it to sit about three feet back from the skiff's stem between the sides. It would only be temporary, he had explained, just a piece to hold the sides as they started bending the back of the boat into place. He didn't want the sides to start pulling out of the rabbet joint in the stem as he bent the sides. The stretcher helped prevent that from happening.

"Okay, take this now," he said, handing her the stretcher.

She wiped a bead of sweat off her nose. The late spring had taken a warm turn suddenly; it could do that around here, she remembered. One day it would be fifty-five degrees, the next eighty. Her T-shirt was sticking to her back. Rabbets, bending chines, stretchers; Lily was fascinated by the words. Every discipline had its own language. She'd learned that early on just being around the water and boats. She had plowed through drifts of legalese during a brief stint covering the state supreme court in Maine, she had parsed the convoluted sentences of school administrators who seemed, ironically, to be entirely deaf to the merits of clarity in education. She found that she loved the vernacular of the woodshop and of boatbuilding.

"Why is it called a rabbet?" she would ask him, and most of the time he would just shrug and say, "Why are you called Lily Rae? It's your name." But then he might go on and explain how it was done, and show her why it was done that particular way. And somehow it always made sense, and this was why she loved it so much.

Usually, what sounded arcane was entirely obvious once he'd explained it to her. They were called biscuits, he said, because the small wafers of wood looked like little crackers or biscuits; consequently it was called a biscuit joiner because it was a tool used to join two pieces of wood using the biscuits as fasteners by sliding them into slots. When you ran a board through a sawmill but left the bark edge intact it was called flitch sawn. She just liked the sound of that word—flitch—and really, that's what that shaggy edge resembled, the sound of the word. One of her favorite terms was to sister a piece of wood. That meant to strengthen or repair a section of wood you might not want to get rid of—or couldn't because it was too structural—by laying in a piece or even two pieces alongside it and fastening them all together, the multitude being stronger than the one. You could do this, Jines explained, to shore up a column under a porch, repair a rafter in your house or a rib in your boat. And bending the chine was just what it said it was: The point in the building process when you began to force a curve into the boat's sides. Chine, Jines explained to her, described the shape and structure of the hull where the bottom met the sides. A hard-chined boat had a sharp edge where the side met the hull at the waterline. A soft-chined boat had sides that curved without that edge. The skiff was hard-chined, as were most traditional Bay boats. For one thing, Jines said, it made them easier to build, since you didn't have to spend a lot of time shaping the sides; you just laid them up, cut them out, then bent the chine, made sure the sides were true and even, and started pounding in bottom planks. And up toward the bow, even those planks took on a separate name: Staving.

"Staving," she said, rolling the word around in her mouth. "Why's it called staving?"

"Aye God, it just is!" he'd snapped.

But every now and then she'd see what she thought was a grin as she asked question after question. And she couldn't help it. The words seemed as unique and integral to the skiff as every step in the process. As if it couldn't be the same skiff, from her father's hands and his shop, without the words going into each joint and cut, and the light smell of the cedar shavings underfoot mingling with the deeper, woodsier scent of the loblollies overhead.

"All right now," he said, finally satisfied with the forward stretcher. "We may have to move her a little as we go along here, but we'll see."

"Why would you have to move it again?"

"Well, this is part of how you decide how a boat's gonna look, how it's gonna go through the water," he said. "You want a boat with a fuller bow, you'll move that stretcher up a little bit, let the bow push out some. You want a finer bow, you ease her back."

"So you can change the shape of the boat as you build it?"

"To a point. It's all in this time now when we decide how she's gonna be. But once we got the transom attached, then you're pretty well set. Then you lay in the ribs, keelson, keel, and start with the bottom." He moved stiffly toward the workbench. "Well, the best of the best around here was Sonny Hudgins, hands down. He was your mama's great uncle."

For a second she couldn't figure out what he was talking about; then she remembered her question about the boatbuilders. Jines was pulling something out from under the workbench, and his comments about Sonny Hudgins, whom Lily could only remember for the sharp smell of the cheroots he always smoked, came in fits and starts.

"There was just something—ah, Jesus—about the way his boats went through the water—goddamn this thing—made 'em slip through just about any seas." He stood up and said, "Gimme a hand with this."

"This" was a contraption of two parallel pieces of wood with what looked like a cat's cradle of half-inch rope between them. It had pulleys on each end. "What on earth is that called?" she asked.

"You honest-to-God got me on that one," Jines said. "I got no idea."

"You're kidding. I thought everything had a name out here." She felt a vague disappointment.

"Oh, no doubt it's got a name, but damned if I know it." He took one side of it and handed her the other. Then he started working it apart, easing the lines between, to stretch it as wide as it could go until there was no line left to slacken. "Gilbert White, of course, down to Foxwells, now he was known for his deck boats," Jines said as he worked the line. "Most of them boys were buildin' boats before the electricity, so they never had anything like the band saw there, nor even so much as a light bulb. Gilbert, he used an axe and a hatchet. That was it. He built a fifty-, sixty-foot boat that way, all by eye and elbow grease." Jines clamped his piece of wood to the stern-most end of one of the skiff's sides, then moved over to Lily and clamped the second piece to the other side right across from it. The cat's cradle of line stretched across the open space of what would become the skiff's transom, once the two sides had been pulled closer together and the skiff took its proper shape. At the moment, it looked to Lily like a giant letter "V."

"There was Alton Smith, down to Pepper Creek, where his daddy started a big railway. Aye God he built a purty boat." The contraption squeaked a little as he manipulated the line. "Your granddaddy was one of the best too, you know that. He's the one invented this thing, whatever it's called. All them other boys used a come-along, or even a Spanish windlass. They work fine, but this thing, it gives you a lot more control over the bending. Those pulleys there let you control and adjust the angles a lot better."

"Spanish windlass?" she asked, but Jines's eyes suddenly went glassy, and he leaned on the sawhorse that was holding up the skiff.

His big hand gripped the edge of the wood, and his face, which had been bright red all this warm day, was suddenly washed of color.

"Jines," she said, and grabbed his arm. "Can you get to the couch? Come on." He leaned on her hard all the way. "I'm going to get you some water. Do not move."

And she ran out of the shed and up to the house, cursing herself for not having a bottle of water right there in the shed all the time. It was stupid. He had recovered so quickly from the stroke, he seemed so normal most of the time, especially when they were working on the skiff, that she forgot he'd been close to the edge only a few months ago. When she came back his head was leaned back and his eyes were closed, but his color was coming back a bit. She handed him the water. His hands shook as he held the plastic bottle. Right out of the fridge, its sides were already sweating with condensation in the humid air. "It's warm today, Jines, I'm thinking maybe you've done enough."

He shook his head. "We get her stretched we can take a break."

"It can wait."

"If every time I feel like hell I stop, I'll be dead and she won't be done."

Lily watched as he took tentative sips of water. "Make sure you drink that whole bottle, Jines."

"Don't boss me, dammit!"

She felt herself tighten up and was surprised that her eyes stung with quick, angry tears. She turned back to the skiff. It was always this, always. She never knew when it would come, but she always knew it would. It was so tiresome, all of it. She had enjoyed his talk of the boatbuilders. She had enjoyed the sound of his voice, not really paying attention to her, just talking to her like she was a normal anybody, not so much his daughter. Now she stood there, waiting, willing back tears and wanting nothing more than to be gone. She was thirty-two years old, for God's sake. Why should she put up with this shit anymore? And why should it still hurt so much? She could just walk out, but who knew what he might get into then? Without knowing the next step on the boat, she could do nothing with her hands or herself. It was this helplessness she hated. And so Jines had assumed control again, she realized, just that quickly. Did he even know he did it? Did he set out to make her feel beaten, or was that just his lifelong habit of pushing people around? She thought, the hell with him. She squared up her shoulders and headed for the door.

"Tell you what," she said, "I'll be in the garden." And she was almost out when his voice stopped her once more.

"You stretch it," he said.

"I don't know how!" She hated the pitch of her voice but it flew out there on its angry, tremulous wing and she couldn't stop it.

"It ain't so hard." Now his voice just sounded tired. "Get over to those pulleys there and just start easing them in."

"Why should I do that, Jines?"

Even as she said it she knew it was a mistake. Why let him know she was still vulnerable, after all this time, still the daughter he could crack like an egg with just the right tap. Did she think that the sweet smell of cedar and the sweat on her back was going to make her someone else? She didn't know where this infuriating hope came from in her, this idea that he could love her after all, but she despised it, for its partner and co-conspirator was weakness, and no one knew better than she that Jines couldn't stomach weakness. Red flag to a bull, knowing that someone might need him for something.

"The pulleys, see, they let you tighten the line nice and even," he said as if he hadn't heard her. "If it makes a little noise as you start that's okay, probably just the skiff sliding on the sawhorses a bit. This wood's been setting so long, though, she's a might dry. We might want to wipe her with some kerosene, just to help her bend."

Kerosene. In the context of the moment, it seemed a nice, neutral word. She took a deep, quiet breath, trying to hold her shoulders level so he wouldn't see it, and she said, "Kerosene."

It was in a small room off the back of the shed, where he kept various solvents and paints. She tried not to look too closely at the rusted cans and tins lining the wooden shelves; it was a mini Superfund site in here. God knows how long these things had been sitting through freeze and thaw, years of cooking, dissolving, transmogrifying into something never intended. She took another shaky breath as she scanned the shelves for the can he'd described and swore she was going to sit on the dock and watch the sunset tonight with a whole bottle of wine to herself, her withering bank account be damned. She found the can and a box of rags and took them into the shop. He was still on the couch. The water bottle was very nearly empty.

"There's rubber gloves in there too," he said to her.

Back she went into the small room, certain that Jines had never once used a rubber glove in his life.

"Interesting way of showing his affection," she muttered under her breath, "making sure my hands don't sting."

At his instruction, she soaked a rag in kerosene and washed the sides of the skiff with long, slow strokes. It seemed a shame to overpower the cedar scent with that of the chemical, but worse still she supposed to suffer the wood to crack under the stretching. It was dry, he'd said. It had sat so long. It needed a little help. I can help the wood, she thought, it won't mind. It might even like it.

Once the sides were soaked he explained how to slowly tighten the pulley mechanism, and the two ends of the back of boat began to bend inward as she tightened notch by notch. The skiff was starting to look more like a boat now, less like a snowplow. He told her to set the stretcher in place, and she inserted it where he had made his marks, tapping it in with a mallet. She realized as she slowly cranked up the tension in the lines that she was nervous. Every now and then the wood would ping, like a sudden crack ricocheting through a long sheet of ice, and each time it made her twitch. She wasn't sure she could stand to be the one to split the skiff's side.

"How much more?" she asked.

Jines heaved himself up from the couch unsteadily. She let him stand there, make his way across to her on his own, and told herself it was because she needed to keep her hand on the pulley mechanism.

He looked down the side, eyeballing it, and said, "Let's stop there and let her set up for the night. A little more tomorrow, we'll set in a stretcher in the middle, stretch her some more and then get the transom in."

"You just leave it like this?"

"You're asking it to do something that don't come natural," he said, already making for the door. He'd grabbed the cane that was by the couch and was leaning on it hard to one side. He resembled a ship that had taken on a debilitating list. "It needs time."

The sunset was promising a glorious flare when Jamie emerged from the culling shed and saw her sitting on the dock. This hadn't been her intention, or maybe it had, but either way he hesitated and then, instead of following the crew he'd taken out today to the trucks parked beside the shed, he waved them goodbye and walked toward her. She watched the fleet of trucks clatter down the driveway as Jamie sat down beside her. He had a beer in one hand and with the other he lit a cigarette. He sighed. "Long day," he said.

"You can say that again."

"How's it coming out there?"

She shrugged. "It sure isn't boring."

He waved his Budweiser toward the glass of wine at her side

and then out toward the western sky. "Gonna be a beautiful evening."

"Yes."

He looked at her quizzically. "Woman of few words?"

She smiled, though she wasn't sure at that moment what she wanted. Did she want to just be alone with the setting sun and the river? Did she want the company of this man who smelled of fish and somehow managed nevertheless to be completely desirable in his jeans and work boots and T-shirt, this man who was once a boy she knew but who now was someone else entirely, the father of a wondrous child? Who couldn't seem to figure out whether he wanted to go forward toward her or backward toward his ex-wife, a woman who pulled his strings with such precision and ease? When did we all get so complicated, Lily wondered.

"Sorry," she said, "I don't mean to be." She took a long sip of wine and let it pool around in her mouth before swallowing it. "Jines and I kind of got into it a little this afternoon. I don't know why it always surprises me, but it does."

"Hurts you, you mean." He didn't look at her, but instead kept his eyes along the river.

"I didn't say that."

Jamie finished his cigarette and stubbed it out on the dock. Unlike most of the other men he never tossed his butts. Instead, he meticulously field dressed them, taking them apart so that he could scatter the remaining tobacco and pocket the filter. The third time she'd noticed this she'd asked him why; he said Belle had given him grief for being a litterbug and finally had brought home from school some information she'd found on the Internet stating that the single most common piece of trash on beaches and elsewhere was cigarette butts. "Something like two hundred million pounds of them a year, just in the U.S., " he had said. "She guilted me into it."

Now he carefully dismantled the spent cigarette butt and

finished his beer with a long head-tilting swig. Lily watched his Adam's apple.

"No," he said to Lily, "you didn't say that." He stood up. "I need another beer, you need some more wine, and this sunset needs a river cruise to truly appreciate it. What do you say?" He held out his hand to her.

"Don't you need to get home to Belle?"

"Belle's with Gina this weekend. They're going to Norfolk to see *The Lion King* or something."

Though she knew she had no right, Lily hated the very thought of it. What kind of grand scheme made it possible for a manipulative witch like Regina to be the mother of this girl who pulled up a yearning in Lily so deep and strong she was sure it must have always been there, the way your body was capable of doing something it had always known to do even if you weren't aware of it. Probably the same kind of grand scheme that had landed her back here in the first place. Somebody up there had a twisted sense of humor. She was feeling sorry for herself and knew it. She had been since Jines had snapped at her in the shed. It wasn't making her feel a whole lot better.

Jamie's hand was still out there, waiting. She took it, and he gave her a tug and she was on her feet. She went up to the house and checked on Jines, who growled that he could fend for himself for dinner, aye God, did she think he hadn't known how to eat before she came back? She grabbed a couple of towels, a hunk of cheese, some apples, and a box of Wheat Thins and the bottle of wine she'd left in the fridge. By the time she reached the dock again the *Jenny Rae*'s diesel was rumbling, and Jamie's big hand lifting her over the gunwale made her feel as light as milkweed down.

Throttled up to cruising speed, the diesel pretty much precluded conversation. She sliced some of the cheese and apple and set it out on a plate on the engine box, then poured herself another glass of wine. It had been an indulgence, this bottle, even though it wasn't anything fancy. She had felt guilty about spending the eleven bucks, but she let it go for now. It tasted lovely. The river stretched out before them as the boat slid toward the darkening eastern sky. Jamie slowed down to let the cable ferry pass. The ferry driver waved from the little shack where he sat at the helm, and Jamie waved back. He throttled back up and the *Jenny Rae* pushed onward. Piney Island passed to starboard. She pointed to it.

"Why don't we beach her there?" she shouted.

Jamie shook his head. He touched her arm as if to make sure he had her attention.

"Ospreys," he said. "They have chicks now. We'd really piss 'em off." He leaned closer to her ear. "Besides, I've got a surprise for you."

Her arm felt warm where he'd placed his hand. She nodded, and they were silent again as the boat cruised past the island and out through the jetties. She sat on the engine box and faced aft, watching the sunset paint its way across the sky. He touched her arm again, this time to point out a bald eagle flying low. The great bird lowered its talons and dragged them in the water, then banked upward and away. Jamie grinned, and Lily realized that in this way he had not changed; he still loved the wild beauty of the river and the Bay as much as he ever had. They had been like river animals themselves as they spent long summer days dreaming up countless adventurous scenarios in their young ramblings. Hidden pirate treasure was a frequent and time-honored source of material, as was the escape-from-the-horrible-orphanage theme, the getaway always being made in the skiff through croc-infested waters. Poking around in the woods they would find bleached animal bones and use them for their stories, or they would pretend to be Indians who had lived here for generations, a tribe that had broken away from the mighty Chief Powhatan to the south. She remembered when they had decided to make their own dugout canoe from an old pine that had fallen, an endeavor that ended abruptly when Lily's mother caught them trying to hollow the log by burning it with flaming branches. She wondered now if Jenny Rae had ever told Jines about that; she doubted it. He would have grounded her for life. She was sure now it wasn't the only time her mother had covered for her.

A surprise. A swirl of pleasure ran though her. Was she getting a little drunk? She hadn't had any alcohol in a long time. Could be. She wasn't sure if this had the potential to be a good thing or not; she decided to reserve judgment and had another swallow of wine. They had cleared the jetties and the sun was nearly down, but the evening was hanging on the way it did at this time of early summer, seeming to stretch itself like a cat that wasn't in any hurry to get to anywhere, even into night. They were just past the lighthouse when Jamie throttled back, cut the engine, and wrapped his arm around her waist. She made a startled sound into the sudden silence, "Wha-?" He lifted her off the engine box and spun her gently around, so she was facing the water, and he put his face next to hers and stretched his arm to the south.

"There," he said.

His voice was so close she thought she could feel it vibrate in her. He smelled of Budweiser, cigarettes, and fish. She didn't mind at all and she had the notion this must be proof positive she was indeed tipsy. She could feel her heart thumping and wondered if his hand still resting on her waist could feel it as well.

"There's the surprise."

She didn't see anything at first, only the flattening of the light across the horizon, and then suddenly in the near distance she saw what looked like a short puff of smoke on the water's surface. Then the rounded grey backs of the dolphins became clear as they arced through the water. There must have been a dozen of them, grey as pewter, the water glistening on the smooth curves of their backs.

"Jamie!" she gasped.

She had seen them before, of course; they were annual visitors to this part of the Bay, coming up from the ocean when the water warmed in late spring. But every time seemed as magical as the first time. She never tired of watching them. Jamie let go of her and leaned over the side, slapping the *Jenny Rae's* hull with the flat of his hand.

"I saw them this afternoon as we were coming in," he said. "Two big pods, working around that pound down there."

He kept slapping the hull, and she watched as the group turned and came toward the sound. She leaned as far over the gunwale as she could when they came close, all of them moving in elegant, powerful concert, so close now she could hear the push and pull of their breathing as they surfaced.

"Wouldn't Belle love this," she said.

"Oh yeah, you know it. First time I showed her this I thought she was gonna go right overboard to chase after them."

"You don't see them much in Maine. Lots of seals instead. Sometimes sharks."

"I reckon the water gets too cold for them up there," Jamie said.

The dolphins were moving off to the east and he fired up the engine again and moved the boat slowly along, not chasing them, just shadowing. Lily loved watching him move around the boat. There was no wasted motion in him, yet he never looked tense or awkward. His loose grace was part of his beauty. It didn't seem like an inappropriate word for Jamie, she thought. It didn't make him any less masculine. He had that same beauty that Isabelle had, a way of carrying himself that was born in his sense of place in his world. It wasn't unlike her boat, *Pelagic*. Small as it was, the boat had an elegance that was part and parcel of its inherent strength and sense of purpose.

"I wish I could take you sailing on my boat," she said.

"Why don't you?"

"It's a little difficult right now. Seeing as how we're down here and she's up there."

"So why don't you bring her down here?"

"I think it might be easier the other way around."

Jamie throttled to neutral and shut down the engine again. The *Jenny Rae* drifted on the silky water. She could see the dolphins in the distance, disappearing into the soft grey of the coming night. A couple of stars had popped out overhead. Jamie sat on the engine box and cut up some of the cheese and apples. He handed her a sandwich of one, apple slice, cheese, apple slice. It tasted delicious. Everything out here tonight seemed delicious, even the rough edges of her father's workboat. His next question was more reality that she wished to face at the moment.

"When are you going back?"

"I don't know." She eased herself down until her back was flat on the engine box, her face to the sky, her feet pulled under her so her knees were bent into two triangles. She balanced the glass of wine on one of them, holding it by the stem. "I have two weeks, exactly, to tell my boss—and former lover, I might add—whether I'm coming back at all."

"You were sleeping with your boss?"

"Well, yes." She giggled.

Okay, she thought, you must be drunk if you even told Jamie about Michael, especially if you think it's funny. She sat up long enough to take another drink of wine, then flopped back down again. More stars were appearing by the second. She glanced over at Jamie but she couldn't quite decipher his expression.

"I know, not the best thing to do. But hey, we all make mistakes, right?"

As soon as she said it she wished she hadn't. He turned his face from her, pretending to look at something out over the water.

"Right." he said.

She sat up. "Jamie, I'm sorry. I didn't mean anything by it. I mean, yeah, it was colossally stupid of me to sleep with my boss. Not to mention the height of unprofessional. I didn't mean—I was more talking about me. But it doesn't matter anymore. It didn't really matter then anyway." Just. Shut. Up, she thought, but her mouth kept on talking. "It was more circumstance than anything else, when I think about it now. Situational love."

"Situational love?"

"I just thought of that, just now. You know, a relationship based more on the situation than what's really between two people."

Jamie got up and went to the cooler. "I think I need another beer." He popped the cap off with an opener that was fastened to the side of the engine box and took a long swallow.

Lily tried to clear her head. "Did that sound awful?"

"Not awful. I'd say, confused."

"Well." She wrapped both arms around her knees. "I won't deny that."

They sat there for a moment. She listened to the water lapping the sides of the boat, wishing she hadn't steered the conversation this way. She didn't feel equipped to talk with Jamie about all this. Not yet.

Finally he said, "Are you still confused?"

"About what happened with my boss? No. I fucked up. It's done. Other things, though."

"Like what?"

Like whether I should go back to my job in Maine or stay here and find something else, she thought. Like how the hell I'm going to pay for my boat's mooring fee next month. Like why I'm really liking how Jines is teaching me to build a boat, and how he can make me so damned mad at the same time. Like why being around your daughter makes me feel like I'm losing some part of me I didn't even know I possessed. Like why even looking at you makes me weak in the knees.

She let out a long breath and said, "Like whether we should go swimming or not."

He grinned at her, that wicked grin that made her breath come so quickly it wasn't really a breath at all, just enough of a bite of air to keep her from falling over.

"I can help with that confusion," he said, stripping off his shirt.

His neck and broad shoulders were pale hillsides in the starlight. He kicked off his workboots, unbuckled his belt and dropped his jeans, standing there before her in nothing but his boxers. She believed her mouth was hanging open.

"The answer," he said, climbing up on the gunwale, "is yes!" And he dove overboard with a whooping yell.

She laughed out loud. Why not, she thought, she'd started it. Halfway through pulling her shirt off she realized she hadn't even worn a bra, so she kept it on. Maybe the evening breeze would dry it out. Jamie had paddled around to the bow of the boat and she followed him. The water was cool and salty on her tongue. Treading water, he reached up with one hand and rubbed the very prow of the boat like a trainer checking the legs on a prized racehorse.

"Your old man may drive you crazy, but he builds a hell of a boat," he said. "Every day I go out I still pinch myself that he went for the idea of letting me work her."

"Maybe he's adopted you," she said. "I think he was always a little disappointed that he ended up stuck with me and not my brother." She dove deep into the darkening water and came up a little ways away from Jamie, who was watching her.

"You know, Lils," he said. "At least you had a dad."

Why don't we trade, she was thinking, but then she realized he was right. She'd grown up without her mother. Undoubtedly it was equally hard for Jamie growing up without a father. All her life she'd been jealous of the attention Jines had paid to other things and other people—his boat, his crew—and not to her. There was no way she was going to let herself be jealous of his affection, if that's what it was, for Jamie. Of all people, Jamie deserved it. The coolness of the water was sobering her up, and she struck out across the surface, stretching her arms hard in a steady, strong crawl stroke. She finally stopped when she heard a shout behind her.

"Lily Rae! Don't go so far!" Jamie yelled. "It's getting dark."

She looked around. He was right about that too. Wouldn't it be wonderful, she thought, if the dolphins would come back and she could swim with them? And if she got in trouble out here, wouldn't they come and save her? Dolphins did that, so the legends of mariners said. Across the water, she could see the worry on Jamie's face. He couldn't leave the boat, she knew that. Someone always had to stay with the boat. She swam back to him, pulling up next to him. He had one hand up on the corner of the stern to steady himself.

"Did you miss me?" she asked.

"I ought to smack you," he said. "That was too far, and the tide's starting to run."

"So you did miss me." She smiled.

He looked up at the star-freckled sky and sighed in what sounded like exasperation. When he brought his blue-eyed, straight-on gaze back to her, his dark hair wet across his brow, she knew she loved him. She had no idea if he loved her, if he still loved his ex-wife, what he wanted. But she knew she didn't want to be afraid of loving him anymore. With his free hand he cupped her cheek and drew her toward him. His kiss was as gentle as his hand, his mouth soft and yielding. The water held them and his kiss was like water inside of her, a long, liquid flame. She wrapped her arms around his neck and her legs around his waist; she clung to him like a limpet clings to a rock. He was steady with his hand on the boat, only his mouth moving against hers, his tongue probing her own, his free hand still content to hold her face.

"Do you want to know," he asked, "how long I have missed you?"

"No."

She covered his mouth with hers. She didn't want to know. She only wanted to know that he was here now, that this was Jamie's rough hand around her waist pulling her even more tightly against him, that this was his smooth wet skin against hers as she pulled her shirt up and over her head and threw it into the boat's cockpit. Their bodies could not get close enough to satisfy her. They could not make enough of their skin touch to calm her.

His hand moved down her body, and for a moment or two he let his fingers move among the folds of her, then he pulled his hand back and up to her face and said, "I have missed you all my life."

His kisses, which had grown hard with the movements of his hand, became soft again. Her body felt like an instrument he was playing, a whole orchestra, fortissimo, pianissimo, then crescendo, again. She was taut as a violin's string. She allowed her mouth to leave his long enough to meet his eyes. What he was seeing she didn't know; she wanted him to see the wonder there, the hope, the wild idea of joy. She slid her fingers into his mouth and the moan that escaped him thrilled her as deeply as the thick feel of him against her. Neither one of them, for a moment, dared to move. Now, she thought, perhaps now our bodies are close enough. She started to move against him, and then he slowed her and pulled himself away. She had a terrible moment of doubt, but she let it fly when he kissed her again.

"Slowly," he said. She was too breathless to answer. "We have time, Lils. Plenty of time." He grinned against her mouth. "Also—" he pushed her gently off of him—"my arm is killing me."

He kissed her again and swam around to the boat's transom. He pulled himself up, his body pale and dripping the starlight. Then he turned to pull her up to him. His wet shorts landed on the deck with a smack, and he wrapped them both in one of the towels she'd brought, pulling her against him.

"Jamie," she said. She felt suddenly afraid of how completely he could undo her.

"Come with me." He led her by the hand to the engine box and spread the second towel out. He laid her down gently. There were goosebumps all over her skin. He started with her mouth, lingering there to kiss her deeply, then slowly moved his lips down her neck, every now and then letting his teeth graze her skin. The contrast made her writhe. He slowed at the little hollow of her collarbone. Then past her shoulder and down, again, to her nipples. She moaned. He flicked them with his tongue, his hands moving down her sides. Then his mouth, down to her stomach. His head moved down her thighs and she tried to twist up to him, force his mouth to her burning center, but he wouldn't let her, teasing her instead with his tongue up and down the insides of her thighs. When finally he came to rest there, it was with the gentlest of breaths. He waited. "Please," she whispered, her fingers in his hair. If she felt any fear, it had been overwhelmed by pure desire. She could barely stand to stay here, held in this beautiful suspension. She wanted him to make her fly apart. Beneath them, the boat moved gently in the low swell. She opened her eyes to see the night sky brilliant above them, and he lowered his tongue into her and against her, forward then back, and forward again. He brought his fingers into her until she cried his name out loud, her back arched high into him with the wave of her orgasm. Then he slowly withdrew and repeated the long journey his lips had taken, across her quivering thighs, up her stomach, her breasts, her shoulders, to her mouth, where he stopped. She reached for his face and pulled her to him. There were tears in her eyes, she could not believe.

He lay down next to her. One of his hands covered her stomach. She rolled herself into him and kissed him over and over, his mouth, his eyes, his chin. She bit his lip gently. She had been wrong about that, she realized; she had been wrong to think their bodies could ever be close enough. She saw the goosebumps on his arms.

"Are you chilly?" she asked.

"Far from it," he said.

"Jamie." She pulled the towel over his shoulder, kissed his neck. "My God, Jamie."

He sat up and looked around, taking a quick measure of where they had drifted. Then he looked back down at her and grinned.

"God help me tomorrow morning," he said.

"Why?"

"I'll never be able to look at this engine box the same way again."

She laughed and pulled her back down to him. He kissed her and rested on one elbow beside her. His hand made a lazy circle over her stomach, up to her breasts, brushing over her nipples in a way that made her shake. Her legs had not stopped trembling. She was watching the eastern quadrant of the sky when she saw a white streak drop across it and flame out just above the horizon.

"I just saw a shooting star," she said.

"Where?" He twisted around, sounding like a jealous kid.

"Right over your beautiful head." She ran her fingers over his lips. "Do you know that every morning I watch you walk down to the boat?"

"You do?"

"Every morning. I hide up in the window. You have a great ass in blue jeans. Out of them too, for that matter. I was always afraid that you'd see me."

"And I was always hoping you were watching."

"You were?"

"But I couldn't very well turn around and look, could I? Then you'd know."

"Know what?"

"You'd know that I wanted to know you were there." He leaned over to kiss her.

She felt herself melting again. "Let's just stay out here forever. Do you think you could catch us enough to eat? And we have more beer, right? How much cheese is left?"

"I think your daddy might wonder why his boat and his daughter didn't come home."

"Well, his boat maybe." She laughed.

"Lils," he said.

She waved her hand. "No, it's all right, really. It's all right. It's been so strange coming back here, Jamie. Everything about it."

"What's strange about it?" He leaned in to kiss her neck, which she found deliciously distracting, but she wanted to finish the thought. She thought he could understand it, if anyone could.

"Well, for one thing, it's pretty strange to go down into your father's room in the morning and sometimes have him think you're his dead wife."

"He thinks you're your mama?"

"It's happened once or twice. He just wakes up and doesn't know what year it is, I guess. One time I caught him out on the front porch taking a leak on the camellias. Really. All over the pink ones. It's okay, you can laugh. It was pretty funny, in a twisted kind of way. He was sound asleep." She shook her head. "I'm just glad he hasn't sleepwalked any more than that one time. I already hid the Browning up under my bed, just in case. Never know when he might think I'm not even his wife but some person come to rob him. Knowing Jines, he'd shoot first."

"Jesus," Jamie said.

"But that's not even what I really mean. About it being strange." She sat up and wrapped the towel around her. She held his big hand in hers, running her fingers all through his while she talked. "I mean, I didn't even want to come back here. At least, I didn't think I wanted to come back. So many bad memories." She glanced up at him, then let her gaze fall over the water so she could focus on what she was trying to say. "I was so sad here for such a long time." He didn't say anything. He brushed the damp hair from her face. "But it was so weird. Have you ever heard of this thing called muscle memory? You know, when you used to do a certain sport, say, or play an instrument, and you haven't done it for a really long time, and you pick up the instrument again after ten or twenty years when you can't even read music anymore, and lo and behold your fingers just go to the places they're supposed to go to make the notes? As if they remember, they know, even if you, in your conscious mind, don't. That's what it's been like. When I walked around the house, when I got out in Mama's garden, even when I started helping Jines with this skiff, it was like I had wanted to come back all along, but I hadn't even known it. Like coming around a bend in a road where you haven't driven for twenty years, and all of a sudden you see the landscape ahead of you, the road ahead of you, and you know what's going to be around that corner, and then you come around the corner and there it is, just the same as it ever was. I thought I wouldn't be able to stand that, you know? At first, I thought, oh everything's just the same, nothing has changed, and so I expected all the feelings to be the same as they were. But they weren't." She stopped and looked at Jamie again. "They aren't. They're different. It's like some part of me knew I wanted to see the river again, and grow tomatoes in my mama's garden again. And be with you again." She paused. "Does this make any sense?"

"Yeah," he said simply. He untwisted their fingers and placed both hands on either side of her face gently. "You're home."

He kissed her again, his tongue seeking hers. And then his cell phone rang. They both froze, as if they'd been caught necking in the back of a car somewhere. A cell phone?

"Cell phones work out here?" she asked.

He got up and reached for his jeans, rooting around in the pocket.

"Once you get past the jetties. Signal comes from a tower south of here."

He looked at the phone, and she watched his whole face change, all the tenderness gone.

"Shit," he said.

He turned his back to her and walked toward the cabinhouse.

"Gina," he said into the phone.

Lily felt suddenly cold in the nighttime air. She wished now she hadn't left her T-shirt on when she went swimming. It was soaked, and she had nothing dry to put on. She put it on anyway, shivering at its clammy feel over her skin, and then pulled on her panties and shorts. Then she wrapped the towel around her and walked to the back of the boat so she wouldn't have to listen to him talk to her. His voice, low as it was, carried on the light breeze that the boat had turned its bow into. "Come on, baby," he said. The quick fear that Lily had felt before returned in the form of a dark fist, clogging her throat and settling in her stomach. She was nauseous. She reached for some of the crackers; they had gone stale in the humid air but she ate a few anyway. They didn't help. Jamie still had his back to her. His head was tilted to one side, into the phone, trying to hide his voice. "Gina, for once just don't, please?"

Lily leaned hard against the boat's sharp gunwale and focused her mind on the fist in her gut. What had she done. She had let down her guard. She had let him in. She had been drunk. No, that wasn't a good enough excuse and besides, she hadn't been that drunk. Buzzed maybe, but not drunk. She had known what she was doing when she was doing it. She had known, when she looked into his eyes, that she loved this man and wanted him to know it. She had believed he could love her. For a second she let herself remember the feeling of their entwined bodies in the water, his hand holding hers—was that just a minute ago?—and tears filled her eyes.

"Gina, honey, you know that's not true," his voice still carrying, and she brushed her eyes angrily.

There was a bit of wine left in the bottle, and she poured it carelessly into her glass, letting it splash down the sides. Then she walked past him up the boat's sidedeck, past the cabinhouse, and sat on the small triangle of the bow, waiting for his conversation to be over. Up here, at least, all she could hear was the slow panic of her heart. After a bit, she heard the engine start, and he called up to her. She walked back unsteadily and jumped into the cockpit. He was dressed again, back in his jeans and boots and T-shirt.

"I gotta get back in," he said.

She didn't trust her voice to ask why.

"That was Regina, seems she's had a change of plans, and she's bringing Belle home tonight." He came close to Lily and reached for her. "Lils?" She let him lift her face up to meet his eyes. "I'm sorry about this. But I can't let Belle just sit there alone. I gotta get back. You understand, don't you?"

What I understand, she wanted to say, is that she still holds you, and I hold nothing. What I understand is that the sky is above me, the water below, and I exist in between, floating on the surfaces of things, alone. Flotsam.

"Sure," she said.

"Lily," he said, "hey."

He bent to kiss her, but she held herself tight. She felt if she moved too quickly all her bones would break. Every person has a dark side, she said to herself. This is what I have learned. All love is, is learning to live with somebody's darkness, figuring out how to protect yourself. And all falling in love is, is living under the delusion that this person doesn't have a dark side, that they're perfect. And these delusions, she would no longer allow herself.

"Don't be angry with me," he pleaded.

"Jamie." she said. "When I see you, I want to sing out loud. But it's a delusion, Jamie, a dream." Her voice turned brittle, flippant. "Actually it's chemicals. They have studies now that prove that when you fall in love your brain produces the same chemicals it does when it's psychotic. Isn't that great?"

"It's not a joke, Lils, What's happening with us isn't a delusion. We're not crazy. We've always been meant for each other."

You still love her, she wanted to say. I see your darkness and I don't want to share it. But she didn't say this to him, she didn't want to hear his denial.

"We should go," she said.

Whether Jamie understood her fear or created his own distance for himself, she didn't know. Nor did it matter. The boat rushed back towards the river in the dark night, the wind of its movement frigid against her skin as Jamie stood at the helm, watching only the water ahead, and she stood by the engine box, watching the boat's wake fall away behind them. No dolphins now, none to save her. After a little while she understood why Jines had always sought refuge within this sound; the diesel's loud rumble drowned out everything else. It made talk all but impossible, paving the way for silence, and all the while pushed the boat onward, giving the illusion, at least, of forward motion, even if she was standing in one place like something cast of stone, helpless to move on her own.

Chapter 15

There had been times in the past when Lily had found safety in work, and so when she walked to the shed each morning now, carefully avoiding Jamie by either waiting until he'd gone or getting out there before him, she walked with a new sense of purpose. So what if the purpose was escape; she'd grab it like a log in a flood. Her work with Jines building the skiff gave her a reason to get out of bed every day. It gave her a place to use her hands and hide her thoughts. The irony didn't escape her that these were the same reasons she'd believed the project would be good for Jines.

Many mornings now she made sure Jines was up and moving, then headed out to the shed first and got the lights on, looked over what had been accomplished the day before, thought about what had to be done this day, at least as far as she knew. After they'd finished stretching the sides they had installed the transom, deck beams, and ribs. They had laid in the keelson, the skiff's backbone that ran its length down the centerline to which all the floor planks would be attached. Then the keel itself, solid oak for strength and durability, glued and fastened. Still upside down on the sawhorses—but nailed firmly to them, and they to the floor so nothing could move—the skiff reminded her sometimes of a great fish undergoing a process of reverse filleting.

She found herself pushing Jines, pushing herself. The clear-cut tasks that faced her in the shed were a relief from the overwhelming sense that she was merely floating, rising and falling with the rhythm of the tides, but not really moving. Out here, at least, something was becoming real. Her hands had toughened, so the sharp quick splinters that had plagued her at first were growing fewer and farther between. She knew they were still working on the easy part of the bottom—Jines always found a way to remind her of that—but still, she was pleased with how quickly now she could make a few cuts in a piece of lumber on the band saw, carry it to the skiff, measure, make her marks, return to the band saw for a more precise sizing, then fit the board in its place. She would clamp each end to hold it, then drill four or five pilot holes for the stainless steel nails. Jines had groused about the stainless steel. He'd wanted to use bronze, but the metal was so soft and the nails bent so easily she'd gone through dozens on just a couple of planks, and both of them ended up snapping at one another over her lack of precision and experience with a hammer. Finally he'd sent her off to the House of Deals for stainless steel, which seemed to withstand her mistakes with greater fortitude. As he'd shown her, she would trim off any excess plank ends with a quick pass of a handsaw, remove the clamps, and the board was in place, and she was moving on. Beneath her hands, the skiff was taking shape. Jines had been right. There had been a boat in there, all that time.

She'd noticed that even while she was pouring herself more intensely into the work, Jines was spending more and more time on the couch. More than once she would ask him for guidance on a particular problem without looking up, and receiving no answer, she'd see that he'd dozed off, chin to chest. She wasn't sure at all that this was a good thing, but she took, perhaps erroneously, a certain pride in believing that he felt sufficiently comfortable having her working there that he would let himself relax enough to fall asleep. She'd call his name and after a moment or two he'd snap awake, and she'd be sure to have her head in her work, supposedly awaiting his answer on this problem or that. It didn't seem right to let him know she watched his sleep, an intimacy she was certain he'd never willingly grant. And his sleep frightened her sometimes. He might get deep into a dream and thrash and moan and weep. It always stunned her, the crying. She wondered if he dreamed about nearly drowning. She wondered if he dreamed of fishing. She wondered if he was seeing her mother.

On this morning it was oppressively hot and humid already. The air seemed thick in her throat, and her shirt stuck to her back like a second skin she didn't want. She measured a piece of planking and zipped it through the band saw. Tall and gangly as a teenaged boy, the saw's single, naked bulb dangled from the questionable socket like some kind of glowing fruit. The dust that blew out of the wood as she made the cut glued itself to her sweaty forearms.

"Getting right cozy with that thing, ain't ya," Jines observed from the couch. She had positioned a fan on the workbench and directed it toward him. Even so, every now and then he swiped his forehead with a blue hankie he kept stashed in his pocket.

"Better watch out, that almost sounded like a compliment." She carried the piece over to the skiff and set it in place. "It's true I guess. I like it. Who would have believed that?"

"What's hard to b'lieve? It's in your blood. The learning how it goes together, that's one thing. You can teach just about anybody that. Nails in a board." He mimed what she was doing, pounding the fasteners through the plank into the bottom. "But the *way* it goes together, the art in it, that's something else. You can't teach that. That's either in you or it ain't."

She dropped her hands and looked at him.

"What?" he asked.

"I don't think I've ever heard you use that word when it comes to something like this."

"What word?"

"Art."

"I ain't so ignorant, you know."

"No. Just defensive."

She went back to her work on the plank. Jines made a humphing noise and settled deeper into the couch.

"It's what it is, though," he said. "It's what makes a boat alive. All the rest, that's just tacking boards together. All them builders you've been asking all about, they weren't just builders. I mean, some of their boats were rough, no doubt, but they were workboats, not some snotty yachts. They were supposed to be rough. And you had to make do with what you had, lumber-wise. Even so, those boys knew more about building boats than any book could tell."

"Somebody ought to write a book about it before it's altogether gone, though," she said.

"May be too late for that." He sighed.

"Maybe I ought to write it," she said. "What do you think; a national bestseller about traditional boatbuilding on the Chesapeake. Hah."

"I bet you'd do all right with that."

"Better do better than all right. Better make *The New York Times* bestseller list."

She drove in two nails with particular emphasis. Her bank account was dangerously shallow. Michael was growing impatient for an answer. The thought of returning to the Portland bureau filled her with emptiness. She didn't even know that she wanted to continue as a reporter, though what else would she do? She realized that it had been a long time since her work had inspired more in her than a sense of duty at best, dread at worst. She remembered an assignment last year that had begun as the story of a child gone missing in a small town up near Wiscasset. He was a boy about Belle's age, and one day he'd been out playing and never came home. For a week, they searched. Every day Lily would drive into the town and follow the police chief, interview the family, friends, and strangers who came to help, walk around with them as they scoured every inch of the place, literally, on foot, bicycle, and by car. Each day, she became less an observer and more a participant.

She couldn't sleep at night, thinking about the boy alone and lost, or worse. People came from all over the region to search. The story "had legs," as Michael said; it was national news. Like a plague of termites, crews from all of the major networks and papers descended on the town, sticking their cameras and microphones into every nook of the community's woodwork. She hated her role in drawing them here; her stories, filed on the national wire, were the tropical rain that fueled the hatch-out. By the fifth day the police chief was so exhausted he'd cried openly in front of her because, he told her, he had a boy that age of his own and he was afraid and angry that he couldn't help this missing child. She had closed her notebook on the table and just sat there with him, letting him cry over his hundredth cup of cold coffee. She'd returned to the bureau that night, deeply shaken, and Michael told her to write it up.

"That's great copy, the police chief breaking down," he said. "And he has a kid the same age. That's your lead, right there. It'll go national again."

"I can't do that!" She was appalled. "I wasn't writing, I was listening. The notebook was closed. He was confiding in me, not conducting an interview!"

But Michael demanded it. She wrote it, sick and bitter with every word. A day later the boy turned up dead in a dumpster. He had been sexually assaulted and beaten. Lily attended the funeral and cried while she tried to take notes. The police chief never spoke to her again.

"I saw that Jamie and the boys didn't go out today. Guess they decided to wait out the weather. Supposed to get right wild later on." Jincs's voice brought her back.

"I guess."

Maybe she could get a job further up the coast in one of the boatbuilding towns, sign on as an apprentice. There was no money in it, she was sure. But she could try and learn to make something worthwhile, something beautiful. She could cut her expenses, find another apartment. Maybe work part-time at a local paper, covering safely quotidian stories like the inner workings of the planning and zoning commission, the politics of the school board.

"Noticed you ain't been seeing him off in the mornings."

"We've had a lot to do out here."

"Uh huh." He cleared his throat in disbelief. "I didn't know we were in such a hurry to finish up. You got something you want to tell me?"

She set down the piece of wood she was working on and turned on him.

"Yeah, I do, Jines. I do. I'm just about broke. I don't really want to go back to my old job, but I don't see much choice. Soon, too, like next week, or I won't have a job to even go back to. And meantime you just sit here—" she waved her hand at him—"like nothing's wrong, everything's just A-okay. And it isn't."

"Here we go again," he said. He rolled his eyes.

"Have you opened your mail lately? You're sixty days late on sixty thousand dollars, plus another twenty for property taxes. What's your plan, Jines, you think Jamie's going to be able to bail you out? Got eighty grand buried in a jar somewhere?"

"Why's it got you all upset? They're my bills. Ain't yours."

"You're right, why should I make it my problem?" She was pacing between the band saw and the skiff, making her measurements, slapping the wood down on the band saw's table to make her cuts. She turned on the saw and its harsh whine filled the shed as she ripped the wood through it. "Crazy as it sounds, I wanted to help."

"I don't need help."

"Yes, you do. I don't know why, but you just won't deal with this thing, and you're going to lose. You're going to lose everything you care about."

His eyes glittered at her. "What makes you think I already haven't?"

She threw up her hands. She had no argument for this.

"So what's your plan? You can't go fishing anymore, so you're going to let some collection agency take the house? Because that's what they'll go after first."

"Didn't know you were so fond of it."

"Well I am!"

She was shaking. Everything was backwards. She was the one ranting and yelling, and there was Jines, just sitting there, watching her. She tried to remember what measurement she was on and marched back to the band saw.

"You just made that cut," he said.

"Shit!"

She spun back to the skiff and laid the piece of wood in the bottom. It was still too long. She hadn't measured precisely enough. The pencil was slippery in her sweaty hands as she raked it along the side of the wood.

"So I reckon you got it all figured out," he said. "Why don't you come clean and tell me about it."

"It's not a question of coming clean," she said, but it was and she knew it.

She'd gone behind his back to meet with Bradford Wilson. She'd arranged it so that Jines was never around when he came out to examine the land. When the surveyors had come she'd made sure they had plenty of time by lingering at physical therapy with Jines, stopping for groceries, even having lunch with him at the Seaside. She knew Jines wouldn't be walking down to that end of the property for any reason—he never walked that far anymore, for one thing—so the stakes with their little orange ribbons would remain undiscovered. She made sure that when they'd perked for the septic that the truck mounded the pile of dirt from the excavation behind a line of trees. She'd been sneaking around like a cheating wife, and if she hadn't lied outright to him, she'd certainly obscured the truth of what she'd been planning. He was sitting there, waiting. She willed herself to calm down, but his forthright quietude unnerved her.

"I've found somebody to buy three acres of the land. He'll pay three hundred thousand dollars. That's enough to pay off your medical bills, property taxes for a long time, maybe get some long-term insurance that would cover any medical bills in the future. Or other things, like a home nurse, if you ever needed one. You could take the rest and invest it and have plenty to live on."

She adjusted her marks on the board she had been working on and before he could say anything she switched on the band saw. She took her time making her cuts. She didn't look at him. The saw whined down to silence.

"This is still my family land, little girl," he said. "I ain't selling shit."

"Jines, before you get your back all up in a hump think about this. The buyer will accept covenants on the land. Restrictions, so that they can only build a house of a certain size, and it has to be set back a certain distance from the river. You can even limit what trees they can take down."

"Who's this buyer?"

"A realtor I met. He'll buy it as an investment and sell it later."

Jines snorted. "You think I'm climbin' in bed with one of them whores?"

"For enough money to let you live free and clear and keep everything else? Yes."

She was back at the skiff now, trying to fit the piece. It wasn't cooperating.

"How'd you know whoever he sold it to wouldn't turn it into

something else like a condo or some other garbage?"

"It's in the deed, the restrictions would be part of the deed. They can't change that."

"Why'd anybody want to buy it if I get to tell them what to do with it?"

"You'd be amazed. The people who want to buy lots around here aren't nearly as bull-headed as you are."

"Pot and kettle."

"Whatever."

She let the slight slide. She was relieved that she'd finally told him. Bradford Wilson was ready to settle as soon as next week. If she could convince Jines to come to the table, she could shepherd the sale and then just go. Deal with the consequences and decisions in Maine when she got back up there. Home, that's what Jamie had said. She was home. But he'd been wrong, and so had she.

"Three acres over on the north side. Through the pine forest there; that way you wouldn't ever have to even see any house they would build. They could take a right-of-way for the driveway way up at the end. You probably wouldn't even be able to hear their cars."

She clamped the wood to the skiff and drilled her holes for the fasteners.

"You're talking about the piece of land where the wood for this skiff came from."

"You have to give up something, Jines," she said. "You owe eighty thousand dollars, and it isn't going to stop. The only assets you have are the house and the land. Jamie can only give you a percentage of the catch, and what happens come winter? Everybody knows oysters are shot. And how long will he be willing to partner with you? He's going to want to own it a hundred percent; he's got his own daughter and Mary Virginia to think about."

She drove the nails into the holes harder than she needed to, using force instead of finesse. One of them bent to ninety degrees. She pried it out.

"Taxes are just going to keep going up, so's fuel oil and everything else. The house needs work, and that costs money too."

"Guess you got it to the nickel and dime," he said.

He was watching her with his down-dark eyes, and she kept waiting for him to blow up at her, but he didn't. He just asked his questions. It was almost as if he'd expected this.

"It's not up to me."

"You're sure acting like it is."

"Here's how I see it, Jines." She chucked the bent nail into the trashcan and rested the hammer on the skiff's bottom. "You know how animals sometimes, when they get caught in a trap, will chew off whatever's caught to escape? That's this deal. You chew off part of your foot. You might limp a little. But you'll be free."

He shook his head. He leaned forward with his elbows on his knees. "It ain't just my foot, Lily Rae. That's the part you don't see. It's my daddy's foot, my granddaddy's. And I thought you'd understand by now, it's yours, too." He shook his head again. "I ain't selling."

"*Fine.*"

She turned back to the bottom piece that had been plaguing her. If he wouldn't go for the deal, she'd have to figure out a way to pay off Bradford Wilson for the survey and the perk test. She felt sick; she already knew the only way, and that was to sell the only real asset she had, *Pelagic*. After that, then what? She'd go back to Maine. She didn't care whether the skiff was done or not or the garden halfway grown; she didn't care if anything was complete. She pounded the last three fasteners into place, and only then did she really look at her work. The board wasn't even flush with the one behind it. There was a gap of at least a quarter inch, and the end that should be snug with the keelson looked ragged too. She threw down the hammer.

"God *damn* it!"

Jines got up from the couch and walked stiffly over to the skiff. He ran his thick finger over the gap. "Shoot, that ain't nothin'. She'll swell right shut once she's overboard. Just move on past it to the next one. This part of the boat can stand it."

"I have to do it again, it isn't right!"

Jines smoothed both of his hands over the boards, his fingers spread wide. The skiff's bottom stretched nearly twelve feet now, a pale yellow-white the color of a snowfield glowing with the early morning sun. "There's plenty of things in this world, Lily Rae, that ain't right. That don't make 'em wrong."

She tossed up her hands in exasperation. "What the hell does that mean, Jines?"

"Means just what it means. You're always wanting to fix things just so. Make them right the way you see them to be. But some things just don't fit that way." He walked along the length of the skiff slowly, pushing his hand along the wood and using it for balance at the same time.

"Nothing's perfect, Lily Rae. When you build something like this, you got to let it have its flaws. You ain't perfect. Why should something you want to care about have to be?"

She looked along the skiff's length, then across it to the workbench and around the shed. The heat was so oppressive that even the wind had shut down, the pines outside were stilled, and with no machine running the shed was consumed in silence.

"I'll call off the deal, then," she said. "I'll be heading back to Maine tomorrow."

He seemed, suddenly, as motionless as the air.

"What about this boat?"

He was up at the bow, holding the stem. On either side of his big hands, the open spaces of the bottom yet to be completed fell away to the floor below. The deadwood, he called this part, the most difficult section to build. Each piece required thicker stock than the rest of the bottom, because each piece had to be slowly shaped to assume the curve of the bow, and the curve changed subtly and continuously. It might take hours to shape just a single piece, Jines had told her, and they would use everything from the band saw down to a sanding block, measuring between each small change they made. Along with the sheer—the long arc from stem to stern along its upper edge—this was where the skiff's beauty was carried. This was the neck of the swan, where what Jines had called the art held sway.

"You can finish it," she said. "All the wood is ready. You don't need me for it anyway."

"Aye God," Jines said softly.

He shuffled back to the davenport and lowered himself down. He looked deflated, picked clean. His hand shook as he wiped his eyes slowly with the blue hankie.

"Aye God, Lily Rae."

"Hello, Willy?"

Lily sat on her mother's bed twisting the phone cord in her hand. The phone was straight out of the 1960s, one of those trimline models that, at the time, must have looked space-aged and hip. It still had a rotary dial, so that each digit she dialed made her wait a little longer for the call to go through. She let her finger slowly spin backward with it each time. It was so hot, so still, that not a breath of breeze flowed through the big house. She tucked the phone receiver under her ear and tried to swipe the wood dust off her arms, but they were so sweaty the dust clung to her skin, refusing to be moved.

"Ah-yuh, this is Willy Perkins."

A tight little smile flitted briefly across Lily's mouth and then it was gone. She wanted to smell the fresh, cool salt air and hear the seals barking on the rocks. She wanted to feel the tiller of her boat in her hand. At this moment, she felt betrayed by the very air she was breathing in this room. "It's me, Lily Evans. Down in Virginia."

"Well, hello, Miss Evans!" Willy sounded pleased to hear from her. "Ah been wond'rin' how you've been."

"How's *Pelagic*, Willy?"

"Well now you know she's just fine, just right as rain, tucked away in a nice safe corner here. Just waitin' on you, I imagine. Might be feelin' a mite lonely this summah."

Lonely. How many hours had the two of them spent together, she and her boat? And as long as she was sailing, somehow the loneliness just disappeared. Boats were never just boats, after all. She knew that. They could make you better than you were, different. They could carry you on the wind, like a bird. Lily cleared her throat.

"You know that man who always comes and tries to get me to sell her to him? The man who owns that big Hinckley and says she would be the perfect daysailer for him?"

"Why yes, that's Mr. McFadden."

"Has he been around this spring at all, around her, I mean?"

Willy's voice, which was always modulated at a sedate tempo, slowed more than usual.

"Why yes, he has. I launched his boat a month ago, but you know he's always one to walk around the yahd and see who's in and who's not."

"Okay, good." Her voice was almost a whisper. She cleared her throat again. "I want you to tell him I will sell her."

The phone cord was twisted around and between her fingers so hard the tips of her fingers were turning white. She felt them absently with her other hand. Sell a boat, lose a finger. Chew off the limb. It was just a boat, she told herself. She could always get another. Liar. You liar.

"Did I hear you correctly, Miss Evans?"

Willy sounded incredulous. She could see his big droopy eyes opened wide over his sweet droopy face. Won't matter if you wait on Channel 13 for me now, Willy, she thought. I'm going off the air. She did not feel the tears as they splashed on her strangled white fingers.

"Yes." She knew Willy would be too discrete to ask her why. "Tell him twelve-thousand."

That would be enough to cover the perk tests and surveys she owed Bradford Wilson, money she might as well have flushed down a toilet. It would be enough to pay her apartment rent and give her something to live on once she got back to Maine and could get far enough from here to sort out what the hell she was going to do.

There was a long silence at the other end of the line. It was hard for her to keep her voice together while she told him that she could mail the title to Willy once she got back. She didn't want to be present when the boat changed hands. He could unload it for her, store the few things she wanted to keep in his office until she could come by and get them later. Much later, when, perhaps, she could stand to drive into his boatyard and not see her boat waiting for her.

"If you can help me with this, I'll pay you commission," she said.

A part of her could not believe what she was doing. It must have been the same part that once knew Willy Perkins, that once had a life far from here, that once found, if not happiness, then at least peace in the teacup of a beautiful small boat that had never let her down, never hurt her or demanded too much. *Pelagic* was fiberglass and wood, inanimate to all but her and, quite possibly, this man she was asking for help. But it was a friend she was selling. As the tears spilled all over her hands, she had no illusions.

"Ah won't take money for this, Miss Evans." Willy's voice was low and tired. He paused. "You're sure."

She nodded, knowing he couldn't hear her but knowing he did. She could almost see him shaking his head up in his little office.

"All right," he said. "I will let you know when it's done."

"Thank you, Willy."

She hung up the phone and untwisted her fingers from the cord. If she could have broken them just then, she would have. Outside the window the river sparkled and she hated it for its beauty, for what everything around here was slowly taking away from her.

She was angling the kayak onto the roof of her pickup, sweat pouring off her in the humid air, when Jamie's truck rolled up the driveway and stopped next to hers. Before he even opened the door Maggie had jumped out of the passenger side window and was wrapping herself around Lily's legs. The dog's unadorned, uncomplicated affection made her want to do the same, and she dropped to her knees and hugged the thick neck. Maggie licked the tears off her face. When she stood up again Jamie was on the other side of her truck, looking past the kayak at her. He looked tired; she imagined she didn't look much different. She reached into the front seat and grabbed a tissue to blow her nose.

"You're going somewhere?"

"Maine."

She threw the tissue into the truck and went about gathering some straps out of the bed to tie the kayak. She was still angry that Jines had left her hanging with the real estate deal; all that work and money she didn't have, for nothing. The family land; he held onto the idea like it was the Holy Grail, and its light was so bright he couldn't even see the train that was about to hit him and smash it to smithereens. She'd done what she could. There was no reason to stick around for more. She wasn't sure she could deal with anything Jamie might have to say to her now. She just wanted to be gone.

"When?"

"Tomorrow."

"I see."

She heard rather than saw the pack of cigarettes come out of his pocket, she heard the snick of the lighter, she heard the sound his lips made when he drew on it. Despite herself, she remembered the feel of his mouth on hers, his eyes. She drew in a breath and uncoiled one of the straps.

"Why?"

"Why what?"

"Why are you going back to Maine? Tomorrow?"

"Because I have to go back to work and my boss wants me back now or I will lose my job. Because Jines has made it clear he doesn't need me around here. Because I don't belong here. There's no reason for me to stay." And plenty of reasons to go, she thought.

"I thought you told me that your feelings had changed about that."

"Must have been the wine talking."

"Uh huh." His voice tightened. "So you're going to go back to your boss. The"—he held up his fingers for quote marks—"situational love?"

She didn't want to hurt him, but she didn't know how else to leave. She threw a strap over the top of the kayak.

"Can you feed that back through for me underneath? Thanks." She made a trucker's hitch and pulled the strap tight against itself, yanking it for extra measure. "I told you I'd made a mistake. But I still have to work for him."

"So it's okay if you make mistakes, but not other people, is that it?"

"I never said that."

"Seems like you don't need to." He tossed a second strap over the top of the kayak and it slapped down in front of her.

"I don't want to argue, Jamie. There's no point."

"No, you'd rather just not talk, period," he said. "You were right about that part anyway."

She rose to it. "What part?"

"When you said maybe you had too much Jines in you for men to take."

It stung and she let it sting. Anger was useful. Anger was shelter. Anger could get a person through a lot.

But Jamie took a deep drag on his cigarette and when he exhaled she could almost hear the bite go out of his voice. He looked up at the sky and he said, "Belle was hoping you'd ask her to come help in the garden. She's wondering why you haven't, lately."

Low blow, she was thinking, don't bring Belle into this. But Belle was part of this. Lily had made her part of it. She dropped her head. "Tell Belle I am sorry about that, I really am. I've been busy helping Jines. I'm sure he'd be happy if she came over and kept the garden going. He likes her."

"It's not the garden she misses, Lils."

She wiped her sweaty face on the sleeves of her T-shirt.

"God I wish there was some breeze."

There was no sun, but the light was forceful all the same, a kind of metallic glare that made her head ache.

"Oh I think there will be later." He stubbed out the cigarette. "I came down to check on the boat, make sure she was tied up proper." He glanced back at her. "Want to give me a hand?"

"I've got some packing to do. I want to leave at first light. It's a long drive."

"Lily." His voice was full and sad, all the anger gone out of it now. He shook his head. "What do you want me to say? That I'm sorry I'm not who you wanted me to be? That I don't want you to go? Because I don't want you to go, Lils, I don't."

"I don't want you to say anything."

She felt herself grasping to hold onto the hurtfulness of what he'd said, to fend off the ache that, if she allowed it, would drill through her bones. This is the only way you're going to get out of here in one piece, she thought, the only way, but even as she thought it she could feel the falseness of it crumbling like something feeble and poorly made. She kept her eyes down in case he could see the wavering in her. His voice came to her even softer. It carried on the thick air so that it sounded as if he were right next to her, his lips to her ear.

"You think you're the only one scared, but you're not," he said. "You think you're protected, but you're not. I used to think I was too, until I had Belle. She cracked my heart wide open. And it's okay, you know, Lily? It's better than okay."

He clapped his hand on the side of the truck. Then he whistled up Maggie, and before Lily could make her voice work again, Jamie's long strides took him away from her and he was gone, down the oyster shell path, down toward the river.

She couldn't get far enough away from either of them—Jamie or Jines—and when she looked back at the house now she felt the same cold indifference she had felt on her first day back here, as if it, too, had closed itself off to her once again. The sky hanging above the roof was a dull grey, as thick and quilted as ticking, and it pressed down ever lower on the earth. She could literally feel the low-pressure system coming. Storms like this one were just cousins of hurricanes, they could spin with the same pinched ferocity, spawning wild thunderstorms at their edges, and the oppression of their cores could force water downward into itself. How many inches? She used to know this, how much the sea would compress around the eye of a hurricane, but it was gone now. Her head had been full of useless facts. What difference did it make how much the sea yielded under pressure? What good did it ever do the sea? The storm still tore it to shreds. She finished tying on the kayak, refusing to let her eyes follow Jamie as he climbed onto the *Jenny Rae*. Jines would be waiting in the house with his shaking hands and that wrecked look he had gotten in the shed. There was no refuge left here. She had fled them all.

Except for one. The one place she had not yet been, the one place she had not yet been able to face. And now it called to her, and she took quick, purposeful strides under the pines past the shed and through the south meadow until she reached a narrow dirt track that slid into a forest of loblollies, whose tall arms enveloped it in silence.

The family cemetery was called the Grove. It was placed on the high ground, such as it was, where the soft pines gave way to a compact grove of hardwoods, tall old chestnuts and oaks, their broad leaves offering shade and solace from the hot summer sun. That was what the high ground around here was for, Lily thought, the cemetery to protect the dead and the house to shelter the living. Everything else was ultimately expendable and so forsaken to the flat, spongy earth that always seemed to abide in uneasy alliance with the river. Yet even the high ground was doubtful in an epic storm like the one that had taken her grandfather. There were always stories after such storms of the river's possession of the land, the upheaval of caskets from the sodden earth found floating downstream or shipwrecked on some point. The Evans plot had never succumbed, not even during the Great Storm of 1933. The Grove always stood firm, the hardwood trees' deep, sinuous roots holding tight to the earth, forbidding the river entry.

Lily walked along the path, which grew narrower and more tangled with every step. Jines had always kept it trimmed like a Marine crew cut. Now it was overgrown with grass that whipped her thighs as she pushed through it. Along the edges, thorny wires of greenbrier ensnared the lower branches of the trees until they looked like wild horses broken the hard way, heads hanging in exhaustion. Jines's care of the Grove and the path leading to it had always been his way of paying respect to their family. He would usually spend a whole day at the task, often inviting Lily along when she was young, and while he worked he would tell her about her great-uncles and -aunts, her great-grandfather and -grandmother, often talking to them all as if the old ones were right there gathered around the family table listening. "Isn't that so, Mama," he would say, nodding to her headstone, as he told a story about Lily's great-grandmother. She was so fearsome a woman, he said, that when she was on her deathbed in the parlor, the Grim Reaper standing right there in the front door and Lily's great-uncle Jimmy weeping at her side, she turned to the young man and snapped, "Aw quit yer blubbering, Jim." Lily never thought it strange that Jines included the dead in on the conversation. She could always feel their benevolent presence in the brushing of the leaves in the wind. It would have been rude to act as though they weren't there. By the end of the day, the stories run out and the cemetery tidy, the tall trees arching their cathedral branches overhead, Jines would sigh with satisfaction. But after Jenny Rae was gone, Jines's visits to the cemetery became obsessive, a religious ritual gone dark. Instead of attending church he would spend every Sunday morning out there alone. He refused to let Lily accompany him. And when he returned he carried none of the Grove's peacefulness.

Thinking about it now, she wondered if he hadn't come to hate the Grove, for it seemed to draw him relentlessly yet sent him away empty. What confronted her was years' worth of neglect on the path. She couldn't imagine the cemetery itself. If he had burned the whole thing down, let the river take it at last, she would have been less bewildered than knowing he had simply abandoned it. All the voices, she thought, out here waiting. Nothing moved in the forest. There was not even the whistle of an osprey fishing out over the river or the tapping of a woodpecker searching for a beetle. Everything waited, hunkered down and uneasy, and silence filled the spaces between.

She came to the rusted gate. Its flap-eared latch squeaked in the stillness, and the old hinges protested with a low screech. She had to push to get it open enough to pass through; the weeds and grass on the other side were knee high. The Grove itself wasn't very large; Lily could walk across it in about ten paces. She was struck at how small it seemed. In her memory it was a vast space, as big as the ground floor of the house anyway. In her adult eyes it was only about as big as the parlor. The entire burial ground was surrounded by a hip-high iron fence that had once been shiny black but had given way to a dull, pitted rust. In some places it was entirely obscured by honeysuckle and the rapacious greenbrier. Just outside of the fence stood the sheltering chestnuts and oaks. Bordering the fence inside were red cedars, what they called junipers. They were planted as a windbreak and also, she had been told, for their clean scent, which could bring healing to those in grief. These had not grown smaller in her eyes. They were majestic trees now, thick and fragrant in the moist air.

She could see the browned remains of daffodils planted at each stone. They must have looked beautiful three months ago, nodding hopefully under the early spring sun. Toward the middle, what looked like a circle of bright green daylily leaves was pushing through a mess of old growth and crawling honeysuckle. Some of the headstones were tilted and sinking, some were mounded over with ivy, and the clear areas of the space were thick with weeds and tufted grasses. The simple headstones were grouped according to relationship. Lily bent down to examine a tall narrow stone in the northeast corner. *Capt. Elijah S. Evans, b. Sept. 21, 1833, d. Feb. 19, 1908.* That would be her great-great-grandfather. *His toils are past, his work is done. He fought the fight, the victory won.* Next to him lay his wife, Susan, born August 14, 1833, died in January 1892. *Loving mother and wife. Angels on Earth here cannot remain.* There were aunts and uncles, cousins and babies whose names were never even inscribed on the small square stones that marked their tiny mounded graves. *Capt. James Evans, b. June 15, 1896, d. October 4, 1933. Oh hear us when we cry to thee, for those in peril on the sea.* Her grandfather, whose body was never found. Some of the stones were so weatherworn the inscriptions were nearly illegible. Rendered soft and indistinct, the markings spoke to her about the gentle nature of time that eventually could allow something even as impervious as granite to release the burden of its message. She felt herself easing up some.

She kneeled next to her grandfather's grave and began clearing the weeds from around the stone, taking care not to tear the flat green leaves surrounding the spent daffodil blooms. When she'd cleared enough space around the browned flowers she carefully bent the leaves and flower stems over on themselves. Using a single long leaf, she wrapped it around the bundle several times and then tied it in a loose slipknot to hold the whole thing together. Eventually over summer it would rot and disappear, the bulbs beneath it doubling and tripling for more blooms next spring. Lily liked the idea of the daffodils and their dependable bulbs in the Grove's ground. After a long, dark winter with only the trees for company, the old ones must've looked forward to their vibrant color. If she could get these spent blooms tied off there would be even more next year. When she would not be here to care for them.

She stood up. There was a newer stone at the southeast corner, the one she had really come to see. Approaching it was like scuba diving, she thought; she could only go so far, let her body equalize to the depth, before she could go further. *Jenny Rae Hudgins Evans, born April 17, 1938, died May 25, 1975.* Next to that one, the smaller stone of Danny's. Reading her mother's headstone now it stuck Lily how spare it was compared to some of the older generations' epitaphs. Danny's too, nothing more than a name, a date of birth and death. Jines's judgment of silence, presiding even here.

In the still air, the mosquitoes smelled fresh blood. Several of them landed on her forearm and Lily brushed them off brusquely. Lord, they were all over the place over here. She'd forgotten bug spray. In the far distance, a rumble of thunder. Sheltered as she was under the trees she couldn't see the horizon but she knew what was coming. It didn't seem possible but the air had grown even more oppressive. It lay against her skin like a web, making it hard even to breathe. There were storms here sometimes that were violent to the point of madness, storms that made livestock run blind in the fields with the relentless thunder and lightning that seemed to come from all directions. She didn't care. She wanted the storm to break over her. It would blast everything clear and clean. The wind would shift into the northwest and blow cool and crisp. Then, she could go.

She knelt and pushed her hand into a clump of grass that was trying to strangle the spent daffodil blooms, loosening it enough to draw it out of the soil without pulling the surrounding dirt with it. She piled up the clumps to dump outside the fence later. As she worked, the image of Belle came to her, working alongside her in the garden. She always wore a red bandanna that she tied across her forehead to keep the bangs out of her eyes, and Lily remembered how her eyes looked enormous set off this way, as big as a doe's eyes. She hadn't meant to hurt Belle. It hadn't been fair of Jamie, dropping that one on her. But even as she allowed that self-pity she knew that she was the one who had breached any sense of what was fair. She hadn't thought it all the way through; if she had, she probably never should have let Belle come close in the first place. She should have realized that it would be hard for the girl to understand why she had to leave. She was the grownup here, right? She was the one who should have been thinking about the consequences of misplaced actions. And she shouldn't have been using a child to get closer to her father, or to fill some hole in her heart that wasn't anyone else's task to fill.

The thunder rumbled closer. As distant as it still was, she could hear the quick shock of it. A chill rushed over her skin. She sat back on her heels and regarded her mother's name etched in the granite. Belle had her own mother; it wasn't Lily's job to take on the guilt of feeling like she'd abandoned her. She was just a friend to her, after all, not some surrogate. But how did that make it any less wrong? She should have been brave enough to see Belle at least; what had happened between Lily and Jamie wasn't Belle's fault. All she knew is that one day Lily was there, a friend, someone to run on the beach with, and the next, she wasn't. When she thought of it in those simple little girl terms, Lily felt ill. Too much Jines in her, she had said. Too much Jines.

Angrily she pulled at the grass too hard, inadvertently yanking a half a dozen daffodil bulbs from their delicate bed in the earth. The pale orbs lay against the dark ground, hopelessly uprooted.

"Shit!" Lily yelled. She slammed her hand against her mother's headstone so hard it stung. "You stupid shit! Why do you wreck everything you touch?"

She started to cry. Why had she ever come back here? She remembered that night in Portland, her hands on the photograph. Jenny Rae plaiting Lily's hair before the mirror. Her mother's hands, so strong and yet gentle. Lily had wrapped up that photograph in a sweater and put it in her suitcase and driven here for her mother, not for Jines or for Jamie or even for herself; she had come for her mother, whose love had compelled her. She remembered the dream of drowning she had had that night in her mother's bed, the ice sealed overhead, Jines's grip on her arm, all the blue sky and possibility of life beyond her reach. There had been a time she felt worthy of love, and that love was strong enough to bring her back here and offer her this: Another chance for that sky-blue possibility, a seam in the ice. And how had she honored the gift, her mother's love? She picked up the daffodil bulbs, her tears washing the soil off of them leaving bright clear, white spots. She had wounded a beautiful young girl. She had alienated an imperfect but good man who might very well love her. And she had, in the end, built a house of solitude within her father's own, its walls tall enough even to drive him out. You think you're protected, Jamie had said, but you're not. And it's okay. A crack of lightning somewhere nearby, and the truth of this hit her like the thunder that followed, rumbling deep into the core of everything it touched.

She heard the first edges of the wind moving in the tops of the trees. A moment later came the cool rush of air that meant the storm was going to be on her in minutes. She could make out enough of the sky to see that it had gone from dark grey and purple to a bilious green. She didn't need to look to see the great bulbous clouds that were mounding, their forward edges bulged like balloons about to pop. The storm cell's wind would dive out of the misshapen clouds to displace the hot air beneath with a violence indifferent to living things. She wasn't protected, and neither was Jines. She had seen the realization in him this morning, when he'd slumped into the couch, when she said she was leaving. When she'd said he could finish the skiff himself. What had he said to her? When you build something, you had to let it have its flaws. Why should something you care for have to be perfect?

And then she understood why the headstone was nearly empty,

why the silence had swept over him like a storm tide that never could recede. He had yearned for something perfect, he had grasped it so briefly, and then lost it before he understood the simple truth, that it didn't need to be. He had no words for his failure, for his grief. Jenny Rae's name and Danny's, the dates that framed their time here on earth, that was the only solid ground left. To step away from that hard truth toward Lily was to drown. And yet, when she had come back and stayed, somehow he'd realized it was the only way to survive. That you had to risk drowning before you could breathe clear, open air again. He had tried to communicate this to her in the only way he knew how. Lily remembered the feel of his rough hands on hers that first day in the shed, guiding the saw. The two of them together, building something beautiful in its imperfection, something that could transcend their silence.

Jines.

The storm was so potent and omniscient she could taste its metallic fingers on her tongue. The hair on her arms was lifting off her damp skin. She started running. The sky split open and Lily ducked and shut her eyes against the lightning. She counted, one-one-thousand, two-one-thousand, three, and the thunder pounded out of the sky like a fist into her chest. She covered her ears. Every instinct in her wanted to bolt, though she knew she should just lay down, make herself as flat as possible. It was too late. The metal gate clanged behind her as she slammed it racing through. The wind was howling, blowing shards of rain ahead of it. Along the path the overgrowth provided some shelter from the wind, but the loblollies whipped and snapped above her. She felt a wild kind of panic rising up inside. She burst from the path and ran across the meadow, past the shed and garden and across the yard. Jamie's truck was gone. The shed door was open. She didn't stop to investigate but took the back porch steps two by two, finally reaching the house's shelter.

The rain pounded on the porch's tin roof and poured like a waterfall past the screens, battering the camellias. Her breath was tight in her chest, coming in short, shallow cups of air.

"Jines?" she called, running into the kitchen.

Between bouts of thunder she heard the television in the parlor. She walked into the hall, and right away she saw it. The front door was wide open. The floor in front of it was soaked with wind-driven rain.

"Jines?"

A blast of laughter came from the television. She knew she hadn't left the front door open; she hadn't gotten around to patching the screens in the screened door yet, and too many mosquitoes had been getting in. They'd been keeping the door shut. She closed the door and walked into his room. On the television screen, a rerun of M*A*S*H was playing. She turned it off. The bed was empty, as was her father's easy chair.

"Jines?"

No keeping the anxiety out of her throat now. She walked to the other side of the bed and checked the floor. He was not there. Lily ran to the bathroom under the steps; vacant. An old fear came to her as she raced through the house.

"Jines!"

The cry came from a place so distant, a child so far away, it came in the wind or from the loblollies straining against the storm, or from the immutable walls surrounding her. "Daddy!" She was standing on the stairs again, watching him turn away and close the parlor door behind him. She was begging at the door for someone who would never come back.

Lily ran down the front steps. The shed door. The shed door had been open. She was yelling into the rain as she ran across the yard, but the shed was empty too. They had warned her about this possibility, the therapists at the rehab, they had told her that Jines could become confused. He could wander off not knowing where he was going, or thinking he knew exactly where he was going except he might be in a different decade altogether. He could walk into the wrong house. He could get lost in his own front yard. She shouldn't have left him; she had been taking it for granted that he was better, that he wouldn't just walk off the dock one day thinking he was walking down the road. That a wild storm might confuse him. What if he had gone out looking for her? She raced from the house across the yard toward the dock. Out on the river it was raining sideways, the horizon obliterated in a grey-white wall. The water foamed with whitecaps. If he'd gone off the dock she'd never find him.

"Daddy!" she screamed as her feet pounded on the slippery boards.

In the thrash of the waves, the *Jenny Rae* backed and strained against her lines like a frightened horse. Rain sluiced off her sidedecks and cabinhouse. To the side of the engine box, his face pale as the moon and streaming with rain, Jines lay where he had fallen.

Chapter 16

The night nurse—the one who snuck cigarettes out on the front porch and hid the butts under the camellias—had the eyes of a shrew, but what Lily disliked most about her was how she belted Jines into the bed. She insisted on it, said it was a safely precaution. All it would take, she lectured Lily, was for her dad to try and get out of bed one night to use the bathroom, forget he needed to get to that wheelchair, and crack his head open, or worse. The straps were a blaring yellow-green and had sturdy ratchets to adjust for tension. Jines's face was usually expressionless when the nurse drew the straps across his chest and his thighs, and then the ratchets made their harsh chewing sound as they took in the slack. More than once Lily had to turn and leave the room. On the nights when the nurse didn't come, the belts lay like a nest of chartreuse snakes in the corner. Lily could not bring herself to strap Jines to the bed as if he were a slab of meat or an insane person in need of restraint. It was risky, she knew. She believed Jines was cognizant enough most of the time to know that trying to climb out of bed in the middle of the night would probably land him on an unyielding reality of hardwood floor. But it was when he didn't know where he was, when he was lost even to himself, that he could try to do something that once was routine and now was nearly impossible.

Three nights of the week the night nurse came, and though she insisted she could, and should, be there seven nights a week, Lily said no. The sounds her father would make in the darkness, the torment of his subconscious revealed in moans and cries, were difficult to bear, but they somehow were easier to tolerate when she was alone to hear them. The enduring walls did not abide a stranger; Lily could feel it. It was better that they shoulder on together alone, the three of them—Jines, Lily, the old house. It was the way of things. When Danny had been sick, it was her mama who had spent every night in his room. And when it was her mama, even Jines, in his desperate and panicked way, cared for her as best he could. This was her duty, Lily knew it, even if it meant her heart would break every single day, and the nearly dead weight of him in her arms as she helped him to the bathroom, in and out of the wheelchair, in and out of bed, sometimes threatened to buckle her knees. How remarkable, she wondered, that she ever thought this burden belonged to someone else.

The strangers always came in the front door, thinking it was the right way. During the daylight hours the therapists came and went, round and round like the Guernsey cow and the Old Bay on the lazy Susan in the kitchen. She knew their names—Connie, Angela, Fran—and they all assured her that with time, lots of time, perhaps her father would be able to do more for himself. "Will he talk again?" she would ask, and ConnieAngelaFran would say that as far as they could determine, there was nothing preventing him from forming words. It was simply a matter of will and desire. Perhaps, they suggested delicately, he was suffering from depression. It happens so often in the elderly and in people who have gone through a traumatic event such as this. They always called it an "event," which made her want to scream, "You mean stroke! Another stroke! Call it by its goddamned name!" Perhaps, they said, medication might make a difference, and some counseling with a professional specializing in stroke victims' mental health. Lily listened to them and wondered at how much they didn't know. What they couldn't understand was that the language between Jines and her had never translated well in this house. It was a language that flowed on the curve of a cedar plank, that existed within a pair of old hands guiding young ones in the intricacies of shaping wood. She couldn't explain to them that it wasn't just Jines who needed to relearn how to make his words into something understandable. And

304

the words she needed to speak to him now, the questions she needed to ask, were like dangerous birds in her mouth, struggling to fly free.

"What were you doing, Jines?" She whispered the questions to him in the dark, thinking it would easier for him to answer with his face in shadow. She asked him in daylight, on the porch, thinking that the sight of the dock and the boat might jog his memory or loosen his tongue. "Were you looking for me? Were you worried about the storm? Did you get confused, think you were going to close the shed against the rain and ended up out there on the dock? Or was it something else?" She asked him in as many ways as she could find to elicit an answer, or even acknowledgment of the questions. She asked while he slept, watching the slow rise and fall of his breath. When he was peaceful, he breathed like the sea. "Why were you going to the *Jenny Rae* that day, Jines, in that weather? What were you after?"

They suggested a motorized wheelchair, whose controls he could manipulate easily, but the old house wasn't built for such a thing. At Mary Virginia's insistence, Kenneth came in one afternoon and added some small ramps to smooth the transit over the front door's threshold and a long one off of the front porch to the sidewalk.

"Cain't see Jines Arley motoring round here in no wheelchair, even one a them with fancy controls."

Kenneth's lips, occupied with their usual cargo of chewing tobacco, were working overtime holding a few nails in the corner of his mouth like fat toothpicks. He pulled a tape measure off his belt, yanking his jeans around so that his T-shirt rose up over his belly, and took a quick measurement of a piece of wood that would help support the ramp. He pressed the button and the tape retracted with a snap.

"Ain't right, a man like him. Gawd ain't got no mercy, y'ask me,

I don't care what Mary Virginia and that preacher down to the church say."

For once, Lily could agree with him. He spat into the bushes.

"Y'ask me he'd a been better off goin' like yer granddaddy." He jerked his head in the direction of the river and the Bay. "Out there, where he shoulda been. Where any waterman worth his shit wants to go. Course then he went and gave the whole damn shebang to Jamie Cockrell, so's now he don't even have his own boat anymore. I swear, I was right pissed off when I heard about all that." From his crouch, where she thought he resembled a troll with an oral hygiene problem, Kenneth glared up at her. "I reckon you had somethin' to say about all that, didn't ya." He pulled one of the nails out, set its tip against the wood and whaled away at it with the hammer. It bent like a flower in a driving rain. "Shee-it." He pulled the mangled nail out and tossed it to the side, where it made a tinkling sound landing on the walk. "I figured if Jines Arley couldn't run the *Jenny Rae* one-hunnert percent he'd a given me first lick at it, seein' as how I'd backed him all those years. Then you come along home and what's next but it's Jamie Cockrell out there. I ask myself, 'Now where in hell'd that idea come from?' "

She wasn't about to rise to the bait the way she had all those months ago when she'd run into him at the Seaside. The futility of it, how little it mattered to her what Kenneth understood or didn't understand, made her briefly embarrassed for that girl who'd thought she was being so damned clever to smart-mouth her way out of that ridiculous scene. What difference did any of it make anymore? What difference had it ever made?

"Ah shit," Kenneth said, turning his attention back to the ramp in progress. He picked up the half-bent nail off the walk and regarded it with something like disgust. "I don't reckon I did myself any favors when that asshole Tyler Jenkins near to killed the man that day at the Seven Brothers. Story of my life, one fuck-up after another." He shook his head and for a minute all the bulk and bluster he'd always carried fell away, and he was just bent over and small, full of regret and self-pity. "Jines Arley deserved better." He reached for another nail and whacked it with far more force than was needed. It bent so abruptly it sprang from the wood and hit him in the leg. Kenneth hurled it onto the walk and spat into the bushes. "Anybody ask him, if he wants a goddamn wheelchair rest a his life?"

"Try a pilot hole," she said.

"What?"

"A pilot hole. With a drill. Helps get the nail started. Easier to drive it in true."

He straightened up stiffly using the porch railing to push up to his feet and regarded her. "Ah know what a fuckin' pilot hole is. Christ, you're more like him every damned day."

She shrugged. "Suit yourself."

"You two ever finish that boat you was buildin'?" He waved toward the shed. "I reckon you could sell it for a pretty penny. Jines Arley Evans' last Little River skiff. Never be another like it."

And suddenly she understood it, all of Kenneth's anger toward her that she had never been able to fathom; he was envious, plain and simple, like a child so bitter in his jealousy he could never see around it. He had spent his life in hero worship for the man who was her father, but he could never be his kin, never be his blood, no matter what he did. That particular gift and curse was hers alone. Lily let her gaze travel past the half-finished ramp, the gingerbread along the peeling porch railing, the waxy green camellias and her grandmother's riot of climbing roses, across the lawn to the dark length of the loblollies where the shed, its doors firmly closed, stood in the patient shade. She allowed herself the memory of the coolness of morning there, the sound of his voice explaining things like pilot holes and the ways of wood. A well of emptiness opened so deeply and suddenly before her it robbed her heartbeat.

"There's a spare drill in the pantry," she said. She turned away from Kenneth to go get it.

The wheelchair arrived a few days later, and while it could maneuver well enough down the ramp and onto the concrete walk to the driveway, its tires ground uselessly on the oyster shell path around to the back. Lily mowed a parallel track in the grass until it was putting-green short, level enough for the wheelchair to amble about the yard. This seemed to give Jines a measure of comfort, or maybe it just made her feel better to see him outside. They would park the chair under the maple tree, the wind chimes she had bought at the House of Deals dinging overhead. He would sit and stare speechlessly at the river in the chair she knew he hated.

One day, when she had left him in the chair on the front porch and had gone to the kitchen to wash up the dishes, she was startled to see him come around the corner of the house on the cut path. The chair bumped and trundled on the trimmed turf, and a puff of wind blew his baseball cap off. He seemed not to notice, intent on a destination, his one good hand on the joystick controls.

"Jesus!" she said, and was nearly to the door before she pulled herself up short.

Hadn't this been why she'd cut the path in the first place, to encourage him to move around? Let him be, she thought. Let him go where he wants. But when he rolled right past the maple tree and off the cut path, heading for the dock, she raced out after him and caught the chair as it wobbled in the thicker grass.

"What the hell, Jines!" she said, stopping him. "Stay here."

She went back and grabbed his hat off the lawn—it was his favorite, a sweat-stained red ballcap with Little River Seafood in cursive across the brim. She put it back on his head and dropped to the grass next to him, feeling suddenly close to tears. Over the river, an osprey lifted out of the water, the fish in its talons squirming wildly.

"I wish you would talk to me," she said, her voice breaking. "I'd cut a path over here, Jines, but I'm afraid you'll try and do something crazy like get onto the *Jenny Rae* again. You just can't do stuff like that right now, do you know that?"

The osprey screamed as it struggled to gain altitude, the fish still writhing beneath it. It hurt her eyes to try and follow the bird as it finally overcame the weight and burden of the fish and soared toward the sun. Jines watched until the bird was out of sight, somewhere over the pines past the shed. His gaze fell to his boat, then back to her. Almost imperceptibly he nodded.

"Okay," she said. "Okay then."

A few days later she extended the path to the dock, but for whatever reason he never followed it, content again, it seemed, to go as far as the tree.

Six days a week, Jamie's truck pulled into the driveway and he and Maggie walked to the boat. Lily could tell he was pound netting by whether his crew came down the drive with him. Since it was summertime, though, most of the time he was alone, which meant he was crabbing instead. Now and then, when the day was done and he had packed up and gone, she would find a couple dozen crabs in a bushel basket sitting on the back porch step. The first time, she steamed them, wheeled Jines out to the back porch table and picked crabs for hours. The table became a battlefield of red, spice-encrusted shell fragments, the white meat of the crabs mounded in the same hand-thrown bowl her mother had always used for this purpose.

"C'mon, Jines," she said, putting one of the wooden mallets in his hand, "I know you're pissed off in there. Smack a couple of crabs, it'll make you feel better."

But he let the mallet slip from his hand, his gaze fixed on the boat waiting silently at the dock, and when she offered him a perfect chunk of backfin meat—the crab-picker's prize, what he always called a lollipop because of the way it came out in one piece on the end of the backfin, like a lollipop on a stick—he turned his head away.

The next time Jamie left a basket on the back step, she sat down beside it, lifted the lid and examined the contents. By any standards they were gorgeous crabs, heavy and clean, their shells a mossy green, their claws tinged with a luminous cobalt blue that faded into white the way night melts into dawn. They were piled on top of one another, quietly waiting their fate. Now and then one would squirt water out of what she presumed was its mouth. It's not as if she hadn't known blue crabs all her life, fierce things that had no compunction about killing and eating their own kind to survive. A few of those on top of the pile were still fighting even while they were motionless, their claws locked in a temporary standoff. She could lift one of them up and they would still hang onto each other this way, so single-minded they could be. Those tourists who stumbled upon the Seaside this time of year would probably pay about sixty bucks for this bunch Jamie had left her, number one jimmies, top of the market. If this is what he'd been hauling every time he filled the back of his pickup with bushel baskets—and those, she knew, were stuffed to the brim—he was doing well this summer. Doing right by the *Jenny Rae* and her father, too. She waved her hand over the basket and one of the crabs, the biggest one on top, swung a pugnacious claw in her direction.

"I ought to eat you," she said, but instead she carried the basket to the dock.

She crouched down there and tilted the basket, watching the pile of crabs slide out and into the water where they let go of one another, skittered away and vanished in seconds. "Aye God, Lily Rae!" She could hear Jines's voice in her head. "The hell is wrong with you, dumping perfectly good crabs overboard? You know what they'd a fetched at market? You know how hard that boy worked to bring 'em in? Jesus H. Christ!"

And she smiled to hear him as the water smoothed itself out again beneath her.

At the hospital, the caseworker advised that she find a lawyer and have a power of attorney made up and signed.

"Your father isn't capable, dear, of making these sorts of decisions anymore," she explained to Lily. "Legally, ethically, in every way, really, you need to take over that role. Otherwise you could find yourself in an extremely awkward position should something else occur."

"For instance."

"Well, for instance—"

Lily thought it odd that the woman should seem so flustered at such a basic question. She waited.

"For instance, should he suffer another stroke, or be in a situation where, for example, you would have to decide whether he should have something like a Do Not Resuscitate order in his chart. You would want to have those things done ahead of time, you see, and since he's not capable of making those decisions, or at least he can't verbalize or show in any other way that he understands what's being asked of him, you as the surviving family might want to make what you believe to be the right decision for him."

"He knows what's going on. He understands his situation."

"But if he can't express his wishes, my dear, if he can't make them clear to a doctor, then someone else has to do it for him." She moved a few things around on her desk, a pencil, a pen, a cream-colored ceramic mug. It said, "World's Greatest Grandma." She cleared her throat a little. "In particular, with stroke patients, when other issues can set in more subtly, such as dementia, that sort of thing, you want to have someone more capable in charge of his affairs."

"So what you're saying is, I get to decide whether he lives or dies? That's my job now?"

"Well of course not in so many words, dear, but yes, there could be a circumstance where this could be a decision you would have to make. And if you have these things set up in advance, you see, it makes it so much easier when the time comes. If the time comes."

Out in the garden, the weeds snarled the green peppers; the tomatoes grew huge and top heavy, forcing their stalks to bend and snap over the edges of the wire cages she'd placed around them months ago; the green bean vines climbed over the tops of the poles and snaked and twisted among themselves, seeking something new to cling to but strangling one another—and themselves—instead; the bolted lettuce towered and twisted like the spires of a bizarre cathedral.

"Why don't you have Belle come over and do some gardening with you, Lily Rae?" Mary Virginia asked one afternoon when she had dropped by with a casserole comprised of noodles and crabmeat and cheese. Comfort food, she called this sort of thing, soft enough for Jines to easily eat. "She's out of school, of course, and off with that woman who's her mother some of the time, and I think Jamie has her enrolled in that YMCA camp over on the Rappahannock for a few weeks, but you know she'd be over here in a heartbeat if you'd just ask. Seems a shame to just let all that work you did this spring in Jenny Rae's garden go to waste. And will you please eat some of this? My word, child, you're skinny as a barn cat."

The money from the sale of *Pelagic* arrived in the form of a cashier's check. She felt strangely numb as she deposited it into a new account at the Northern Neck Savings and Loan, then paid off Bradford Wilson. Most of the rest she distributed among the most overdue of Jines's medical bills, fending off their assignment to

312

collection agencies.

Summer held them in a kind of warm, liquid amber, everything around them growing wild and rich while she stood poised, suspended, waiting for what, Lily wasn't sure.

She is kneeling on the dock. Splintery planks under her knees and shins. The river frozen in great sheets, jagged seams between them etched like the lines in a skull. The ice groans as the current moves beneath pulling little strips of dead grass and tattered leaves toward the Bay. She leans over the ice watching the ebbing tide. She remembers this place. The foghorn at the lighthouse offshore moans. Suddenly Jines is floating there, his face like a bright moon pressed up against the ice. His eyes are open, his pajamas blooming around him like a pale exotic flower. His mouth open as if he is speaking but all she can hear is the slow call of the foghorn, filling her with melancholy. He is sinking, his face falling away into the darkness. His arms reach up to her. Just as he is about to vanish a seam in the ice opens with a snap. She plunges into the water and dives deep to find him. She grabs his wrist. She expects him to be heavy, but he is light as down as she pulls him up. They are in the shed. He's wearing his fishing clothes, his bib overalls and sweatshirt, his boots. He is sitting on the couch, smiling in a way she has not seen for so long. She feels overwhelming relief and joy that she has saved him from the ice. He says nothing, but his face is bright with light, there is light beaming all over his body. Her mind is confused, her memory tells her there are no windows here, there is never any sunlight on this couch in this shed. But Jines is safe and dry, whole again, in the light that doesn't belong.

Lily jolted awake in her mother's wide bed. Not a sound in the house. The light of the waxing moon streamed across the white sheets and into her eyes, disorienting her completely so that for a moment she was unsure if she was awake or still in the dream. The light. The dream. He's dead. Jines is dead. She bolted from the bed and raced downstairs to the parlor, but before she even got there the yawning front door stopped her in confusion, the cool breeze from outdoors a chilly palm on her neck. Some part of her fell back in the thick ebb and flow of the dream. Had someone broken in? Had a noise woken her? "What—?" she started, then turned slowly into his room.

"Jines?"

The empty bed was stripped to the bottom sheet, the blankets fallen to the floor. She walked to the other side, terrified to find him sprawled there, even while a calmer, more rational part of her brain asked why would he be on the floor over there, if the blankets are over here? The oak planks whispered into the dark corners of the room. The pile of straps lay there accusingly. The wheelchair was gone. A low animal moan escaped her throat. She was into the hall, through the front door and across the porch, past the wicker loveseat in its swing, down the steps and banked hard left—too hard off the last step—and crashed on her side into the grass, a searing pain shooting up her shoulder as she landed. Gasping for breath she looked down the path cut in the grass. Two tracks, level and straight, carved a clear wake in dark lines against the dew-laden grass that shimmered in the moonlight like a silver sea.

She pulled herself up and flew around the corner of the house into the back yard, under the maple tree where the wind chimes toned slowly, each perfectly round note an individual murmur in the gentle night breeze. Down on the dock, the glinting metal of the wheelchair flickered in the moonlight. As she raced she yelled his name; she didn't slow down as her bare feet left the yielding grass and tore across the oyster shell path in her effort to halve the distance. At the dock she stopped dead. He was hunched over in the *Jenny Rae*'s cockpit, one arm braced against the sidedeck, the other holding something she couldn't make out. He looked up at her, his face wet in the moonlight, whether from sweat or fever she couldn't tell.

"Lil'Rae."

His voice creaked like a rusty hinge on a heavy door. Then he turned away and shuffled toward the boat's stern.

"What the hell are you doing down here? God, you scared me, I thought you were gone!"

She stumbled into the cockpit and grabbed his arm. He was holding a hatchet. Her feet stung, and she looked down and saw blood on the deck. Her brain felt slow and drugged, nothing was making sense to her. Then she remembered the oyster shells; she'd run straight across them. She must have cut her feet. She felt the *Jenny Rae* move oddly beneath her with a restless jerk, and then the boat's transom ground into a piling, startling her with a sharp squeal. Jines stumbled into her with the boat's movement. She grabbed him around the waist and suddenly he seemed to lose whatever it was that had been holding him up. She sat down heavily with him on the engine box, breathing hard. His head dropped to his chest and something like a sob escaped him. She wondered what else was wrong here. The forward dockline, which should have been fairly taut with the work of holding the boat's bow in place, hung straight down the piling. Up on the bow, she could see that its other end was still cleated to the boat, but it, too, lay limply over the edge. Like a horse nudging open a gate to a meadow's freedom beyond, the *Jenny Rae*'s bow nosed away from the dock, swinging on the tide, only the spring line at the boat's midships slowing her movement. Aft, the protesting stern squeaked again as it jammed up against the piling. Lily stood up and walked forward. She grabbed the dockline still attached to the forward piling and pulled it up; it had been cleanly cut. The hatchet. How had he managed the strength to cut it? How had he managed any of it—getting into his chair alone, getting from the chair to the boat, any of it? And why?

"Jines? Her voice was deliberately light. She made an exaggerated check of the watch she had begun wearing when he had her up at all hours; it read four a.m. "Don't you think it's a little late for going fishing?"

And then, looking at his fallen face, she knew the answer she hadn't wanted to know to the question she had never been able to find the words to ask, and her breath caught in her throat. He continued to stare vacantly into some distance. The thin sweat that covered her skin began to cool. She shivered.

"I want to believe," she said softly, carefully, "that you got confused again. You must have been dreaming." She took the hatchet from his lap and slid it back into the leather holster that held it, for emergencies, against the side of the engine box. Its handle was smooth in her hand.

"No dream."

A helpless fear flooded into her. She walked brusquely to the cabin and opened the door, the thick smell of diesel and oil and sweat rolling into the night. The moonlight coming through the windows clearly lit up the helm to the right, the old vinyl seat and the spoked metal wheel. He'd gotten that wheel from a skipjack that had been hauled up to die in a marsh. The *Miss Emma*. She even remembered the name. Opposite the helm was a small bench seat with a hinged lid, which she yanked open and started throwing out its contents—two moldy orange life jackets, some cans of motor oil, a rusted tool box that took both hands to lift out of the space, her shoulder stabbing with the effort, a brown plastic tackle box with bits of monofilament line escaping the lid. A line. Any kind of rope would do. She marched back out to the cockpit. "A line, Jines. Where're the spare docklines?" When he didn't answer she stormed back into the cabin, this time pulling up the board over the small V-berth forward. Bingo. She pulled the topmost coil off the pile, its thick strands rough and stiff in her hands. The line was so old and unused it took her a good five minutes to work out its kinks enough to get a loop around the forward piling and then snake it back through the bow chock and onto the cleat. When she was done, and the *Jenny Rae* was riding properly alongside the dock again, she cleared away the line Jines had cut and let the two pieces drop into the water. In the waning moonlight, she watched them slowly sink from view.

"Lily Rae." For so long she had wanted to hear his voice; now she willed it to silence for fear of what he would say. "Lemme go."

She turned on him. "I have to get you back to the house, out of this boat and into that chair and back to the house."

She would not give in to the panic that was seizing her breath. She would not ask him the question; she would not allow the words to become real in this, the dark hour before dawn. She would put everything back the way it was. No one would have to know. No one could know. She went back into the cabinhouse and closed the V-berth, put everything back into the small seat.

"Please." Tears rained down his cheeks.

"No!"

She leaned down in front of him, grabbing him under the arms intending to pull him away from the engine box so she could get behind him and lift him, but he was so heavy in her arms, so heavy, and it was nothing like in the dream, when he had been so easy to pull up from the darkness, but rather the opposite, as if, with her arms around him, all of the physical weight of him seeped into her bones and she could feel for the first time the true crushing burden of memory that he carried, the current of time that was pulling him down and that she knew wouldn't ever let go until it carried him from her.

She slid to the floor with him there in her arms and cried, "I will take care of us, Jines, you don't have to go, you don't have to go. We'll be okay, I'll make it okay. Don't ask me again, please don't ask me again." And she was still weeping there when the slow glimmer of dawn began to push back the night, the sound of

Jamie's truck came to her ears, and he called her name and found them leaning against one another and the *Jenny Rae*.

Chapter 17

The world had contracted like the pupil of an eye suddenly exposed to too much light. Though the old house stood at the end of the long drive as it always had, and the river murmured just beyond, fear had narrowed the breadth of Lily's horizon to the most cautious and circumspect of movements. Boundaries defined her, the walls determined by her father's presence and need. He wanted to die, and he wanted her to let him do it. She could barely stand to be in the same room with him for fear he would ask her again, yet she was afraid to leave him alone thinking he might find some other way to fulfill his wish. Every time his eyes met hers she knew his mind, and the weight of that secret made her feel as though she were swimming in the abyss, the paralyzing compression of a hundred atmospheres bearing down through the column of water above her.

Nights when the shrew-eyed nurse came, Lily sometimes would allow herself out of the house where she could breathe. The dark sky of the new moon let her keep the secret safe, though in the starlight the white decks of the *Jenny Rae* still whispered its name. Whether or not Jamie believed her explanation of what had happened—that Jines had gotten confused in the night and had wandered—he promised her he wouldn't mention it to anyone. And though she knew he would keep his promise, it did little to ease the burden of the knowledge she carried. Outside she would lie back in the damp grass and let a million stars rain over her. Through the shimmer of tears they were her mother's arms, in streaks of white. They fell on her skin like snow-white kisses. A hundred gentle hands would move across her in the breath of the night, and she would think of the voices in the Grove, and the scent of junipers. All the voices, out there waiting.

Jines refused to work with the therapists anymore. He would sit in whatever position they propped him like some kind of overgrown doll and allow them to manipulate his arms and hands and whatever else they felt needed manipulating. His distance from every day expanded; he seemed to be focused in some other place or time. ConnieAngelaFran peppered him with questions, enticements, advice, but in the end they came to Lily. He'll never improve, they told her, if he doesn't try.

"I can't make him want to try," she said, which was true enough, though she knew it was only a fragmented truth.

He'd come within one blow of the axe from freeing the *Jenny Rae* from the dock. All he'd have had to do then was turn a key to start the engine; it would be easy for him, she knew, to rest on the side of the cockpit and steer the boat down the river. Even if he couldn't stand for the duration, he could sit, or lean. Once he got far enough, ultimately it was just a matter then of letting go.

He was more capable and stronger than they imagined, but they kept on with their exercises, asking him over and over to do this and do that, until one afternoon, as ConnieAngelaFran insisted that, now, Mr. Evans, I know you can hold this marker, let's just make this letter over here, Lily could stand it no longer. She ran off the back porch with no clear idea of where she wanted to run to—just that she wanted out—and then she heard voices down by the water. Jamie and the boys had just come in from the Bay. They were all under the tin-roofed, open-sided shed built on the far end of the dock, standing around the culling table sorting the catch. They were laughing about something, probably some Cro-Magnon humor involving sex in some form or another, a rich deep sound that belonged inevitably and easily out here. The reek of fish wafted out on the humid summer air, refreshingly rank and real, and she suddenly realized she hadn't been outside, other than her stealthy

320

forays into the night, in weeks. She felt like some kind of burrowing animal emerging from a hole, blinking against the light. When she walked up their laughter stopped. With the exception of Jamie, they all ducked their heads like embarrassed schoolboys, suddenly finding something intensely interesting in the pile of fish they were sorting and boxing.

"Hey, Lils," Jamie said. He smiled at her.

"Don't stop laughing on my account," she said to the men. "Please. I could use something funny."

But the spell was broken, and they shifted uneasily in their work. She stood there feeling stupid and self-conscious, suddenly aching to be a part of something normal, something completely ordinary that had nothing to do with death, pain, or illness. The physical logistics of caring for Jines had never been particularly easy, but lately they seemed straightforward compared to what was in her head and heart. His hopelessness had become like a pool of spilled ink spreading across every page of what her life had once been, consuming everything in shadow and muted sound. She hadn't quite realized it until just now, when she'd heard the men's throaty laughter. That people could still laugh seemed a kind of miracle. She longed for the uncomplicated job of sorting one fish from another, of boxing them, icing them, sending them to market. She needed to know that a world still existed where such a simple and useful task was even possible. But even as this yearning rushed into her, the men's awkwardness at her presence only underscored her isolation. Was she so lost that it was written all over her face? Did doubt and fear have a smell as unmistakable as this pile of fish? Nighttime was safer after all; no one could know her there. Only the old ones, the dead ones, who watched and waited. She was halfway across the lawn when Jamie caught her by the arm.

"Lily, wait."

She turned her head from him, hiding tears. "I don't belong out here, it's too bright," she whispered.

"Of course you belong out here," he said. "You *need* to be out here. What's the point of having all those people around to help if you don't get out and get some fresh air? You don't need to be in there all day every day."

She shook her head, not trusting her voice.

"Lils." His voice was gentle. "I know you don't know how to help Jines Arley. But you gotta help yourself. How can you be strong for him, if you aren't strong for yourself first?'

Strong, she thought. When was the last time she felt strong?

"Listen to me now. Tomorrow, I'm going crabbin'. I've got sixty pots soaking out by Motorun Creek—you know that little spot I'm talking about?"

She did know the place. It was only a few miles inshore of the lighthouse.

"If I work fast maybe I can get to the other sixty I put overboard down near Dividing Creek, but either way, I gotta get those first sixty pulled and reset. You got one of those therapists coming tomorrow?"

She nodded. "At one," she said.

"Perfect. Mama'll come with me in the morning and take over for you till then. You're comin' with me tomorrow. I could use a hand. Okay? Okay." And without waiting for an answer he turned and started walking away. "Be ready at five!" The shout came over his shoulder, and she watched him all the way back to the dock.

Morning dawned exquisitely clear and quiet, the river like a satin ribbon subtly changing color every moment the sun crept higher, from the palest lavender to silver, then copper to hammered gold. The birds busied themselves as she walked down the back porch steps and onto the oyster shell path, the swallows chattering up under the eaves of the porch, the goldfinches teetering on the stalks of bolted lettuce out in the garden, the Carolina wrens belting out

322

their prodigious songs from the woodpile. Beneath it all came the rumble of the *Jenny Rae*'s diesel; Jamie was already waiting for her, ready to go. She hadn't really thought twice about his idea. The urge to get away from the house and the whole situation, once she'd allowed it a foot in the door, kept her up half the night in anticipation. God, to see a clear horizon again. To feel the breeze straight off the water, untainted by land. To feel a boat under her feet, even if it wasn't *Pelagic*. How had he known that she needed these things, when she'd barely realized it herself?

Mary Virginia had loaded her down with sandwiches, potato salad, sugar cookies, summer fresh peaches and tomatoes, water and sweet tea.

"That's a lot of food, Mary Virginia."

"Make sure he eats, will you, honey?" she said, as she laid some plastic bags full of ice in the bottom of the cooler bag. "I know he'll go out there and work hard all day and never even take a moment for a bite. These boys, they do it all the time. You can make them the food and they just plain forget about it unless you wave it under their noses. Live on coffee and Snickers bars. Ridiculous."

"Thanks for letting me go."

"Oh now, honey," she said, hugging Lily tightly and then holding her at arm's length. "I love you both, you know that. But Jines Arley has plenty of help. It's you I worry about the most. You hold it all in there, same way he did, and you don't need to. People love you, do you know? You need to trust that. It won't let you down."

Lily gave a short laugh. "That hasn't always been my experience."

"Well, Lily Rae." Mary Virginia gave her that look that made her feel like a wayward pupil. "People aren't perfect. We're human beings, honey, it's our nature to rush from the fryin' pan into the fire."

"Funny. Jines said almost the same thing to me a while ago."

"Well if anyone should know, it's him. But darlin', it's a two-way street. You want love to come to you, you got to open the door to it and then send it right on back out, double-time." She zipped up the cooler bag smartly. "Now, it's way too early in the morning for a debate, so you just agree with me and then get on out there and make sure my boy eats lunch today. Okay, honey?" And she more or less shooed Lily out the door like she was sending her off to the bus stop.

When she got to the boat and hefted the cooler bag over Maggie's wagging body and into the cabin Jamie said, "Jesus, what's all that? It's only us out here today, not a full crew!"

"Talk to your mama. And you'd better eat lunch or I'm in for it."

They cast off the *Jenny Rae* and headed into the sunrise, and she could not help but think about the last time the two of them had been on this boat together motoring down the river. It seemed so long ago, almost as though it hadn't happened. The ache she felt high up in her chest when she saw Jamie or heard his voice hadn't diminished, but everything that had happened since that night had put some distance from it that made it more bearable. He too seemed to have been willing to give it some space, and for this she was grateful. For now, she was content to know that he was close by and that they shared a small piece of the same world. The river she saw in the nighttime would be the same he saw the next morning; the boat he worked was the same she had known from childhood, plank by plank. She wondered about that night out by the lighthouse and thought it had all happened too fast, and maybe that was why she'd run from it. Maybe it had less to do with her jealousy of Regina and more to do with her need to approach him more slowly. She'd worried that she'd blown it, especially after her harshness toward him on that terrible day of the storm. But perhaps not. Looking into the bright morning light, she allowed herself the notion that perhaps today could be one of hopefulness.

As before, the noise of the boat's engine made talking difficult, and so provided a comfortable cover for any awkwardness that lay between them. She leaned against the engine box, her hand idly scratching Maggie's head, and now and then she would glance over at him. He would be concentrating on where he was going, though once or twice she caught him looking at her and the smile he threw her was an easy one. Once they'd passed the jetties, it took about half an hour to get out to the string of pots Jamie had set near Motorun Creek, and as he came upon them he idled the engine, the steady growl easing down to a grumble. He waved her to come close.

"So, what we're gonna do is, you steer the boat and see how it goes. It's a lot easier than handling the pots, and I reckon you're a natural at it. The bigger issue is the pace and timing, so you'll have to listen to me for that, okay, at least at first."

There was a flutter in her stomach that had nothing to do with his closeness to her and everything to do with nerves.

"You may find this hard to believe, but I've never driven this boat."

"First time for everything," he said. "Come on over here." He positioned her next to the aft helm station, so she could steer using the vertical tiller. "You steer back here, that way you and me can talk clearly and you can see what I'm doing. You lean out this way—" he gently eased her shoulders over the gunwhale so she could see around the cabinhouse—"and you can see the pots as they're coming. I'll be busy getting 'em up and dumped and baited, so I won't have time to tell you where to go."

"You sure you don't want to drive? I can handle the pots."

"I don't doubt it, but I think this will be a more efficient system. And it's sixty pots. No offense, but that's a lot of lifting.

Let's try it anyway, and we'll go slow as we need to for the first couple just to see how it all works. You ready? Okay then, now just ease on up to that first one there, nice and slow. No wind out here yet and the current's pretty slack, so it's a good time to start. By the time it gets real tricky you'll have it down."

"Glad you think so," she said nervously.

"Have a little faith, Lily Rae, have a little faith."

Compared to *Pelagic*, steering her father's workboat was like riding a Clydesdale after an Arabian. Where her sailboat had been so agile, quick to catch her mistakes but just as quick to forgive them, the *Jenny Rae* was a much bigger, heavier boat with a lot more momentum. It took longer to do everything with her, to speed her up and slow her down, to feel her respond to the helm. Lily had the tiller in a death grip as she approached at a crawl the bright orange float that marked the first pot. "Little closer here now, come on, baby, don't be shy," Jamie was saying, as he stretched his arm and the hickory boathook out to catch the line attached to the float. He drew it into the mechanical roller mounted on the boat's coaming behind the helm and flicked a lever whose well-worn knob shone in the light, and it drew the pot up and out of the fifteen feet of water it had been resting in until it was right alongside the boat. "Neutral now, neutral!" Jamie called, and Lily eased the throttle straight up and down. Jamie hoisted the pot over the coaming and into the cockpit. The pot, which was a boxy trap the size of a coffee table and made of heavy gauge chicken wire, stank to high heaven and was crawling with crabs. "Yeah, now, look at that," Jamie said, as he lifted it onto one edge, opened a hinged wire door on the top and hooked it in place. Then he tilted the trap all the way over until the crabs poured out into a huge plastic tub on the floor of the boat's cockpit. Most of the crabs fell out of the trap and hit the tub in a furious scramble, claws swinging. A few clung tenaciously to the inside; Jamie poked at them with his gloved hand and, if they still didn't let go, he pried them off with a set of orange-handled pliers that jutted from the back pocket of his jeans. Once the last ones had dropped into the tub, he pulled out the reeking remains of the old bait, flung it over the side, and stuffed handfuls of frozen fish into the bait compartment. Then he closed and latched the trap door and slung the whole thing overboard. Around the boat, clouds of gulls screamed and dove for whatever scraps they could find. Amid their clumsy squabbling a few nimble terns with their gimlet eyes darted like arrows to the water's surface.

Jamie and Lily looked at the crabs skittering and clawing around the tub. With lightning hands he grabbed the ones with orange-tipped claws and flung them over the side before they could get a pinch on him.

"You only keep the jimmies?" Lily asked.

"I got guys who'll buy the females and sell 'em to the tourists down in Norfolk," Jamie said. "But Belle'd have my ass if she found out I was keepin' 'em. You know how she is. She says to me, 'Even if the law says it's all right, Daddy, you know it isn't. One female crab can produce a million juveniles in one lifetime,' or some such thing, and what can I do? You know how it is with that girl. I'm not so foolish as I'm going to try and argue with her." He reached down and grabbed one of the jimmies from behind, his hand positioned so that the crab couldn't maneuver its claws around to pinch him. "Watch this."

He dropped the crab to the floor. Maggie, who had been observing with the calculating focus inherent to Labradors when there's a ball, a bird, or food in range, raced after the crab when it took off, grabbing it gently but firmly in her mouth. As she held it there, the crab's pincers found the soft skin around her jowls and latched on, forcing the edges of the dog's mouth up into a goofy smile. A bit of drool leaked out one corner of her mouth as she settled down on her stomach, tail wagging slowly, crab securely in place.

"My God, doesn't that hurt her?"

Jamie shook his head. "Damndest thing. You'd think it must, right? But look at her. Happy as a lark. She'll sit there with that one crab for hours. Watch her."

"Maggie, you are crazy!" Lily laughed out loud, and when she turned back to Jamie she caught the fleeting longing in his eyes.

"I gotta tell you, Lils. That is a beautiful sound." Then he turned to look across the water. "So there's the next one. You think you got this? More we can speed it up the better. Don't be scared of the throttle."

All of her life she'd seen workboats out on the water, watched how, when they worked a string of pots, the watermen would roar up to the float, then drop to neutral, then power up again and charge away with a belch of diesel smoke. They seemed to know two speeds: full tilt and stop. They'd show off their skills at the festival held each July in Reedville, where the docking contest drew the highest honors for speed and accuracy. By himself and under the clock, the driver would have to sprint off the starting line, rush to the dock, slam into neutral, leave the helm and race to drop two lines over two pilings to secure the boat. It wasn't unlike a calf-roping contest in the speed with which they charged their quarry, but the trick was to bring the boat to heel without hitting the dock, and since boats don't have brakes, everything relied on perfect timing with the throttle. Lily wasn't nearly that confident in her boathandling, and the first six pots or so were more like a slow waltz than any kind of tango. Jamie was patient though, giving her advice now and then but generally letting her get the feel of it herself. After they had cleared the first six pots and she hadn't run any of them down, overshot, or had to double back because she'd been too far off, she started feeling more comfortable with the job. She also became aware of how much she didn't want to screw up.

She wanted to do well for Jamie, but more than that, she wanted to do well for the boat. For Jines Arley. She was an Evans, after all; by God, she'd better know how to drive a boat well. As the morning stretched away she allowed her mind to focus entirely on the feel of the tiller in her hand, the rumble of the boat under her feet, the distance to the next pot and whether she could afford to speed up a little this time. The uncertainty about the future, the fear about Jines, all of it slipped briefly and blissfully away as she concerned herself only with driving the *Jenny Rae* as well and as accurately as she could, helping Jamie get his work done. It was clarifying to think only about the moment at hand with a clear task to accomplish, and as they cleared pot after pot and she watched the patch of sweat that had blossomed between Jamie's shoulder blades soak his T-shirt straight through, she felt a deep gratitude. He had known what she needed without even asking. This single day—the sweat and the engine's rumble, the unending stretch of blue-green water and the rhythm and pace of the work—all of it was a gift only someone who loved her could have given. The understanding came with a kind of steadying warmth, filling a part of her with the same depth and inevitability as a flood tide slowly filling a creek.

It was going on about eleven in the morning when he launched another pot and waved at her to stop the boat. He took a long, deep drink from one of the bottles of water Mary Virginia had packed and handed the rest to Lily, wiping his face on the shoulder of his T-shirt. "That's thirty, we're halfway there. You're doing great, getting faster with every one. I reckon the rest of it'll only take us a couple three, four more hours. I told you you'd be a natural."

She smiled despite herself, pleased. "It's fun, really. I love being out here." She paused. "Thanks, Jamie."

"Shit," he said. "You're the one helping me. I'm thanking you. Pretty nice having some company besides old Mags, too." The dog, hearing her name, wagged her tail. She still hadn't dropped the crab. "You're whacked, you know that?"

Lily handed Jamie the water and he took another swig. "See that over there?" He pointed far off in the distance, where the water looked darker. "That'd be the sea breeze, making her way up the Bay. By three she'll be blowing fifteen, twenty out of the southeast, you watch. We want to be on our way in by then."

"Are you hungry?"

"Yup. But no time now. Let's get the rest of these done, get back into the river. We can stop by Piney Island and put a dent in that food. That ought to make Mama happy."

"You're okay with just getting this first sixty done today? I'm probably slowing you down, getting used to how fast to come up to the pots."

"I'm more than okay. You'll be that much faster next time. Let's go."

Next time. The promise glowed.

By the time they cleared the last of the pots it was going on three in the afternoon, and just as Jamie had predicted, the breeze was building to a solid fifteen knots. Maneuvering the *Jenny Rae* had become trickier by the minute as the wind and choppy water conspired to push the bow off in the wrong direction when she least expected it or throw the boat for a sudden roll. Still, the sky directly above was the color of a bluebird's wing, and the building wind filled her with that old restlessness that always came when she stepped onto *Pelagic*. It was a powerful yearning that in any other place would have left her frustrated and empty, but with nothing but a clear horizon in front of her and a strong boat beneath what she felt was a stirring of hope and possibility. She drove the *Jenny Rae* through the waves and chop back toward the river while Jamie tossed the crabs into the bushel baskets, packing them down on one another until he could top the basket with a flat wooden lid, secured in place with clips made of bent wire. The bushels crowded the back of the cockpit under a tarp he'd rigged to keep them out of the sun, and after the last one was shoved into place, Jamie washed down the deck, the roller, and the bin. They cleared the jetties just as he finished, and as they came into the river's flat, protected water he waved her to throttle down. He smiled as he looked at her there.

"First time I've seen you look halfway happy in a while," he said. He waved his hand back toward the open water. "It's always the same. I get done and I'm whipped, but I'm as alive as I could ever be."

"Free," she said.

"Free." He stood close to her as the boat peeled back the water. "I wouldn't have this if you hadn't suggested it. And if your daddy hadn't given me the chance."

"It seemed to make sense," she said. "For both of you. I think it made him happy, you know, that the boat was still out here working. Even if he couldn't."

She was talking about Jines in the past tense, as if he weren't there anymore. A quick shiver ran through her, a shadow, and the urge to turn the boat around, clear the jetties and keep going was powerful and dark. She thought about him sitting back there in the house haunted by all the old footsteps, and it seemed as though he was already a ghost caught between two worlds. She could come out with Jamie again, she could romance the horizon, but for Jines it was over. He would never be able to go back to what he truly loved, what fed his soul and made him feel free and strong. Always her anger and her need for his love had burned through any compassion for him. Always he had failed her in what she thought he should be. But the failure wasn't his alone; it was hers as well. Only now had she begun to see it. She felt the breeze calling to her and tried to imagine what life would feel like with no hope, with everything that made you whole past and gone. She thought about how heavy he felt in her arms that night in this very cockpit, the weight of his grief crushing them both.

They were approaching Piney Island, and Lily gave Jamie the helm. As he had done in his skiff *Belle* that early morning that felt like years ago, he pushed the bow quickly up onto the sand bank, letting it anchor the boat while the stern hung out in the deeper water. The ospreys lifted off from their nest shrieking their displeasure, and this time, two feathery heads popped up to see what was going on.

Jamie pointed. "The babies are getting really big."

Maggie jumped off the bow and trotted happily off into the grasses, and Jamie shut the engine down. For the first time all day they were left with only the sounds of the river around them. Lily's ears were ringing as she opened the cooler bag and half-heartedly started pulling out the food. She wasn't so hungry as she'd felt out on the Bay.

"Can I ask you something?"

She bit into a peach, then grabbed for a napkin as the juice dribbled deliciously down her chin. Peaches, sweet corn, tomatoes, crabs. The definition of a Chesapeake summer.

"Anything."

"What would you do if you couldn't come out here anymore? What would you want?"

Jamie slid a slice of thick tomato between the cheese and ham Mary Virginia had already put together into a couple of sandwiches. He handed her one, then took a huge bite of his own and chewed thoughtfully. "I don't see how I could not come out here. I mean, if not in the *Jenny Rae*, doing what we did today? Then in *Belle*. Or something. You know how that is. Even up there in Maine, you have your boat."

"Not anymore," she said softly. She reached over and flicked a dab of mayonnaise from the corner of his mouth.

"What?"

"I sold her. That day of the storm? The day Jines had the second stroke? I asked Willy—he owns the yard I keep her in—I asked him to sell her."

"Why the hell?"

"It was an expensive spring. And I owed that realtor money for the surveys and perk tests on a piece of land I was trying to get Jines to sell to cover his medical expenses. Among other things. He wouldn't do it."

"Jesus, Lily, that'd be like me selling *Belle*. It must've broken your heart."

"Well, I didn't build her like you did *Belle*. But still, yeah. I tell myself I can buy another one like her sometime, but it won't be quite the same."

Jamie handed her some iced tea. "You okay for money now?"

"Now?" She put the uneaten half of sandwich down. "Now, I have the power of attorney. I get to make all the decisions. Stupid thing is, now that I could sell the land, I can't seem to do it. He would know. I don't know how, but he would know, and I just can't do it. One more thing taken away from him, you know? One more piece. Bit by bit, it all goes away."

"What have the doctors said?"

She shrugged, a tremble in her shoulders and breath. She hadn't wanted to dwell on her problems, not on this day, but it was a relief to finally talk to Jamie about these things. The sudden energy that had swept through her while steering the *Jenny Rae* through the building wind had left her just as quickly at the thought of Jines waiting at the house.

"They really don't know. He could have another stroke, one big one or a series of smaller ones. He could get better, but how much better nobody knows. And they can't define 'better.' And they don't know how long it might take, either, whatever 'it' is. What they don't know is a lot more than what they do, really. The thing is, he just seems to me like—" she didn't really want to say it; that would only make it more real. Nor did she want to burden him with this secret and her fear. Jamie waited for her. "Maybe Jines knows. I look at him, and he seems emptied out. He doesn't want to do anything; he doesn't seem to care about anything. It's like he's just waiting."

"For what?"

"For it to be over."

Jamie dropped his head.

"I mean, what future is there for him? Everything he loves is past." She threw the sandwich over the side.

"Not everything." Jamie reached over and tapped her hand for a second.

"And that's just the thing, too." A harsh laugh like a sob escaped her. "All these years I had hoped, I had wanted, you know, to know that he cared about me. And now?" She wiped her eyes impatiently. "I mean, I feel like I've just now started to have a father, and now he's going away."

"Not by his choice, though, Lily. You can't blame him for getting sick."

"I can if he does it on purpose."

"What are you saying?"

"He's giving up, dammit! That's what I'm saying. There's a chance he could get better, a chance. But he's already decided." She shook her head, reaching for a napkin to blow her nose. "Shit. The most stubborn man in the whole world, and he's giving up. It's so stupid it makes me crazy."

Jamie was quiet for a while. He looked out across the river and she followed his eyes. Another workboat was on its way in, its white hull sharp against the blue sky. A bright red Confederate flag snapped from a short mast on its cabintop.

"Who's that?" She blew her nose hard and sighed. God, but she was sick of crying or always feeling like she was about to.

"Frankie Barnes. Usually crabs out of Locklies. A real piece of work."

Jamie stood up slowly, one hand on his lower back. He walked to the cabinhouse and came back out with a cigarette between his lips.

"Maybe, Lily, it's like this. Maybe Jines Arley just wants to choose." He took his time lighting the cigarette, then slid the lighter into his jeans pocket. "It's not about how he feels about you; anybody who's been watching you two building that skiff knows that story. There's nobody else he'd do that for. *Nobody*." She started to interrupt him and he held up his hand. "Just listen a second. Jines Arley is a proud man, a man used to running the whole show. Like you say, stubborn, but what comes right along with that is independence. Freedom, like you said." He swept his hand back out in the direction of the Bay. "Now he has none of it. There's only one thing he still has any say-so over, and that's how he wants to live what's left of his life. All the rest is out of his hands. How do you think that sits with a man like your daddy?"

"So you think I should just go along with it, let him sit there in that chair like he's dead already? I can't do that, Jamie, I can't. He's *not* dead. He *could* get better. He could try."

Jamie took a few more drags on the cigarette then put it out, stripped it to the filter and pocketed it. He started gathering up the food and putting it back in the cooler bag.

"We'd better be gettin' these crabs in."

"Don't, Jamie, don't." She put her hands on his to stop him from cleaning up. "More than anyone else, what you think means the most. You understand better than anybody."

"I don't want to hurt your feelings."

"Just say what you think. I can't see straight anymore, about any of it."

He put his hand on her cheek and held it there. "I know you want him to stay with you, to get better, if that's even possible. I know you want to take care of him and make things right. But maybe this shouldn't be about what you want. Maybe it should be about what he wants, what's the best thing for him. He needs *you*, Lily. Don't you see it? All this time you've been thinking it was you needing him. But now, it's him that needs you most of all. Don't be scared of it. Be strong for it."

It was late afternoon when they rounded the last curve in the river before the old house hove into view. The long day's sun had begun to wear them both out, but Lily knew they still had the bushels of crabs to load into the back of Jamie's pick-up, and he had to get them down to Little River Seafood before the end of the day. She was thinking that nothing would feel better than to flop down in the cool grass under the maple tree when she heard the engine throttle down and felt his hand on her arm, pulling her toward him.

"You take her in," he said, moving from the helm and gently pushing her in his place.

"What?"

"You dock her. It's good practice."

"No way, I can't do that yet!"

"Hell you can't." He stepped aft and got the boathook out to grab the mooring lines left on the dock.

"But—"

"There's nothing you can do to this boat I can't fix, short of sinking her, and I don't see that happening with this little maneuver here. Now come on. Look, you've even got a cheering section."

Running down the oyster shell path was Belle. She was waving both hands over her head and yelling something Lily couldn't hear over the engine, but she didn't need to hear it to know what it was. She had been that girl, long legs, ponytail and all, running to meet her daddy at the dock at the end of a long day. She had felt that rush of pure happiness at knowing he was home and hers again, at least until tomorrow. The memory made her breath catch in her throat.

"I thought she was still at camp," Lily said.

"Came home this afternoon." Jamie grinned. "Thought you could use a little surprise."

"Wow." She couldn't wait to hug the girl, feel all the power and energy of that young life. "Now I really can't screw up."

"You won't."

Gauging the breeze, she approached the dock letting the boat get blown a little sideways, and for a second she'd thought she'd miscalculated the speed, but Jamie covered her with a quick grab of the lines, and before she knew it, the *Jenny Rae* was snugged in with hardly a bump. Her hand was shaking as she pushed the thick black button that killed the diesel.

"Nice." Jamie grinned at her.

"Lily, that was awesome!" Belle yelled.

"Not half as awesome as seeing you!" She jumped over to the dock and grabbed Belle up in a bear hug, lifting her off the ground and swinging her around. "I missed you."

"I missed you, too. But listen, the garden looks terrible. What have you been doing?"

"Jesus, baby girl, don't nag. You sound just like your grandma," Jamie said. He kissed her cheek.

"Don't swear in front of me, Daddy, you know it's not polite."

"Yes, dear."

"Did you keep some crabs for us? Grandma says she got some sweet corn from Mr. Hudgins that's the best yet, and she made cole slaw the way I like and a peach crisp, and we're gonna have a big feast for dinner right here on the back porch."

"I got your crabs, baby. Only jimmies, don't worry. First I got to get these bushels here to the market, though, and I'm runnin' a little late." He turned to Lily. "If you can help me load 'em, I'll run 'em down there and you and Belle can maybe catch a swim or something before dinner."

The enticement of a swim sent Belle racing back up the path to get her bathing suit, yelling all the way to Mary Virginia that they were home and they had crabs for dinner. And it was all Lily needed to find the energy to help Jamie heft basket after basket into the back of the Ford. By the time they were done she was thoroughly exhausted, loving the feel of each and every sore muscle earned from a hard day's work.

"God, I'm tired," she said, as Jamie climbed into the truck's cab and closed the door. "It's fantastic. Do you think Belle'll mind if I just fall in the water in my underwear? Walking all the way to the house for a suit seems a long way."

"Belle won't care," Jamie grinned. "And you know I don't mind." And before she could swat him one he was off, the sound of his laughter following him as the truck pulled onto the drive.

Lily and Maggie walked slowly down to the swatch of beach where she usually launched the kayak, and she was already wading into the water by the time Belle galloped straight across the sand, dropping some towels without pausing, and splashed into the water alongside her. It was surprisingly cool for this time of year, deliciously refreshing. She floated on her back, filling her lungs to stay on the surface without needing to move her hands. The sky had lost the bright glare of midday and was softening now, easing into the coming evening. "So, how was camp?" she asked Belle, and that got a flood of stories going about the kid who was homesick and cried every single night, how hot it was because she hadn't known that she could have a fan but she could have, and everybody else did but they didn't want to share, how much she liked the hamburgers but hated their spaghetti because it always stuck together and the sauce was too spicy, how her favorite counselor was from Jamaica and had the funniest way of talking so that it sounded like music was coming out of his mouth all the time instead of just words.

Lily let the cool water and Belle's voice float her along, until suddenly Belle stopped and said, "Daddy told me you were going crabbing with him today. I was really jealous 'cause I wanted to go too, but he said you needed some time out there just for doing, not talking."

"Did he now."

"Yup."

"Well, he was right. He even let me drive the boat."

"Wow. He never lets me drive *Belle* yet. Wanna go build a sand castle?"

"Sure."

They sat at the edge of the little beach while Maggie lay down next to them contentedly gnawing a stick. The wet sand dripped out of their hands and down their fingers. The castles looked like stalagmites covered with soft, pale petals. Lily tried to remember the last time she had made one, and with that same rush she'd felt at seeing Belle run down to the dock she was small again, kneeling with Jines in this very same place, showing him how to hold his finger so that the sand would drip down just so. His fingers were so rough and thick that the sand would hopelessly clump up, and she'd always have to help him with the more delicate spires and steeples or he'd crush his whole castle. That was the summer he'd brought back the sea turtle, and he would come down here almost every evening just to spend time with her. How long had it been, she wondered, since she'd remembered that time?

"When I was about your age, I used to come down here all the time," she told Belle. "Jines caught a sea turtle in his nets, and it was injured. He helped me build a big pen that started right about here, so the turtle could swim around and eat and get better."

"What was its name?"

"Granny."

Belle giggled. "That's a funny name."

"It fit her, though."

"That must have been so cool. A pet sea turtle."

"Well, she wasn't a pet. She was wild. But I got to keep her for awhile."

"You mean you had to let her go? Why?"

"She got better. By the end of summer she was all healed up."

"But you could have kept her, didn't you want to?"

"Yeah, sure, of course I did. But she was an endangered species, and it's against the law."

"There's a kid in my class at school who catches sliders and keeps them, and that's not legal either. I found out when I asked the librarian, Mrs. Huckins, and she gave me an article about it. I showed it to him but he keeps them anyway."

"Well, he shouldn't." The sun was dropping low, and Lily shivered. "We ought to get back up to the house and help your grandma get those crabs steamed up. Your daddy'll be back before you know it, and I'll bet he's hungry."

"So did you just let her go here, out the river?"

"No. We loaded her into the *Jenny Rae* and took her all the way down past Cape Charles, where the ocean meets the Bay. That way she wouldn't have so far to go to get back to where she belonged."

That night had been so like this one, twilight seeming to last forever. She remembered how the turtle struggled to be free when she sensed the sea. Jines and that scientist could barely hold on to her as they lifted her out of the tub, her flippers were paddling so wildly. She remembered how in an instant, she was gone. And how Jines had wrapped one arm around her all the way home, steering with his other hand.

Belle traced her fingers through the sand thoughtfully.

"Did you ever see her again?"

Lily shook her head. She stood up, brushing the sand off her shins, and held out a towel for Belle. She threw a second towel over her own shoulders and picked up her clothes. Maggie stood up heavily and shook, sending out a fine spray of sand, water, and wood chips from the demolished stick.

"Sea turtles live a really long time, you know. I learned about them in science class. They have to come back to land to lay their eggs. Maybe she comes back, and you just don't see her."

"Maybe."

They walked in the trimmed grass alongside the oyster-shell path toward the old house that watched over them, and when Belle's small hand slid into Lily's and gripped it tightly, she wanted to believe, more than anything she'd ever wanted to believe, that Belle was right.

Chapter 18

The moon rose fat and gold, dripping cantaloupe light. As it traveled across the night sky it would grow lithe and silver. It would illuminate the *Jenny Rae*'s deck like a snowfield and reveal all of the water's nighttime secrets, the dozing of gulls on the glimmering surface and the blowing of dolphins out near the lighthouse. All through the night it would hold sway. Then the eastern sky would lighten, nudging aside that longest hour before dawn, and the moon and sun would share the sky briefly before the sun asserted its dominance over day. Lily sat by the window in her mother's bedroom and watched the solstice moon's progress across the sky. It glinted off the roof of the shed, it limned every shaggy detail of the garden. She had hoped that its luminous beauty would show her something she hadn't seen, reveal a miracle, turn away time. From downstairs came only silence, and she knew that he, too, was awake. From across the yard, deep in the loblollies she heard the call of a barred owl.

The parlor was darker. The moonlight had to work its way across the river and under the porch roof to wander through the single window on that side of the room. There was enough light, though, to see his eyes, and they were watching, as if he were drawing the silvered river into himself. All she had to do was let him go. All she had to do was love him enough to do that. She wiped her eyes with the heels of her hands. His eyes never left the river, and they were level and calm. How incredible, she thought, for him to be calm. But he had been this way for weeks, detached in a way that was no longer threatening, a distance that didn't seem hurtful. She took a long, tremulous breath and pulled a chair next to his bed. She laid her head against his chest, seeking some of the certitude he seemed to have found. She felt his good hand on her hair, resting heavily. She heard his heart thudding in his chest and from outside again came the call of the barred owl, and she knew that these two things were linked, the brilliant nocturnal hunter who flew in pure silence and this powerful wounded heart that belonged to her father. She knew that she wouldn't be able to change these things. Nor, she understood as his hand touched her hair, did she need to.

"I can't help you leave, Jines. I'm sorry. I don't want you to go," she whispered, her voice breaking.

Once more she drew in a deep breath against his chest. Then she stood. The straps that had held him in the bed every night since she'd found him with the hatchet on the *Jenny Rae* glowed an unhealthy neon yellow in the light. Slowly she loosened the buckles on each one, drawing the ends through. She let them fall to the floor.

"But I understand, I can't make you stay."

His eyes came to hers. The deep darkness of them glimmered with tears. She kissed him, then turned and left through the front door. In the deep night, the path through the trees to the Grove seemed almost tropical in the lush moonlight, the loblollies tufted as palms, the greenbrier draped like Spanish moss. She walked slowly, feeling like the moon had removed her, too, from time and place, as if these were not her feet falling softly on the pine needles below, as if this was not her body moving through the cool night air. If she let herself breathe too deeply she might break the moon's spell. It took all of her will to allow the moonlight to carry her, to not turn and run back to him, yet all the same for a moment panic seized her throat like a wolf. She had to stop him. He would go and never come back. She had to stop him.

"My God," she gasped, and spun about to bolt back down the path when the owl dropped from the trees and flew directly for her. Its silence and speed shocked her to a standstill. Like a hole in the night it came at her, more shade than living, and at the last second before colliding with her it swooped up and over her head, so close she imagined she could feel the whisper of its passage even though its wings muted all sound. Her breath left her in a gasp, and she stood stunned and shaking as the owl melted into shadow among the trees further down the path toward the cemetery. Moments passed, her breath quick and high in her chest. Away, then, away. She would follow the owl, not her fear.

She came to the cemetery, where the gate opened with a rusty squeak.

"Mama?"

Her mother's headstone stood in the moonlight. Around it, the tall stalks of the summer's daylilies stood poised, waiting for dawn to open their bright orange and yellow flowers. She dropped to the ground beside the grave and leaned against the stone. Her fingers traced her mother's name while the tears wet her face.

"Make me strong, Mama, like you were," she cried. "Make me strong enough to love him."

And after awhile, when she couldn't cry anymore, she leaned back against the stone and looked up through the swaying trees to the night sky above, where the breeze was coming on slowly as the moon settled deeper into the west. The scent of junipers was thick on the air, and the rustling of the chestnuts and oaks surrounding the Grove was like a thousand voices melding into one true song, a song that settled into her like peace.

A schooner carrying tourists on a dolphin-watching cruise out of Cape Charles found the *Jenny Rae*, not long after sunup. She was drifting peaceably on the inbound tide, about a mile southeast of the Chesapeake Bay Bridge-Tunnel. No one was aboard. The Coast Guard called a towboat operator to retrieve her, but the Little River brethren wouldn't allow it. With Jamie leading the group in his skiff

Belle, they brought the *Jenny Rae* home. Then they all went back out again to search for Jines. Lily knew this was necessary, a ritual she always found to be selfless and respectful to the point of wonder. But they wouldn't find him. She knew the place he had gone; she remembered its blue-green horizon from that evening long ago. He wouldn't have wanted to be found, and he would have let himself go on the sea-bound tide.

The Coast Guard sent the same young lieutenant who had come to the hospital after the Seven Brothers accident. He had that same loose-leaf notebook with the crossed anchors of the Coast Guard insignia on the cover, and he opened it to a page with, Lily presumed, a casualty report form. He asked her standard questions such as what time she had discovered Jines and the boat missing, what were the boat's exact specifications, Jines's date of birth, the exact spelling of his name. He asked her to show him the wheelchair, the ramp from the porch, the path to the dock, the hatchet, the cut lines. Mr. Evans had done all of this without waking her, the lieutenant asked? Had she not heard the boat's diesel when he started it? She allowed as to how having to care for her father full-time at home was taxing her physically and emotionally. Last night, she said, desperate for a decent night's sleep, she had taken one of the sleeping pills that Mary Virginia had offered her a week ago. She had never taken a sleeping pill before, she said, and it had knocked her flat out. If he'd like to see the pills, she'd be happy to show them to him, as long as it wouldn't get Mary Virginia in any kind of trouble. He didn't want to see the pills. He looked again at the cut lines, at the boat now back beside the dock. He squinted across the river glittering in the sun.

"Miss Evans," he said. He seemed to be struggling with what he was trying to say. "I, it—" he took off his cap and rubbed his forehead, as if a headache were gathering there. He looked so young to her suddenly, a boy perplexed over some bewildering situation. "It just doesn't seem possible to me that he could do this."

"Not possible that he could take his boat out by himself?" she asked. "Or not possible that he did not come back?"

"Both, I guess," he said, putting his hat back on. He closed his notebook and met her eyes, then dropped his gaze to the immutable water beside them. Almost imperceptibly, he shook his head. "Both."

"No," she said. The tears fell out of her like rain. "It doesn't."

The memorial service, which was held at the Bethany United Methodist Church a week later, filled to overflowing with people, only half of whom Lily remembered or knew. Many of them were sun-beaten and old, and she realized that she was seeing the last of a generation, people whose river-bred way of life, born of necessity and nurtured in stoicism and self-sufficiency, was vanishing with them. The service was fairly brief but infused with a religious fervor Lily was quite certain she had never seen in her father and so found rather hypocritical. She had wanted no service at all for this very reason, but Mary Virginia had argued with her that it would be flat out unkind to not give those who knew Jines Arley an opportunity to pay their respects to him in the House of God. "Why can't they just say goodbye in a way he would have appreciated?" Lily asked. "Is this about them, or about him?" But when she saw them there, all gathered together one more time to praise a hard life well lived and now ended, to lift their trembling voices to *Amazing Grace*, she was glad she had acquiesced.

"He went on his own terms," Kenneth said gruffly to her outside afterward. He had managed to get through the entire service without a plug of tobacco, but she could see his hand working in the pocket of the blue polyester jacket that was straining to compress his bulk, and she expected it was turning a bag of Red Man over and over in there. "That's how it should be. You oughta be proud."

"Should I be?" Lily asked. "You think suicide is something to be proud of?"

"I wouldn't call it that."

"What would you call it then? Self-euthanization?" Kenneth looked at his feet. "Whatever you want to call it," she said, "it doesn't matter. He's gone."

That night a cold front blew through Ophelia, pushing ahead of it thunderstorms that pulled her from a sleep she'd largely tranquilized herself into with the better part of a bottle of wine. The old house groaned around her, and lightning illuminated her footsteps down the stairs and into the parlor. The hospital bed was gone, along with all of the straps, the wheelchair, the paraphernalia of infirmity she had donated to the rehab center. The space still stood largely empty, only a few pieces of furniture he had placed here, she imagined, when he'd first moved into this room after her mother died. A flash of lightning lit up the room and she noticed the night table that had stood by his bed. The table had been pushed back against the wall when the people had come to remove the equipment. What had caught her eye? She walked toward it, and another flash illuminated the object on its surface. She picked it up. It was a small model of a workboat like the *Jenny Rae,* the kind of souvenir summer people and tourists would buy at a museum or gift shop. She turned it over and over in her fingers, feeling where his hands had been. She carried it with her over to the big soft chair where his sweatshirts were still heaped and curled her body to fit there, cradling the model and catching his fading scent on the clothes. Outside, the rain pounded the porch's tin roof, and she tried not to think of him out there somewhere, alone on the sea in a night so wild.

When she woke, the world had been washed clean. The northwesterly wind that always followed a cold front was blowing pure and clear, and the leaves on the camellias and her grandmother's climbing roses shimmered in the dawn light. In the kitchen, sunlight streamed through the big window as she made a pot of coffee. The sugar was on the lazy Susan, and as she turned it, the pill bottles paraded past. Her knees went out from her again, stunned at all of the ways in which he was still present. She wondered if it ever had an end, the depth of the place inside of her where he had once been. Eventually she became conscious of the sound of barn swallows chattering under the porch eaves and her wind chimes singing hard in the breeze. There was the *Jenny Rae*, too, shifting restlessly in the wind. She dumped the coffee that had gotten cold and walked outside. The sky had shed its white summer haze and was sea glass blue. God, what a beautiful morning. There was a time he would have loved this.

She walked slowly across the yard, trying to pay attention to what the morning was giving her. When she stopped and looked up she was in front of the shed. Its sides were still rain-darkened from the night before, and the loblollies surrounding it bent hard now and then in the gusty breeze. When she unlatched the doors, they sprung open with the wind as if they'd grown impatient with how long it had taken her to show up. She entered the shed with the same careful steps she'd entered the old house all those months ago, not sure how she belonged anymore in that space.

The skiff waited on its sawhorses. Sawdust scattered from her steps like sweet-smelling snow. The hammer and a fistful of nails, the carpenter's pencil and drill, were resting just where she had left them long ago, on the last plank she had worked. The one that wasn't perfect. The one that suffered her mistakes but still managed to fit. She held her breath, as time seemed to have stopped in here. If she turned around now, would he be on the path coming down to meet her, the sight of him filling up the early daylight?

"You know, I met a man at the church yesterday who knew

your daddy about a hundred years ago."

No, she remembered, Jines wouldn't be there. Time rushed up to itself again, and she turned to see Jamie in the door. He was outlined against the morning light, his shoulders broad and strong, standing in that easy, hip-slung way he had. She had been walking with ghosts for so long, and Jamie suddenly seemed intensely real.

"He was real interested when I told him that Jines Arley had been working on a new boat." Jamie walked past her and over to the skiff. He crouched down and eyed the curve of the sheer as it arched from one sawhorse to the other. "Back in the day, sounds like he built as much as Jines did, only his boats mostly went over to the Eastern Shore. He says he has a whole shed full of old boats that he's looking for a home for. Thinks somebody should start a kind of boatbuilding school, you know, a place where people could restore these old boats and build new ones. Keep the old techniques alive." Jamie stood up and brushed some dust off the skiff's sides. "Says he has plenty of time on his hands these days, seeing as how he's retired. Says he still knows where some of the old builders are, the ones still alive."

"Does he now."

"Mm hmm." Jamie started to reach for a cigarette until she whacked him gently on the hand.

"Not out here, are you crazy?" she said, waving to the cedar shavings all over the floor.

"Oh, yeah. Sorry." He took her hand and cupped it like a bird between his two roughened ones. He held it so she could feel the warmth there. He looked around into the dusty darkness of the shed's far corners. "Looks like you got some extra space here. Plenty of room to expand, too, if you had, say, a bunch of Belle's classmates out here learning how to build a Jines Arley Evans Little River crabbin' skiff."

Lily allowed a small smile at the image. She let her hand rest within his. She wasn't prepared to ask if any of the old builders could help her finish the skiff that still waited here. She wasn't prepared to lose the feeling of Jines's hands guiding hers.

"It's an idea, anyway," Jamie said.

"It's a good idea," she said.

She allowed the image to bloom a little in her mind, the sound of saws and hammers working, the bright voices under the tin roof, the hopefulness inherent in watching something come alive.

"Well okay then," Jamie said. He let go of her hand and made for the door. "I'll be out to the *Jenny Rae*."

"Isn't today Sunday?"

"Yup. But there's a pod of dolphins been hanging around the jetties, past couple of days. Belle wants to see 'em. Tide's just about right soon." He threw her that grin, and she couldn't do a thing but smile back at him. "I'll bring the coffee," he said, and he vanished out the door.

The shed was suddenly big and quiet around her. She waited for the silence to grow too unbearable. But the space, for all its dusty vastness, did not feel empty. She let her gaze fall to the old pot-bellied woodstove, the long mad clutter of the workbench, the ugly, mouse-infested sofa, the gangly bandsaw and the square tonnage of the Beast, the patterns for the skiff's sides hanging on the wall, the skiff itself. She walked around it, her hand trailing on the wood as she went, until she came to the unfinished bow, its fine curve sweeping back seamlessly into the unwavering rigid strength of the keel. She put her hands on either side of it where Jines's had last rested. She had thought it would feel different out here with him gone, emptier, but it didn't. In some strange way his presence felt even larger, and she wondered if it was because he seemed to be in everything, every piece of machinery, every smooth-handled saw, every pale piece of cedar. Everywhere she looked, all the places and things he had loved. And he was outside too. He was up in the green tips of the pines, he was on the osprey's wings, he was the glinting shine of the river. He had spread out somehow. He had opened up. And she knew that his arms would be among the white streaks of stars now, his hands coaxing the nighttime breeze to her face. Silence was no longer possible for him. He had loved her. What came into her was a deep gentleness, an opening out of her own. She thought about the sound of dolphins breathing, the rise and fall of his chest, the constant, inevitable breath of the tide. She thought about the sunrise pouring down the river, the warmth of Jamie's hand holding hers, Belle's arm draped over Maggie's yellow back. Lily laid her face against the smooth grain of the oak stem that Jines had shaped, and she let all that remained imperfect and incomplete come away from her and drift out like an ebbing tide, out and upward into the sighing loblollies outside.

The End

Acknowledgments

This novel is my love song to the Chesapeake Bay, but I could not have sung it without a chorus backing me. Its members, whether they know it or not:

George Butler, who let me spend hours in his boatbuilding shop in Reedville, Virginia, where I filled chilly winter days with endless questions, and never once did he seem to mind. Without his generosity, grace, and fathomless knowledge, the cedar heart and soul of this book would never have taken shape under Jines's and Lily's hands.

Tim Sayles, my longtime boss at *Chesapeake Bay Magazine*, who always gave me free rein to explore—as a writer and as a water rat—and who loved it when I turned an ordinary profile story about a waterman into an award-winning piece of creative nonfiction. That story was the genesis of this book.

Beverly McMillan, who asked me to write a book of Chesapeake essays, and who learned my heart and became a dear friend and fellow writer. She and her brilliant marine scientist husband, Jack Musick, introduced me to the late Walter Coles Burroughs.

Walter Coles Burroughs, who took me pound-netting. He was a gentleman, caring of me though he didn't know me, and his voice, his singular loneliness, and his kinship with the water speaks of the very best of the Chesapeake Bay and its complex, proud waterman's culture.

The late Edward Pritchett, who walked me through his beautiful old family graveyard in spring when it was covered in daffodils that bloomed despite being strewn with loblolly pines, which Hurricane Isabel had shattered.

My oldest brother, Bill Mitman, and my sister-in-law, Cathy Wilson, for falling in love with Miss Lucy's house on Flood Point and always keeping the doors open.

My most wonderful writing group: Jan Linley, a soul mate I knew from the moment we met at The Writer's Center in Bethesda, Maryland; Louise Farmer Smith, who assured me that I could survive being workshopped and live to write again; and Fiona Jane Mackintosh, whose knife-edged wit and ruthless clarity kept me honest and more succinct than I could ever be on my own. Without these three, I would be a much lonelier writer (and I probably would weigh a few pounds less given all the cheese and wine in which we indulged).

Andrea Barrett, my first fiction teacher at the Bread Loaf Writer's Conference, who reminded me that sheer tenacity is a writer's greatest talent, and Kevin McIlvoy, my second teacher at Bread Loaf, who helped me begin to believe I could be an artist.

Connie Bond, Mike and Roberta Hilbruner, Nica Waters, and Hannah Gardner. They continue to remind me of who I can be, even when I think I can't.

Marcia Landskroener, colleague, soul sister, and one of the best writers I know, who copy-edited this manuscript's next-to-final version, and who helps keep my feet on the ground and my head in the stars, every day we work together.

Nancy Taylor Robson, writer, sailor, and mother-in-arms, who encouraged me to share the story and is almost entirely responsible for it being in your hands, dear reader.

Joe Evans, editor of *Chesapeake Bay Magazine*, and its new publishers, who happily offered to support this book at its publication.

Mike Kaylor, Master Printer at Washington College's Rose O'Neill Literary House, who type-set this book's title using the Lit House's antique letterpress, along with the care and heart he brings to his work and his mentorship.

And last but never, ever least: Bird, for being my inspiration, Kaeo, for being my young hero, and Johnny, for always believing in me.

Wendy Mitman Clarke reported and wrote for The Associated Press in New England before returning to the Chesapeake Bay, where she grew up sailing with her family. She was Mid-Atlantic Bureau Chief for *Soundings* in Annapolis then Executive Editor for *Chesapeake Bay Magazine* where for many years she has chronicled the Bay, its history, its people and its environmental issues. Her first book, *Window on the Chesapeake, The Bay, Its People and Places* (Howell Press and The Mariners' Museum, 2002) is a collection of essays.

After years spent sailing the Chesapeake with their young children on 34-foot *Luna*, she and her husband moved the family onto 45-foot *Osprey*, and from 2008 to 2012 they sailed throughout the U.S. East Coast, Bahamas, Central America, and western Caribbean. During their travels while also homeschooling the children, she wrote an awardwinning monthly column ("Osprey's Flight,") for *Cruising World* magazine.

Her work has won numerous awards, including several from the Society of Professional Journalists, MD, and Boating Writers International, the Monk Farnum Award for Excellence in Editorial Commentary, and an Emmert Memorial Award for "The Water and Walter Coles," which inspired **Still Water Bending**. Her poetry, which won the Pat Nielsen Poetry Award, has appeared in *Blackbird*, *Rattle*, and the *Delmarva Review* and was nominated for a Pushcart Prize.

In addition to being director of media relations at Washington College in Chestertown, MD she is a contributing editor at *Cruising World* and a regular contributor to Smithsonian.com. Her work has also appeared in *Smithsonian*, *Preservation*, and *National Parks* magazines, in addition to many marine and boating publications. She lives with her family on the Eastern Shore of Maryland.

https://www.wendymitmanclarke.com